MW01153958

LAS VEGAS SIDEWINDERS: DOMINIC

KAT MIZERA

Heather —
Thanks for your support!
All the Best —
Kat M

Copyright @2016 by Kathy Mizera, all rights reserved

All rights reserved. No part of this book may be used or reproduced in any manner whatsoever, including internet usage, without written permission from the author, except in the case of brief quotations embodied in critical articles and reviews.

These are works of fiction. Names, characters, places and incidents are either products of the author's imagination or are used fictitiously, and any resemblance to actual persons, living or dead, business establishments or locales is entirely coincidental.

Cover Design: Dar Albert, Wicked Smart Designs

OTHER BOOKS BY KAT MIZERA

The Las Vegas Sidewinders Series:
    Dominic
    Cody's Christmas Surprise
    Drake
    Karl
    Anatoli
    Zakk
    Toli & Tessa's Wedding
    Brock
    Vladimir
    Royce

The Inferno Series:
    Salvation's Inferno
    Temptation's Inferno
    Redemption's Inferno
    Tropical Inferno (formerly Tropical Ice)

Romancing Europe Series:
    Adonis in Athens
    Smitten in Santorini

The Alaska Blizzard Series:
  Defending Dani
  Holding Hailey
  Winning Whitney
  Losing Laurel (Coming 2019)

Other Books:
  Special Forces: Operation Alpha: Protecting Bobbi (Susan Stoker's Special Forces World)
  Brotherhood Protectors: Catching Lana (Elle James's Brotherhood Protectors World)

ACKNOWLEDGMENTS

The Las Vegas Sidewinders became a reality in my head years ago, long before there was ever any talk of bringing a real NHL expansion team to Las Vegas, simply because I love hockey and I love Las Vegas. The characters I created are a conglomeration of every hockey player I've ever met, watched play or read about, with a touch of all the things we love (and hate) about men in general. The casual references made to players like Carey Price, who really plays in the NHL, are only meant to bring a sense of context to the story for people who know the sport. I tried to be extremely careful with the frames of reference so that it never impacts real games that were played or their records. I do apologize for changing the winners of the Stanley Cup in the years that the Sidewinders do it because, when it's all said and done, this is fiction and it's supposed to be fun!

Special thanks to the Florida Panthers, who made me fall in love with hockey in 1993—you'll always be my #1 team!

This book wouldn't have been a reality without my husband, Kevin, whose insight into the sport pales in comparison to his insight of me. All the long nights of writing that left me asleep while he got up with the kids for school, listening to me describe a scene and giving me a comeback line, and most of all, reminding me that I could do this. I love you, babe.

For my parents—who gave me the heart, support and love to believe I could do anything.

For Mary Bevilacqua, my high school English teacher, who started me on the road to being a writer and gave me the foundation for all things written. You are forever my mentor and friend.

For my besties—Jodie, Lisa, Christine and Tasha—who always have my back and whose faith in me never wavered. Who listened and laughed and pushed my limits. My partners in crime. I look forward to the next adventures!

BIG thanks for Jodie for her expert editing and endless advice.

Nothing would have been finished on time if it hadn't been for my trusty assistant, Lisa Sealey. Thank you for your hours of research and the thankless job of keeping me organized. Really, nothing would have gotten done without you!

And very special thanks to Joanna Campbell Slan who took me under her wing and helped make this dream a reality. Her friendship, insight and willingness to help made all the difference in the world. I could not have done this without you!

PROLOGUE

MARCH 2012

There were ten minutes left in the game and Nashville was down 2-1. Montreal was playing hard tonight and Dominic Gianni watched the game unfolding on the ice with a practiced eye. His team, Nashville, needed this win, and Montreal wasn't going to make it easy. As the clock slowly wound down, Dom felt the usual surge of adrenalin that came with knowing he would be on the ice in another minute or so and that it would be up to him to make something happen.

He watched Montreal's rookie forward Bobby Thomas skating up the ice fast, chasing someone on the other team. The two were neck and neck when Thomas stole the puck just before they reached the goalie.

Skating back in the other direction, Thomas headed towards Nashville's goal with two guys on his tail and Dom clenched his jaw as he watched the rookie closing in on the goalie. Just as Thomas was winding up to shoot, Nashville's captain got the puck away from him and turned to head in the opposite direction. Frustrated, Thomas wheeled and threw an elbow into the goalie's face, sending him sprawling.

"Are you kidding me?" Dom was on his feet, yelling at the refs who'd missed the illegal hit. The goalie was still on the ice with the trainers tending to him and Nashville's back-up goalie was warming up: a tall Canadian named Rob Rousseau. The backup seemed like a stellar guy and teammate, though Dom didn't know him very well.

"Go get him, Gianni!" the coach shouted. Dom leapt onto the ice and joined Rob skating out to the net.

"That hit was bullshit," Rob groused under his breath.

Dom nodded. "Don't worry—I got this." He exchanged glances with Thomas, who arched an eyebrow at him, as if inviting him to make a move. Dom mentally shook his head; rookies were way too cocky these days. Barely 20 years old, Thomas should have been a little more respectful; Dom would make sure he learned that.

The ref dropped the puck, and Dom watched Thomas win the face-off and immediately head for Nashville's net. Dom deftly angled in and cut him off before he got in front of Rousseau. Giving him a dirty look, Thomas pivoted back and passed the puck to one of his defensemen. Dom turned to follow the play, but kept his eye on Thomas, positioning himself to keep the rookie off to the side so Rousseau would have a clear view of any coming shots.

Thomas came back around to fight for position in front of the net, but Dom was ready for him. Older and more experienced—not to mention three inches taller and at least 25 pounds heavier—Dom knew what the kid was up to: circling around, Thomas was building up speed, thinking he would come in fast enough to push past Dom, using a combination of speed and momentum to overcome Dom's 6'5" frame.

Dom braced his legs and almost laughed when Thomas collided with his shoulder and practically bounced backwards. "Not this time, hothead," Dom chortled, sliding back a few feet.

Thomas watched in frustration as his teammate shot the puck and Rousseau easily kicked the rebound into the corner. Dom followed the puck and in one motion banked it up off the glass as one of his forwards streaked up the ice to intercept. Dom caught a glimpse of Thomas coming up behind him and turning to follow the play. Thinking Thomas was going to keep going, Dom turned his head to follow the puck just as he felt a sharp stabbing pain at the back of his right knee.

The pain momentarily stunned him: almost anyone else would have gone down. *Sonofabitch!* Dom had to clench his fist to keep from dropping his stick. The pain from the unexpected assault made him growl deep in his throat; that little fucker had just used his stick to slash him in the back of the knee, one of the only areas not protected by a pad. A quick look at the refs told him everything he needed to know: neither of them had caught the bastard! Again.

Now Dom was pissed. Exchanging a look with Rousseau, who'd seen it and was shaking his head, Dom experienced a surge of pure fury so intense he literally saw red. Powering through the pain, he started to move forward. He was too angry even to entertain the notion of heading back to the bench to have his leg looked at; all he could think about was getting revenge on the little bastard wearing number 87.

He moved through a haze of pain and rage, his mind blank except for his focus on the back of Thomas's jersey as it got closer and the numbers got bigger. Unaware of the blood dripping down his leg, it was as if his mind had shut off everything except what he had to do. The cocky little shit was going to pay—for what he'd done to their goalie as well as what he'd done to Dom. *No one* fucked with Dom Gianni or his friends, that was for damn sure.

The puck was heading his way and Dom picked up speed as he crossed the red line. Thomas wasn't far away now, watching the puck and tapping his stick to let his teammates know he was open. The scraping of Dom's skates grew louder as he sped up, and Thomas heard him at the very last second. Instinctively bracing himself, Thomas bent his arms at the elbows and brought his hands up as he ducked his head, but it was too little, too late; Dom left his feet and drove into the numbers on the back of Thomas's jersey, sending him headfirst into the boards.

Underneath the thud of the helmet and pads hitting the boards was a sound unlike anything Dom had ever heard: an unmistakable snap, like King Kong cracking his knuckles. Breathing hard, Dom stopped and watched in a kind of slow motion as Thomas' head made contact with the glass and snapped back before he slid to the ice and lay motionless. The refs blew their whistles frantically and motioned for the team trainer.

Dom still hadn't moved when one of the refs skated up to him. "That's five and game, you're done." Five minutes and a game misconduct; no surprise there.

Dom nodded slowly, his eyes still on Thomas's prone figure.

What the hell had he done?

"Get Gianni off the ice," the ref was saying as several of Montreal's players moved in Dom's direction.

Was Thomas dead?

Someone nudged Dom. "Dom, come on, man. You need to go."

"Yeah, I know." Dom felt a wave of nausea as he skated back towards the bench.

Rob was getting another bottle of water. "I saw what he did," he said. "I'll let them know."

"Yeah. Thanks." Dom had to force his legs to keep moving as he started down the tunnel.

"Did you break his fucking *neck*, Gianni?" someone yelled from Montreal's bench.

"You're toast, Gianni!" someone else called out.

Dom had to pick up speed to get to the locker room in time to heave into the nearest garbage can. He held on to the edge, swallowing down the bitter taste of bile, sweat and remorse. *What the fuck had he just done?*

As the adrenaline left his system and he started to crash, he slowly sank to the ground and hung his head, resting his arms on his knees. He'd done it again. What the hell was wrong with him? Everything inside him told him it was bad this time; this time, he was going to have to pay.

"I'm sorry, Brian," he whispered into the stillness. "I'm so fucking sorry."

1

JUNE, 2012
   Las Vegas, Nevada

D om stared out the window of the elegant condo feeling mildly irritated. He'd just arrived in Las Vegas and apparently he was here for good. For the next year, anyway, and this was the last place he wanted to be. Who the hell had thought it would be a good idea to bring a professional hockey team to the desert? He certainly didn't, and he definitely didn't want to be part of it.

After finishing his seventh season in the NHL, having played for Detroit, Buffalo and, most recently, Nashville, he'd been shipped off to the desert, warned by the NHL that one more on-ice "incident" of unsportsmanlike conduct and he'd be out for good. No one wanted to play with him now, much less if anything else happened. The only reason he was here was because Brad Barnett, his coach from college, was the head coach of this Las Vegas expansion team, and because Dom's best friend Cody Armstrong, who had been recruited as well, had talked him into it.

"This is your last chance," Coach Barnett had told him on the phone. "We're going to have a serious conversation when you arrive. Then you'll come to dinner at the house—Andra can't wait to see you."

Dom smiled as he thought of Andra. Mom Andra, they'd called her in college. Most of the team had spent nearly every weekend they weren't traveling at the Barnett household, being fed, having their laundry done and generally being mothered by Andra, who wasn't only their coach's wife but their teammate's mother: Coach's son Brian had played with them at Boston College, and they'd been about as tight as a group of men could be, more like brothers.

"So, what do you think?" Cody asked him, startling him out of his reverie.

"It's nice."

"You said furnished, so it's got everything. Did you sell all your stuff?"

"Yep. Decided if I was going to get a fresh start, I'd do it right. Sold almost everything except the two big screen TVs, my mom's dining room set, and some random crap. I'll keep the dining set in storage until I figure out if I'm staying long enough to buy a house, and figure out the other crap when it all gets here in a week or two. "

Cody nodded. "You can store stuff in my garage too—plenty of room."

"Thanks. Make sure you let me know how much I owe you for the deposit."

"I've got the paperwork right here." Cody passed over an envelope.

Dom glanced at the contents. "Thanks," he said again.

"You all right?"

Dom made a face. *"Really?* I got traded for the second time in two years, to an expansion team in the freakin' *desert*, living in a suburban condo and on probation with the league for being an asshole. Does it sound like *anything* in my life is 'all right'?"

"It doesn't have to be this way, you know."

"Oh, God, please tell me you're not going to give me another lecture. I've gotten them from everybody and I have a meeting with Coach first thing tomorrow."

"I'm picking you up at 8:30, by the way. After the meeting we'll go car shopping. You know what you want?"

Dom was grateful for the reprieve and change of subject. "I don't know. Feels like I need to get past the sports car phase."

Cody arched an eyebrow. "Seriously? You're twenty-eight years old, single, making seven figures and playing professional sports. You're going to buy an SUV?"

"You have one."

"I'm married with a kid!" Cody laughed. "I spend more time dragging him places than I do playing hockey!"

"How's Suze?" Cody's wife Suzanne had also gone to college with them.

"Good. We don't see each other much. I'm on the road or at practice, and she has her life, her friends. Cody Junior keeps her busy."

"You just moved to Vegas in April. She already has friends and a social life?"

"Well, as soon as she enrolled Cody in school she started meeting other moms, and she's pretty tight with Dave Marcus's wife Tiffany." Dave Marcus had been named an associate coach on the team.

They were quiet again as Dom took in the view, wondering how the hell a kid from upstate New York was going to live in a place like this. Nashville had been bad enough, but the desert? He probably deserved it, but right now the punishment didn't seem to fit the crime. He hadn't meant to hurt Bobby Thomas, or even to hit him that hard; he had just hit him. Dom didn't know the kid was going to put his head down at the last minute and hit the boards head-first. Now he was out indefinitely with a broken neck and a concussion, and Dom was banished to the desert with an expansion team, a hefty fine that had taken a chunk out of his bank account, and the warning that this was his last chance.

"You want to talk about Bobby Thomas?" Cody asked, reading his mind.

"There's nothing to say. He was playing dirty and needed to be taught a lesson, but I left my feet and smashed him into the boards. Dumbass put his head down; I didn't mean to hurt him. Everybody knows I hit hard—why did he put his head down?"

"I don't know. But that was the third time you've been called for boarding, and this guy might not come back. The only reason you're still here is because it's obvious he put his head down and Rousseau told them about the slashing."

Dom sighed. "Believe me, I know."

"When do you start anger management?" Cody knew anger management classes during the summer were part of his probation.

"Next week."

"You want me to go with you?"

"You don't have to babysit me."

"I'm not babysitting. You're one of my best friends—I don't play games— with them or with *you*. You have to give yourself a break, man. I know what you're going through."

"Okay." Dom was somewhat taken aback. Even in college, Cody had been the quiet one of the group. He was six feet, two inches of lean muscle with short sandy blond hair and blue eyes. He'd been a leading scorer in the NHL the last few years, and no one understood why he'd opted to leave his successful career in Canada to come to a brand-new NHL team in Las Vegas. Dom had a funny feeling it had something to do with him—in addition to a potentially humongous contract —and they had to talk about that soon. He just wasn't sure what to say. Friendship was one thing, but Cody putting his own career on the line took everything to another level. He was grateful but didn't feel like he deserved it.

When Cody was ready to go, they wandered out of the building and down the street, walking towards the adjacent block where he'd parked.

"The coffee place over there has fresh scones and croissants every morning— really amazing," said Cody. "Suze sends me down here sometimes on weekends for a dozen of them and freezes them so we have a few during the week."

"Good to know."

Cody pointed out an art gallery that had fun Friday night exhibits that included alcohol and lots of eligible women, as well as a few restaurants and a store that sold vintage sports paraphernalia.

When they ran out of small talk, Cody said evenly, "I know you don't want to talk about it, but don't you think we should?"

"Talk about what?" Dom ran a hand through his tousled dark brown hair; it fell to his shoulders and often stuck up when he didn't want it to. The longer it got, the better it behaved, but he'd gotten a bad haircut before he left Nashville and now was anxious for it to grow out.

"Maybe it's time to forget the past and move past all this," Cody said. "Find a good shrink and talk it out. It could be time to focus on finding a nice girl, settling down…"

"Yeah, right. Aside from the puck bunnies that are after either my bank account or bragging rights about banging an NHL player, there's no decent woman out there who's going to want my messed-up life."

"You're a smart, good-looking guy who makes a ton of money. How do you know there's no one out there? Just because you have some anger issues on the ice doesn't mean you would ever take it out on a woman."

"Who the hell knows what I would do if I spent a lot of time with someone?"

"You know, the doom and gloom is getting old already. You have to look at this as a second chance—the NHL is letting you play. Coach brought us here to start a whole new franchise. New city, new fans, new teammates—"

"Oh, give it a rest!" Dom snapped. "We're all a hot mess and you know it! Look at you and Suze—I mean, she had a one-night-stand with her fiancé's best friend, got knocked up and wound up being married to a guy she doesn't love! How is that less fucked up than my life?"

"First of all—" Cody's voice went cold "—don't talk about my wife like that. We were grieving. We made a mistake, but we got married and are raising a beautiful little boy we love very much. We've moved on, though, while you're still floundering and getting in trouble."

"Look," Dom took a deep breath; he didn't want to fight with Cody. "I appreciate your putting in a good word for me—"

"I didn't. Coach called me and asked if I'd come. He said you were coming—this was your last chance and he didn't know if you could get through it without someone like me here to have your back. Suze didn't care about Toronto one way or the other, so here we are. We thought all of us being together might be healing for us. We've moved on, but you're right—it hasn't been the same, and Suze and I have had our share of problems. Being here together could be cathartic, damn it, so you're going to try, even if I have to beat you into submission."

Dom rolled his eyes. "That didn't work in college, and I'm pretty sure it's not going to work on the dirtiest player in the NHL either."

Cody grinned. "Oh, but I've been watching, my friend—and I'm onto you!"

They chuckled, a moment of familiarity washing over them. Finally, Dom cleared his throat. "I know I've been a dick the last few years. I haven't been a very good friend, but you know there's nothing I wouldn't do for you guys—you're all the family I have, and even though I don't always act like it, I love you."

"We know that. Suze can't wait to see you. Coach says Andra is going to spoil us."

Dom laughed. "I can only imagine—"

His words broke off as a loud scream tore through the air.

"What was that?" Dom turned, his eyes darting up and down the street. There were fewer people here near the building than further up the street by the restaurant. There was an alley across from his building that led to a parking garage, and they both darted in that direction.

A woman was crying, and they could hear a man shouting.

"You stupid cow! I should throw your ass off the side!"

"Do it!" the woman screamed. "Go ahead—you're the big man! I dare you!"

There was the sound of a thud and a muffled scream.

Cody and Dom ran up the ramp of the garage towards the sounds. A stocky man in his 40s was holding a woman by the throat, pushing her perilously close to the edge of the railing. She wasn't fighting, her arms and head hanging limply despite the anger in her eyes.

"You dumb, fat bitch—you don't lie to me and get away with it! You understand me? I will kill you!"

"I already told you to—what's the matter, Tim? You chicken?" Her body was limp but there was spirit in her voice that belied her helplessness. "You don't love me! You don't want me! You can't stand to touch me—so go ahead!"

"That's too fucking bad! You're mine and you will not get off that easily!" He pulled his fist back and smashed it into her stomach just as Cody and Dom got to the level they were on.

"Hey!" Dom yelled, sprinting toward the couple. "You need to settle down."

"I'm a police officer." The man turned, a badge in his hand. "This is a private matter. You don't need to involve yourself."

"I just saw you punch an unarmed woman," Dom shot back. "Where I come from, that's not what police do."

The man turned and eyed them, his eyes squinty and mean. "You need to turn around and mind your own business. This is my wife, my business."

"You made it our business when you went public with it," Cody said, standing next to Dom with his arms folded across his chest and his phone visible in his hand.

"Just go," the woman whispered, sliding to the ground. "I'll be okay. Don't get involved."

"Shut up, bitch!" The man kicked her in the side and she whimpered from the pain.

"I'm not going to tell you again to step away from her," Dom said, moving into a threatening stance. He was an imposing figure on or off the ice, and with shoulders as broad as a truck and biceps the size of small trees, he wasn't a man many would stand up to.

Cody had discreetly begun recording the altercation. If there was going to be a fight with a cop, he was going to make sure there was video of it.

"You need to just walk away," the man said. "This is between my wife and me."

"She needs medical attention," Dom said, taking a step closer.

"She needs her ass beat so she learns to listen when her husband tells her not to leave the house!"

Dom had to force himself not to react to such an idiotic comment. "She's not a child or a dog," he heard himself saying. "And whatever it is she did, it's still *illegal* to hit her."

"Do you understand who I am?" The man pulled his jacket aside and revealed a holster with a gun.

"I've got 911 dialed into the phone," Cody said. "And I've been recording this whole conversation. You need to find somewhere to cool down."

The men stared each other down, the policeman looking from Dom to Cody and then back again. "You messed with the wrong cop," he spat. "And you're going to be sorrier than she is."

"I think you misunderstood the part where I don't give a fuck *who* you are," Dom said in a voice that would have scared any other man. "Now step away from the lady and get out of here."

"If this shows up on the internet," the man to his wife, "you'll regret ever meeting me!"

"I already do," she whispered before doubling over in pain.

"Bitch!" He went to kick her again but Dom moved so fast the man never had a chance. Grabbing him by the scruff of the neck, Dom growled, "You don't know how lucky you are. On any other day, I'd break you in half. Today, however, I have a boss to impress and can't afford to go to jail. Now get out of here!" He shoved the other man, hard, in the opposite direction. The two men stared each other down for a moment before the policeman turned and jogged away.

2

DOM KNELT BEFORE THE CRYING WOMAN. "WHAT CAN WE DO FOR YOU, MISS? YOU need to go to a hospital and—"

"No!" Though one eye was now swollen shut, the other one, which was bright green, widened in horror. "He knows everyone at the hospitals. He'll find a way to make it look like this was my fault! Please, just leave. I can find a way home later, after he cools down."

"You're bleeding, one eye is swollen shut and you might have some broken ribs." Dom spoke gently. "We play for the new NHL team that's coming to Las Vegas—we're not going to hurt you. We can help."

For a moment their gazes locked, her one thick-lashed green eye and his dark brown ones, and something deep in his gut twisted almost painfully. Her mere closeness made his entire being yearn to hold her tightly and make all her pain go away.

Finally, she spoke in a tiny voice. "There's no one who can help me—he'll hurt anyone who tries. It's better for you to let me be. He has a lot of friends on the force—helping me will bring nothing but trouble to your life."

For the first time in weeks, Dominic laughed. "Sweetheart, that tiny little man has no idea what trouble is if he thinks I'm going to leave you here or let a cop torment his wife." He reached out his hand. "Come with Cody and me—I'm Dominic, by the way."

"Molly," she said automatically. When someone introduced themselves to you, you told them your name too, even though it seemed kind of ridiculous under the current circumstances.

"Let us help you."

"It won't matter," she said after a long moment. "He'll find me, and I have nowhere to go. I can't go to my friends because he'll cause trouble for them, and the longer I stay gone, the more he'll beat me when I get back."

"So don't go back," Dom said simply.

"I have nowhere else to go. No money, no savings, no family. I'm all alone."

Dom and Cody looked at each other. There was no way they could leave her here, but where could they take her? Finally, Dom reached out both his hands.

"Come with me. I just moved here—literally today—and I have a big apartment all to myself. You can lock yourself in my guest room and never see anyone. He'll never be able to find you, and in the meantime, we can figure out a way to help you."

Cody was gaping at him and Molly just stared at him with her one beautiful green eye. "Why would you do that?" she asked at last. "You don't even know me."

He sighed and looked away. For a long time, there was silence. Then he said, "Because once upon a time I knew someone who needed to be saved, and I couldn't save him. I'm not letting it happen again."

While Cody ran to get his SUV, Dom sat beside Molly and gently asked her questions about where she could go or if she needed medical attention. She said very little, grimacing from the pain in her abdomen where Tim had hit her. He'd been hitting her for so long, she couldn't even remember a time when there was no pain. Usually there was a big blowup once every month or so, but today had been bad. There was a chance she was pregnant, and Tim had forbidden her to leave the house because she'd had so many miscarriages.

He'd insisted if she stayed home she might actually carry this child to term, but they'd needed groceries. He expected dinner on the table when he got home, no matter what, so she'd gone to the store. Apparently he'd put a tracking app on her phone and could see where she was, so he'd found her at the bakery up the street, dragged her out and pulled her into this parking garage where he threatened to kill her, like he always did. Except this time, she was done; this time, she was tired of him hurting her.

Then along came two knights in shining armor, with their broad shoulders and bulging biceps, saving her from Tim and, if she was honest, from herself. She wasn't listening to what Dom was saying anymore; his voice was so soothing, she found herself just resting up against the wall, half falling asleep. He had the most beautiful voice, deep and slightly gravelly, like a television announcer, but sexier.

"Come on," Dom was gently reaching for her. "We're going to put you in the car and drive you over to my place. He won't be able to see you in the back seat, and he won't know where you went."

"He has a tracker in my phone," she whispered.

"Give it to me." Dom held out his hand and she pulled it out of her pocket, handing it to him. It occurred to her that this was probably the stupidest thing she'd ever done, but honestly, what could they possibly do to her that hadn't already been done? She'd almost been ready to die half an hour ago—surely these guys couldn't beat her worse than Tim did, and God knew getting attacked by someone as gorgeous as Dom or his blond friend had to be better than any sex she'd ever had with her husband. Though she felt a tiny prickle of fear, she was already resigned to whatever was to come.

She watched him take a small chip out of her phone and put it in his pocket before handing the phone back to her.

"The tracker won't work now," he said with a smile. "And Cody will toss it out the window on his way home."

"Okay." She let him lift her into the back seat of a massive SUV and she melted into the soft leather as he shut the door.

"Do you know what you're doing?" Cody asked Dom.

"What choice do I have?"

Cody shook his head. "You can't afford to get into more trouble, Dom."

"How can I get into trouble by helping someone? Don't worry about me. I got this."

"*That's* what I'm worried about!"

Molly normally would have been awed by the big, beautiful condo with the fabulous windows, sleek décor and gourmet kitchen. But right now she just wanted to curl up somewhere and succumb to the sleep she so desperately needed. Tim kept her up half the night wanting sex, food, or to beat her. She rarely slept through the night because she was so accustomed to being awakened, but right now she couldn't think about anything else.

She couldn't hear what Cody and Dom were saying, but Cody gave her a short nod before leaving.

Dom approached her slowly. "Look, I just moved in, hours ago, so I don't know where anything is. There's a bathroom in there, by the guest room. I can give you one of my t-shirts and some shorts to sleep in. They'll be a little big, but they're clean."

"That's okay. I just want to sleep."

"Good. I won't bother you. I'll be in my room, and then I'll be out early in the morning. I have an 8:30 meeting with my new boss."

"Thank you," she said after a moment. She limped into the guest room, closing and locking the door behind her. She took a deep breath. No matter what happened, she reminded herself, it had to be better than life with Tim. Besides, Dom was gorgeous and looked to be in his twenties. She was almost forty, overweight and a complete mess. It's not like he would be interested in her. She just wanted to be left alone.

H er door was still closed in the morning when Dom arose, and he didn't disturb her. He left a note to tell her there were muffins on the counter and some coffee she could warm up in the microwave, and scrawled his cell phone number at the bottom in case she needed anything. Hopefully he would be home by early afternoon and they could talk. He had no idea what he was going to do with her, but he had to get her away from her husband.

Cody was waiting downstairs. "Morning. Ready to face the music?"

Dom rolled his eyes. "Not really, but let's get this over with."

"So what happened with Molly?"

Dom shrugged. "She locked herself in the guest room and I haven't seen her since. Sounded like she was still asleep, but I didn't bother her."

"She's not a stray puppy, Dom. I mean, you can't just *keep* her."

"I know that!" Dom scowled. "But seriously, should we have just left her there to cops who probably weren't going to help her, and a man who's obviously been abusing her a long time?"

"No, but you're setting yourself up for a world of trouble if he figures out where she is and tries to get to her."

"Look, I'm going to talk to her and see what she wants to do. If she really wants to go back, I have to let her. I just want to give her the chance to escape. If she chooses not to take my help, well, at least I tried."

"Most abused women go back. Suze and I looked up some information last night. There are shelters and programs, but without a family, and him being a local cop, I don't think those would work for her."

"Me either. But right now I've got to get my head in the game and think about what I'm going to say to Coach."

Coach's new office was a far cry from the one he'd had as a college coach. This one was upscale and beautiful: professionally decorated with plush leather furniture and expensive-looking artwork. The colors were warm and inviting, and Dom had a feeling Andra had something to do with that—she'd always insisted that their places be made to feel inviting, even their tiny dorm rooms. It felt like such a long time since he'd seen Andra, and he'd missed her. His own mother had died when he was a teenager, and had been an alcoholic for years before that, so Andra had given him his only real experience with having a mother.

"Dominic!" Brad Barnett came into the room, grinning broadly. The two men embraced with genuine affection. "You look good, son! I'm glad you're here."

"I'm glad too, Coach." Dom forced a smile.

"Don't bullshit me," Brad laughed, sinking into the chair behind his big desk. "You hate being here and you think Vegas is a dumbass place to have a hockey team."

"It is—but that doesn't mean I'm not grateful to have a chance to play for you again."

"There is that, I suppose." Brad looked at his protégé and couldn't help but shake his head. The kid was so damn good. An offensive defenseman who could play forward or defense, he could also fight, rack up the penalty minutes, score goals and, when he wasn't in an anger-infused haze, had the potential to be a great team captain. But Dom had never recovered from his best friend's murder—Brian had been Brad's son—and nothing any of them had done could get Dom to comprehend it wasn't his fault. Brad probably should have had this talk with Dom a few years ago, but he'd been busy with his own career and his own grief.

"Coach, why did you bring me here?" Dom never beat around the bush. "We had a close relationship in college, but I've totally dropped the ball since Brian died. Why am I here? If this is pity—"

"It's *not* pity." Brad made sure the younger man was looking at him. "It's a favor, it's almost nepotism, but it's not *pity*. Listen to me. As a man, as a human being, as a father, I owe you everything for what you tried to do for Brian the night he died. You had his back—even though he died anyway, you were there. As his father, I can't ever thank you enough for jumping in knowing you could have been killed too. You stepped in front of those thugs and protected him—"

"I didn't protect him!" Dom felt his heart thudding in his chest as he pictured his friend's body lying in that alley. "He *died*!"

"That's not your fault! He was dead before you got there, son! You couldn't save him, but you didn't know that and you put yourself in the line of fire in case he was still alive. Nothing I'll ever do can repay you for that—and besides all that, you were my shining star! Better than the rest of the team put together, better than my own son—God, you are one of the finest hockey players to ever come into the NHL. You could be another Gretzky if you didn't keep playing dirty. You're the only one who doesn't believe it. That's why you're here—because I believe you're better than what people see. I know the real Dominic Gianni, and I'll be damned if I'll let you continue down the path you're on.

"You're on my team, but this isn't college anymore. I won't coddle you; I expect you to do everything the NHL has mandated in your probation, and I expect you to fucking score goals and *legally* knock the living shit out of every team we play. Do you understand me?"

"Yes, sir."

"I also expect you to go out of your way to coddle my wife." His arched an eyebrow. "Technically, I can't enforce this rule, but I'm asking you as someone who thinks of you as a son, to spend some time with her. Brian was our only child, and when we lost him we lost all of you. You and Cody went off to the NHL, Sergei went back to Russia, and even Suze dropped out of sight, as though sleeping with Cody the night of Brian's funeral was going to make us hate her."

"That's what she thinks."

"I know, but she won't take any of the olive branches Andra's offered. I know it's a burden for a single guy like you, but she needs something to do, and I've moved her so many times the last few years, she's all alone."

"It's never been a burden to spend time with Andra," Dom muttered, trying to figure out why he was choked up. "I just feel like I let her down. Brian..." His voice trailed off. "I know she expected me to save him."

"Andra and I had the police reports and medical reports independently examined. Brian's heart was still beating, but he was brain-dead before you got there. The men who jumped him are still in jail, and Andra plans to be at every one of their probation hearings. Trust me—she doesn't blame you. The only one who blames you is *you*."

"Okay." Dom cleared his throat, trying to regain his composure. "So now what?"

"You have anger management classes twice a week for ten weeks, as well as the shrink they want you to see. Cody said he lined up a special trainer for you guys to work out with five days a week, and I expect you to help me prepare for when the rest of the team arrives. Cody's the unofficial captain right now, because it's a new team and we're going to need leadership over the summer while guys get settled, and you're going to be part of that process. We'll probably have a couple of rookies, so they're not going to have any experience with you, none of them have a personal beef with you, and you're going to make it clear to them that you've got their backs."

"Got it."

"All right. We're done." Brad paused. "Dinner tonight?"

"Sure."

"Dinner's at 7, but come early."

"Okay."

"See you tonight." Brad turned, put on his reading glasses and picked up a stack of papers. Dom figured that was his cue and slipped out.

3

CODY WAS IN THE HALL TEXTING SOMEONE, A FAINT SMILE ON HIS FACE.

"You look like you're texting a woman," said Dom.

Cody jumped, his eyes narrowing slightly. "What's that supposed to mean?"

"Just what I said. You had a kind of wistful look on your face, and that used to mean a girl."

"I'm married, so there are no girls." Cody stuck the phone back in his pocket.

"Dude, I saw you at the hotel in Boston with that redhead a few years back. I know there are *girls*, even if they're one-night-stands."

Cody clenched his jaw. "Look, we've been friends a long time, but you need to butt out of this."

"Suze deserves better."

"Suze doesn't sleep in my bed!" Cody spat back before he could stop himself.

"Because you cheated? Or do you cheat now because she stopped sleeping with you?"

"I don't know," Cody admitted. "All I know is she won't sleep with me. I mean, we tried for a while, but Brian was somehow always between us. Then one night I lost my temper and accused her of still pining for him, and she told me I was right. Then she moved into the guest room. These days, she's back in our room and we share a bed because CJ is old enough to notice, but we live separate lives."

"Do you still love her?"

Cody's eyes met Dom's sadly.

"You always loved her," Dom said, "from the first time you saw her, but she never had eyes for anyone but Brian. Sergei and I figured out how you felt, but I don't think Brian ever did."

"Yeah, I've always loved her. But she doesn't love me, and she knows there have been other women, so now she never will. I'm not going anywhere because —well, you know why."

"Yeah." Dom shook his head. "And everyone thinks *I'm* the hot mess?"

Dom didn't see Molly when he got home that afternoon from car shopping; the guest room door was still closed, but the food was gone and the cups and plates washed, so he knew she'd been out. He left her another note, telling her to order Chinese food or pizza for dinner because he had somewhere to go, and left a credit card next to it. That was probably the dumbest thing he'd ever done, but he couldn't picture the timid, frightened woman going online and charging thousands of dollars of clothes or jewelry on his credit card. Something inside him told him he could trust her, even though he had nothing to base it on.

He dressed in pressed slacks and a button-down shirt, picked up a bottle of wine he'd bought earlier, and went downstairs to wait for Cody. Waiting for someone to drive him places was getting old fast, and he needed to buy a car sooner rather than later. Maybe tonight he could coax Molly out of her room, show her the brochures he'd picked up for the cars he'd seen today and get her opinion. A woman's opinion was always good, even if he already had a good idea what he wanted. It would also be a safe topic to get them talking, because at some point they were going to have to.

He was happy to see Suze in the car when Cody pulled up. She jumped out and hugged him tightly. "It's *so* good to see you," she exclaimed.

"You too, gorgeous." He shook his head. "Damn if you don't look good enough to eat."

"You're still a pig, Gianni!" she teased.

"Hey! That's my wife!" Cody yelled.

Dom and Suze had always had a playfully flirtatious relationship, and they fell back into the routine now as though no time had passed. Suze did look good, though. Her naturally blond hair was still long and straight, but she'd curled it a little tonight and it fell almost to her waist in soft, sexy waves. Her bright blue eyes had long lashes, and her lips were full and pink. In a slinky turquoise halter dress and matching low-heeled sandals, there was no sign she'd ever had a baby. Everything about her was almost the same, and a wave of nostalgia washed over him as they headed towards the interstate.

"So what do you think of the desert?" Suze asked Dom.

"It's hot. How do you like it?"

"I love having a pool, and the shopping is pretty damn amazing."

"You had a pool at your old house."

"Yeah, but we could never swim in it. It was in Toronto, for God's sake—it was always freezing!"

"It was heated," Cody protested.

"Yeah, but the minute you stepped out it was like having brain freeze all over your body."

"The winters are pretty harsh up north," Dom agreed. "But I miss it. I miss Boston."

"You'd go back to Boston?" Cody glanced at him in the rear view mirror.

"Probably not to the Bruins. I don't have a lot of friends on that team, but I'd go back to the area."

"Not me," Suze said with a shudder. "If I never set foot in Boston again it'll be too soon."

Silence fell over the car.

"Sorry," Suze said after a minute. "I didn't mean to kill the mood."

"It's fine," said Dom.

"So tell me about the car hunt," she prompted.

They fell back into easy chatter all the way to Brad and Andra's, but quieted again as they drove into the gated community. The Barnetts had lived modestly in Boston, and Dom, Cody and Suze were surprised to see how big their new house was, considering it was just the two of them now.

They walked to the door and rang the bell, all of them suddenly nervous.

"I haven't seen Andra in ages," Suze murmured. "We've been here for almost two months, but I haven't made it over here."

"We've been busy unpacking, and getting CJ settled in school," said Cody. "She knows that."

The door swung open to reveal a smiling Andra. "Oh, my goodness, look at my kids, home again!" She threw her arms around Suze. "Look at you, still the prettiest girl on campus."

Suze blushed. "If people keep telling me that, I'm going to start to believe it."

"As you should!" Andra reached for Cody next. "How are you, handsome?"

"I'm doing great. Thanks so much for having us over."

"It should have been sooner. I was just waiting until we got settled in." Andra turned to Dom, placing her hands on either side of his face. "Look at my Dominic. So grown up now."

"I've filled out some," he replied, returning her embrace.

"Jesus, Andra, are you going to invite them in or keep them in the hallway?" Brad bellowed from inside the house.

"Come in, all of you," said Andra, taking Dom's arm. "Let me show you around."

They made their way through the spacious home as Andra pointed out a few items of artwork and furniture. It was clear how much work she'd put into making her home beautiful and welcoming.

They entered a warm, cozy eat-in kitchen with a granite island bordered by six leather stools.

"Have a seat," said Brad as he uncorked a bottle of Chardonnay. "We'll have a drink and chat before we eat," he added as he placed the bottle next to open bottles of cabernet and pinot noir.

After everyone's glass was filled, Brad raised his for a toast. "To old friends and new beginnings."

"New beginnings." Everyone touched glasses.

Andra brought out appetizers and soon everyone was engrossed in conversation.

Dom wandered into the adjacent family room and was joined by Andra. They stood before a huge fireplace, looking at the framed photographs displayed on its mantle: Brian as a child; Brad in his Montreal Canadiens uniform from his years playing in the NHL; Brad and Andra's wedding photo... and then the one that made Dom's heart thud in his chest. He could handle looking at Brian as a kid, but the picture of the group of them celebrating after winning the Frozen Four just days before Brian's death, got him every time. They all were there: Dom, Cody, Brian, Brad and Andra, Suze, Sergei and his then-girlfriend, Maria, and Sergei's older brother Toli.

God, they'd all been so young and innocent. Brian's face was alight with laughter as Toli made rabbit ears behind his head. Suze's head was thrown back, her long blond hair flowing behind her. Sergei and Toli were grinning broadly, each with an arm thrown around the other's shoulder. Dom and Cody were flashing thumbs-up signs, and Brad and Andra looked so much younger and happier. The haunted look he saw now in her long-lashed grey eyes hadn't been there that night.

Even as their team mom, Andra had always been a beauty. Petite and trim, she was absolutely stunning, with shoulder-length ash blond hair and the amazing grey eyes she'd passed on to her son. People always had commented on how much alike they looked: and of course, Brian always had girls after him, but he'd never looked at anyone but Suze from the day they'd met in their freshman English class.

"You look sad," said Andra, coming to stand beside him.

"That picture brings back a lot of memories."

"They should be good memories. We had so many good times."

"We did." Dom looked down at her. "I'm sorry I haven't been around for you, Andra."

"Oh, sweetheart, we've all grieved in our own way." Her eyes roved across the line of photos of her son. "But life does go on, especially for you young people. Now that we're together again, we need to try harder. Brian wouldn't have liked this at all."

"I know." Dom looked back at the picture. "He'd be pissed that Cody and I haven't been there for you."

"It's not your job to take care of me. I'm the mom—I should have been taking care of you." She glanced over at Cody and Suze, who were laughing at something Brad was saying. "And I certainly should have taken better care of Suze. She looks so sad."

"It's been a long time since I've spent time with them, so I'm not sure."

"Well, maybe now that will all change." Andra squeezed his hand. "I'm here for you. You know that, Dom, don't you?"

"I know." He bent to kiss her cheek. "I've always known. I just didn't know how to reach out. And I was scared."

"That I was angry?"

Dom hunched his shoulders. "It was my fault, even though I didn't do it. I should have known something was wrong and—"

"That's the dumbest thing I've ever heard!" She wagged a finger in his face. "You had no way of knowing where he was going. He was a 22-year-old man who took a shortcut and ran into criminals. That is not in any way your fault. So let's move on from that nonsense and go back to being a family."

"I have a long summer ahead of me before I can get back to anything."

"Yes, I heard about the anger management classes and the psychologist." She paused. "Dom, have you thought about being treated for post-traumatic stress disorder?"

He shook his head. "I've been reading about it, and it's part of what I'll discuss with the therapist, but it's really more about being pissed off that it happened. They put me on antidepressants for a while after Brian died, but they didn't help. There's no real diagnosis."

"So do you think you're going to be okay now?"

"I don't have a choice. If I get into any more trouble, I'm done with hockey, and that's not an option."

"We're here for you," she said gently, squeezing his arm. "And I have faith in you."

He smiled. "Thanks, Andra."

"So," Andra said with a smile, "Tell me what's new."

Dom felt a twinge of guilt as he realized how easily his thoughts had turned from Brian to Molly. "Actually, there is something interesting that happened almost the minute I got to Vegas." He told her the story of how he and Cody had found Molly.

"And she's at your apartment?" Andra gaped at him. "Dominic, have you lost your mind? Is this about sex? You could have had any number of puck bunnies without giving them access to your credit card!"

He shook his head. ""It's not like that."

"Okay. Then tell me what it *is* like."

"I don't know anything about her. I can't even tell how old is she is—she's really beaten up; one eye is swollen shut, and she looks kind of dumpy, but there's something about her eyes... I just couldn't walk away. Her good eye is bright green, and when I looked at her, I knew I couldn't leave her there and let that asshole could kill her. She'd given up—I saw it in her face—and I couldn't let her."

"Dom... Saving her won't bring Brian back."

"I know—but it might make me feel like I didn't screw up again."

"You didn't screw up the first time," she reminded him. "But being kind to another human being is never a bad thing."

"She hasn't said a word to me since I brought her home. I know she's terrified. You had to be there, Andra. Cody was horrified too. That's why he taped it on his phone, in case that guy tries anything with his police friends. I don't think he figured out who we were, but eventually she's going to have to either go home, or serve him with divorce papers, and she's going to have to show some sort of address…" His voice trailed off. "I don't even know what I'm talking about. Jesus, Andra, am I in trouble already?"

"No, sweetheart. You're being the kind, gentle Dominic I remember. Saving a woman from a wife-beater is a good thing. You just have to go home and find a way to get her to talk to you without scaring her, and make sure she's on the up-and-up. Other than that, you're doing a good thing. Maybe it's the best thing that's happened to you since Brian died." She touched his face gently and then turned back towards the others.

"Dinner time!" she announced, and ushered them all toward the dining room.

4

It was a fun evening: filled with laughter, good food and shared memories. When they left, Andra made them promise they would come back soon.

There was a peaceful silence in the car as they headed back towards Dom's apartment. Finally, Suze turned to look back at Dominic.

"Did you tell her?"

"No. Not my place. But you have to, Suze, because she's going to find out now that you live here."

Her eyes filled with tears. "I don't know how."

"We'll figure it out." Cody immediately reached for her hand. "Come on, don't cry. It's been one big misunderstanding after another, and now it feels like everything has come together for us to do what we should have done years ago."

"It could ruin your career. Which could hurt Dom if you're not here for him! It could fuck up everything! "

"It's not going to hurt my career," said Cody. "I could go back to Toronto tomorrow if I wanted to—it's not like I committed a crime. If Brad wants me off the team for personal reasons then we'll deal with it, but now that we're here we have to come clean."

"And then what?" Suze whispered. "Are you going to leave me?"

"What? No!" Cody glanced at her and then back at Dom. "Can we talk about this in private?"

"Why? I'm sure Dom knows about what you do on the road and—"

"What I *did*." Cody emphasized the word. "I do *not* do that anymore. I was still grieving too, and while Dom was beating the shit out of guys on the ice, I had sex with a lot of women. I'm not saying it was right. I'm just saying I've been faithful—and celibate—for close to two years."

This time the silence in the car was almost palpable, and Dom wished he could drown in the leather seats.

No one said a word until they arrived at Dom's condo, and he jumped out quickly after kissing Suze's cheek and nudging Cody's shoulder.

"So, the gym at 9, lunch, and then car shopping?" Cody asked as if nothing had happened.

"Yeah, I'll see you in the morning." Dom was inside the building even before Cody pulled his SUV away from the curb. Dom didn't know what was going on between Cody and Suze, but he wanted no part of it. He'd never been in a serious, adult relationship, and theirs looked about as complicated as they came. No, he'd much rather deal with the strange, abused woman who was hiding in his apartment than anything going on with his friends' personal lives.

When he opened the apartment door, he could see a light coming from down the hallway, but everything else was dark. Without turning on the lights, he headed towards his room, but stopped when he saw a bar stool out of place... and a shadow in the recess beneath the granite bar's overhang.

It was Molly, with her knees pulled tightly against her chest and her hair hanging down around her face. He paused, unsure whether to leave her alone and just go on to bed, but something about her was radiating fear. Slowly, he knelt in front of her.

"Molly? Are you okay?"

She didn't say anything, merely dipped her head in the barest nod.

"Did something happen? Why are you sitting here?"

"Someone knocked on the door," she whispered. "I thought it was Tim."

"He has no way of knowing where you are. He could try going door-to-door at every condo on this street, but this building has good security. Even a cop can't get up here without a warrant. You haven't been out since you got here, so there's no way anyone could have seen you."

For a moment she met his gaze in the semi-darkness, then closed her eyes and let her head fall back against the cabinets. She didn't say anything else, and finally, not knowing what else to do, he moved another bar stool and eased himself to the floor beside her, making sure to leave several feet of space between them. He too leaned back against the cabinets and was surprised to find it somewhat soothing, despite the hard tiled floor.

For long minutes, neither spoke. Finally, Dom couldn't help himself: he needed to talk to someone, and she seemed to be more in the mood to listen than to speak. "I had a stressful evening. Cody and his wife Suze and I had dinner with my boss—his name is Brad. He and his wife Andra have a beautiful house about twenty minutes north of here. There's a lot of history between us, and I'm kind of in a weird situation."

Molly said nothing, but he saw her glance at him.

"We were all in college together in Boston. Brad was our coach. His son Brian and I were best friends. Cody was on the team too. We were one big happy family for almost four years. Then Brian died, and everything went to hell, even though Cody and I both got picked up by the NHL. It was like I couldn't stop being angry, so I took it out on guys on the ice—fighting, unsportsmanlike behavior; you name it, I did it. Now I'm on probation with the NHL, and this new Las Vegas team is my last chance. No other coach wants to take me on, and the only reason I'm here is because of Brad. He knows I've never forgiven myself for Brian's death, so he's trying to let me know that he doesn't blame me. But *I* blame me." He sighed, staring up at the bottom of the granite overhang.

"Why do you blame yourself?" she asked suddenly, her voice soft but well-modulated and a little bit raspy.

"It's a long story."

"We're not going out tonight, are we?" She looked completely serious, and he would have laughed if he didn't think it might hurt her feelings.

"No, I guess we're not." He shifted to rest his arms on his knees. "It started in our freshman year of college. I was there on a hockey scholarship, and I roomed with a couple of other players: a Minnesota farm boy named Cody Armstrong, and a Russian brainiac named Sergei Petrov. Sergei is really smart, and he helped us with the hard classes like chemistry and calculus.

"Second semester, we had one of those massive lecture classes, World Litera-ture, and sitting in the front row was one of the most beautiful girls we'd ever seen. We all took the class together because A, it was mandatory, and B, we figured if Sergei was with us we'd do okay. Sergei always used to sit down front so he could see and hear better, so of course we had to follow him if we wanted him to help us, and there she was. Suzanne Conway, with this hot body, long blond hair that fell to her ass, big blue eyes, beautiful smile, and tremendous tits. We fell all over ourselves to get her attention, but she only saw Brian. Within days they were a couple, and Suze, she was right there: drinking, trash-talking, hockey-loving—she was one of us. That was the great thing about Suze—she fit in with the crazy hockey players, all while painting her fingernails, getting straight A's and talking science and physics with Sergei.

"We had so much fun. Sergei's older brother Toli was already playing in the NHL, so whenever they were in or near Boston we'd go hang out with the team. We were playing our asses off. We won two championships in four years, and life was pretty great. We spent almost every weekend over at Brian's house—his mom and dad were just amazing. At any given time, there were five or six of us sleeping over. I don't have any family, so it was like nothing I'd ever experienced. My dad died when I was six and my mom became an alcoholic. She died when I was sixteen and I moved in with my hockey coach. He was a bachelor, so I stayed with him until I got my scholarship to Boston College. The Barnetts were the only family I'd ever had."

He stopped talking and looked over at her. She hadn't said anything, just watched him with her one bright-green eye. Even in the darkness, he could see how beautiful it was. He could tell she was older than he was, especially now with a big purple bruise around one eye, several cuts on her lips; and she appeared completely shapeless within his oversized t-shirt and baggy shorts. But her eyes were bewitching. When she looked at him, it was as if he'd known her forever.

"They sound wonderful," she whispered.

"So, senior year," he continued, "Suze was planning a huge birthday party for Brian. His birthday was April first, and we had just won our second championship. She wanted to make it a big deal; combination celebration for the win, graduation, and Brian's twenty-second birthday. What she didn't know was that he was planning to propose that night. And Brian didn't know there was a party planned, so Cody and I were helping *him* plan his proposal and *her* plan her birthday shindig.

"The night of the event, Suze was a crazy woman. She had everything set up at this little bar where we used to hang out. The setup was Cody and I were taking him there for a birthday drink before he took Suze out for a romantic dinner. We were halfway there when Brian freaked out because he'd forgotten the friggin' ring. He told us to go on ahead and he'd meet us there in ten minutes—our apartment wasn't far. We tried to go with him, but he insisted we go on, and there was no way to do it without making him suspicious. When we got there, Suze was pissed we let him go back alone because he was notorious for getting sidetracked. He was always forgetting things, showing up late, waking up late, going to the wrong place—he was like that."

Dom paused before telling the hardest part of the story, the part that always made him sick to his stomach. He wasn't sure he could get through it—he'd never managed to before. Not to Coach Brad, not to any number of therapists, not even to Cody, even though Cody had been there and lived it with him.

"It's okay," said Molly, gazing at him intently. "Whatever it is, it'll be okay."

He took a deep breath and continued. "After about half an hour, Suze sent us to find him, even if it ruined the surprise. Brian wasn't answering his phone, so we were a little worried. Brian was scatterbrained, but he would never stand up his buds on his birthday. Cody, Sergei and I headed back. It was still chilly in Boston, and there had been snow the day before, so we were slipping and sliding down the streets. We split up, and Cody and Sergei went back towards the apartment while I went the other direction to follow a shortcut we always took when we were drunk and wanted to get in the building without any of the R.A.'s seeing us."

Dom's mind whirled with the details, even though it had been seven years. "Then I heard it. Men were yelling, cursing in Spanish, and somehow I just knew Brian was involved. I yelled for Cody, knowing he couldn't be far off, and I just ran. I skidded into that alley and saw Brian's body on the ground; they were kicking him, over and over." He gulped in a breath. "I don't... I don't even remember what I did next. I remember grabbing two of them and slamming their heads together and screaming for help. I just kept punching and hitting..." His voice trailed off before coming back as a whisper. "There was so much blood. All I could think about was getting them off him.

"Cody and Sergei got there a minute later and they say I had Brian in my arms. There were four of them, gangbangers who'd been in the middle of a drug deal when Brian stumbled onto them. He fought hard, but one of them hit him in the back of the head with a pipe..." Dom felt the familiar wave of nausea, and had to lower his head so he wouldn't heave all over the floor. His heart was racing, just like when he relived it in his dreams, and he fought to regain control. This was how he felt on the ice sometimes, and that's when he would hurt people.

He was barely aware she'd inched over until he felt a gentle hand on his arm. "It's okay," said softly. "You don't have to tell me the rest. Unless you want to."

"Yeah," he rasped, trying to breathe. "I do. I have to tell somebody. I've never told anyone before."

"Okay." She leaned over and rested her head against his shoulder. "I'm right here. Those guys can't hurt Brian anymore. Or you."

His throat tightened, as though he might cry, but he swallowed the urge and forced himself to finish. "They hit him so hard his brains came out. When I finally had taken all four of them down, I grabbed him and saw pieces of his brain all over the ground. I tried to hold it together. I held him and begged him not to die. He was still breathing, but we found out later that even though his heart was beating he was already brain-dead. There wouldn't be any way to repair that damage, but I tried to keep his skull together. I wrapped his head in my scarf while Cody and Sergei tied up the bangers. Then we all just sat there in the alley, crying, watching Brian die." Tears began slipping down his face and he tried to wipe them away.

"Oh, Dom, that's the saddest thing I've ever heard." Molly wrapped her arms around his shoulders and pulled him close to her so his head was buried in her shoulder. "Go ahead and let it out—how long have you been holding that in?"

"Seven years," he choked, his tears soaking through her shirt.

She stroked his long, silky hair but didn't say anything. For a long time, after his tears had dried and he was calm again, she held him against her. She kept stroking his hair, whispering that he was okay now. She didn't know what else to do for him, but for the first time in more than a decade she felt someone else's pain could actually rival her own. She'd had a moment the day she met him where she had been positive the only solution for her was death; now she knew that couldn't be true. Dom had watched someone he loved die, and it was slowly destroying him; somehow, it made her feel ashamed he'd had to watch her try to goad Tim into killing her. Death wasn't really a solution for anything; the only way to fix things would be to live. A few days ago she wouldn't have believed that.

"Cody is the guy who was with you when you found me?" she asked finally, sensing he was ready to talk again.

"Yeah. He and Suze are married now. They left Toronto to come here and play with our old coach." He explained the situation.

"So you're back with your friends. Isn't that a good thing?"

"It is, but it's complicated. Cody and Suze had sex the night of Brian's funeral, and she got pregnant. So they got married, and then he got picked up by Toronto. I went to Buffalo and Sergei went back to Russia. We all went our separate ways and although we've stayed in touch, it's not like it was."

"Of course not," she said, leaning back and moving slightly away from him. "You've all grown up."

"Yeah, but we needed each other and didn't take care of each other. Brian was the glue that kept us together, and without him, we fell apart. He'd be pissed."

"He would know you did the best you could under the circumstances."

"Maybe." Dom sighed heavily. "I feel like I just ran a marathon."

"Seems like it was a long time coming."

"Maybe," he acknowledged. "What about you? Are you going to tell me about you?"

She looked away. "What's to tell? A stupid 18-year-old marries her first boyfriend right out of high school, finds out too late he has a mean streak and then isn't strong enough or smart enough to leave him. Now I'm almost 40 years old, married to a cop who keeps me under lock and key, and I've got nothing to look forward to. I almost had him mad enough to kill me this time, but you stopped him." She paused to look at him. "At first I was annoyed about that, but now I'm glad, because it meant I could be here for you tonight."

"You really wanted to die?"

"I wanted the pain to stop," she said. "You have to understand I've lived all of my adult life in terror. I've had twelve miscarriages because of him beating me. My family is mostly dead, and he doesn't let me have any money or credit cards. Hell, he barely lets me leave the house. I don't have any friends because he uses them to manipulate me. I've never been on a vacation, or had a party, or celebrated the holidays. I've been married twenty-two years and I don't think he's ever made love to me—I don't even know exactly what that means. I'm thirty-nine years old and I've never had an orgasm." She laughed suddenly. "And I'm sitting here telling all this to a complete stranger."

"I don't think we qualify as strangers anymore," said Dom. "We've lived together for two days, and you know my life story."

She managed a smile. "I suppose there's that."

"I can help you," he said. "Let me help you."

"I don't know what you can do. He's a detective in Henderson. He knows everyone, has connections everywhere, and he'll find me. Then he will make you, and everyone you care about, miserable, until he gets what he wants."

"Which is what?"

"I don't know," she admitted. "I don't think he wants to kill me. He just has a temper, and there's no way for me to be perfect enough to make him happy. It started with the first miscarriage. I talked to the doctor—it happens in about a third of first pregnancies; so often that many women never even know they're pregnant. But we knew, and he was furious, convinced it was because I was working and going to school. So he made me quit, and we got pregnant again about six months later. We had an argument when I was about 15 weeks along, and he shoved me into a wall. I miscarried the next day.

"He made all the noises about being sorry and how it would never happen again, but it did. Every time I got pregnant, he got meaner and meaner, and I miscarried every time. The doctor told me I should get my tubes tied—every miscarriage caused more damage—but Tim wouldn't allow it. He's still saying he wants a son, but he beats me every time I get pregnant. There's nothing left for me. I'm so tired, Dom." She rested her head against his arm again. "And eventually I have to go back."

"What?" Dom took her by the shoulders, making sure he was firm but gentle. "Are you kidding? You think I'm going to let you go back? Have you lost your mind?"

"What other choice do I have?" Tears filled her eyes. "I have nothing."

"No!" He stood and reached down for her hands. "Come here."

"Where?" She put her hands in his without even realizing she did it.

He pulled her to her feet and led her into the kitchen. He got his wallet off the counter, opened it and pulled out a copy of the picture that had been on Andra's mantle. He kept a smaller version of it behind his driver's license. "See this? This is Brian, Cody, me, Suze, Sergei... this is us before everything changed. Brian's death killed all of us in a way, yet we're still fighting to be here. *You* can't give up because *we* haven't given up, and because if Brian was here, he'd tell you to knock it off."

"You're young and rich and successful," she said, running her finger over the photograph. "I'm getting old, and I have nothing."

"You have me," he whispered, pressing his forehead to hers. "I don't know why Cody and I found you in that garage the other day, but we did. Now you're a part of me. Somehow, for whatever reason, you were brought into my life. I'm not particularly religious, but if there is a god or a heaven, Brian is definitely responsible for this. We crossed paths for a reason, and I'm not letting you go without finding out what it is."

"Dom, I have nothing to offer you," she said, her eyes meeting his.

"I'm not asking for anything."

"I can't even give you sex."

"Are you hurt?" he asked.

Her eyes widened. "No... not like that. But I mean, I, uh, I'm probably old enough to be your mother! You couldn't possibly want to..." Her voice trailed off and she seemed wary.

"That's not what I meant." He rolled his eyes. "I'm not looking for casual sex; you're not anywhere near old enough to be my mother; and how did we get into this conversation?"

They both burst out laughing and laughed until they were on the floor again, side by side, holding their stomachs.

"Okay, we have to stop," she pleaded. "I have some bruised ribs and it hurts to laugh."

"I'm sorry." Then they dissolved into laughter again.

"All right, no more!" she begged.

"No more," he agreed. They both nearly started to laugh again, but instead he reached out to touch her bruised eye. "I'm sorry he hurt you. If you let me, I'll make sure no one ever hurts you again."

For a moment she looked startled. "That's very sweet, Dom. *You're* very sweet. You're also very good-looking. Why are you single?"

"I didn't meet the right girl in college, and then I was always afraid to get into a relationship because of my temper. So I don't do relationships."

"Well, we're quite a pair. You have a bad temper and I'm apparently one of those women who make men mad enough to hit them."

"I don't think that's true. The man I saw in that parking garage the other day was an asshole. I don't think I could ever treat a woman the way he was treating you."

"I don't think you could either," she whispered, realizing she actually believed it. Maybe that made her naïve, but somehow she didn't think so.

"So stay and let me help you."

"What am I going to do? Stay locked up in here for the rest of my life? You might want to get married or something someday, and what's your new wife going to say? 'Oh, sure, the strange old lady in the guest room can stay'?"

He began to laugh again. "Of course not. We're going to find a way to get you away from him. Being a cop doesn't make him above the law. I'm a professional athlete, and I know people too. We just have to lay low for a while: let you heal, and give me time to get through my probation with the league. In the meantime, we can do some research. We'll figure out if you can get a divorce without going to court, see about a restraining order, stuff like that. You probably will have to stay here in the apartment for a little while, but we'll go out on the weekends—we can drive to L.A. or Reno and just hang out. You can help me work through all this shit I'm dealing with, and I'll help you get away from that creep you're married to. Deal?"

She smiled at him, her one visible eye sparkling in the pale light. "Deal."

"And one day," he added mischievously. "If you wanted me to, I would make love to you. Because no one should go through life without having an orgasm from Dom Gianni."

Her eyes widened and she almost felt young again. "Why would you want to do that?"

He laughed again, now completely in his element. "Because I'm a guy?"

She couldn't help it; she laughed too.

5

MOLLY KNEW SHE WAS GOING TO HAVE ANOTHER MISCARRIAGE EVEN BEFORE IT happened. Sitting on the floor of the bathroom in Dom's apartment, she practically felt the life of the baby inside of her draining out of her as she bled. Emotionally raw after so many other miscarriages, this one was almost a non-event. She'd long since stopped wanting Tim's baby, and it was almost a relief to know there wouldn't be one. Her only regret was that this had probably been her last chance; there would be no more babies for her at her age.

She cleaned up as best she could and found a washcloth she could stuff in her panties to absorb the blood; Dom would have to take her to a clinic for a D&C. Then maybe this would be over. She didn't know where she could go or what she would do, but being away from Tim was liberating. She could breathe again, despite the strange circumstances. She didn't understand what had happened, or how she'd fallen into this bizarre arrangement with a young, incredibly hot and somewhat messed-up hockey player, but this was the hand she'd been dealt. Looking at it from the perspective of an outsider, it was definitely strange; but it was the only interesting thing that had ever happened to her.

Nothing in her life before this would have prepared her for the gentle, tortured soul that was Dom Gianni, yet listening to him tell her his story made him human and showed he was almost as broken as she. Despite his money, success and good looks, he had as many demons as she did. She didn't understand it at all: it was foreign to her, the idea of having friends and money but being unable to get past the things that haunted you. He was living proof, though, and something about his little-boy-lost persona melted her heart. If she'd never had a reason to get up in the morning before, she had one now.

When she heard his key in the lock, she tried to get up but it took too much effort. She was weak from lack of sleep and probably from blood loss as well, so she leaned back against the sink and waited. He would find her; she had no doubt of that. She sensed that about him, even after knowing him just a few days, and it was comforting.

"Molly?" Dom tapped on the door.

"I'm not feeling great," she called back.

"Can I come in?"

"Yes," she replied, and the door opened.

"What's happened?" he asked, dropping to his knees in front of her, his dark eyes narrowed with concern.

"I had another miscarriage. I need to go to a clinic—I know of one that will treat me for free."

"I have money. I can take you to a hospital."

"No." She shook her head. "This clinic deals with a lot of abused women. They won't call Tim. That's what's important."

"Can you get up?"

"I don't think so," she admitted.

He lifted her in his strong arms and she closed her eyes. For now, she would lose herself in his strength and the security he provided. Later, when she was physically healed, she would find a way to leave Tim for good. Even if she only had a few days to figure something out, it was better than anything she'd ever had before. She still had nothing, but Dom made her remember she had herself. Maybe that was enough.

Molly awoke and blinked groggily in the semi-darkness. Spying Dom in a chair at her side, tapping at his phone, she watched him for a few minutes. He was so good-looking she couldn't help but stare. She hadn't thought about men being attractive in years but Dom wasn't just attractive, he was downright hot. With his rakishly long dark hair and brooding dark eyes, it was hard not to just reach out and touch him. The cleft in his chin gave him a dangerously sexy look, and his full, wide mouth was the kind you wanted to kiss. Not that she thought about things like that anymore, but she could still appreciate the man he was.

He looked up. "You're awake," he said. "How are you?"

"Tired, but okay."

"The doctor said he stopped the bleeding and cleaned everything out," he told her. "But your body won't be able to take another miscarriage. If you have another one, you're going to have to have a hysterectomy."

"I know." She swallowed hard. "Thanks for being here. You didn't have to stay."

"Of course I did. No one should wake up from surgery alone."

"They take good care of people here, even when you don't have money."

"I'm paying for everything. Don't worry about that."

"I can't take money from you!" she said, tears pooling in her eyes. "You barely know me!"

"I thought we made a deal that I would help you get through this and you would help me get through my issues?"

"But your issues don't cost money!"

"My issues could cost me a $25 million contract," he said mildly. "I would say they cost quite a bit."

She choked back a sob. "Why are you doing this? I'm just a messed up, abused woman who stumbled into your life. Helping me isn't going to bring Brian back, Dom."

"I know." He took one of her hands between both of his and gently rubbed it. "If I can make a difference in someone's life, everything I've worked for is actually worth something other than money. Maybe Brian's death wasn't a freak accident that ruined me forever. Maybe you're my second chance. Maybe saving you makes up for being three minutes too late to save him. In my heart of hearts, for whatever reason, I truly believe Brian sent you to me to take care of. Maybe it was his time to go, but I refuse to believe it's yours."

For what seemed like forever, they just looked at each other. Finally, she smiled faintly. "You know I have nothing? I have a purse and a driver's license and there might be some loose change in the bottom of my bag, but that's it. Even the clothes on my back are ruined."

He shrugged. "Suze can take you shopping."

They looked at each other for another long moment before she spoke his name. "Dom?"

"Yeah?"

"If I agree to this, I go from being an abused prisoner to being a pampered one. I still have to hide from him."

"Not forever." He squeezed her hand as the doctor came in. "We're going to take care of it. And you'll never be a prisoner with me—you can walk out the door any time you like. But I want you to stay and get well and let me help you. Okay?"

"Okay." She looked deep into his long-lashed chocolate-brown eyes. For a moment, she was entranced by his good looks and realized she couldn't remember what it was like to feel that way about a man. She smiled again. "Thank you," was all she said.

"You're welcome."

M olly woke up the next morning feeling disoriented. This wasn't her room at Dom's, and for a moment she panicked, afraid she was home again. Then she remembered, and settled back into the comfortable bed. They'd decided she might be more comfortable at Suze and Cody's house, so now she was getting charity from even more people she didn't know. But they'd made her feel welcome, and both seemed easy-going and sweet. Molly had been a little nervous about coming here, but Dom could talk her into almost anything. When she'd gone to bed, he'd lain next to her and promised not to leave until she was asleep.

He was gone now, and she looked around for some clue as to the time. The clock on the nightstand said ten-forty-six, and she realized she'd slept for more than 12 hours. She got up and went into the bathroom, staring at herself with growing alarm. She was wearing a pair of Cody's old sweats and a T-shirt, with a pair of Suze's maternity underwear. Her right eye was finally open, though the bruise was still dark purple and ugly. The cut on her lip was beginning to heal, but it hurt if she didn't keep it moisturized. Dom had bought her some lip balm, but it was back at his apartment.

Suze had given her a new toothbrush, toothpaste and a hair band so she could pull her hair back out of her face. She washed up the best she could and then padded downstairs.

Suze was sitting at the kitchen island working on her laptop. She looked up at Molly with a smile.

"Good morning! How did you sleep?"

"Pretty well," Molly said, sitting on one of the stools.

"Would you like some coffee? I kept it on for you."

"That would be great." Molly gratefully accepted a steaming mug and took a sip.

"No cream or sugar?"

"Nope. I like it black."

"Sugar is my weakness," said Suze. "I love sweets. Luckily, I exercise enough that I don't have to watch everything I put in my mouth." She laughed.

"Is Dom working out?"

"Yeah, and then they had a meeting because the two assistant coaches arrived, plus a new trainer. There's a big meeting with them and the GM and the owner."

"I know close to nothing about hockey," Molly admitted. "It's embarrassing."

"We'll watch some videos on YouTube. I'll show you Dom and Cody's most shining moments. Watching Dom fight, when he's not angry, is actually a beautiful thing, because—"

"You think fighting is beautiful?" Molly looked confused.

"You have to remember fighting is a tradition in hockey," Suze said slowly. "Yes, sometimes it gets out of control and guys do things they shouldn't, but in general, when a couple of guys drop the gloves and throw a few punches, it adds momentum, it boosts morale on a team that's struggling. It's rare that anyone gets hurt. After the game, a lot of these guys are friends, or at least acquaintances with respect for each other. Fighting isn't usually serious. Of course, there's always a jerk out there who goes after everyone and intentionally tries to hurt guys, but that's the exception, not the rule."

"What does Dom do?"

"Sometimes he can't stop himself. He gets caught up in whatever it is that haunts him and then…" Suze's voice trailed off. "Anyway, hopefully this anger management stuff and us all being together again will help."

"It must have been a terrible time."

Suze glanced at her. "Did Dom tell you our history?"

"Most of it. I know about the night Brian died and how you and Cody got pregnant and all that. I know how close you all were and how everything fell apart when Brian died."

"It's never been the same. I thought I knew exactly how my life was going to go. Brian and I would get married—he'd already been drafted—and we would have babies and a wonderful life with our family and friends. But then…" She paused, biting her lip. "One freak incident changed everything. I wound up married to a guy who was great but I didn't love, with a beautiful baby boy who became my whole world."

"At least you're married to a man who cares about you," Molly said after a moment. "It may not be perfect, but it's better than a man who can't stand the sight of you, who drinks and calls you names, then forces you to have sex night after night in the hope of producing a son, but then beats you until the child is dead." She looked away sadly. "I'm sorry. I shouldn't have said that."

"No." Suze reached out and covered one of Molly's hands with her own. "You're right. I have a pretty great life. Cody and I don't have a perfect marriage, but he's kind and gentle; he's a wonderful father and a great provider. He's smart, funny and good-looking, and it would never cross his mind to hit me. I can't complain, although sometimes I still do." She shrugged sheepishly.

"Brian's been gone a long time," Molly said. "Don't you think you could ever love Cody?"

"Oh, but I do!" Suze shook her head. "It's so complicated. When we first got married, the guilt almost killed me, and of course we were both mourning. I was pregnant, and there was no sex during that time. After CJ was born we tried to be a "couple," but Brian was always the elephant in the room. Eventually, I just couldn't do it anymore, and after a while Cody started looking elsewhere. I finally told him it would be a marriage in name only, and if he wanted a divorce, I was okay with that. But he said no, we were going to raise CJ together and if I didn't want to sleep with him that was okay too. He was determined to take care of me and be a family with CJ. He said Brian would have expected that of him. So here we are."

"But if you're in love with him, and he's always been in love with you—"

"What are you talking about? Cody's never been in love with me! We had drunk sex the night of Brian's funeral and when I found out I was pregnant, we immediately got married because he knew Brian wouldn't want me to do it alone. Cody never loved me."

Molly looked at this woman who was practically a stranger to her and frowned. "Look, I'm late to the party. I wasn't around back then, and I don't even know what I'm doing here now—but I can tell you, based on what I've seen and what Dom's told me, Cody is one hundred percent in love with you. He always has been, but you've never loved anyone besides Brian and Cody couldn't compete with him. Not when he was alive, and even less now that he's dead."

Suze gaped at her. "What exactly did Dom tell you?"

"That he, Cody, Brian and Sergei all fell in love with you freshman year. All four of them wanted you, but you were only interested in Brian. Dom and Sergei moved on—they knew the ship had sailed—but Cody compared every girl he dated to you, and even when he was cheating, apparently no one measured up."

"You mean he's really stopped cheating?"

"That's what Dom said. It's killing him, but he's determined to find a way to win you."

"Shit." She rubbed her eyes. "I never knew. I mean, I know they all used to tease me about having a nice ass and stuff, but we *all* said that about each other. In fact, Dom has the best ass out of the lot of them! Brian was hot—everything a girl could want—but in the ass department? All Dom. Sergei, now he was pure Russian hotness. All blond and blue-eyed and chiseled, with the *best* abs you've ever seen. Someday, if I can find the picture online, I'll show you Sergei's abs. Holy Jesus, makes a woman go into heat." She giggled. "And Cody? He's movie-star material—by far the best-looking guy in the NHL. He's been approached by all kinds of companies to be their spokesperson, but he's pretty embarrassed by it."

"And what did Brian have?" Molly asked with a smile.

"Eyes." Suze sighed. "They were like steel—with these long gray lashes—the absolute epitome of bedroom eyes. I have a few pictures I can dig up one day when the boys aren't about to get home. His eyes could swallow you up." She smiled then, resting her chin in her hand. "My beautiful Brian—what a wonderful love we had. I didn't think I would ever love again, but Cody is so good too… I realized after he started cheating that I wasn't angry—I was jealous. But I had cut him off, so he had every right, and now, well, now we dance around the issues."

"It can be fixed."

"I don't know," Suze sighed. "I really want another baby, and he said that's fine with him, but I don't want to stay together because of a baby. I miss being in a relationship, where we laugh and finish each other's sentences and hold hands…" Her voice trailed off. "Anyway, enough of that. How are you feeling? The doctor said you should take it easy for a couple of days so I figured maybe Thursday or Friday we could drive down to the Strip, go to the mall and buy you some stuff. Dom said he'll give you cash and he doesn't want to hear anything about it. You need clothes!"

"I need to lose weight and stop looking like a hobo. I'm a mess." Molly rested her chin in her hands. "I'm so out of shape, I can't believe Dom wants to be seen with me."

"You're beautiful!" Suze said firmly. "Yes, you're a little beat up right now and you could lose a few pounds, but you've got gorgeous eyes, beautiful skin, and sexy lips. We'll get you healthy and then you can start coming to the gym with me. Maybe we can all take boxing together—Cody and I already got Dom to agree to come with us!"

"Boxing?" Molly looked dubious.

"Trust me—it's empowering, a great workout, and fun."

"Well, we'll see."

"Okay, the guys will be home by around 12:30. I have a quiche in the oven and I'm going to throw together a salad."

"Can I help?"

"Nope. You're just going to rest and heal. Let me know if you need anything from the drugstore."

"I think I'm good with what you gave me last night," Molly said. "But thank you." She was overwhelmed by the kindness she'd been shown over the last week. This was definitely not how she'd expected her leap of faith to go, but she was truly glad that it did.

6

THE AFTERNOON PASSED QUICKLY, HAVING LUNCH WITH THE GUYS AND THEN chatting for a while. Finally, Molly was exhausted and went to take a short nap before dinner. Dom followed her up to her room and lay beside her.

"You don't have to lay with me," she said with a smile. "I'm okay. I feel comfortable with Suze and Cody now."

"I like laying here with you. It relaxes me, keeps out all the bad thoughts and makes me focus on my life; my career, my friends... and you."

"Me?" she said curiously. "Dom, I'm not what you need."

"How do you know what I need?" He brushed a lock of hair out of her face. "I've known you for less than a week and I've found more peace in that time than I've had in seven years. Apparently, you *are* what I need. Maybe we're destined to be friends, maybe something more—but whatever it is, I definitely need you as much as you need me."

She gave him a beautiful smile, the first one he'd seen since he met her, and it nearly took his breath away. "That you need me is the greatest thing anyone has ever said to me."

Voices and a child's laughter downstairs roused Molly, and she realized it was after six o'clock. She hurried to get up, splash water on her face, fix her hair again, and then make her way downstairs. She really liked these people and wanted to be a part of them for however long this lasted. If nothing else, she had a feeling she and Dom would always be friends. because with his money, connections and physical strength, she didn't think Tim would be able to easily intimidate him. He might try, but Dom had repeatedly told her he had powerful friends too—

both within the NHL and outside. A cop from a small Nevada town couldn't hurt him without repercussions.

She found Suze in the kitchen checking something in the oven and Dom on the ground with a young boy on top of him pummeling him with his fists as "Uncle Dom" squealed with fake appeals for help.

"He's so cute," Molly said, standing beside Suze.

"Dom, CJ or Cody?"

"Well," Molly glanced around the room. "All three, to be honest."

"Yeah, but I think CJ wins the cuteness category!" Suze gave a surprisingly sharp whistle that brought the wrestling on the floor to a stop. "CJ, come say hello to our guest. This is Molly. Molly, this is our son, CJ."

"Hello, Miss Molly." CJ scrambled up and into the kitchen, giving her a big grin, showing off his two missing front teeth.

"Hello, CJ." Molly stared at the child and then glanced up at Suze before forcing herself to look down again. "Aren't you a handsome boy?"

"Thank you. Are you Uncle Dom's new girlfriend?" he asked.

"CJ!" Cody laughed and scooped him up. "You're not supposed to ask about things like that."

"Why not?" The child looked at him in confusion. "She's a girl but she's not his friend?"

Molly snickered. "Yes, CJ, I am Uncle Dom's new *girl* friend." She patted his head and he gave his father a look of satisfaction that made them all chuckle.

"Okay, time for dinner!" Suze hustled them out of the kitchen and into the dining room, leaving Molly to try to remain composed. The child she'd just met had the most beautiful eyes she'd ever seen; big and grey, with long lashes that would one day make a girl's heart beat faster. If she had to take a guess, especially after seeing both Suze and Cody's bright blue eyes, CJ was *Brian's* son, and Molly didn't understand that at all.

"So if she's up to it," Suze spoke without looking at Molly although she undoubtedly knew what Molly was thinking. "I thought we'd go shopping in a few days and get her some things. We can go to the Fashion Show mall. No one who lives here shops on the Strip, so we'll blend in with the tourists."

"Why don't you call Andra?" Dom suggested. "Ask her to go with you so she can meet Molly too."

Suze blinked. "Um, maybe, I guess."

"Coach says she's lonely," Dom continued. "And right now I've got anger management, my workout regimen and Molly to take care of. Maybe you could spend a little time with Andra."

"You know it's awkward for me," murmured Suze.

"Wait a minute," Molly said, suddenly comprehending that no one knew that CJ was Brian's son. "I mean, what…" Her voice died off as she looked at CJ and forced herself to stop talking. "No one knows?" she finally asked, looking around the room.

Dom looked down, focusing on his food. "Bet I can finish my chicken faster than you!" he teased CJ, who began furiously shoveling food into his mouth while Suze gave Dom a hard stare.

"We were gone before we found out," Cody said after a moment. "And then there was just never the right time."

"For what?" CJ asked, his mouth full of chicken.

"Don't talk with your mouth full," Cody admonished him. "And nothing for you to worry about. Just grownup talk."

CJ rolled his eyes. "Grownup talk is boring. Can I go watch TV?"

"After you put your plate in the sink and finish your milk," said Suze.

CJ downed his milk in one gulp, grinned at his dad and stuck his tongue out at Dom. "I win!" he shouted, and ran for the kitchen.

Suze shook her head. "Must you encourage him?"

Dom laughed, "I'm Uncle Dom. I get special privileges."

"Great." Suze put down her fork and looked at Molly. "We meant to tell Brad and Andra, but the longer we waited, the harder it was... and now it's been more than six years."

"But as soon as they see him... I mean, I don't know them, but if it were me and you'd kept my grandson from me, I wouldn't be very happy."

"Honestly, we didn't know right away," Cody said defensively. "His eyes were blue until he was a year old. Once they turned gray, we knew we had to do a DNA test, but by that time we were in Toronto, and they were in Boston. We didn't know how to tell anyone, and frankly, at that point we were finally starting to get past the grieving process and we didn't want to dredge it up again. Yeah, we screwed up, but we're going to fix it."

"When?" Dom asked.

"Soon," said Suze. "Very soon."

It was Monday before Suze and Molly left the house to take CJ to school. From there Suze headed to the salon where she got her hair done. She figured Molly would balk if she'd told her where they were going, so she opted for the element of surprise. It felt good to do something nice for someone. Her circle of friends in the last five years had been rich, spoiled NHL wives and after a while it had become tiresome.

This team in Las Vegas was a new beginning in more ways than one. She was sort of glad to get out of Toronto, where everyone knew about all things hockey, and as the wife of a player that's all she'd ever heard about. It was unfortunate a good number of players wound up married to puck bunnies who cared about nothing but money and status. Those women all thought it was so 'cute' that she and Cody had been together since college. The status of being an NHL wife had never even crossed her mind when she and Brian had talked about their future; she hadn't thought about it when she and Cody got married either. By then, all she'd cared about was making sure her baby had a father.

Pulling into a strip mall, she said to Molly, "I have a little surprise for you."

"What? What are we doing?"

"You're getting your hair done," Suze said with a grin. "All girls want to have great hair, and this place will make you feel like a princess."

"Suze, I'm wearing Dom's old sweats and an oversized t-shirt. I can't go into a salon."

"You'll be fine. This isn't a fancy place—I found it by accident, and my stylist is quirky but absolutely amazing!" Suze pulled into a parking spot and jumped out of the car. "Come on!" She slammed the door and Molly was forced to follow.

They checked in, and before she knew what was happening Molly was wearing a smock and had pieces of foil all over her head. Suze and her stylist Mags, a tall, skinny woman with bright pink hair and black lipstick, chatted casually. Mags wore all black, her fingers were swift and sure as she looked Molly over carefully. She didn't say anything about her bruises, only complimented her thick, wavy hair.

"These auburn highlights are natural," Mags said with admiration. "So I'm just going to add some lighter ones to give depth, plus some lowlights to cover the hint of gray here and there. I'll cut some layers in to give you volume and natural bounce. With a round brush, you can…" Her voice was soothing and Molly closed her eyes to enjoy having someone pamper her. She'd never had her hair done professionally before; she'd always trimmed it herself. She didn't even own a blow dryer and had no idea what to do with a round brush.

"Do you have a round brush?" Mags was asking her.

"Oh. No. I don't."

"We'll take one like mine," said Suze. "And we'll need one of those curling things you sold me last time I was here—it's awesome! I can get my hair to do anything with it!"

Mags laughed. "Darling, with a face like yours, you don't need to do anything with your hair."

"Oh, stop."

"How do you usually fix your hair?" Mags asked Molly.

"I just wash it and let it dry by itself. It's almost always in a ponytail anyway."

Mags blinked at her. "That isn't right. You have to show off a glorious head of hair like this!"

"Well, we never really had the money…" Molly's voice trailed off.

"Bad divorce," Suze interjected. "She's staying with Cody and me until she gets back on her feet, so we need to get her the basics… a good hair dryer, that round brush, the shampoo and conditioner I use, and that curling iron thing."

"Suze…" Molly started to protest but Suze cut her off.

"This is my treat, not Dom's. Even though we come from different backgrounds, I know what it's like to hit rock bottom, and luckily I married a guy with enough money to make it a lot easier to crawl out. I like helping someone else, so you should be gracious and let me."

"Okay." Molly bowed her head. "Thank you."

"It's all good."

When her hair was finished, Molly acknowledged Suze was right—Molly did feel like a princess. Her hair draped in soft waves around her face and curled just below her shoulders. Her natural auburn color was highlighted, and the gray at her temples was gone. Despite the bruises on her face and Dom's ill-fitting clothes, she felt prettier than she had in years.

It was like that for the rest of the day. They went from store to store buying the essentials, and it was like starting completely from scratch. They bought underwear and bras, a couple of casual tops, shorts, capris, sandals, and a pair of yoga pants with a matching top. Then they found sneakers and socks, plus hair accessories and every toiletry from deodorant to razors and shaving cream.

By the time they stopped for lunch, Molly was exhausted. "I can't shop anymore!" she groaned. "This is more than I've owned in my whole life!"

"Didn't your husband even let you buy clothes?"

"In the beginning, I got things now and then, and I've had to buy a few things in the last few years because I've put on weight; but up until five years ago, I was wearing the same clothes I had in high school."

"How is that possible?"

"My parents passed away in a car accident right after we got married, I don't have any siblings, and Tim scared away all my other relatives. I have a cousin in Ohio, and my mother's sister is in Texas, but I never hear from them anymore." She sighed heavily. "I don't know how I will ever repay you for today."

"We'll have more days like this," Suze promised. "After your face heals, we'll go get makeovers! Then we'll get manicures and pedicures."

"I've never had any of those," Molly confided. "I always did my own nails when I was younger, and then I stopped doing even that. I stopped caring a long time ago about how I look. Subconsciously, I figured if I was ugly he would leave me alone."

"You're not ugly. And you're going to be okay now. We're going to take care of you."

"I don't understand why," Molly said helplessly. "I understand you guys are all wealthy, and the money you spent today is probably just a drop in the bucket for you, but why *me*?"

"Because Dom lights up when he talks about you," said Suze. "I've never seen him like this before—not even in college. I mean, I don't know what's going on with you two, but—"

"Nothing!" Molly looked horrified. "God, I'll be forty in July and he's 28! I'm old and fat, and he's young and..." She stopped abruptly.

"...Hot?" Suze supplied with a giggle.

"*Really, really hot*," Molly murmured before clapping a hand over her mouth. "Oh, my God, did I say that? I'm still married!"

"I'm thinking you're not, really. I mean, I guess you are, legally, but you need to find out what you can do to change that."

"He's never going to give me a divorce."

"Molly, it's time for you to take back your life. He can't keep doing this to you. Not only is it illegal, you're terrified of him. Why not grab some happiness while you have a chance?"

"Because at the end of the day, I have nothing to give back."

"Not everything is about giving and taking. We're giving because we can, and because we want to. Dom seems drawn to you, and for the first time since Brian died, there's hope in his eyes again. He's a really special guy—absolutely a guy I would go out with if I wasn't married!"

"He seems wonderful," Molly agreed.

"He is. I've never seen him angry except on the ice. Every once in a while, he just loses it, and you can tell when it's about to happen. Something in the way he moves changes, and he's charging down the ice like a lunatic. Then it's over and it's like the fight literally drains out of him—you can see it happening."

"He hurts," Molly said simply. "And sometimes, when you hurt that way, you just need release. The day he and Cody found me, I was begging for Tim to kill me... not because I'm suicidal, but because at some point you just want the pain to stop. That day, I'd had enough. I guess when Dom has enough, he goes out and does whatever he does. Until you've experienced the kind of pain that makes you want to die, you can't understand."

"Which is why you need each other. All we've been able to talk about is finding a way for Dom to get past what happened, and then there you were. So buying presents and doing nice things for you is our way of keeping you around. It's really a bribe." She smirked and Molly laughed aloud.

When was the last time I laughed, she wondered? "Well, then, I guess I'm easy, because I'm happy to be bribed." She'd changed into shorts and a top at the last store, putting on her new sandals and letting her styled hair flow behind her. Sitting here on the Las Vegas strip watching the hordes of tourists, she felt free, anonymous and safe. It had been twenty years since she'd felt truly safe; it was the greatest feeling in the whole world.

7

THEY GOT HOME AFTER THREE O'CLOCK TO FIND CODY AND DOM PLAYING WITH CJ in the family room. CJ came running when he caught sight of his mother. "Mommy!"

Suze gathered him into her arms. "Hey, buddy. How was school today?"

"It was great! I got to be line leader."

"Good job!"

"Look out, Uncle Dom!" CJ attacked him and Dom allowed himself to be thrown to the floor.

Suze rolled her eyes. "I swear to God, you guys, if he starts acting up at school..."

"Come on, Suze!" Cody nudged her. "He's a boy!"

She made a face at him. "I'm well aware he's a boy."

Molly had come in a minute or so later, carrying the bags with all her new purchases. She put them down and smiled at the wrestling going on in the family room. "Looks like the boys are working up an appetite," she remarked.

Dom glanced up and froze. She was standing there in a pair of denim shorts and a short-sleeved white top. Her legs were long and tanned, despite a handful of bruises. Her newly colored and cut hair was thick and wavy, framing her face and bouncing below her shoulders. Today, both eyes were open and focused on him, as he allowed CJ to mock wrestle with him. The bruises on her face were fading, and he found himself drawn to her mouth: the cuts were almost gone and her beautifully-shaped lips were a pale red. It occurred to him he wanted to kiss her someday, but a sharp jab in the ribs jolted him back to reality.

"Hi," he managed to say, fending off a playful swing from CJ as he sat up.

"Hi."

"Your hair looks great," he finally said.

"Thanks." She gave him an embarrassed smile and then turned to Suze. "Should I put this stuff upstairs?"

"You're welcome to stay here as long as you like," Suze said. "But I know Dom needs to start sleeping at his own place. We're really out of the way for his therapy and stuff."

"Whatever you want," Dom said quickly. "If you're comfortable at my place, we can go back there, or we can stay here a few more days."

Molly hesitated. She liked being in the big, happy household and having a live-in girlfriend to hang out with. But Dom needed to live his life too, and she wasn't ready to be away from him. At night, he still sat with her until she fell asleep, and last night she'd awoken from a nightmare to find him gently wiping the tears from her face.

"Why don't we make the move tomorrow?" Suze suggested. "We're going out tonight, so—"

"'*Going out?*'" Molly's eyes widened in alarm.

"Just to Coach Brad's house," Cody assured her. "Our associate coach Dave Marcus and his wife Tiffany have been away, so Brad and Andra wanted to have a little get-together. I think the coaches are going to set us up for what's coming."

"What's coming?" Molly asked.

"She's not a hockey fan," Suze reminded the men as they stared at Molly in disbelief.

"I am a *little*," Molly protested. "We'd put it on if it was on TV. Tim's originally from Michigan, so he grew up with hockey. But no, I don't know anything about expansion teams or stuff like that."

"Well, technically, we're not supposed to be here yet," Dom explained. "I'll be an unrestricted free agent on July first, which means my contract is expiring and I know the Predators are letting me go. Coach Barnett wants me on his team, but per league rules he can't actually offer me a contract until July first. But it doesn't really matter right now anyway, because I'm not allowed to play next season until I've met all the requirements the NHL set for me. That's why I'm in anger management twice a week. I also need to have a psychological evaluation at the end of the summer, and then a sit-down with the Department of Player Safety. So the organization can only offer me a contract with the stipulation the NHL okays me to play."

"And technically, I'm still part of the Maple Leafs," Cody said. "But after Dom, Brad and I talked, we decided we were going to do this together, so Suze and I sold our house and rented this place to be here with Dom over the summer. I've already made arrangements with Toronto—they had a couple of young players they needed to protect for the expansion draft, and I volunteered to fall on my sword, so to speak, for the future of the team. I'll be Las Vegas's first pick during the draft because the other expansion team will be picking as well."

"There's a chance that Cody could get picked up by Anchorage, which is the other team," Suze added. "If they get first pick in the draft, it could happen, but Brad already has a gentleman's agreement in place with the head coach over there. I don't know the details, but he says it's a non-issue." She made a face at Cody. "And let's be clear: I am *not* moving to Alaska!"

Cody laughed. "I know, dear. No more northern teams."

Suze shivered. "I am *so* tired of those winters!"

"And I'm not allowed to play in Minnesota or Boston, either," Cody made a face behind Suze's back that made them all laugh.

"I'm not enduring that kind of winter unless we're in New York," she said. "In Manhattan, I guess I could suck it up, but there will be no Minnesota winters in my future, and I'm never going back to Boston."

No one said anything, and Suze turned away. "Come on, Molly, let's figure out what you're going to wear tonight."

"I don't think I should go," said Molly. "I mean, how will Dom explain me?"

"You're my friend?" Dom suggested.

"Look at me!" She glanced down at herself. "Why would a guy like you have a frumpy old 'friend' like me?"

"Stop." Dom reached out and took her chin between his fingers. "You're beautiful, and you're my friend. People in general can wonder all they want, but not *this* group of people. Coach Dave married a stripper. Everyone who heard about it was horrified, taking about mid-life crises and how he'd lost his mind. But Tiff is the best thing that's ever happened to him. She makes him happy, and we all know there's a lot more to Tiff than how she looks. So relax. The people you're going to meet tonight are not going to be overly curious—well, they'll be a little bit curious because I've never lived with a woman before—but not in a bad way."

"It's gonna be fine," Suze tugged on Molly's arm. "Let's go start getting ready."

"My face is still a mess," Molly objected, trailing Suze up the stairs after exchanging another long look with Dom.

"I can cover it with makeup. And the rest, well, no one is going to wonder about anything except whether or not you're sleeping together."

"Sleeping together? No one would think that!"

"Molly, you have to stop being so hard on yourself. You're a beautiful, vibrant woman who's had a rough time. Don't worry about what others presume about you or Dom. Just be yourself and focus on getting better."

"Thank you, Suze. You've been so great and I appreciate it."

"We've all gone through hard times. It's nice to be able to help someone else for a change."

Arriving at Brad and Andra's large, beautiful house, Molly was nervous. Riding beside Dom in his new Mercedes SUV, she wasn't sure how she fit into this group of people. These strangers had shown her more kindness and affection in a week than Tim and his friends had in more than two decades. For the first time in many years, she wondered if it was possible she could truly find happiness. And it was all because of the gorgeous man who sat beside her, this incredible stranger who'd swept in like a knight in shining armor to save her from Tim, from her life, and even from herself. Never in her wildest dreams had she imagined such a man existed. Even though she had a hard time believing he would be interested in her romantically, she had a feeling their shared experiences gave them a bond that would last a long time.

"You ready?" Dom asked as he turned into the driveway.

"No. I'm not sure how to behave, or what to say. These people are totally out of my league."

"Out of your league?" He chuckled, reaching out to touch her cheek. "Molly, these are some of the very best people in the whole world. They're going to welcome you with open arms, just like Cody and Suze did."

"They're going to pity me and think I'm a leech hanging onto the rich, young hockey player who happened to be in the right place at the right time." She sighed. "I may not be worldly, but I know how people think."

"They're not like that."

"How can they not be?" she demanded. "If these people care about you, then they're going to be worried about you. This older woman, married to a dirty, abusive cop, has latched on to a rich kid like you. If you were my friend and I saw you doing what you're doing with me, I would try to talk some sense into you."

"First of all, I'm not a kid. I don't give a damn what anyone thinks, and neither will my friends. You and I... clicked. Sitting there in the dark underneath the bar, I cried on your shoulder like a baby. For the first time in seven years I told the story all the way through without wanting to hurt someone. Our friendship is whatever we want it to be, and the rest of the world can suck big donkey balls."

She snorted with unexpected laughter. "Then what do we tell people?" she was still chuckling. "Because you know they're going to ask."

"We're friends and roommates. You needed a place to go during your divorce, and you bring a sense of calm to my life that I desperately need."

"Okay." She took a deep breath. "Then I guess I'm ready."

Dom got out of the car and walked around to her side to open her door. She smiled up at him, charmed and overwhelmed. He offered her his arm and she took it without hesitation. Whatever this was, she was going to try to stop questioning and just enjoy it. She'd already lived through hell; even if this only lasted for a little while, she was going to hang on to every moment of something so wonderful.

Brad and Andra met them at the door, greeting them warmly before leading them into the beautifully-decorated great room where Suze, Cody and another couple were already enjoying a glass of wine.

"Hey!" Suze greeted them with a smile. "Molly, this is Dave Marcus and his wife Tiffany. Dave's an associate coach, which is basically an assistant coach."

"It's nice to meet you." Molly shook their hands and tried not to stare at the gorgeous woman in front of her. If Suze was movie-star beautiful, Tiffany was super-model-beautiful. Almost six feet tall, with deep hazel eyes and brilliant golden-red hair falling past her shoulders, she was any man's wet dream. She was absolutely stunning, yet the older man beside her seemed oblivious to it, casually playing with a lock of her hair as they chatted. He was probably in his early fifties, with pale-blue eyes and thinning blond hair. He was lean and muscular, with the body of a retired athlete, a bright smile and a crooked nose that gave him what people might call character.

"So, are you a native?" Tiff was asking her.

"I was born in California," Molly replied. "But I've lived here since I was five."

"I can't imagine growing up in Las Vegas. But I guess I'll be raising my kids here, so I'm going to find out firsthand."

"How many children do you have?"

"We have twin boys, Derek and Duncan. They're two and a half."

"Twins! That must be a lot of work."

"I have lots of help," Tiff said. "Although because we just got here I'm still getting settled and trying to find sitters and such."

Molly listened as the women settled into easy conversation about local restaurants and favorite shopping areas. Though she'd lived here most of her life, she had no idea what most of these places were like. Tim had never taken her anywhere special, and she certainly didn't have the money to shop where they shopped. Though it made her feel a little awkward, she was happy to sit and listen, soaking in their sophistication and experiences. She liked these beautiful, interesting women, despite how different they were from her.

"So, Molly, what do you do?" Tiff asked, trying to draw her into the conversation.

"I've been a housewife, for the most part," Molly swallowed hard, trying not to be embarrassed by her lack of a more interesting answer. "And now I'm in limbo. Dom is trying to help me figure out if I can get a divorce without having to actually see Tim again."

"And then what will you do?" Tiff's eyes were kind, but Molly sensed her underlying question.

"I have no idea," she admitted after an awkward silence. "I was originally going to be a nurse before I got pregnant the first time. After my miscarriage, my husband insisted I quit school and stay home. If I qualify for any kind of alimony, I'd like to use that money to go back and finish my nursing degree."

"Will you stay with Dom?"

"I don't know." Molly shrugged slowly. "He's been a really good friend to me and I'm trying to be there for him this summer while he does everything he's supposed to do to get back in the NHL's good graces."

"Molly has been good for Dom," Andra said. "I've never seen him so content. Regardless of the circumstances that brought you together, it's been lovely to see him focused on something other than the past."

The men came back in the room then, keeping Molly from having to answer. She moved to Dom's side, breathing a sigh of relief. She looked up at him gratefully, wondering how she'd gotten so lucky to meet him.

The doorbell rang and Cody and Dom glanced up. "Are we expecting someone else?" Dom asked.

"Maybe." Brad grinned like a kid. "Why don't you and Cody go see who it is?"

Cody frowned. "Coach? What's going on?"

"Oh, go answer the damn door and let an old man have some fun!".

Dom and Cody went to the front door as the bell rang again and Cody opened it. There was a moment of silence and then whoops of laughter.

"Toli!" Dom and Cody hugged their old friend, shocked to see him.

"Surprise!" he laughed. "Toli has come to see friends in America and talk to Coach about playing with NHL again!" He had a fairly heavy accent, but his eyes gleamed with mischief and affection as they led him into the family room.

"Toli!" Andra hurried over to greet him. "Look at you! It's so good to see you!"

"Toli has missed Mama Andra!" he exclaimed as he hugged her. He stepped away and turned to Suze. "*You* are still Toli's favorite!"

Suze giggled in delight as he swept her off her feet and swung her around.

"Stop flirting with my wife." Cody said good-naturedly. "Are you really coming back?"

"Maybe is time for Toli to play in the NHL again. KHL is not so interesting. And Tatiana says no wedding." He shrugged.

Though she thought it odd he referred to himself in third person, Molly found Toli delightful. Tall and rangy, with short, spiky blond hair, deep-set blue eyes and crooked teeth that gave him a boyish look when he smiled, he was handsome in an offbeat kind of way.

"How's Sergei?" Dom asked.

Toli said something unintelligible in Russian and then shook his head. "Sergei is... what is the word? Pussy whipped? Puck bunny."

"What's a puck bunny?" Molly asked blankly.

"Hockey groupies," Tiff said in a stage whisper.

"Oh." Molly turned back to the conversation.

"After divorce, Sergei has not been good." Toli shook his head. "Toli tried to make him come to NHL too, but he is in difficult period."

"And what about Tatiana?" Cody asked. "You've been with her since high school, right?"

"Yes, many years. She is difficult, always with the schooling and training." He rolled his eyes. "She listens to nothing, so Toli is single again!" He made the announcement like it was a great thing, but there was no mistaking the shadow of pain that crossed his eyes as he said it. It seemed as though all of them had demons.

8

THEY HAD A MAGNIFICENT DINNER IN THE FORMAL DINING ROOM, WITH champagne and expensive wine, cloth napkins and beautiful china. Molly was awed by the beautiful things, though she tried not to show it. She and Tim had never owned formal china or crystal, and she couldn't imagine a time when they would have used cloth napkins. He was definitely a beer-and-hamburgers kind of guy; he would never even meet people like Brad and Andra.

After dessert, they moved back into the great room to enjoy coffee and cocktails. Brad, Dave and Cody were deep in conversation about hockey. Dom and Andra had moved off to the kitchen, and Suze and Tiffany were chattering about clothes. Molly slipped out onto the deck by herself to enjoy a golden desert sunset. There were many things she wanted to change about her life, but one thing she wanted to remain the same was living here. She loved the dry heat and warm sunshine, the mountains and the unpredictable winters. Though she thought living someplace with four seasons might be nice, she knew she would miss the Southwest.

"Molly looks thoughtful." Toli spoke from behind her and she jumped.

"Oh! You scared me."

"Sorry." He flashed a grin. "I am Anatoli. I did not know Dom had a new girlfriend."

"I'm not his girlfriend. We're just friends and roommates. I'm getting ready to go through an ugly divorce, and he's helping me."

"And you are helping him?"

"I'm trying. He's been very kind, so if I can help him accomplish what he needs to, I will."

"Why do you divorce?" he asked bluntly.

"Because my husband hits me." She raised her chin a notch.

Looking deep into her eyes, he studied her face. "Your husband did this?" He touched the spot just below her right eye with his thumb. Though it was almost healed, there were still yellow-green bruises that the makeup couldn't completely hide.

"Yes, and much more." She shuddered suddenly, realizing how terrified she was of going back to him after just a little bit of freedom.

"Toli will also be your friend," he announced. "I am single; you are single. We can be friends?"

She laughed. "Yes, I'd like that very much."

"Will Molly go to dinner with Toli?"

"Um…" She hesitated, blinking in confusion. She hadn't expected this.

"Not a date," he clarified as he noted her hesitation. "Just friends. Like you and Dom."

"Then yes. I'd like that. We just have to go places where I won't run into my husband. He's a policeman here and has a lot of friends."

Toli muttered in Russian again. "Do not worry—we will go to Los Angeles or Reno. Someplace this asshole cannot find Molly!"

She smiled. "Thank you. That sounds lovely."

"Is a date." He turned and walked back into the house, leaving her staring after him in confusion that was coupled with happiness. She had friends, a wonderful place to live and now an almost-date. Things were happening quickly, and she was hanging on for the ride.

T he next morning, Suze helped Molly pack all her new belongings in a suitcase and listened in amazement as she told her Toli was going to take her to L.A. for dinner one night next week.

"You're going out with *Toli*?" Suze was gaping at her. "Dom is *not* going to be happy."

"What are you talking about? We're just friends. He's way too young for me, and anyway, it's not like *Dom* would date me!"

"Well, if you're going to look at it that way, why would Toli? He's rich and successful and also younger than you!"

"Dom is eleven years younger than I am, Toli is only five. That's not quite as embarrassing."

"I don't know why you're embarrassed. Dom likes you!"

"I can't afford to get involved with anyone right now. I'm still married, and in a precarious situation. Anyway, Toli is safe because I think he's still in love with his girl back in Russia."

"Girlfriend, you need to grab life by the balls and stop worrying about what's safe."

"I know."

Suze zipped up the suitcase. "Now get on home and think about what I said."

"I will." Molly took the bag and headed downstairs to where Dom was waiting.

"Ready to go?" His smile made her heart beat a little faster. Could he possibly be any better-looking than he was? He was really tall, probably close to a foot taller than her own 5'7", with shoulders as wide as a house. But it was really his eyes that held her captive: so dark and mysterious, surrounded by high cheekbones and a great mouth. There was a scar across his cheek, but it just made him seem rugged and even sexier.

"I'm ready." She forced herself to stop staring at him and hurried out to the car. As she fastened her seat belt, she hoped he hadn't noticed how flustered she was. She didn't know how she was going to continue to live with someone who made her feel like a foolish teenager. Maybe going out with Toli was a good thing. Suze might be right that Dom wasn't going to like it. Though he'd never made any kind of sexual overtures, she recalled his offer to make love to her if the opportunity arose. He might not be interested in a relationship with her, but he was definitely the kind of guy who might be a little possessive given their shared experiences. It made her nervous because of the way Tim had treated her, but it was also thrilling because the reality was that Dom wasn't Tim. She clung to that hope because the alternative was unacceptable.

"I'm going to go to dinner with Toli next week," she said slowly. "Is that okay?"

"What?" He turned to stare at her. For a moment neither of them spoke and then he shook his head in apology. "I'm sorry," he said. "You caught me off guard. You don't have to ask my permission to go out."

"I know, but I wanted to make sure you didn't mind. He just got here and he seems really broken up about Tatiana. So when he mentioned dinner, as friends, I said okay."

"You should absolutely go out with him," Dom said, though he had to force the enthusiasm. "He's a great guy. He was a mentor to us while we were in college. I was really bummed when he and Sergei went back to Russia."

"Do you think he'll play here?"

"I don't know. Whenever there's an expansion, there has to be a draft. Each of the existing teams can protect a certain number of players, and then the new teams pick from those who aren't protected. In Cody's case, he asked not to be protected, to give them a chance to keep some of their young talent, and also so he could come here. I don't know how a free agent from the KHL fits into management's plan, but he's a damn good player and a leader on any team. His numbers weren't as high in the KHL as they were in the NHL, but Sergei says that's because of Tatiana."

"Would you like him to stay here?"

"Hell, yeah! He's amazing on and off the ice."

"That's good to know."

"So where are you guys going to go for dinner? Are you sure it's safe?"

"We're going to drive to L.A. for the day. He said we could leave in the morning, do some sightseeing, have dinner and then drive home after the L.A. traffic dies down."

"That's a lot of driving."

"But there's almost zero chance of running into anyone who knows me."

"That's true," said Dom. "It'll be great. I'm glad you're making friends."

"Me, too. Thank you."

"You don't have to thank me. I told you I was going to help you, and I have every intention of doing that."

She reached across the seat and laid her hand on his. "I may never stop thanking you."

He glanced over at her. Their eyes met briefly and something sparked between them once again. Molly forced herself to turn away. She had to stop letting him get her so worked up. She was in no position to get involved with anyone, much less someone so young and hot. But he sure made her want to.

The next week was busy, with Dom and Cody helping Toli find an apartment and all of them spending a lot of time at the gym. Dom was also meeting with a psychologist once a week, in addition to his anger management classes, and Molly could see it was wearing on him. When Dom came home after a day that began at the gym and was followed by anger management and a visit with the psychologist, plus taking Toli to see a few apartments, he was grumpy.

"You look tired," she said as he came in and sank onto the couch.

"I'm just over all of this. I know I screwed up and that this is what I have to do to get my career back on track, but it's a pain in the ass running from one place to another where all they want to do is talk."

"You just have to remind yourself how much it means to you to play in the NHL," she said, placing her hands on his shoulders as she stood behind him. He reached up to cover her hand with one of his.

"Thanks," he said. "They just don't understand. I don't have anger problems—I have grief and guilt problems."

"So why don't you tell that to your therapist?"

"I'm afraid she'll tell the NHL I'm in denial or something."

"She's supposed to be helping you. You have to trust that she can. Don't say you *don't* have anger issues; instead, mention that you're *also* struggling with guilt and grief. See where it leads."

He looked up at her gratefully. "That's pretty smart."

"I try," she said. "So, would you like a beer? I've got dinner in the oven. It should be done soon."

"You didn't have to cook. You don't owe me that."

"I'm not cooking because I *owe* you anything. I'm cooking because I love to cook, and I think maybe I've found someone who will actually appreciate it."

"I love to eat," he admitted. "Whatcha cookin'?"

"Homemade stuffed shells, garlic bread and a Caesar salad."

"I might have to marry you if you go on spoiling me like this."

Molly felt her cheeks grow warm. "Don't be silly." She turned and headed back to the kitchen. "Five more minutes!" she called over her shoulder. "Why don't you go take a quick shower and then we can eat?"

"Will do!" he called back, disappearing into his room.

Out of his sight, Molly leaned against the wall and closed her eyes. She would do anything to hold on to this moment. Tim had never been so relaxed and easygoing, not even in the beginning. She'd never been with anyone who made her feel happy and needed. She'd really never wanted anything but a family to take care of. She'd wanted to be a nurse for a while, but Tim had quashed those dreams long ago. Now Dom was giving her the ability to dream again. If she could just keep her emotions in check, everything might be okay. Maybe once they were alone together, she would be attracted to Toli the way she was to Dom, and then she would stop having this kind of reaction to a man she could never have.

The drive to Los Angeles was fun, with the top down on Toli's rental car, music blasting on the radio and them singing at the top of their lungs. Molly couldn't remember the last time she'd felt so carefree. Toli was probably the funniest person she'd ever met, and he'd had her laughing from the moment he picked her up. Her only regret was the odd look on Dom's face when she'd left.

"Be careful," he'd whispered as she'd been about to step out the door. "Make sure Toli understands how dangerous Tim is."

"I will," she'd whispered back, as if they had some special secret. He was so sweet and thoughtful, as well as sexy and mildly possessive, she almost didn't leave. But he'd already gone back to the baseball game he had on the TV, so she slipped out. She was excited about going to L.A. and spending the day with Toli, but part of her wished it were Dom taking her.

"How is possible Molly never goes to LA.? Is only three or four hours—if you drive very slow." Toli looked at her questioningly once they were on the road.

"We never had any money when I was growing up, and Tim never took me anywhere."

"Stupid man." He shook his head. "You are beautiful woman—why does he treat Molly badly?"

"I don't know," she said. "I used to think there was something wrong with me, but now I know it's him. His eyes, they almost turn black when he looks at me, as if I'm evil, and I've never done anything except try to make him happy."

"Asshole." Toli touched her arm. "He loses. Toli wins."

She couldn't help but giggle. "And what about Tatiana? Why have you been together so long without getting married?"

"Tatiana is a doctor," he said with obvious pride. "But never happy. Always more school, more training, more specialty. Toli asks for this to stop. Tatiana says no. Big fights. Toli wants wedding, maybe a baby. Tatiana wants success. Not money," he added hurriedly. "Just pride and accomplishment. Her parents always say Tatiana is stupid, not good enough. They are also doctors, and always trying to prove Tatiana is not so good. So Tatiana shows everyone she is not just good, but the best. At everything."

"Except making Toli happy," Molly said gently.

"Yes, very bad at this." He sighed. "No more talk about Tim and Tatiana?"

"No more." She rested her head against the seat. "This is the best day I've ever had."

"We have done nothing yet."

"No one is asking me about dinner, no one is hitting me, no one is yelling or throwing things. I have sunshine, a friend, good music—for me, this is heaven."

He smiled. "Yes, Toli thinks so too."

9

TOLI OBVIOUSLY KNEW HIS WAY AROUND L.A. TAKING THE 405 FREEWAY SOUTH towards Santa Monica, he parked and escorted Molly to the pier, making her laugh with stories from the NHL and the KHL; about his brother Sergei; and even about Dom, Cody and Brian. Molly laughed until her sides hurt. They walked on the pier and rode the Ferris wheel. He bought her a wonderful dinner at a restaurant on the water in Venice, and then they walked back towards Santa Monica along the shore, holding their shoes in their hands. He reached for her hand at one point, and she let him pull her as they ran through the puddles as the tide came in.

"We're getting wet!" she squealed.

"Is summer," he said with a laugh. "You will melt?"

"No. I just don't want to sit in wet clothes all the way home!"

"Toli will buy dry clothes." He pulled her close and looked down into her sparkling green eyes. "Molly is happy?"

"Yes."

"Toli likes this." He leaned forward slowly, and Molly all but stopped breathing. Was he going to *kiss* her? She had no idea what to do as his lips lightly touched hers. He hovered, waiting for a response, and she gently returned pressure but kept her mouth closed. He paused, leaning his forehead against hers. "Toli's kiss is not interesting." He made a simple statement, without any kind of censure.

"It is," she protested. "It's just…"

"Molly thinks of Dom and Toli thinks of Tatiana." He sighed. "No spark?"

"I'm sorry."

"No." He shook his head. "Toli thought maybe this would be good for both, but is obvious is nothing there. Friends?"

"Of course."

"Do not be sad," he said, throwing his arm around her shoulders as they began to walk again. He nudged her with his hip. "This is okay. Friends are important. Friends maybe more important than lovers—friends are always there. Lovers... they go."

"I won't go anywhere," she assured him. "I hope you're not angry with me."

"That is not how Toli works," he said. "Toli is also to blame."

"I would really hate to ruin the best day ever over a kiss."

"Kiss was not bad. Toli and Molly have other thoughts."

"I'm trying so hard not to like him!" she sighed, "but I can't help it."

"Why should you not like him? Dom is great guy. Does Molly still love Tim?"

"What? No! I can't stop thinking about Dom, but—" She bit her lip.

"What?"

"Look at me! I'll be forty in July! Dom is twenty-eight. He's gorgeous and rich."

"Toli is not gorgeous and rich?" he teased, taking her hand and swinging it between them.

"Yes, but Toli is only five years younger than me—not almost twelve," she said. "And Toli is probably going back to Russia, so I don't think you're serious about me."

"Toli is still confused about Tatiana, but Toli doesn't play games with women. If there was no interest, there would be no date. Casual sex is nice, but not between *friends*. This is not appropriate. Today is all for Molly, to be happy and see L.A. and leave the place that brings pain for one day. Maybe not *love*, but interest is real."

She smiled, comfortably holding his hand as they walked back towards the car, the sun setting on the horizon and the breeze blowing through her hair. The sun was low enough in the sky that she could look out over the water and ruminate over everything that had happened in the last couple of weeks. "I'm sorry there was no spark between us. I really like you, but..."

"But heart beats for Dom." He smiled too. "This is okay. Dom is lucky."

"Dom doesn't look at me like that."

"No?" He raised his eyebrows. "Maybe Molly doesn't see."

"What's to see? I'm too old and fat and boring for him."

"Not true." He paused, taking her by the arm. He brought her fingers to his lips and gently placed a kiss there. "Do you think Toli cannot find a date?"

"I'm sure you can, but—"

"But what? Why would Toli ask Molly for date and then a kiss? Because Molly is fat and old? No. Molly is beautiful—if Dom does not see this, other men *will*. I know many men who will like Molly very much. And if Tatiana does not change, Toli will ask Molly out again."

For the first time in her life, Molly felt nothing but joy. With a grin, she tugged at his hand and they continued walking. She couldn't remember the last time Tim had held her hand and she didn't care if this was friendship, a budding romance or simply a wonderful day; she'd never felt more alive.

W atching them pull up in front of the building, Dom let out the breath it felt like he'd been holding all day. Although he'd bought Molly a cell phone, he didn't feel he could call her while she was out with Toli. He wasn't a lover with a right to be jealous, and he had no doubt he would lose her friendship if he tried to keep her on a leash. Tim had done enough to her, and he refused to cause her any more distress. He wanted her to be happy, but he'd hoped she would be interested in him, not in one of his best friends. He watched unhappily as she and Toli got out of the car. Molly approached him and she and Toli laughed about something as he wrapped his arms around her.

Stepping away from the window, Dom sighed. Damn. Maybe he'd been wrong about her. Maybe she *was* just looking for a rich husband to save her from her awful life. Well, of course she was, he told himself. Who wouldn't want to get away from a guy like Tim?

He honestly couldn't blame her. She hadn't asked for anything and had been honest about the fact she had nothing to offer him other than friendship. In fact, he couldn't blame her for looking at a man who had immediately made it clear that he liked her. Why shouldn't she take a chance on a great guy like Toli?

Toli was older, Dom reasoned as he stretched out on the couch. He and Molly probably had a lot in common, despite the language barrier. Toli would be good to her, and she would definitely be safe. Toli acted like a goofball, but he was fiercely protective of those he cared about. No, Molly would have a good life if she and Toli were together. He found himself wishing she were interested in him and didn't know why. She was a bit older than he and probably not as attractive as many of the women he'd been with over the years, but there was something about her that made his heart pound.

First and foremost, her eyes mesmerized him. He loved looking at them, and at her. Her long legs made his mouth water and he'd dreamt about having them wrapped around his waist. Her mouth just begged to be kissed, and the fact that she'd never had an orgasm drove him wild. He'd initially thought his attraction to her was simply because it had been a few months since he'd had sex, but the more he got to know her, the more he liked everything about her.

The fact she could cook just added bonus points, and although he wasn't 100% sure, she had to feel the sparks when their eyes met. Maybe she thought him too young for her, but their bond was evident every moment they spent together. Their friendship was already solid, and he wouldn't disrespect that, but he didn't know what he would do if she got into a relationship with Toli without even giving him a chance. Somehow, he had to make her notice him as more than a friend.

He didn't know what he felt for her, but he had to try to figure it out. He'd gone a long time convincing himself that he might be a danger to any woman he got in a relationship with, but he knew in his soul he would never hurt Molly. Being sure of that gave him strength, and he made the decision that he would work on trying to get her to see him as a potential lover, not just as a friend.

Hearing the door open, he forced himself to relax. He had no right to be jealous, and he wouldn't ruin her new relationship, no matter how hard it was for him.

He would try to figure out how serious she was about Toli, and then he would talk to Toli if necessary. In the meantime, he would go slowly.

He looked up as she stepped in and locked the door behind her. "Hey!" he called out. "How was it?"

"It was glorious!" She sank onto the couch with him. "We had so much fun! We walked all the way from Santa Monica to Venice and back again. It was amazing."

"Next time you should rent rollerblades," he said. "There's a great trail that goes between the two beaches."

"Have you been?" Then she laughed at her own question. "Of course you've been! What did you do today?"

"The usual. Worked out, all that crap," he shrugged. Unable to stop the jealousy eating away at him, he stood up and faked a yawn. "Okay, well, I'm going to turn in. Do you need anything?"

"No, I'm just going to watch a little TV, if that's okay?"

"This is your home, Molly. What's mine is yours."

She looked at him with something in her eyes he couldn't interpret, but he just smiled and went to his room.

AS THE NHL'S EXPANSION DRAFT APPROACHED, DOM, CODY AND TOLI SPENT more and more time with the team's management. Meanwhile, Molly and Suze spent almost as much time together: shopping, working out, and getting to know each other. It had been years since Molly had had a real girlfriend. Suze too had been lonely, because even though she had a lot of friends in Toronto, they all had been involved with the team and sometimes she needed a break from hockey. Besides, there hadn't been people she could trust the way she did Molly. Suze could tell her anything, and Molly was happy to listen.

Hanging out by the pool at Suze and Cody's house, Molly lay in the hot midday sun with a glass of ice water in her hand. She and Suze had gone to yoga in the morning and then run two miles before coming home to have lunch and lie by the pool. She was tired and sore, but in a way that made her relaxed and happy. CJ was at camp for another hour or so, and the guys had said they might be late. The expansion draft was in four days and they were huddled over stats and the projected performance of every NHL player. Of course, she had no idea what that meant, except that they were busy.

"You're quiet today," Suze commented, handing Molly the bottle of sunscreen.

"Am I?"

Suze laughed. "Just tell me what's up."

"Dom is acting funny."

"Funny how?"

"I don't know. Ever since my date with Toli he's been different: kind of distant, like I have a boyfriend or something."

"Are you still hanging out with Toli?"

"Some."

"You said you talk to him every day."

"We're friends. I talk to you every day, but I'm not dating *you*."

Suze threw back her head and laughed. "Girlfriend, you do understand that unless you *tell* him nothing happened, he's going to assume you two are dating, and he's not going to do anything to betray his friend's trust."

"Wouldn't they have talked about that?"

Suze rolled her eyes. "You don't know much about men, do you?"

Molly narrowed her eyes. "What's that supposed to mean?"

"Men don't talk like we do! And if Toli thinks Dom has a thing for you, he's probably purposely *not* telling him that you two are just friends just to mess with him. Men are funny that way—it's all about their ego."

"What am I supposed to do?"

"Well, I'm no expert, but I think you're going to need to give Dom some motivation."

"I don't want Dom losing his temper, especially over me."

"You could tease him a little."

"*Tease him?*"

"You know, come out of your room half-dressed or something."

"That might scare him away!"

"Would you stop?" Suze scolded her. "You've lost weight just in the few weeks you've been here, and you're all tan and sexy with those green eyes of yours. Cody even commented how great you look."

"*Cody* thinks I look good?"

"Of course he does. The only person who doesn't believe you're beautiful is you," said Suze. "Enjoy life, Molly. It's short."

"The truth is, I have no idea what to do. Dom is amazing—sexy and kind and good to me. Toli is a riot. He's not as good-looking as Dom, but he's no slouch either. He's also wonderful to me, and when we're together we can talk about anything. He's still pining for Tatiana, though."

"So that leaves Dom, who's completely single. What are you waiting for?"

Molly shrugged. "With Toli, there's a *chance*—he's closer to my age and not quite as hot as the sun. He's more down-to-earth and the biggest thing is, he already has a kid."

Suze was surprised. "I didn't think he told anyone about Anton."

"Yes. Anton lives with his mom in Texas. Toli sees him pretty regularly—he flies to Texas, or they go somewhere together in the summer. He's almost 15 and plays hockey too, so they're close."

"I can't believe he told you all that."

"We're good friends. Just like you and me, except we flirt a little." She blushed. "But that's all it is. The truth is, Dom is probably going to want kids someday, and we both know that isn't going to happen with me."

"You don't know that!" Suze protested. "You've never been pregnant without someone hitting you. Maybe a pregnancy without abuse would be okay."

"I'll be forty this year. My time is running out."

"Then you should hurry up and seduce Dom."

"I'm not getting pregnant unless I'm married. No guy would ever trust a woman in my position who got pregnant."

"Okay, but marriage isn't going to happen without you being a little proactive."

"I don't even know if I want to get married again. I mean, I don't know how I feel after what I've lived through with Tim."

"Most guys aren't like Tim," Suze reminded her. "Remember, I married a guy I wasn't in love with and we've had a nice life. Yes, it could be better, and all the cheating stuff made me want to strangle him—but we had a whole set of other problems that make our situation unique. Yet, despite all of that, if Cody and I were to separate, I would get married again. Being married is great, assuming the person you're married to isn't a psycho."

Molly sighed. "It's just that my focus right now is on *not* being married anymore; Dom and I are going to see a lawyer this week. Even though Nevada is probably one of the easiest places in the country to get a divorce, Tim is going to fight me and I'm not sure I can do it without a lawyer."

"Cody still has that video of him getting all crazy," Suze pointed out. "That should help."

"Yeah, we're going to show it to the lawyer. Maybe once Tim's lawyer sees it he won't fight me. I don't want anything except my share of the house—it's only fair. I don't even want alimony. I just want him out of my life."

"Amen to that."

The meeting with the lawyer was one of the scariest things Molly had ever done. He asked questions she hated answering, and took a strong stance on the abuse, insisting they had to make it public knowledge, or at the very least threaten to do so, which could effectively end Tim's career. But there was no way to file the paperwork without listing an address, and Dom was adamant they not list an address where Tim could actually find her.

Cody and Suze had offered to let her use their address, but Molly refused, saying that they had a child in the house and she didn't trust Tim not to try and hurt the Armstrongs. This was why she no longer had any friends: on occasions when she didn't do what he told her, Tim had threatened the few that she had, and eventually she'd had to stay away from them for their own safety.

"Use Toli's address," Toli said that night at dinner at Cody and Suze's house. "There are two bedrooms. One will have some of Molly's things—like situation in Dom's apartment—but Molly will never be there."

"I would be putting you in danger," she said, shaking her head.

"Toli is big, strong Russian hockey player. American policeman with small penis is not scary." He folded his arms across his chest. "Somewhere has to be address—and Molly must not be there."

She sighed. "Toli, if something happens to you…"

"Nothing will happen." He put his big hands over hers. "Everything will be fine."

"That's the only address we can use," Cody said. "I think Toli's place is set up perfectly for our situation. There are security cameras in the building, a doorman, and special keys needed to get up to each floor in the elevators. The doors to the stairwells require keys as well."

"Is settled," said Toli.

Molly sighed. She hated everything about this situation, especially endangering her new friends. She didn't know what else to do, though, because she couldn't stay married to Tim and still move on with her life. This was dangerous, but necessary.

"You okay?" Dom asked, following her out to the pool, where she sipped a glass of wine.

"I hate putting Toli in danger. You guys don't know how dangerous Tim is."

Dom blinked at her. "Do you recall how we met? I know damn well how dangerous he is, but let's be clear: He's only a tough guy when it comes to his smaller, weaker wife. You think he's going to be so tough against one of us?"

"I think he carries a gun and has no qualms about using it."

"Toli grew up in Russia and was in the military before he got drafted by the NHL. He's comfortable with guns and Cody lent him one of his for this very reason. If anyone can handle Tim other than me, it's Toli. I have absolute confidence in his ability to keep you safe."

"You say that like he's responsible for me," she returned. "We're just friends, Dom."

Dom glanced at her. "You spend an awful lot of time together."

"Because he asks me to do things—we've gone to the movies, dinner, Los Angeles, all kinds of things I've never done thanks to my dillweed of an ex. If you asked me to go places, I'd go with you." She swallowed hard as she watched his face.

"I thought you guys were dating."

"We're *friends*. He's all tied up in Tatiana—he still talks to her every day, so there's no room for me in that situation."

"What about me?" he asked. "Where do I fit into your life?"

"You're my *best* friend," she said, putting her drink down and taking his hands in hers, channeling her inner strong, confident woman. "You're my rock and support system. Without you, none of this would have happened, and without you, I wouldn't have the strength to get up every day. Toli and Suze don't hold my hand when I wake up in a panic—you do. Toli and Suze didn't sit on the floor with me in the dark until I was strong enough to turn on the lights—you did. No one else in my life holds a candle to you—and I don't know that anyone else ever will." She hadn't meant to say it quite that way, or to look at him quite the way she was, but she couldn't help herself.

"Molly..." He ran his fingers over her cheeks. "There's so much—"

"Uncle Dom! Aunt Molly!" CJ came running outside, crashing into them and nearly causing Molly to stumble.

"Easy, kiddo." Dom caught CJ with one arm and Molly with the other, keeping her from toppling into the pool.

"CJ!" Cody came running out after him. "Sorry about that! You okay, Molly?"

"I'm fine," Molly was laughing. "It wouldn't be the worst thing in the world if I'd fallen in the water. I do know how to swim."

"Still, he needs to learn a little more control." Cody knelt before his son. "CJ, tell Aunt Molly and Uncle Dom you're sorry."

"I'm sorry." CJ looked up, his lower lip trembling. "I didn't mean to make you fall, Aunt Molly."

"That's okay, sugar!" She gave him a hug. "Everything's fine. You just need to slow down a little."

"Okay." CJ glanced at his father, who ruffled his hair.

"Go on inside, son."

"Mommy said it's time for dessert!" CJ called over his shoulder.

"Sorry," said Cody. "I tried to grab him before he got out the door, but he's a fast little bugger.".

"It's okay. He's a kid."

"I know. He's just so much like—" He stopped abruptly and looked away. "Anyway, Suze said it's time for dessert."

"So much for all the weight I've lost," Molly sighed.

"You look fabulous," Dom said in her ear. "You don't need to lose any weight."

She flashed him a smile. "Flattery will get you everywhere."

11

Toli was on the phone with Tatiana when he heard his doorknob rattle. He moved into his bedroom, pulled Cody's .357 Magnum from his nightstand and stuck it in the waistband of his shorts. Dousing the lights, he spoke quietly into the phone.

"Will call you back," he said in Russian, disconnecting. Tatiana would undoubtedly blow a gasket, but he turned off the ringer and then typed in 911, though he didn't hit send. Waiting, he stood in the shadows listening. Someone was actually trying to pick the lock on his door. He hit 'send' and waited for the police dispatcher to answer.

"Someone is trying to break into my home," he said abruptly, giving the dispatcher his address. He had a chain on the door, but he figured once they got the locks open, they would make short work of the chain. Ignoring the dispatcher who was still talking to him, he found a chair and quietly wedged it under the door handle. It wouldn't keep them out for long, but it would give the police an extra minute or so to get here.

Strangely, he wasn't afraid. Knowing this was probably the man who had been beating Molly for the last twenty years, he was almost looking forward to an opportunity to put his fist in the man's face. Guns didn't scare him either, although he wasn't naïve enough to think he could outshoot a man professionally trained to use a weapon. He was proficient, but he wasn't a killer, and the military had been more than a decade ago.

As he expected, Tatiana had called back twice already, but he ignored the incoming call notifications as he stayed on the line with the police. He heard the click as the dead bolt was finally turned and he shook his head in frustration—he was definitely having better locks installed! He heard the chair scraping across the floor as someone pushed until the door began to open.

Toli whispered into the phone that the burglars had picked his lock and were now pushing against the chain. As the dispatcher told him to hide and that the police were only a minute or so away, he made his way into the kitchen and picked up one of the metal pans Suze had bought for him.

"You need to be able to boil water for pasta and make a scrambled egg," she'd insisted, giving him two fancy pans he would probably never use. "Even a bachelor has to cook a few things!"

Now he held the frying pan in his hand, trying to decide if it was hard enough to knock someone out or if he should take the chance of firing the gun. Though he wouldn't hesitate to do it if it meant saving his life, it would most likely cause him all sorts of problems and bring bad publicity to the team he wanted to play for next season. Taking a deep breath, he put his phone back in his pocket and raised the metal pan in the air. Someone put their full weight on the door, finally breaking the chain and pushing the chair across the room. The door swung open and someone stepped inside. Toli brought the frying pan down on the man's head, rendering him unconscious. Someone shouted and Toli yelled, "Police are on the way—enter at your own risk!"

"This is the police," someone yelled back. "You need to cease and desist! Drop your weapon and put your hands in the air."

"Not a chance in hell," Toli yelled back. "When the police I called on 911 arrive, then I will *cease and desist*." He enunciated the words sarcastically, knowing this had to be Tim or his friends.

He heard muttering, whispered voices, and then the sound of footsteps in the hall.

"You will get out of my house," Toli called back. "I will defend myself."

"This is a police matter and you need to step back."

"Do you have a warrant?" he asked.

There was more silence as someone whispered something to someone else. "There have been reports of violence on this floor and we're searching for a battered woman. We're searching all the apartments on this floor."

"There is no woman in my apartment—I'm home alone." Toli could hear sirens outside and let out a sigh of relief.

After that, everything happened in a blur. Police swarmed the apartment, with a lot of whispered voices and people searching each room. He watched as they looked under the beds and in all the closets.

"Who else lives here?" the man in charge asked him abruptly.

"That would be my friend, Molly McCarran, who is the wife of the police officer I believe sent these men here—Tim McCarran. She recently filed for divorce and has been trying to stay away from him." Toli didn't hesitate to look at each of the men in the room carefully. Although he often downplayed his command of English by talking in third person and using grammatically incorrect phrasing because it didn't require as much concentration, he'd been speaking English most of his life. He had no difficulty leaving behind his class-clown persona and going head-to-head with a room full of dirty cops. He wasn't playing around with these guys and he wasn't going to let them think he was some dumb jock.

"You broke into my home without a warrant. There is no possible way anyone heard any kind of problems coming from this apartment because Molly has been out of town with a girlfriend for a couple of days," he lied, folding his arms across his chest.

"How, exactly, did a Russian national who's only been in the country a few weeks become friends with Mrs. McCarran?" one of the policemen asked.

"She's a hockey fan; I'm a hockey player." He arched an eyebrow. "She asked me for an autograph at a restaurant and, after a pleasant conversation, I asked her if she could help me find a place to live. I need someone to take care of my place when I'm on the road, and we decided it would be a perfect arrangement since she was currently without a place to live."

"So you invited a total stranger to live in your home?" the man asked dubiously.

"She's hot," Toli said with a telling shrug. "Who wouldn't want a good-looking woman living in his house?" He hated making her sound so cheap, but the policeman was right in questioning his letting a total stranger move in with him, and the only way for that to make sense was to hint they had some kind of relationship.

"We're going to need to follow up with Mrs. McCarran to make sure she's all right," the policeman said.

"My understanding is she'll only deal with the police through her lawyer," Toli shrugged. "I don't know much about her divorce, but I know she doesn't trust any of you."

The man in charge narrowed his eyes slightly. "That's a serious accusation."

"So is a group of off-duty policemen breaking into my home late at night without a warrant." He cocked his head and glanced at the man's nameplate. "You do not want this kind of trouble on your record, Officer Valdez. I have plenty of money to spend on making the lives of bad cops miserable. Harassing me will not end well for any of you." He focused on the man on the floor who was finally coming to, making sure he understood he was talking to him. "And you should tell your friend Tim that Molly wants to be left alone. Otherwise, we're going to spend a lot of time in court, and I'd be willing to bet I have more money to waste than any of you."

There were more questions and forms to be signed, but by midnight they were gone and Toli was left to shove another chair under the door handle until he could get it repaired in the morning. Exhausted but unable to sleep, he stared at the TV for a long time. As crazy as all of this was, it seemed a hell of a lot better than what he'd left behind in Russia, which made no sense at all.

With the passing of the NHL entry and expansion drafts, Cody, Dom and Toli had more time to relax. Most of the players would not be arriving in Las Vegas for at least another month, so now they could focus on vacations and enjoying their time off. Dom and Toli both signed contracts on the first of July, and because of the July 4th holiday, they agreed to go on vacation to celebrate.

"San Diego," Dom told Molly. "The Hotel Del Coronado is incredible. I think you'll love it."

"I'm sure I'm going to love anywhere we go, since I've never been anywhere!"

"You should go shopping." He pulled some cash from of his wallet.

"What? No, I have what I need. You shouldn't—"

"Shut. Up." He moved closer to her and pressed the bills into her hand. "You're going on your very first vacation. With me." His eyes met hers meaningfully. "Buy a pretty dress—something you can wear at night, slow dancing by the ocean. Buy a sexy pair of heels so I can look at your legs. Buy something pretty to sleep in—because we're sharing a room and although I will never do anything you don't want to do, I seem to remember making you a promise."

Molly swallowed hard, knowing exactly what he was talking about and feeling her stomach doing flips at the very thought of making love with him.

"Dom, you're too young for me."

"Says who?" He gently lifted her chin and looked into the green eyes he'd been mesmerized by since the moment he'd met her. "And what difference does it make?"

"It makes a lot of difference—men like you don't date women like me."

"What kind of women is it that I don't date? Beautiful ones? Divorced? Green-eyed?"

"Old," she said tiredly. "You're young and have your whole life ahead of you. One day you're going to want children—and I probably can't give them to you."

"Would you stop over-thinking everything? I have no idea if I want kids, and we both know life is too short to think about that stuff. Just go shopping. Please?"

"Fine." The jolt of excitement that passed through her as he bent his head and lightly brushed his lips across hers almost made her blush.

12

Driving across San Diego Bay on the bridge that led to Coronado, Molly stared in fascination at the fabulous and historical hotel. She'd looked it up before they'd left, and discovered it was built in 1888 and was the second largest wooden structure in the United States. Featured in many films over the years, including the Marilyn Monroe classic, "Some Like It Hot," Molly was excited to be seeing it in person. She'd always dreamed of visiting places like this, and now she was actually here. It was as gorgeous as she'd imagined and she couldn't wait to explore every inch.

Though the drive was longer than the drive to Los Angeles, they'd broken it up by stopping in Los Angeles for lunch. She and Dom were in his car, and Toli was riding with Cody, Suze and CJ. Dom had taken the week off from therapy and anger management: he was allowed a vacation and it was a short week anyway due to the holiday.

Molly felt like a teenager as they drove for miles with their hands linked between them. She was playing with fire, and risking a broken heart, but she couldn't help herself. After what had happened at Toli's apartment, she had no doubt Tim would be coming for her. Although she wouldn't go down without a fight, she also wouldn't risk her friends' lives. If he found her, she would go with him before allowing him to hurt anyone. That meant her time with these wonderful people was possibly coming to an end, so she was going to savor every moment of it. Though Dom promised her he wouldn't let Tim get to her, he would eventually find her and there was no way of knowing whether Dom could protect her.

Not today, though, she thought as they pulled into the parking lot of the hotel. It was just as beautiful in person as in the movies, and she snapped a picture with her phone.

"Pretty cool, huh?" Dom said as he pulled their suitcase out of the SUV.

"Can I go swimming?" CJ was already asking.

"In a little while," Suze promised him. "We have to check in and then get your bathing suit on. You can go for a quick swim before dinner, okay?"

"Okay!" CJ happily ran in circles in the parking lot.

Walking into the hotel, they checked in and then separated. Dom and Molly were going to relax a little before dinner. Suze and Cody were taking CJ to the beach, and Toli said he had a few phone calls to make.

Opening the door to their suite, the bellman pointed out the various amenities. Dom slipped a bill into his hand and the man disappeared. Molly went to the double doors that opened to a view of the beach and sighed with delight.

"I've died and gone to heaven," she announced, leaning back against Dom as he came up behind her.

"You like it?" He placed a kiss on her neck that sent shivers down her spine.

"Yes." She turned to face him, her green eyes sparkling with excitement. "It's absolutely beautiful. Thank you for bringing me here!" Throwing her arms around his neck, she leaned up and kissed him. But instead of letting her go, his arms tightened and his lips slowly parted hers. Her mouth responded without hesitation, and he deepened the kiss, his tongue finding hers. He stroked it gently, caressing her as she came alive under him.

She'd never been kissed like this and her heart hammered against her ribs as he continued to kiss her, hands slowly traveling across her back and settling in her hair.

"God, you're beautiful," he whispered. "I could do this all night."

"I want you to," she whispered back, tugging at his T-shirt so she could run her hands along the skin of his beautiful, hard chest and gloriously flat stomach. She'd never seen anything quite like him, and she had to admit it was heady. He was absolute perfection, and when he pulled off his shirt she sighed happily. Touching him was like an out of body experience, and she traced a line with her finger along the tattoo of a hawk that spread across his chest, up to his shoulder and over to his right bicep. When he kissed the spot behind her neck, she shivered against him longingly.

He pulled her to the bed, where he fell back and brought her down so she was resting on top of him. His mouth found hers again and she could feel his erection growing against her thigh. A whimper of need escaped her as he unbuttoned her shorts and slipped his hand inside to explore the curve of her hip.

"Is this okay?" he asked softly.

"Yes," she breathed against him. "It's wonderful. You're wonderful."

He kissed her again, easing off her shorts and slowly running his fingers along her soft, smooth skin. He could tell she was nervous, but he intended to make this a trip to remember. He was determined to convince her they were a good match. He understood her reservations, but he wasn't worried about the age difference. He'd never met anyone like her before, and in the month they'd been together, he'd learned so much about himself. Mostly that he didn't want to live in the past anymore; he wanted to move forward and he wanted Molly to be with him. He'd never really believed in love at first sight, but he'd known the moment he saw her in that parking garage she was going to change his life.

Focusing on her now, he pulled away long enough to look up at her enraptured face.

"What's wrong?" Her eyes opened in surprise.

"Nothing." He rubbed his knuckles across her cheek and smiled. "You're just driving me crazy."

"Is that good crazy or bad crazy?" she smiled back.

"Oh, it's good." He found her mouth again and slowly ran his hands along the indentation of her waist. She was curvy but far from fat, and he was enjoying the hell out of touching her. When he slipped her panties off, his big hands slid along her thighs, the swell of her ass and the warm mound between her legs. He felt her jump slightly as he moved his hand there, and he stroked her slowly. "It's okay," he whispered. "Trust me, Molly."

"I feel like a virgin again," she said in a whisper. "It's always been so... uncomfortable."

"We can stop any time you want," he said, brushing kisses across her neck.

She nodded, but put her hands on the back of his head and brought his mouth back to hers. This time when he slipped his hand between her legs, she moved against him, completely immersed in his touch and the way he made her feel. She yearned for him to make her feel like the women she read about in romance novels; she'd never found pleasure in Tim's lovemaking but something told her Dom would be very different.

"You okay, baby?" he asked, as she shivered.

"Yes," she closed her eyes as he slowly explored her body. She'd never felt sexy before, and her nervousness was slowly replaced with desire. Every stroke was pure magic, and she'd never been wet like this. When he slipped one finger inside of her she was sure nothing had ever felt so good. A tiny moan escaped her as he moved, finding the rhythm that made her sigh with pleasure. Using his finger, he found her clit and her eyes popped open in surprise.

"Is that the spot?" he asked with a small grin.

"Oh, yes!" Moving against his hand, she couldn't believe how incredible this was. Her body was on fire, and he was only using his fingers. She hadn't been sure she even had a clitoris because Tim had certainly never found it, but Dom knew exactly where it was. An unfamiliar fluttering between her legs made her arch towards him. "Oh! Dom! Don't stop..." Her voice faded as he sped up, bringing her over the edge with a cry of delight. "Dom!" His mouth devoured hers as she had her first orgasm against his hand.

"That's it, baby." He laughed gently as she gasped and clung to him, the ripples making her shudder.

"Oh my God." She looked at him in amazement. "That felt so good."

"I'm glad you enjoyed it." He kissed her again, less urgently this time, relaxing against the bed as he brought her against his chest.

"Don't you want to..." Her voice trailed off as she ran her hand along his bulging erection.

"Not right now," he said. "I'll wait until later. I want the first time I make love to you to be romantic and special, not hurried or distracted because we have dinner plans. I just wanted to give you a taste, so you would think about what it felt like when I give you an orgasm."

"I'm going to be thinking about it all night!" she giggled, wrapping her arms around his neck.

"You'll be doing more than thinking about it," he chuckled, kissing the tip of her nose.

D inner was a casual affair, outside on the terrace where CJ could run around while the adults shared a bottle of wine. Wearing a new sundress that was as green as the ocean with pink accents, and nude high-heeled wedges, Molly felt sexier than she'd ever felt in her life. Both Cody and Toli had told her she looked beautiful, but Dom had come to her when she'd come out of the bathroom after getting dressed and whispered all the ways he was going to touch her after dinner. She could feel the heat rushing to her cheeks just thinking about it and forced herself to take a sip of wine.

Conversation turned to hockey, and Molly listened intently, trying to follow a subject she knew so little about. She knew the basics of the game and the teams, but she really had no idea about the inner workings of an organization, or who the best players were.

"I think Karl is going to be an amazing back-up," Cody said, referring to a goalie they'd signed.

"Karl Martensson?" Suze asked, her eyes twinkling.

"Yeah, why?" Cody eyed her.

"Because he's also going to bring *girls* to the game," she chuckled. Glancing at Molly, she said, "He's this big Swedish kid—hotter than hell. And single! Every unattached woman in Vegas is going to be coming to games just to try to catch his eye."

"How do you know he is single?" Toli asked, frowning at her.

"Are you kidding? All wives in the NHL know the relationship statuses of the hot players, because we all have single friends who might be interested."

Dom rolled his eyes. "Really?"

"Well, yeah. You'd rather he go out with a puck bunny?"

"Drake Riser is going to be hot this season," Dom said, changing the subject as he casually slipped his arm around the back of Molly's chair. "Did you see him during the playoffs last season? I think he's hit his stride and I'm really excited to play with him."

"Me too," Cody nodded. He glanced at Suze. "Is *he* single?"

"Last I heard, he hasn't seriously dated since his divorce."

"Do you know everything about *everyone* in the NHL?" Cody asked.

"Not everyone." She glanced at Dom and Molly. "But almost."

They laughed as the guys continued talking about the other players on the team. Molly finally excused herself to go to the restroom, and Suze hurried after her. As they washed their hands, Suze pounced.

"You're glowing! Did you do it?"

Molly laughed. "Not *that*, but we had a pretty intense make-out session."

"Was it hot?"

"Totally hot." Molly fanned herself and they both dissolved in giggles.

"*And?*"

"And what?"

"Are you *gonna* do it?"

"Probably."

They burst into laughter again. "I'm so glad we met," Suze whispered, giving her a hug. "I haven't had a girlfriend in a long time."

"Me either." Molly hugged her back. She turned back to the mirror and reapplied her lipstick, trying not to think about the evening of hot sex that was inevitable.

WATCHING HER COME ACROSS THE RESTAURANT, DOM FOUGHT THE URGE TO immediately drag her back to their room and have his way with her. She'd driven him crazy this afternoon, listening to her moans and sighs. He was dying to make love to her and show her what it was like to be with a real man. The more he heard about her husband, the more baffled he became by the crazy people in the world. He didn't understand how a man could hurt a woman, over and over, for more than twenty years. He also didn't understand how she could stay, but he understood she really had nowhere to go. He was grateful he'd been able to save her that day that seemed like so much longer than a month ago.

She dropped into the seat beside him and he couldn't resist leaning over to brush his lips across hers. She smiled into his eyes but turned to find CJ staring at them.

"Are you going to get *married*?" the boy asked, and Suze snorted.

"I don't know yet," Dom told CJ calmly, despite the laughter he was holding back. "But I like her a lot. Is that okay?"

CJ squinted at them. "But will you still be Aunt Molly and Uncle Dom if you get married?" He seemed worried and Molly reached over to tousle his hair.

"Of course we will! Nothing will ever stop us from being Aunt Molly and Uncle Dom!"

"Promise?"

"We promise, buddy," Dom gave him a smile.

"Okay." He still eyed them suspiciously and Suze fought not to laugh out loud.

"Does he skate yet?" Toli asked Cody.

"A little," replied Cody. "I guess I'm just not sure I want him becoming a hockey player, you know? It's a tough life sometimes, and even though I love it, I can't ever remember having a *choice*. I went to the rink four or five times a week for my whole life. Even my sister played. I'd like him to decide on his own—because no one ever asked me what I wanted."

"I want to be a goalie!" CJ announced, startling everyone.

"When did you decide that, honey?" Suze asked him, her eyes wide with unshed tears.

"When I was little," the child said. "Being a goalie is cool! Five hole!" He immediately dropped into a split on the ground with his hand in the air as if catching a puck.

"All right, we can talk about that when we get home," Cody said. "But we don't practice goalie moves in a restaurant."

"Okay." CJ hopped back into his seat and stuffed a piece of bread in his mouth.

Molly gave Dom a quizzical look at Suze's reaction and crinkled her forehead. *Brian,* he mouthed silently. Molly immediately understood; Brian had been a goalie.

"Hey, would you guys watch CJ for a few minutes?" Cody rose slowly, pulling Suze up with him. "We're just gonna take a quick walk on the beach before dinner, okay? We'll be right back, buddy." He leaned over and kissed the top of CJ's head.

"No problem," Molly waved at them. "We'll keep him entertained."

Cody pulled Suze off the terrace and onto the sand, where she slipped off her shoes before moving against him. He whispered something in her ear that made her smile and they strode off and out of sight.

"So, how's your son doing, Toli?" Molly asked.

"Anton is very good," he grinned, pulling out his phone and showing them a video. "This was high school championship," he said proudly. They watched Anton score a goal and put his hands in the air. He was built just like Toli, with the same grin and blue eyes, but hair that was longer and a straight nose that more than likely came from his mother.

"He looks good," Dom said, impressed. "Is he looking at the Juniors?"

"One more year," Toli said. "Mother wants to wait. This is okay—he will grow more. He is six feet tall—maybe taller than Toli soon."

"Are you going to see him?" Molly asked.

"Next week. Toli was thinking to bring him here for the rest of summer, but after situation last week…" His voice trailed off as he glanced in CJ's direction.

"I'm sorry," Molly sighed.

"Is not problem," he said. "Toli will go to Dallas. Anton's mother is good, no problems with visits."

"Is she married?" Molly was curious.

"Yes, she has another boy and one girl. Husband is nice, very good to Anton. Nice family. Toli is lucky the *situation*—" He refrained from saying one-night-stand— "turned out so well."

"It could've happened to any of us," said Dom. "There were probably a few times I got really lucky in college, before the word AIDS actually sunk in."

Toli nodded. "True."

"I wasn't doing any of that until I got married," said Molly. "So I've never even thought about AIDS." For the first time, Molly wondered if Tim cheated on her in addition to everything else he did. Would he have been careful? She couldn't picture Tim being conscientious enough to wear a condom—he never would with her, no matter how many miscarriages she had.

Her thoughts were interrupted by CJs voice. "Aunt Molly, I have to go potty."

"Okay, honey, I'll take you." She got up and held out her hand. He put his small one in hers and they left the table.

"You must not hurt her," Toli said to Dom as soon as she was out of earshot.

"What?"

"Is simple request. Please do not break Molly's heart. Toli would be unhappy."

"Why do you think I would do that? I adore her."

"Because you are young, but Molly is special."

"I know she's special." Dom scowled at him. "Why do you think I'm trying to protect her from Tim?"

Because you are human being," Toli grumbled. "He is pig. But loving Molly, *sleeping* with Molly, will bring her much unhappiness if you are not ready for commitment."

"Why? Are you thinking about going out with her?" Dom was getting irritated.

"Toli already thought about it, and did it." He gave him a look when Dom's eyes narrowed. "Not sex—she was not ready. But now she is, and Toli sees the way she looks at you. You must know what you want, Dom."

"Toli, no offense, man, but I got this. Molly and I are good."

Toli saw the younger man's scowl and decided to let it go. He really had no right to be so protective of Molly, but he couldn't help but worry about her. Dom was a good guy, but he was on his own journey trying to get back into the NHL's good graces and bring back his top game. His intentions were good, but he might not be thinking beyond having this amazing woman in his bed. Toli himself had almost fallen into that trap, and if she hadn't called him out when he'd tried to kiss her, he might have continued deluding himself about his conflicted feelings for Tatiana. Dom, however, didn't have another woman distracting him—which could be good or bad.

Molly and CJ came back from the restroom around the same time Cody and Suze came back from their walk. Suze had composed herself in that time, and now she sat at the table sipping wine as though nothing had happened. Whatever they'd discussed in private had obviously calmed her down, but Molly noticed a slight tremor in her hand when she picked up her wineglass. Maybe tomorrow she would try to talk to Suze.

TWO HOURS LATER, SHE AND DOM WERE HEADED UP TO THEIR ROOM, ARMS around each other as they walked.

"I'm sorry we didn't get to dance," he said softly.

"There will be other times," she said, looking up at him.

"You bet there will." He opened the door and let her walk in before him. The room was dark, with just some lights from outside illuminating them, and Dom kept her from turning on the lamp. "Leave it dark," he said softly. "Come here."

She moved into his arms easily. "Except for CJ's announcement about becoming a goalie and freaking out his mother, tonight was perfect."

Dom chuckled. "Yeah, he managed to send his mom into a tailspin. I'm glad Cody's got her back because she sure is carrying a heavy load by keeping Brad and Andra in the dark."

"I think she's getting tired of hiding CJ's secret."

"I'm sure." Dom looked down at her before he bent and kissed her, taking her breath away. "You taste like red wine," he mused, running his tongue along her lips.

"So do you." She reached for his hand. "Come here."

"Where are we going?"

"Balcony." She opened the doors and stepped outside. "I want you to kiss me here in the moonlight, with the ocean in the background."

"I can do that." He kissed her thoroughly, his fingers finding the smooth skin on her back and arms as she clung to him. When he couldn't stand it anymore, he backed her into the bedroom, kissing her all the way. "Don't move," he said, going over to his bag and pulling out a handful of condoms.

"That many?" she laughed.

"You never know, and I don't want to have to stop and go looking for them."

He put them aside, lay back on the bed and held out his arms.

Slipping off her shoes she crawled over to lie on his chest. She slowly unbuttoned his shirt, pulling it free of his slacks. She ran her hands over the hair curling on his chest. "You are so... perfect." She placed a soft kiss on his navel and heard him groan with desire as she kissed her way back up to his lips. "I have no idea how I got lucky enough to find you."

"Baby, I'm the one that's lucky." He curled a lock of her hair around his finger. "You make me want to do better, be better... knowing you has made me realize just how much I've missed while I've been wallowing in grief. I don't know I ever would have seen past all that if you hadn't come into my life."

"I'm really glad I did then." She lowered her face to his, wanting to feel him touch her. She'd never yearned for sex before, but when Dom touched her, she could barely remember her name.

Dom tried to pace himself. It had been months since he'd had sex, and Molly had been driving him crazy since the first time he laid eyes on her, but he knew she needed him to slow down. Though he didn't consider himself jaded by the number of women he'd had sex with, he wasn't used to romance either. This was fairly new to him, and he wanted to please her like he'd never pleased anyone before.

Molly hesitated when he reached out to pull her dress over her head.

"What's wrong?" he murmured against her ear.

"I'm self-conscious," she admitted. "I don't know what kinds of women you've dated before, but they probably don't look like me."

"You look great," he said, rubbing his fingers across her cheek.

"With clothes on, I look okay, but underneath..." She swallowed. "My boobs aren't perky anymore, and my stomach is kind of jiggly." She looked down, biting her lip.

"Honey, I don't care about that. A woman's body is a beautiful thing." He slowly tugged at the dress until she finally lifted her arms. Lying there in the strapless bra and matching panties Suze had insisted she buy, she'd never felt so exposed in her life. His sigh of pleasure surprised her and before she could say anything he kissed her again as she took his shirt off for him.

His bare-chested torso was simply breathtaking, she thought, forgetting about her own insecurities as she ran her hands over his broad shoulders and bulging biceps. His pecs and abs were any woman's fantasy, causing her to pause and inspect his entire body with appreciation. Moving to his slacks, she undid the button at the top and unzipped them. They slid down and he kicked them off, sending them flying off the bed. Feeling bolder, she made short work of his boxers, and then sat there taking in how glorious he was naked. She'd never seen anything like this, not even during the ridiculous porn videos Tim made her watch. Dom was far better than any porn star she'd ever seen.

"Seen enough?" he teased, licking her neck and softly blowing into her ear. "Is it my turn to see you naked yet?"

"Maybe." She smiled before reaching back with trembling fingers to unsnap her bra. She'd never undressed herself—Tim usually just ripped off whatever she was wearing or simply pulled her pants down.

"Don't be nervous," he caught her trembling fingers in his as she tossed the bra to the side. He brought her fingers to his lips and kissed them one at a time. "You're beautiful, and there's no one else I want to be with."

Gripped by a kind of desire that was completely overwhelming, Molly lay back as Dom kissed her, making love to her with his mouth. She'd never been kissed so wonderfully, or thoroughly, and she slowly relaxed. When he moved his head lower to brush tiny kisses across her breasts, she whimpered with pleasure. It was wonderful torture that made her ache for him. He used his fingers to bring her the kind of pleasure she'd never dreamed of. A simple brush of his finger across her cheek left her breathless; this was tenderness she'd never experienced and tears stung her eyes.

"What's the matter, baby?" Dom paused, his face inches from hers, his dark eyes filled with concern.

"You're just so wonderful," she whispered. "I'm terrified of the things you make me feel. Before I met you, I didn't care about anything, but now I'm terrified I might have to go back to a life without you. I think that would kill me long before Tim ever could."

"You're not going back to that life," he said firmly, taking her chin in his fingers and forcing her to meet his gaze directly. "Do you believe me?"

"I believe you mean it, but I don't know if anyone can stop him."

"I can. I will." He kissed her again, gently and repeatedly, until he was sure she wasn't thinking of anything but him.

When she was panting and breathless, Dom kissed a trail up her stomach, leaving her shuddering with pleasure. He focused on her most sensitive parts—her neck, the spot just behind her ear, and then her breasts. He could feel her heart pounding in her chest and he reached up to move her thick, silky hair off her face.

"Don't be nervous, babe."

"Can't help it," she murmured. "This is exciting and terrifying at the same time."

"Never be terrified when you're with me." He touched her face and then stroked her hair, kissing her everywhere except on the mouth as he struggled to keep his own desire under control.

It had been years since Molly had been excited about sex. Losing her virginity to Tim had been underwhelming. Then he'd insisted on doing it every day the first few months of their marriage, never really giving her sore private parts time to heal. He wasn't big on foreplay, so her readiness for him had been mild, at best, and it always hurt at least a little. That was definitely not the case now.

When his lips found her breasts she lost herself in the sensations of his velvety tongue. His mouth was so gentle it sent shivers down her spine. Her nipples puckered against him and he continued to suckle first one and then the other, until they were heavy and sensitive. She moaned with need, fingers buried in his long hair. He kissed his way down her stomach, lingering after each kiss so she vibrated against his mouth. When he gripped the edge of her panties with his teeth, she sighed heavily. He pulled them off carefully, looking up to find her watching him. Her lips were parted slightly, her eyes hooded.

With a smile, he kissed the inside of her thigh and used his fingers to slowly part the petals of her sex. He heard her sharp intake of breath and made sure to take his time; he had no doubt no one had ever done this for her before. Using his tongue, he slowly licked the spot where his fingers had just been and he felt her tense.

"Just relax, baby. I won't hurt you."

"I know." Her breath caught. "I just—" She gasped as he spread her thighs wider and buried himself between her legs. "Oh!" She grabbed the sheets, her hips shooting up against him.

The things he did with his tongue made stars float in front of her eyes, and she didn't know how much she could stand. Nothing had ever felt this good, and she couldn't believe he seemed to know exactly how to make her quiver with need. He made swirls with his tongue, kissing and licking until she was bucking under his mouth.

"Dom!" She could barely move; the pleasure was so intense.

Knowing she was close, he found her clit and sucked it between his lips. Without warning, she shattered against him, crying out his name over and over as she rode the waves of her orgasm. Refusing to move away, he continued his assault, making the pressure lighter now because she was so sensitive. She whispered his name, clawing at him.

"Once more, baby," he instructed, fucking her with his tongue.

"Oh, no, I can't..." she gasped. It felt so damn good she wasn't sure how much more she could take.

"Yeah, you can." He just kept going, sliding a finger inside of her at the same time. He could feel her shaking, her soaking pussy milking him with urgency. When her second orgasm overcame her, she went wild, unable to control herself. Holding her in place, he rode it with her until she finally threw her arm across her eyes.

"Oh, my God."

"What?" he laughed. He moved across her body and found her lips.

She turned away, embarrassed for him to kiss her after doing that, but he moved her hands and claimed her tongue. "You don't like how you taste?" he whispered. "Well, I do. I could do that *all* fucking day."

She sighed, giving in to the pleasure he brought her. "I've never done that," she admitted.

"I know," he ran his hands on her soft, round ass. "And I loved being the first man to make you come like that."

"You're the first man to make me come, period," she whispered against his mouth. "I never had an orgasm before."

"Not even by yourself?" he asked in surprise.

She shook her head. "Tim said that was a sin. He's Catholic."

"He's an idiot," he muttered.

She reached out to cup his erection in her hand. She ran her hand along it, not surprised he was so much bigger than Tim. It was almost frightening, thinking about something that big being inside her, but she couldn't wait. Being with him had changed everything she knew about sex and now she was dying to discover more.

"I want to make you feel as good as you just made me feel," she whispered. "But I don't know if I know how."

"As you can see," he glanced down. "You're doing a great job."

"I want to... you know..." Her voice trailed off and she hated how unsure she was.

"Are you embarrassed, baby?" He met her gaze. "Why does my lovemaking embarrass you?"

"I don't know," she whispered. "I'm afraid of doing something wrong."

He laughed softly. "That's not even possible." Opening the condom package he'd left beside them, he rolled it on in one fluid motion. Then he kissed her again, burying his tongue in her mouth and drawing a whimper that told him she wasn't nearly finished yet. He pushed her back and crawled over her. Clasping both of her hands in one of his, he pinned them above her head and poised himself between her legs. He claimed her lips again as he slowly slid into her hot, wet sheath. She exclaimed softly at the intrusion and he paused, letting her adjust to how it felt to stretch around him.

She moaned deep in her throat, her hips arching towards his. Moving slowly, he began to thrust in and out with practiced strokes that had her straining at her hands.

"Dom!" She writhed under him, her eyes glassy. "Oh, God, please..."

"Please what?" he whispered against her mouth. "Harder? Faster? What do you want?"

"Harder," she begged.

He was happy to comply; being gentle felt great but it had also been killing him. She was so tight it was like having a tiny vise around his cock. He picked up the pace, driving into her heated flesh until he felt her starting to tighten around him. He had to let go of her hands so he could leverage himself better, and now her nails dug into his back as she let out a strangled scream.

"Dom! Dom!" She lost control, her third climax hitting her hard. He pumped faster, sliding his hands under her sweet ass to grip her against him as tightly as possible. He could feel his balls drawing up and knew he was lost. With a growl, he slammed into her one final time before he was spiraling into wonderful oblivion. This wasn't like any sex he'd ever had before, and there was no doubt in his mind she owned him now.

"Damn, baby." He rested his forehead against hers.

"You can say that again." Her eyes met his with so much desire; he couldn't stop from kissing her again.

"Are you okay? Was I too rough?"

"No." She shook her head slowly. "You were perfect. I just have one question."

"Yeah?" He looked down curiously.

"Can you do that again?"

He laughed, rolling onto his side and pulling her with him. "As many times as you want."

AFTER FIVE GLORIOUS DAYS IN CORONADO AND SAN DIEGO, THEY HEADED BACK to Las Vegas. It was Sunday, so traffic was a little heavy and it was late when they got home. Dumping a load of laundry in the washing machine, Molly made short work of getting them unpacked while Dom took a shower. They'd had dinner on the road and she was ready to crawl into bed and sleep. It occurred to her the guest room was technically her room, and she wasn't sure where she was supposed to go after sleeping next to Dom for five nights.

With bravery she didn't know she had, she pulled on the pretty nightgown Suze had made her buy but she'd been too shy to bring to San Diego. After five days of being ravished by him in bed, she worked up the courage to crawl into his bed and wait for him.

She was on her phone texting Suze when Dom came out with nothing but a towel on. He looked her up and down with a smile of appreciation.

"Hi." She crooked a finger at him.

"Hi." He went and sat on the edge of the bed, letting her pull him closer for a kiss.

"I wasn't sure where I was supposed to sleep, but decided I liked your bed better than mine." She gave him an impish grin.

"Works for me." He kissed her once more before standing up. "Give me another minute and I'll be right in."

Molly put her phone on the nightstand, and pulled the sheet over her as she inhaled the smell of his aftershave on the pillows. Comfortable and relaxed, she fell fast asleep.

LAS VEGAS SIDEWINDERS: DOMINIC   81

W hen she opened her eyes in the morning, she didn't know where she was
at first. Slowly it came back to her and she felt Dom's warm body beside
her, his arm thrown over her waist. Closing her eyes to enjoy the moment, she
smiled to herself, thinking he continued to make her life as perfect as it had
ever been.

While they were in San Diego, they'd talked at length about ways for her to
protect herself. He'd bought her a second disposable cell phone, and they'd agreed
she would have it somewhere on her body whenever she wasn't with him, Toli or
Cody. Her regular cell phone, the one he'd given her that was linked to his
account, was separate, and she would keep it in her purse or wherever she wanted.

The second phone would always be kept on another part of her body and
always powered on. If Tim grabbed her, he would probably take away her purse
and any phone he found in it, but he might not think to search her for a second
phone. Dom's, Suze's and Toli's were the only numbers in it, and they were on
speed dial. They'd also come up with special codes for her to text in an emergency. Even if Tim or one of his friends saw she'd sent a text, they wouldn't be
able to identify it as a call for help.

Feeling safer than she had since she'd moved in with him, she slipped out of
bed and went into the bathroom to wash her face and brush her teeth. She pulled
her hair up in a messy ponytail and then stepped out and picked up her phone.
Dom was still asleep, so she padded into the kitchen to make coffee and maybe
breakfast, if there was any food that hadn't gone bad while they were away.

Her phone buzzed, alerting her to a text and she glanced down to see Suze's
name pop up.

*Can you come over today? We're going to tell Brad and Andra about CJ—I
could really use your support!*

She typed back hurriedly. *Dom has anger mgmt and then a meeting with his
psych. I'll see if he can drop me off before he goes. What time?*

*As soon as you can get here! They're coming for lunch... If he doesn't have
time, I can send Cody to get you!*

I'll text you back.

Molly finished making the coffee and then poured a cup for each of them
before heading back to the bedroom. She hated to wake Dom, but Suze needed her
and he would need time to take her to Suze's house and then get back to his anger
management class, which was just down the street from their apartment.

She put the coffee on the nightstand and then leaned over to nuzzle his neck,
just as his arms snaked out to grab her and pull her on top of him. She shrieked
with delight, laughing as he kissed her.

"Thought you were going to sneak off, did you?" he laughed.

"I made coffee,"

"I guess I'll have some then." He paused to kiss her. "Good morning."

"Good morning." She smiled down at him before handing him his coffee cup.

"You're bouncing," he murmured, taking a sip of coffee. "What's up?"

"Suze and Cody invited Brad and Andra for lunch. They're going to introduce

CJ to them. Suze asked me if I would be there for support. Do you have time to drop me off before your class?"

He glanced at the clock. "We'll have to get a move on."

"She said Cody could come get me."

"I don't mind taking you, but you'll need to hop in the shower right now."

"Okay." She got up and glanced over her shoulder. "Coming?"

"I took a shower last night!"

She met his gaze, arching her eyebrows, and he sat up. "But I guess you can never be too clean."

M olly and Suze sat in the kitchen talking quietly as they waited for Brad and Andra. Suze was a nervous wreck, wringing her hands and pacing back and forth. Cody had disappeared upstairs with CJ, playing a game with him to keep him out of Suze's hair while she mentally prepared herself.

"I'm not worried about me," she confided to Molly. "I'm more worried about Cody—he gave up a good position in Toronto. He was a fan favorite, and got along great with everyone in the organization. If Brad and Andra are really angry with me, I don't want Brad to make Cody's life hell."

"If they make Cody miserable, he'll get himself traded and take their grandson somewhere far away," Molly pointed out. "Besides, it's not like you knew he was Brian's ahead of time. Since you and Cody were drunk, it was entirely feasible you hadn't used protection."

"I know, but I'm going to *die* talking about details like that," Suze buried her head in her hands. "I feel like I'm going to puke."

"Have a glass of wine," Molly went to the refrigerator and pulled out a bottle of chardonnay. "It will calm your nerves."

"Maybe half a glass."

Molly got out a glass and poured two inches of liquid into the glass. Suze grabbed it and downed it like she was dying of thirst.

"All righty, then," Molly chuckled. "You need to chill. It's 11:51, so they will be here any minute. I'm going upstairs to play with CJ. Call when you're ready for me to bring him down."

"Thanks." Suze watched Molly disappear up the stairs and a moment later she heard Cody pounding back down. He came into the kitchen, took one look at her face and pulled her close.

"Suze, you have to relax. Whatever happens, we're in this together. I've got your back. I'll always have your back."

"What if he says he doesn't want you to play for him?"

"Technically, I have a contract and he can't just kick me off the team because of a personal matter. He can make me *want* to quit, but he can't fire me. And if he goes that route, I'll go back to Toronto and they'll never get to see their grandson again."

She smiled wanly. "You can be fiercely overprotective."

The doorbell rang and he brushed a kiss on the top of her head. "It's going to be fine." He winked before heading to open the door.

Suze heard Brad and Andra in the foyer and took a deep breath, getting a pitcher of raspberry iced tea out of the refrigerator. There were already glasses out and she forced a smile as she greeted them and poured drinks. They settled in the family room and Suze nearly had to sit on her hands to keep them from shaking. Seeing her dilemma, Cody took one of her hands in his and squeezed tightly.

"I'm so glad we finally got a chance to come over," Andra said brightly. "I've been looking forward to meeting CJ!"

"That's actually what we wanted to talk to you about," Suze said, deciding to jump right in.

"Pardon?" Brad glanced at her with a confused frown.

"When I found out I was pregnant, I was mortified," Suze continued, looking down. "I couldn't believe what Cody and I had done the night of Brian's funeral. It was so embarrassing, but there was never a question of whether or not I was going to keep the baby."

"Suzanne, you know Brad and I understood all of that." Andra cocked her head slightly. "That can't be what this is about."

"Not entirely." Suze lifted her gaze. "CJ was born a week early, and he had bright blue eyes, just like me and Cody." She swallowed. "But after he was a year old, his eyes started to change."

"That happens all the time," Andra said. "What color are they now?"

"They're Brian's eyes," Suze whispered.

Brad gaped. "Brian's eyes?"

"Brian and I made love the morning of the day he died, April first. We buried him on April sixth, which is the night Cody and I had sex. There were only five days between the two times, and Brian and I always used protection. Cody and I were so drunk, I was sure it had been *his* mistake, not Brian's. CJ was almost two before we had him tested." She blinked back tears.

Andra gasped, her hand flying to her mouth. "You mean—" She looked at her husband. "What is she trying to tell us?"

Brad was choked up too. "I think, maybe, she's telling us CJ is Brian's son."

"When we found out, I was mortified all over again," Suze had tears streaming down her face. "I kept telling Cody I would tell you in my own time, but the time was never right."

"Until now," Cody put in, pulling her close as she wept against his chest.

"I'm sorry," she whispered. "I wasn't trying to keep him from you; I just didn't know how to tell you what a mess I'd made!"

Andra was crying too, with Brad putting his arms around her. No one said anything for a long time. Finally, Andra looked up and around the room. "Is he here? Can we meet him?"

"You both have to stop crying first," Brad insisted, swiping at his own eyes. "We're don't want to traumatize the boy."

Suze got up and brought a box of tissues. "I'm sorry," she said to Andra. "I'm really sorry."

"I don't even know what to say," Andra sniffed. "We've lost all these years with our grandson..."

"You should have come to me!" Brad looked at Cody sternly. "Even though you knew the women weren't going to handle it well, you should have come to me."

"I know," Cody sighed. "But I was caught between you and my wife—and I've done enough to hurt her already."

"It wasn't Cody's fault!" Suze interjected. "I asked him to let me tell you in my own time, and then I didn't... Don't be mad at him."

"We're not mad," Andra said quietly, looking at her husband. "But we're so very disappointed—in both of you. How could you do this? You had to know how much it would have meant to us to have Brian's child in our lives."

"He was two before we knew for sure, which was almost three years after Brian died," said Cody.

"It's still not right," Brad replied

"Nothing about this was right," Suze swallowed hard. "I know that, but I'm trying to make it right now."

"So you want us to move on as if nothing happened?" Brad was still staring hard at Cody.

"Well, either we move on or Suze and I pack up and go back to Toronto," said Cody. "I came here for you and Dom, but if this changes your feelings for me, I'm pretty sure they still want me elsewhere."

"It doesn't change our feelings for you!" Andra smacked her husband's arm and looked at them. "You're not going anywhere!" She gave her husband a stern look. "We're just surprised—it never occurred to us the child might be Brian's."

"Now you have time to get to know him," Suze interrupted, looking from one to the other. "Cody and I have had problems but—"

"Cody, that's something else we need to talk about. I won't have the captain of my team running around with puck bunnies behind his wife's back," Brad said with a scowl. "It's not right, and that's not the image we want to portray."

"Nah, Coach. That's been done for a while now. Suze and I are working on our marriage, and there are no other women."

There was a small awkward silence before Brad got up and walked around. "This is still a real slap in the face, Cody."

"I'm sorry, Coach." Cody stood up and looked at the older man. "I wanted to tell you so many times, but she asked me not to. What would you have done if Andra had asked something of you that was so important to her?"

Brad looked out the window at the bright sun. He'd missed his son every single day for more than seven years, and finding out he had a grandchild was both a blessing and a curse. He had no doubt seeing the child would bring back all the pain of losing Brian, but at the same time they now had a piece of him. Maybe that would fill the gaping hole in his heart.

"I don't know, son," he said after a moment. "But I would have tried harder to convince her."

"I can't say I'm sorry more than I already have," Cody said. "Just tell us what you want us to do."

"We want to meet him," Andra reached out her hand to Brad and he walked back to the couch.

"Are we good?" asked Cody. "We're not going to keep him from you, but if there are going to be ongoing hard feelings, we need to discuss that now. I won't have my son feeling uncomfortable about any of this."

For a moment everyone froze and Cody looked at them carefully. "You know I love that boy? You understand Brian was my *best* friend—my *brother*—and there is no question I'm raising his son as *my* son. There's no DNA test that changes the fact he's *my son*."

"No, there's no doubt about that," Brad said quietly before he reached out his hand. Cody hesitated a moment before shaking it. "I know that you love Brian's son like your own."

"Can I meet him now?" Andra asked softly, her eyes watering. "Please?"

Suze got up and walked to the bottom of the stairs. "Molly? Will you bring CJ down?"

"Coming!" Molly called back. Looking at CJ, she said, "How about we finish our game after lunch?"

"Okay." He got up, grabbing her hand as they came downstairs. Once at the bottom, he took off running and skidded to a stop when he noticed there were visitors.

"Hey, buddy." Cody reached for him. "Come here. I want you to meet some very special people."

"Who are they?" CJ looked curious, glancing at the older people in the room.

"Well, you know how you have Grandma and Grandpa in Minnesota and Grammy Pammy in South Carolina?"

"Yeah—Grammy Pammy makes the bestest blueberry pancakes in the whole world!"

Suze smiled at the reference to her mother's pancakes; they really were the best.

"Now you have another grandma and grandpa, Brad and Andra."

CJ frowned. "But my grandmas and grandpa are your parents," he said. "How can I have more?"

"Before you were born," Suze pulled him onto her lap. "You had a different daddy, but he had to go to heaven. Daddy—this Daddy—decided he wanted to be your daddy since you didn't have one anymore, so you really have two daddies. Brad and Andra are your first daddy's parents."

CJ looked around the room curiously. "They're my *first* daddy's parents?"

Suze nodded. "Yup."

"What was my first Daddy's name?"

"His name was Brian." Suze swallowed hard, willing herself not to cry.

"That's my middle name!" CJ said brightly, smiling. "Did he want me to have his name?"

Suze nodded. "He sure did."

"Why did he go to heaven?"

"Well, you know how we talk about 'stranger danger'?" Suze said carefully. "He ran into some strangers who hurt him so bad he couldn't get better."

"Were you sad?"

"We all were," Cody said gently. "But now his mother and father wanted to meet you, because they don't have any other grandchildren."

"I like grandparents!" CJ looked over at them. He got off Suze's lap and walked towards Andra first. He extended his hand. "I'm Cody Brian Armstrong. What should I call you?"

Andra blinked back tears as she looked at the carbon copy of the child she'd lost. "I'm Andra Barnett," she said, shaking his hand. "What would you like to call me? You already have Grandma and Grammy Pammy. Would you like to call me Nana or Grandmother, or something else?"

CJ wrinkled his nose. "I don't like Grandmother—that's too long. What about just Gran?"

"That fine with me." Andra smiled. "Could I have a hug?"

"I like hugs!" He gave her a big hug before turning to Brad.

"Hey, there, kiddo." Brad reached for him, slowly pulling him onto his lap. "What do you think you want to call me? Gramps? Poppy? Papa?"

"Poppy!" CJ agreed with a big smile.

"All right then. Poppy it is!" Brad hugged him tightly and CJ seemed content to let him.

Watching from the kitchen, Molly felt tears threatening too. She'd never yearned for a baby as badly as she did right now. Just the thought of having Dom's baby made her insides turn to jelly. She'd never been able to carry a baby to term, but she clung to the hope it was because Tim had hit her. Maybe she still had time. It seemed unlikely, but everything that had happened in the last few months had been unlikely; now she felt like she could do almost anything.

Going back upstairs to give them some privacy, she pulled out her phone and texted Dom she was ready to go.

Dᴏᴍ ᴘɪᴄᴋᴇᴅ ʜᴇʀ ᴜᴘ ᴛᴡᴇɴᴛʏ ᴍɪɴᴜᴛᴇꜱ ʟᴀᴛᴇʀ, ᴀɴᴅ Mᴏʟʟʏ ꜱʟɪᴘᴘᴇᴅ ᴏᴜᴛ ᴏꜰ ᴛʜᴇ house with a quick good-bye. She was glad Suze's ordeal was over. Of course, she and Cody still had their marriage to work on, but Molly figured they would tackle one issue at a time. In the meantime, she was thinking ahead to the rest of the day.

"We have no food in the house," she told Dom. "Want to get groceries?"

"Sure. Where do you want to go?"

"I don't know. Tim and I always shopped in Henderson, never in Las Vegas, so we shouldn't run into anyone I know, but anything is possible."

"Look," he reached over and took her hand. "You can't live in hiding. You've filed for divorce and he's obviously been served since those guys promptly showed up at Toli's. Now we just have to wait for the court date, and then it'll all be over."

"I hope so."

"Baby, I'm not going to let anything happen to you."

"In a few months, you're going to be on the road, sometimes for a week or more at a time. He'll wait until you're gone. Don't underestimate him."

Dom was quiet for a while, thinking about what she said. The truth was, the only way to really protect her was to leave Las Vegas. He could probably make Coach understand why he needed to go, but he was contractually bound to the Sidewinders for two years, and the chances of anyone else taking him right now were slim to none.

"What are you thinking?" she asked.

"I'd feel better if you weren't in Las Vegas," He said. "But I just don't think I can make that happen this year."

"Dom!" She squeezed his hand. "I don't expect you to leave your job! This is where you have to be."

He nodded. "Yeah but if something happens to you, I don't know if I'll be able to play."

"Let's not think about it, okay? We have contingencies in place, and Toli, Cody and Suze all being extra careful. Dwelling on things won't change anything."

Dom nodded but he was still worried because he knew, despite what she'd just said, she was scared.

Molly's fortieth birthday fell on a Tuesday in late July and she woke to the smell of something wonderful. Dom was standing at the foot of the bed with a tray in his hand.

"Wake up, birthday girl," he grinned. "Happy birthday!"

She blinked awake and smiled. "Morning!"

He moved towards her with the tray and she stopped him with a grin. "Wait, let me go to the bathroom first!" She hurriedly did her business, washed her face and pulled her hair back in a ponytail. She'd had it trimmed and colored again yesterday—every six weeks, Suze had told her firmly, so she'd done it. She looked tired, but that was because they'd spent most of the night making love—it seemed as though neither of them could get enough.

Getting back into bed, she laughed as he put a cloth napkin on her lap and then put the tray on her knees.

"This smells amazing!" she said, taking a bite of stuffed French toast.

"I've got skills!"

She raised an eyebrow. "At what? Placing an order online and having it delivered?"

"You wound me!" He burst out laughing. "But you got me!"

She laughed too. "You didn't have to order anything! I like to cook. And where's yours?"

"In the kitchen."

"We can eat in there," she said. "Breakfast with you, even in the kitchen, is still pretty romantic."

He reached for the tray. "Okay, let's go then, because I'm hungry."

She laughed and followed him to the kitchen. They sat on the stools at the bar, feeding each other and talking about the day. He wouldn't tell her where they were going or what they were doing, but apparently she needed to eat relatively quickly, shower and get dressed.

"How will I know what to wear?" she demanded as he pushed her into the bathroom to get ready.

"Casual and cool," he winked. "We'll be doing a lot of walking."

She frowned as he shut the door behind her. Shaking her head, she got ready as quickly as she could, wearing a pair of white shorts and a light blue sleeveless top. She stuck her head out the door.

"Do I need sunscreen?"

"I'm bringing some, but if you want something special for your face, you might need that."

"Okay." Still confused, she put on sunscreen and then a little makeup on her eyes and lips, deciding to forego foundation or blush. Apparently they were doing something outdoors even though it was probably over a hundred degrees. She pulled on the silver bracelet she'd bought with the money she'd gotten from pawning her wedding ring. It looked good on her tan skin and it was the only jewelry she had right now, but it represented her new life.

"Are you ready?" Dom was impatient, his dark eyes sparkling with excitement.

"Is this my birthday present or yours?" she teased.

"If it was *my* birthday we'd spend the whole day in bed!" he ducked as she playfully took a swing at him.

They made their way down to the parking garage and he pulled onto the street, heading out of town. She didn't recognize any of the signs and she glanced at him in surprise. She didn't do much traveling but knew all the local roads and attractions.

"Where are we going?"

"It's a surprise!"

"What about therapy?"

"I'm making it up tomorrow."

She pursed her lips. "Okay, then."

Three and a half hours later they pulled into Grand Canyon National Park and she gaped at him as he parked. "Oh, my God! I'm so excited!"

"I kinda thought you might be. Plus, I've never been here before either, so I thought it would be fun for both of us."

"Yay!" she let out a little squeal of happiness and then clapped her hand over her mouth. "Wow, I didn't know I was capable of making that sound."

Laughing, he looped an arm around her shoulders. "I've heard you make all kinds of sounds!"

She giggled. "Don't say that out loud!"

"Why not?" He frowned.

"We're in public!" she cried, her face getting red.

"I'm not sure why that bothers you, but let's go!" He pulled her towards the entrance.

An hour later, as they took in the breathtaking view, his phone rang and he saw it was Toli. It was odd because Toli knew where they were and that they were celebrating, so he wouldn't be calling unless it was important. Pausing from their hike and sinking onto a bench, he answered hesitantly. "Hello?"

"It's me." Toli always spoke better English when something was wrong and Dom recognized the lack of accent immediately.

"What's going on?"

"Apparently, I'm a suspect in Molly's 'disappearance.'" Toli sounded annoyed.

"I'm assuming someone is there listening?"

"Of course."

"They think she's missing?"

"Because she's never here when they come. I've called my lawyer, but they are threatening to arrest me."

"So, what, someone wants to talk to her? How will they know it's really Molly?" He paused when Toli remained silent and then hissed under his breath.

"What's wrong?" Molly was whispering at his side.

Dom covered the phone. "If you don't talk to Tim, they're going to arrest Toli as a suspect in your 'disappearance.'" He grimaced.

Her eyes widened.

"Listen, he can't hurt you," Dom said. "As soon as we hang up, I'll turn off my phone so they can't track it. You just need to be brave and talk to him so they don't make more trouble for Toli."

She nodded. "Yes, of course." With trembling fingers, she reached for his phone. "Hello?"

"Wait," Toli said abruptly.

A moment later, another voice came on the line. Molly winced as she listened to Tim's voice, sounding more soft and gentle than she'd ever heard it. "Molly? Honey, is that really you?"

"Tim, what are you doing? I filed for divorce—I didn't disappear!" She had to take deep breaths to keep her voice from trembling.

"Sweetheart, if you'll just come home, I'll make everything right."

"No, Tim, we're done. You need to leave Toli alone, or I'll get a restraining order."

"Listen, you can't treat me this way!" His voice turned hard. "We've been married for twenty-two years and—"

"And our divorce will be final soon. Do I need to call my lawyer?"

"I don't know where you got the money for your fancy lawyer, but—" He stopped talking abruptly and she heard a kind of gargled sound before Toli got back on the line. "We are finished," he said to her. "Enjoy your day. I'll see you when you get back to town." He disconnected and she handed the phone back to Dom. He immediately turned it off and looked around. He found a trash can and tossed it in.

"I'll get a new one," he shrugged. "I'll say it was stolen so they'll transfer my contacts and give me a new number."

"I've got both of my phones," she said, still shaking.

"Give me your regular phone, in case we get separated. Make sure the disposable phone is in your pocket, not your purse."

"Okay." She handed him her phone and then moved into his arms. "Dom, what are we going to do? He's going to go after you…"

"He can fuck right off," Dom muttered, holding her close and stroking her hair. "I'm going to talk to Coach about this and see if he or the owners know anyone in Henderson—the Police Chief or the mayor or something. He can't get away with this crap.

"Come on." He held her face in his hands because she looked like she was going to cry. "It's your birthday. I'm sure Toli didn't tell them where we are, and with my phone off, even if they got my number, they can't trace us here. I'm surprised we even have service!"

"Why does he ruin everything?" She sank onto a rock and buried her face in her hands.

He sat beside her. "We're going to find a way to make him leave you alone. If we can't, we'll leave Las Vegas and I'll find a Canadian team to take me. His badge won't mean shit in Canada. If necessary, I'll send you away somewhere until this season ends. It's going to be okay."

"I hate him!" she whispered against his shoulder.

They sat for a while, baking in the sun, until he finally tugged at her hands. "We can't sit here all day. It's going to be okay. Look how beautiful it is—don't let him ruin this day for us, okay?"

She smiled faintly. "You're right." Taking his hand, she forced herself to wander the trail with him, stopping to take pictures and talk quietly together. Though she was having a good time, she couldn't shake the feeling something bad was going to happen. She didn't know what she would do if something happened to him or one of their friends.

Suze had decorated the house for a birthday party, and Molly laughed when she walked in the door. A big banner hung in the hallway leading to the family room that said "Happy Birthday." There were streamers and balloons all over the room and Suze opened a bottle of champagne as soon as they walked in.

"You look like you need this," Suze put a glass in Molly's hand.

"I do, thanks." Molly took a sip gratefully.

Dom got a glass too, and after a quick kiss, followed Cody and Brad out to the deck where they were grilling.

Suze and Andra led Molly to the kitchen where they were nibbling on appetizers. Suze hugged her friend tightly, sensing how tense she was.

"I don't know what to do," Molly said.

"The lawyers are going to make this go away."

"The only way I can protect Dom is if I break things off," Molly whispered.

"Molly, no!" Suze looked horrified. "He's crazy about you—you're going to break his heart and he could totally spiral out of control again!"

"I'd rather have him out of control than dead!" Molly said firmly. "Don't you understand? What they're doing to Toli is just the beginning. The only reason he hasn't really escalated things is because he hasn't actually caught me with someone. If he sees me with Dom, and realizes we're a couple, he'll kill both of us!"

Andra looked horrified. "Brad said the owner of the team, Lonnie Finch, is friendly with the mayor of Henderson. We're going to talk to him."

"But in the meantime, Dom isn't safe." Molly swallowed hard. "At the very least, I have to move out before Tim figures out where I'm living!"

"Move in with us," Andra said automatically. "There is nothing they can use to hurt us—right now, no one knows CJ is our grandson. And Brad is far too powerful within the world of hockey for some two-bit policeman in Henderson, Nevada to touch him. The entire NHL would come down on that little man."

"I don't know," Molly looked worried. "You barely know me and—"

"Nonsense. Dom put his life on the line the night Brian died—now it's our turn to help someone *he* loves."

Molly flushed. "I don't know that he *loves* me…"

"Of course he loves you!" Andra laughed and shook her head. "Love is truly wasted on the young."

"Who wants a steak?" Cody called, coming into the house.

"I've got potato salad in the fridge," Suze yelled back. "And corn on the cob!"

Everyone moved to the kitchen for plates and Molly tried to eat, but nothing tasted good. All she could think about was how she was going to protect Dom.

"I have a present for you." Dom said a little while later, glancing at Suze, who disappeared for a moment and came back with a small, beautifully wrapped package.

"What is it?" Molly's eyes widened in delight she couldn't quite hide.

"Open it." Dom's dark eyes were bright as he watched her.

Quickly ripping off the paper, she found a jeweler's box inside. She glanced at him questioningly.

"Open it," he repeated.

She did as she was told and gasped. Inside was a pair of the most beautiful emerald earrings she'd ever seen. At least two carats each, in a gold setting surrounded by diamonds, she'd never seen anything so beautiful. "Dom!" She threw her arms around him, bursting into tears. "They're stunning!"

"Happy birthday, baby." He kissed her gently. "I got them because they remind me of your beautiful eyes. I think I fell in love with you and your eyes the first moment I saw you."

Her mouth opened in a small "O" as she tried to comprehend what he'd said. "Thank you," she finally whispered.

"You're welcome." He watched with pleasure as she put them on, and turned to smile at him. God, she was beautiful. He couldn't wait to take her home and make love to her wearing nothing but those earrings. As if she could read his thoughts, she gave him a shy wink.

17

THE NEXT COUPLE OF WEEKS PASSED QUICKLY. BY MID-AUGUST, PLAYERS HAD started to arrive even though training camp didn't start for another month. The ones with families wanted to get their kids settled in school, and some of the others came because Las Vegas was a great place to party. They were out most nights, having dinner or drinks with friends, visiting with Suze and Cody, or helping some of the new players get settled. Though Molly hadn't met any of the other wives yet, she'd liked Dom's friend Drake and his roommate, Karl. They were fun, easygoing guys who seemed to get along well with Dom, Toli and Cody. She hoped everyone was as nice as they were.

Mostly, she spent time with Suze and Andra. Occasionally, Tiff would join them but she was focusing on her dissertation for her doctorate during the off-season, while Dave wasn't traveling. Later, even with help, she would have to divide her time between the kids and her studies. So most of Molly's days were spent at Suze's or Andra's: talking, playing in the pool with CJ or cooking big meals for the guys Cody and Dom were particularly close to.

It was probably the longest period of time she'd ever gone without a bruise or a cut, and she realized she'd lost twenty pounds over the summer without even trying. Even the clothes she'd bought for the trip to San Diego were loose on her now. Going to the gym with Suze had been fruitful, and she'd fallen in love with boxing. She, Dom, Suze and Cody went as couples at least once a week, sparring with each other and everyone else who attended.

Though she knew she couldn't fight Tim physically and hope to win, it still felt good to have some sort of power. She and Suze had taken a self-defense class too, and the guys often tested them on their reflexes. They made sure they had back-up phones and pepper spray, took different routes everywhere they went, and Molly never went out alone.

Dom and Molly took care not to show public displays of affection unless they were out of town, and their close-knit group was extra careful all the time. Tim hadn't made any other moves since Lonnie had talked with the mayor, but Molly couldn't shake the feeling he was just biding his time. He would never give up so easily, but her lawyer had assured her the divorce decree would be arriving in the mail shortly.

Supposedly, their old house was up for sale and she would get half the profit—somewhere around ninety thousand dollars. She hadn't realized they had so much equity in the house, but it was a pleasant surprise because she was looking forward to having some of her own money. She couldn't decide if she would go back to school or buy a car, or both. Even though Dom had said he would buy her anything she wanted, she didn't like to ask; it was still too new.

In the back of her mind, she knew she was going to have to move out when training camp started. Dom would be busy and she would be a distraction if he was always worried about her safety. She didn't want to, but instinct told her Tim would wait until the team went on the road and then strike. He wasn't stupid, and he was nothing if not sneaky. That was part of what made him a good detective, his ability to figure out who the bad guys were. In her case, she was the ultimate bad guy and he would stop at nothing to find her.

Coming back from a weekend trip to L.A., she was quiet and Dom reached out to take her hand. "I know it's stressful thinking about how busy I'm going to be in the near future, but we've got our plans in place."

"I don't trust Tim," she said, frowning.

Dom squeezed her hand. "His pockets can't be that deep, and I promise you, Lonnie Finch is not screwing around with this team. He put a boatload of money into it—if his players are unhappy, he's going to raise hell."

"What if he just tries to get rid of you and this problem goes away for him?"

"You mean fire me? I guess he could do that, but I'm not the only person involved now. There's not a chance in hell they're letting Cody go. Toli? Brad and Pierre Bouchard, the General Manager, wouldn't allow it. When all the other guys get here, it's going to be tough to justify the number of people who would be on our side that he would have to get rid of. There are at least five NHL players who are friends that would step up and say something—you think the league won't notice?"

"Women get abused all the time—by professional athletes, no less! Why would the NHL care about our situation?"

"Because in *our* situation, it's an NHL wife getting picked on by a dirty cop—who isn't one of us." He shook his head firmly. "He has no idea what a close-knit community this can be. We've got friends in probably every big city—guys either played together in juniors or college, roomed together as they got moved around the league, played on an All-Star team together, etc. Tim won't find professional hockey players as easy to intimidate as his wife."

"Dom, I really think I should move out," she took a breath as the words rushed out.

"What? No!" He slammed on the brakes as they got to a red light. "Are you kidding?"

"He's already been making life hell for Toli—how long do you think it will take him to figure out where I'm really living?"

"Molly, I can't protect you if you're living somewhere else!" he said in frustration.

"But he won't find me if I'm away from all of you!"

"Where, exactly, are you thinking of going?" he demanded.

"To Brad and Andra's. She's already offered, and I think it would be safer if I'm not living with you."

He gripped the steering wheel as the light turned green. "Babe, you can't live your life like this. At some point, we have to face this guy down and make him understand we're not going to give in. You're not going back, and he doesn't get to hurt you anymore. If he pushes us, we'll release the tape to the media and get him fired."

Molly didn't say anything, knowing he would fight her on this. Though the last thing she wanted to do was leave, she didn't think she could stay either. Although they had every contingency in place, she couldn't shake the feeling Tim was out there just waiting for the right time. If she moved, he might lose his advantage.

"Look," Dom glanced over at her. "I have to go to New York next week to meet with the NHL. Why don't you come with me? We'll spend a few days in Manhattan before I have to get back and get ready for training camp. It'll be another new place I can take you, plus we'll be away from Vegas, and you can relax before we think about something as major as you moving out."

"What happens if they don't clear you?"

"Well, I can't imagine they would do that after how hard I've worked all summer. Coach, Cody and both my therapists are going to bat for me, and physically I'm in the best shape of my life. Coach said he's kept them updated and although I still have to meet with them, they're pleased with my progress."

"Are you going to be okay once you get back on the ice?"

"I haven't had a nightmare since the night I told you about Brian, and I've learned how to handle the anxiety when I start thinking about unpleasant things. I've also got the most wonderful woman in the world at my side." He paused to smile over at her, causing her to flush with happiness. "I'm in a good place. I'm ready to play."

"I don't know how I'm going to adjust to your being on the road for weeks at a time," she admitted. "You have no idea how much I depend on you emotionally."

"For the most part, I'll be gone a few days at a time, sometimes four or five. There will be a few east coast trips that will probably last 10-14 days. We'll prepare for those. We'll go over the schedule carefully and make sure you're okay. When we go east, maybe you and Suze can meet us there. You could do some shopping in New York, follow us around in a rental car... I think in February we go from D.C. to Philly and then up to New York and Buffalo."

"Okay." She nodded half-heartedly. He was doing the best he could, but it was still going to be hard for her.

"So, what do you think?" He tried to distract her. "New York City next week?"

Despite everything going on in her head, she couldn't help but agree. "Well, yeah!"

"It'll be fun."

The phone rang and Dom put it on speakerphone since it was plugged in and charging. "Hey, Cody! We left L.A. a little while ago."

"Yeah, good." Cody paused. "Listen, Toli was arrested today."

"What?" Dom gripped the steering wheel again. "Is he okay?"

"Yeah, you know Toli. His lawyer bailed him out, and he's not showing any emotion, but it's bad. They planted drugs in his apartment."

"Sonofabitch!" Dom grimaced and looked over at Molly, who was suddenly very pale.

"They came with a search warrant, saying he'd been seen in shady parts of town. I don't know how they got a search warrant, there's no way they had probable cause, and his lawyer is already making a huge stink about it. But at the end of the day, he was arrested and is out on bail. It's all over the sports networks."

Dom felt his gut clench uncomfortably. "What should we do?"

"There are reporters staked out at Toli's, Brad's and Dave's, so everyone is here at our house. I'm thinking you guys should come here too. That way, we show a united front, and with everyone in a big group, there won't be any way for Tim to put you and Molly together."

"Yeah, but if there are any reporters, they'll see us drive up."

"Pull over when you're a few miles out, Molly can get in the back on the floor, and I'll leave a spot for you in the garage. You drive in by yourself, as far as anyone can see, and then I'll close the garage and no one will see her get out."

"I guess that's a plan. See you soon."

"Drive safe."

"Thanks." Dom hung up and looked at Molly's drawn face. "It'll be okay."

"It will *never* be okay! Look at what he's doing to Toli and I'm not even dating *him*! Do you know what he's going to do to you when he finds out you're the guy I'm sleeping with?" Molly felt tears threatening.

"I will destroy him," Dom said grimly. "That's all there is to it. He can try, but nothing is going to happen to us!"

Molly wouldn't argue with him. She knew better than anyone else what Tim was capable of; she refused to let him hurt these people, no matter what they thought. Tim had upped the stakes now, and she knew it was because he was doing what he always did; using her friends to manipulate her. He knew her well enough to know she wouldn't allow him to continue hurting Toli. Drug charges could not only ruin his life; it could also get him kicked out of the U.S. She wouldn't sit back and let Tim hurt these people. Leaving Dom would break her heart into a million pieces, but if it had to be done, she would do it.

Moving out of Dom's apartment, and making sure to leave no traces she'd ever been there, was one of the hardest things Molly had ever done. Dom wasn't happy at all, but she'd done it while he was at the first day of training camp, with Suze and Andra's help. Although they didn't like her doing it while he wasn't home, they understood her need to protect him. He'd arrived at Brad and Andra's a few hours after she'd settled in and they'd fought for the first time since they met. Finally, he'd accepted she wasn't going to change her mind and wound up staying the night with her.

18

AFTER LIVING APART FOR A WEEK, THEY WERE BOTH GRUMPY AND UNCOMFORTABLE with the situation. Molly was trying her best to stay tough, but she missed him as much as he missed her, and he couldn't spend every night at Brad and Andra's; that would defeat the purpose. The press had been all over the team since Toli's arrest, and Molly had to stay inside a lot of the time so no one would see her. Andra did her best to entertain her, inviting Suze and Tiff over almost every day, and having a big party on Saturday night for everyone who had been invited to training camp.

For the first time, Molly was nervous. She was going to meet the whole team and their significant others, and Dom had been adamant he wouldn't pretend that they weren't together. The team was going to have to know, and that was all there was to it. Besides, she already had a lot of friends in their group and he didn't care if anyone else was friendly or not.

Molly, of course, had heard a lot of Suze's stories about some of the wives in Toronto, so she had a feeling she wasn't necessarily going to fit right in. Once they looked at her closely, there would be no doubt she was quite a bit older than Dom, and while she didn't have to tell people she was divorced, she wasn't going to live a lie either.

Dressing in a flowing white lace skirt that fell below her knees and a matching embroidered top with lace cap sleeves, she thought she looked nice. Probably not like a lot of the women who were coming, but she couldn't change who she was. She'd curled her hair so it bounced around her shoulders in pretty waves, and Suze had taught her how to do her makeup so that it accentuated her eyes and lips.

I have crow's feet, she thought as she gazed into the mirror. Well, there was no help for that either, so she slipped on a pair of silver sandals that matched the fabulous jewelry Dom had bought her in New York. He'd been so excited when the NHL cleared him to play, he'd taken her on a shopping spree she would never forget.

She headed downstairs, glad to find Suze had already arrived and was helping Andra keep everything organized. Molly had never been to a party that was catered, so she watched in fascination as waiters wandered around the house setting up tables, chairs, food and drinks. There was a bar by the pool and a dessert bar in the great room that made her mouth water. She'd never seen a chocolate fountain and she moved toward it with delight. Although she didn't dare try some now, she would definitely be sticking her finger in it before the end of the evening!

"No touching!" Andra smacked her arm as she breezed past. "Would you keep an eye on the door, dear?"

"Sure." Molly smiled at her and headed outside to see how everything looked.

"Hey!" Suze joined her, a glass of wine in her hand. "Isn't this beautiful?"

"Gorgeous." Molly stared off into the distance. "I'm going to miss this."

"Miss what?" Suze asked sharply.

Molly blinked. She hadn't meant to say that aloud. "Just all this excitement, you know. Once the season starts it'll be different."

"That's not what you meant." Suze narrowed her eyes. "Girlfriend, we may have only known each other a few months, but I already know you really well. You're not planning anything stupid, are you?"

"Suze, you know how dangerous Tim is. At some point, he's going to find me if I stay here—the only way no one gets hurt is if I leave."

"Molly, you can't *leave* us. Not just Dom, but all of us. You can't let that idiot dictate your life."

"I have to do what's right, not what's easy," Molly said firmly. "I stayed with Tim all those years because it was easier than fighting for my freedom—I can't go back there again. But I can't put all of you in danger either. Look what he's done to Toli!"

"Oh, Molly." Suze squeezed her arm. "Promise me you won't do anything rash."

"I can't—"

"Promise!"

"I promise." Molly gave her a quick hug, hating that she would undoubtedly break that promise.

"Where is party?" Toli came striding outside with his usual big grin. Both women rushed to hug him. He put his arms around both of them, kissing the tops of their heads.

"You're early!" Suze teased.

"Toli is first to arrive," he corrected. "Life of party is here—where is vodka?"

They laughed, moving to the bar together where Molly got a glass of wine and Toli got Grey Goose vodka on the rocks. Talking quietly, they walked back inside. Suze went to help Andra with something, leaving Molly and Toli alone for the first time since his arrest.

"I need you to know how sorry I am about everything that's been happening to you," she said, reaching for his arm.

"No worries." He shook his head. "Lawyer handles everything. Search was illegal—charges will be dropped. Everything will be okay. Toli will move into a house with other players—and much security."

She grimaced. "I hate that I did this to you."

"Molly is my friend." He brought her fingers to his lips. "Toli only wishes happiness for you—and for Tim to go fuck himself."

Choking on a mouthful of wine, she burst out laughing.

"Toli made you laugh."

"Yes!" She smacked him playfully and he nudged her with his hip.

Other than Suze, Molly had to admit Toli was probably her closest friend. They talked almost every day, and though he'd never made another pass at her, she had the feeling he would be the one she would stay closest to if she left. She was grateful for his friendship, lucky he was the easygoing guy that he was. Dom wasn't overly fond of their closeness, but he'd been quick to assure her he trusted them both and wasn't jealous. Toli, of course, went out of his way to *make* Dom jealous, but at the end of the day, their friendship and history forced an unspoken trust each of them respected.

"Chocolate fountain!" Toli announced in surprise as he caught sight of it. He grabbed Molly by the hand and dragged her towards it.

Suddenly a loud voice called across the room. "Anatoli Yuri Petrov!"

They both turned in surprise and Molly couldn't help but stare in amazement at the couple on the other side of the room. The man looked familiar, a slightly shorter and stockier version of Toli, with the same blue eyes and blond hair, but more chiseled good looks. The woman was tall, probably as tall as Tiff, with shoulder-length blond hair and the brightest blue eyes Molly had ever seen. Right now, they were sparkling with irritation as she stood there with her hands on her hips. She spouted something off in Russian that made the man beside her chuckle, but Toli was less amused.

"English!" he said, obviously irritated. "Don't be rude." He moved finally, giving Molly's hand a squeeze before went to stand in front of the man. "You are big liar!" he said sternly.

Then both men laughed and embraced tightly, murmuring in Russian. Finally, Toli turned to Molly. "Molly, this is little brother Sergei. Sergei, my friend Molly McCarran."

"Hello!" Her eyes widened as she moved forward to shake Sergei's hand. "I've heard so much about you."

"And I you." Sergei gave her a brief smile.

"This is Tatiana Stepanova," Toli still looked irritated. "Tanya, my good friend, Molly."

"Yes, I see." Tatiana looked at Molly carefully.

Deciding she would not be intimidated by this Amazon of a woman who had broken Toli's heart, Molly stared back, meeting the other woman's gaze directly. After a moment of uncomfortable silence, Tatiana smiled. "I can see why Toli likes you—you have fire."

"Thank you." Molly glanced at Toli. "It's nice to meet you—Toli speaks of you often."

"Does he?" She looked over at Toli and he shrugged.

"So what are you doing here?" Toli asked them, looking from one to the other.

"I've come to see you and then will join the Bruins for training camp," Sergei said mildly. "I think it might be time to come back to the NHL."

Toli gaped at him. "What are you talking about?" He began chattering in Russian. "You said you were never coming back to the U.S.! What the hell is going on with you? And why would you come without telling me?"

"Easy, big brother," Sergei switched back to English with a wink at Molly. "He's flustered. He can't think that fast in English."

"I can, too!" Toli glared at him.

"He really can't," Sergei laughed as Toli started cussing at him in Russian again. "Toli, stop. We can talk later. Maybe you should say hello to Tatiana."

"You did not say you were coming," Toli turned to her coldly. Molly could see the hurt in his eyes and wanted desperately to touch him, let him know she was there for him, but she figured that wouldn't help anything. It was obvious they had a lot to talk about.

"Why don't we go to the bar—" Molly spoke to Sergei but Toli held up a hand.

"No." He shook his head. "Whatever Tatiana has to say, she can say to my brother and best friend." He folded his arms across his chest. She seemed hurt by his behavior, but he'd spent more than a decade waiting for her while she refused to marry him and refused to compromise. He loved her, but he wanted to be part of a couple, not continue living like this.

"I'm sorry," Tatiana spoke softly. "I should have warned you, but I, we, were worried about you. You were arrested!"

"You know I was set up; I would never risk my career for marijuana!" He looked at them in disbelief. "You did not think I really did this?"

Sergei shrugged slightly. "Toli, we don't know what's happening, and the truth —" He glanced at Molly regretfully. "We don't know her. We don't know anything because you don't tell us."

"I would tell *you* if you would answer your phone!" Toli snapped, glaring at his brother. "But you're always in bed with a whore or hungover. And Tanya, she knows enough. She knows Molly is my friend and married to a very bad man." He looked at Tatiana. "But as usual, you don't trust me. You don't listen. You do what you want."

She sighed heavily. "Toli, I didn't come to fight. I was worried."

"You worried only because you thought I found someone else," he said sadly. "Not because you want things to be better between us."

They glared at each other until Molly finally reached over to touch Toli's arm. "People are starting to arrive," she whispered. "You're going to have to behave."

He snorted. "I am fine. Tanya, *you* are not my date."

"Fine," she shrugged. "I am Sergei's date."

Sergei rolled his eyes. "Are Dom and Cody here yet?" He turned, looking around.

"Not yet," Molly shook her head. "They were getting the cars washed first."

"Come, Toli," Sergei motioned with his head. "Let's go get a drink. Molly, will you stay with Tanya for a moment?"

"Of course." Molly felt her stomach churn uncomfortably. She certainly didn't want to have a private conversation with this woman, especially seeing the power play going on between her and Toli. This was one of the most uncomfortable positions she'd ever been in, but the truth was, they hadn't done anything and even if they had, Toli and Tatiana were no longer a couple.

"You don't like me," Tatiana stated flatly, looking at her.

"I don't like the fact you broke Toli's heart," Molly answered honestly. "He's one of my best friends, and I want him to be happy. Whatever it is you're doing makes him unhappy—that's my only issue with you."

"Are you in love with him?" Tatiana asked.

"No. And he's not in love with me. We're friends. Is it so difficult for a man and a woman to really like each other and not be sleeping together?"

Tatiana chuckled. "Not someone as charming and rich as Toli."

"I already have someone charming and rich," Molly said, meeting the other woman's gaze defiantly. "I'm sorry you don't believe me and even sorrier you don't trust Toli—he deserves better." She started as Dom's arms slid around her waist.

"Hey, beautiful!" He kissed the side of her face.

"Hey!" She smiled up at him before looking back at Tatiana with a slight tilt of her head. "Dom, do you remember Tatiana?"

"Oh! Hey!" He gave a small smile before glancing between the two of them. This couldn't be good. Some of the guys were already teasing him about Molly's close relationship with Toli, so he was sure Tatiana was pissed about it.

"It's been a long time," Tatiana said. She was startled to see Dom and Molly together. Dom was one of the best-looking men she'd ever known, much hotter than Cody in her opinion, all dark tousled hair and eyelashes that made women swoon. He reminded her of a pirate; she couldn't believe he was with this older woman who would be rather plain if not for her incredible green eyes.

"Toli didn't tell us you were coming," Dom finally said after another moment of uncomfortable silence.

"He didn't know," Molly said with a sigh and turned back to the other woman. "Look, I'm sorry you think I'm sleeping with your *ex*-boyfriend and getting him in trouble, but I'm not. I'm doing everything I can to get my ex to leave him alone, but like a lot of people, he seems to have trouble understanding that a man and a woman can be *friends*." She looked up at Dom for good measure.

He raised his eyebrows questioningly, but wisely said nothing, wondering if she thought he didn't trust her and Toli, because he did. He often wished they weren't so close, but he knew Toli would never, under any circumstances, try to steal a woman from him. He might even have feelings for her, but he would never get into a relationship with her without having a conversation with Dom, and he couldn't even entertain the idea Molly would lie or cheat after what they'd been through.

"Hey, guys!" Tiff came into the room like a whirlwind, her strawberry blond hair flowing down her back in tight sexy curls, tan legs long and lean under a short denim skirt, white tank top and tan leather sandals that laced up her calves. With a dozen gold bracelets up one arm and gold chandelier earrings hanging from her ears, she was a force of nature as she swooped in, kissing Dom on the cheek and hugging Molly tightly.

"Hi, Tiff." Dom smiled at her affectionately. She was truly stunning and it still amazed him that quiet, unassuming Coach Dave had won her heart. Of course, they were both ridiculously smart too, so that probably had something to do with it.

Tiff turned and glanced at Tatiana, easily dismissing her as the girlfriend of one of the players she didn't know. No wedding ring often meant no long-term status, and Tiff didn't bother to get to know the ones who would probably be gone by the next event.

"Tiff, do you know Tatiana Stepanova? She's Toli's friend, from Russia." Molly glanced over at Tiffany, making a slight motion with her eyes. Tiffany understood immediately that this was the woman who broke Toli's heart and turned to the woman with a fake smile pasted on her face.

"Oh, yes, we've heard *so* much about you." She purposely held out her left hand, showing off the diamond ring on her hand. Though Tiffany didn't usually behave this way, they all knew how much Tatiana had hurt Toli, so she wasn't cutting the woman any slack either. If she wanted to be one of them, she would have to make it up to Toli first.

"Nice to meet you." Tatiana nodded curtly, taking the woman's limp hand-shake grudgingly, suddenly understanding these people were loyal to Toli only and she would not be accepted into the fold unless she made things right. "If you'll excuse me, I need to speak with Toli." She hurried away, and Molly and Tiffany held back giggles.

"I'm sorry," Tiffany murmured near Molly's ear. "I usually try not to be so..." Her voice trailed off.

"Bitchy?" Dom supplied, laughing out loud.

"Well, yeah, I guess you could call it that." Tiffany snorted and looked over at her husband. "Honey, get me some wine, would you?"

"Sure, babe." Dave grinned at her before disappearing around the corner.

"You guys are mean." Dom said with a shake of his head.

"She hurt Toli," Molly frowned at him. "He loves her and she's been stringing him along for years. We're on his side."

"I am too," Dom said, holding up his hands in mock surrender. "But you could have been a little nicer. I mean, she doesn't know anyone here and she's already on the outs with him."

"Then she shouldn't have shown up unexpectedly at an event like this," Tiff said firmly. "She showed up here thinking he would fall into place at her side, like he's always done, and she'd make a claim on him. The people here are the core group of people he'll be playing with this season and she wanted to make sure everyone knew he was taken."

"How on earth do you know that?" Dom demanded.

"It's a woman thing," said Molly.

Dom rolled his eyes. "On that note, can I go get a drink?"

"Absolutely." She offered him her cheek and after kissing her, he ambled off towards the bar.

"Let's go eavesdrop." Tiffany grabbed Molly's arm and pulled her towards the pool where Tatiana and Toli were talking. Molly followed with a happy grin; she'd never felt like she belonged anywhere before, but now she did.

19

MOLLY MOVED FROM GROUP TO GROUP IN A BIT OF A DAZE. THOUGH SHE HADN'T done a lot of socializing over the years, she'd never been shy or unsure of herself in a crowd and she was pretty confident with her group of friends here. These women, however, were cut from a different cloth. Some of them seemed nice enough, but there was no doubt in her mind others were going to look down their nose at her once they figured out she was with one of the younger players, and not married to one of the coaches or trainers.

It was going to be a long night if these women started making snarky remarks, and Tim's abuse over the years left her feeling inadequate. She'd tried hard to listen to everyone telling her she was beautiful, but she was still forty years old, with the beginning of crow's feet around her eyes and hints of gray at her temples. She'd lost weight and was working out, but she couldn't compete with these women.

She knew she looked pretty good, but not like Suze or Tiff. Sometimes she got so caught up in her new life she forgot she wasn't one of the beautiful people. These last three months had been better than the entire rest of her life all together, so she'd been focused on enjoying what she had instead of worrying about keeping up with women almost half her age. Now that she could see them in front of her, she realized it might be harder than she'd thought.

"Sorry!" A petite brunette with a pixie haircut and big brown eyes smiled up at Molly as she stumbled out of her high heeled sandals and stepped on Molly's foot.

"Ouch!" Molly reached down, rubbing her foot, but smiled back. "No problem. Be careful—the floor is slippery in here."

"I can't walk in these stupid things," the young woman looked down at her feet in despair. "I'm Cassidy Rousch, Marco's wife."

"I'm Molly." Molly shook her hand. "Dom Gianni's girlfriend."

Cassidy glanced up. "Oh, wow, you're really pretty! I thought you would be older—" Suddenly her eyes widened and she clapped her hand over her mouth. "Shit, Marco's always telling me I have no filter!" Her cheeks turned red. "I'm really, really sorry—I shouldn't have said that."

"It's fine." The young woman looked genuinely contrite, and technically, she'd given Molly a compliment. But now Molly was more aware than ever that people were already talking about her age. Damn, she'd thought she'd at least get through training camp before the gossip started, but apparently not. "Excuse me." She started to walk away, but Cassidy touched her arm.

"I really am sorry. I'm always sticking my foot in my mouth."

"It's okay." Molly gave her a small smile. "I guess I'd better get used to it if tongues are already wagging."

Cassidy shrugged. "Oh, I wouldn't worry about it. Most of us were just curious—Dom's never had a serious girlfriend before. The girls who aren't nice about it, well, they're just jealous."

"Thanks. I'll remember that." Molly quickly escaped and slipped up the stairs to her room. Closing her door, she sat on the edge of the bed and leaned back on her hands. She was already terrified Tim was going to find her and hurt her or one of her new friends; she didn't want to think about other people hurting her too. The age difference between herself and Dom didn't bother him, and she knew it shouldn't bother her, but it did.

Standing up, she went to the window and looked down at the pool. A lot of people were here now, swarming the pool and bar areas, and she saw Tiff holding court by the Jacuzzi. She was surrounded by four or five young players who were gazing at her in adoration. Sergei was near the bar with Dom, Cody and someone she didn't recognize. Toli and Tatiana were nowhere she could see. Andra was talking to more people Molly didn't know, laughing and at ease. Cassidy was hanging onto the arm of a lanky man with red hair, looking uncomfortable and quiet.

Molly couldn't help but wonder if she'd told him about their conversation or if she'd let it go. Were they gossiping about her now? Shaking her head, she moved into the bathroom, staring in the mirror self-consciously. She reapplied her lipstick and added another layer of mascara. Fluffing her hair, she reminded herself Dom loved her, regardless of any signs of aging. She might not be perfect on the outside, but they had a special bond and she couldn't let herself think about every little thing that could go wrong. If their relationship was going to end, it was much more likely to be because she left him, not the crow's feet around her eyes when she smiled.

Starting to get depressed, she took a deep breath and forced herself to put the negativity out of her mind. She was going to go downstairs and make sure Dom was making friends with all the guys that had been invited to camp; he'd told her he had no idea what some of the younger guys had heard about him and it worried him. He didn't want them to think he was a jerk who hurt people. Andra had asked her to keep an eye on Dom to make sure he was doing okay too. Although Brad and Andra trusted him, they also knew Dom had never gotten close to any of his teammates since college and they wanted that to change here.

Opening the door to her room, Molly yelped in surprise as she came face to face with Toli. "You scared the crap out of me!" she gasped.

"Sorry!" He gave her his typical goofy smile. "Toli saw you come up and you are gone long time."

She shrugged. "Just taking a few minutes to compose myself. I've already been told I'm prettier than they heard I was."

Toli's eyes narrowed. "Who said that? Toli will smack him."

"It was one of the wives," she said wryly. "I think people would frown on you smacking her."

Toli reached out to lift her chin with his fingers. "Molly is not okay. Toli knows this face. What is it?"

"It's nothing." She shook her head. "She hurt my feelings, so I came up here to get myself together."

Fighting off tears of melancholy, she started to move out the door, but Toli gently grabbed her arm. He looked into her face and squinted. "Tell Toli what is making Molly have the tears in eyes?"

"I can't," she whispered.

"You will leave us, yes?" He looked at her knowingly. "This is what pains you."

"I have to." She turned her back, burying her face in her hands as she struggled to keep herself from bursting into tears.

"Toli can take you to Russia," he said softly. "We can go. He will never find you."

"You have to be *here*. You can't worry about me."

He scowled at her. "All the months of friendship and *now* Toli should not worry about you? I was arrested to protect you—of course there is worry! You do not understand friendship if this is what you think!" He crossed his arms in annoyance.

"I just mean I have to solve this myself. You guys have all been wonderful, but it's time for me to fix this without anyone else getting hurt. I have to find a way be free on my own."

"So you will run." He spoke flatly. "And go where? Miami? Memphis? Mexico? Molly, how will you live?"

"I don't know," she admitted. Her heart was overflowing with fear and hurt and a million other emotions she couldn't express to anyone, not even Toli. "But Toli, you're all I have right now. I can't let Dom know how scared I am—he'll get into trouble by trying to kill Tim or doing some other crazy thing. No one really understands how dangerous this is except you." Her tearful eyes pleaded with him to understand, even if he didn't.

"What is Toli to do?"

A soft knock on the door startled them and she sighed. "Come in."

Dom stuck his head in, frowning slightly. "What's wrong?" He asked, looking from one to the other.

"Someone said something stupid," Toli made a face. "Molly has hurt feelings."

Dom glanced at him. "Tatiana's at the bar surrounded by a bunch of young, single guys—you might want to go rescue her."

"Rescue *her*?" Toli burst out laughing. "She will snap like twigs." He grinned at them. "Okay, Toli will go." He winked at her and strolled out, shutting the door behind him.

"What did they say?" Dom asked, reaching for Molly and pulling her close.

She rested her head against his chest, breathing in his after shave and snuggling close. "It doesn't matter," she said softly. "It was actually a backhanded compliment, that I'm prettier than she thought I'd be or something." She tried to chuckle but it sounded more like a sniffle. "I guess I didn't think they'd be gossiping about me *before* they even saw us together."

"Honey, people talk."

"If people are already talking, and the media gets hold of it, Tim is going to find me sooner rather than later."

"I don't think we've reached the media with our relationship yet," he gave her a small grin. "But if one of the wives heard about you, then Suze or Andra or Tiff told someone they thought they could trust, and the NHL wives' pipeline is better than the CIA."

"Great." She sat on the edge of the bed.

"Molly, don't you trust me?" He looked uncomfortable standing in front of her and she glanced up at him with a frown.

"What do you mean?"

"Someone hurt your feelings and you turned to Toli instead of me. Why?"

"I didn't turn to Toli!" She got up quickly and reached for him, hating that he would even consider that idea. "He saw me leave and followed me when I didn't come back down. I'm just trying to protect you—I don't want you to get into trouble because of me!"

"So you don't trust me not to lose my temper." He was hurt.

"No!" She sighed, taking a deep breath and then blowing it out. "I'm not explaining myself very well. It's just that you've done so much for me—I don't want you to see someone hurting me and get into trouble by standing up for me. You just got clearance from the NHL—the last thing you need is to pick a fight with another player because his wife is immature and doesn't know how to keep her mouth shut. You're too important to me."

He gazed at her steadily, his dark eyes boring into her bright green ones. She wasn't afraid of him, but she was still afraid of what he might do to someone else. He didn't know why that bothered him so much, but it did. He'd made so much progress, yet even the woman he loved didn't trust him completely.

"Dom, what are you thinking?" She touched his face. "Tell me."

"You're afraid of what I might do." He spoke flatly, looking away.

"No! You're supposed to want to protect me, aren't you? Isn't that what you've been telling me? You've spent all summer telling me to trust you to protect me—and I do! But that should go both ways! I don't want you to get into trouble over something so trivial! If it was Tim trying to hurt me, that would be different, but you've worked so hard this summer—I don't want our love to be the reason you start off on the wrong foot with your new team." She paused, practically holding her breath as he looked back at her.

"*Are* we in love?" he asked.

"You have to ask?" She was taken aback. "I mean, I thought we were, but we never actually talked about it..." Her voice trailed off. "If that's not how you feel—"

"How *I* feel? I told you once, and have shown you repeatedly, but you've never said it! And you spend so much time with Toli..." He felt uncertain with a woman for the first time in his life. "I'm really not sure how you feel, Molly."

"You're not?" She asked in a tiny voice. She ran her hands up his chest and then wrapped them around his neck. "Really? You can't tell I'm crazy about you? That I'm constantly terrified I'm going to wake up and find out you just want to be friends? That I'm too old for you? That I can't give you kids? I have nothing to offer you—but you're still here. How could I not love you?"

"Then tell me!" he nearly growled at her, pulling her up against him.

This was going to make things so much harder, but she couldn't—wouldn't— let him think she didn't love him. "I'm crazy in love with you," she said softly.

He bent his head and kissed her, passionately, until her fingers were tugging at his shirt and he grasped her by the arms. Her breath escaped in gasps of delight as he covered her with kisses.

He slowly backed her onto the bed and she moved her head to the side. "Dom! We can't do it *now!*"

"Sure we can." He stood long enough to lock the door and pull a condom out of his wallet.

"Dom!" She was protesting even as he pulled down her skirt. "People might hear us!"

"Then I guess you'll have to be quiet," he smirked, yanking off his polo shirt and finding her mouth again.

"They're going to come looking for us!" she gasped, giggling as he tugged off her panties.

"They'll have to wait." He kept kissing her, silencing any more protests, and she couldn't stop a whimper of delight from escaping.

No matter how often they made love, she could never get enough. She wanted him all the time, and the moment he touched her, she couldn't think straight. It had always seemed so silly to her, reading about these kinds of lusty romances in novels. She'd never imagined it could be real, or that she herself would be the kind of woman who wanted sex all the time. Dom was so hot, and so good in bed, she didn't know if she'd ever be able to sleep with anyone else. It was like nothing else in the world existed when they were together.

They finished undressing each other with care, relishing in small touches and whispered endearments. When they were skin to skin, she dug her fingers into the long hair she loved so much, her head falling back as he peppered her throat with kisses and gentle love bites. Running his hands over her possessively, he moved her thighs apart with his knee.

"Dom?" Her voice was husky and she gazed at him shyly.

"Yeah, baby?"

"Can I be on top?" Her voice was barely a whisper.

He captured her mouth with a kiss that told her she could do anything she wanted. Without breaking their kiss, he flipped them over so he was on his back and she was straddling him.

"You make me want things I never knew I wanted," she whispered, placing her palms flat on his chest.

"What do you want?"

"You," she admitted. "All the time."

He chuckled. "You're a late bloomer. It's okay."

"It makes me feel trashy sometimes."

"Trashy?" He reached up to grip her by the waist and pull her down so her face was close to his. "*I love you.* There is nothing trashy about this, or anything we do. Hearing you call out my name makes me so fucking hard, I feel like a teenager again. I've never reacted to a woman like this, ever, and there is no feeling in the world like knowing you want me as much as I want you."

"I love you too," she whispered against his mouth. She ran her hands along his face, kissing him as lovingly as she knew how. Adjusting her position, she sat up and reached down to find his throbbing dick with her hands. She held him in position so she could press down, letting him fill her. A tiny groan of pleasure escaped her when she took him all the way in, a wave of ecstasy washing over her. Her eyelids fluttered closed and his hands closed around her hips. He lifted her gently, guiding her until she found her own rhythm. Gradually, she picked up speed, coming up almost all the way off of him and then sliding back down. Her breath grew shallow and a familiar tingling was beginning low in her belly.

"Dom!" She gripped his shoulders.

"Just like that, sweetheart," he ground out. He was holding back, wanting her to find release first, but she was so hot and tight he had to take a deep breath to hold on.

"Dom…" Her voice faded to a whisper as the first waves rocked her, taking her over a cliff that left her trying to breathe through shuddery bursts of pleasure. She fought valiantly to keep from screaming out his name, but a shriek burst from her unwittingly.

"That's it, baby, come for me!" He thrust up hard when he felt her spasm around him, his own release washing over them both.

"Oh, don't stop!" she begged, her head thrown back.

He continued to move inside her until she collapsed against his chest. He stroked her back, waiting for his heart beat to return to normal. She made him feel like the most important man in the world. He loved watching her sexuality blossom in his arms and he loved when they touched. He'd known he was falling in love with her, but now he realized he loved this woman more than he'd ever thought possible.

Lying on their backs side by side, Molly glanced over at Dom's relaxed, satisfied face and smirked at him.

"Now you're going to have to sit here and wait for me to get myself put together again!" she chuckled.

"Okay." He grinned amiably. "I'll be right here."

She managed to get up, grabbing her clothes from the floor before going into the bathroom. She got dressed, fixed her makeup and curled her hair again.

Finally, looking as presentable as she figured she was going to get, she opened the door. Dom had gotten dressed too, and he brushed past her with a quick kiss.

"Give me a sec and we can go."

"Okay." She sank back on the bed and sighed with pleasure. She didn't know what was going to happen once they went downstairs, but he would be with her every step of the way. Despite all the strangers, she had friends down there too. With Dom and her friends by her side, she wasn't afraid of bitchy hockey wives or anyone else. Sometimes, she wasn't even afraid of Tim anymore.

He certainly still had the power to hurt her physically, but he no longer held any power over her emotions. She had learned so much about herself, and her own strength, she refused to allow herself to think about what she would do if he found her. She would fight, or she would die. There would be no going back to that life, not ever again. She didn't relish the thought of having to leave Dom and the others to keep them safe, but she would do whatever she had to because she loved them.

The bathroom door opened and Dom came out looking as handsome as she'd ever seen him. His long hair was parted on the side and curled a little at the bottom where it touched his collar. His red polo shirt showed off his amazing arms and chest, and the shorts he wore made no mystery of his strong legs and terrific ass. She sighed with undisguised desire and he arched an eyebrow at her.

"Don't tell me you want more?"

"I'm forty," she said. "They say we get hornier as we get closer to menopause."

"Well, then I'd say we're just about perfect for each other!" he chuckled, reaching out his hand to help her up. "Ready to go or you want to spend more time in bed?"

"I'd *much* rather spend more time in bed!" she laughed.

2 O

WALKING DOWN THE STAIRS AND JOINING THE PARTY WAS LIKE A SPLASH OF COLD water after their recent intimacy. People were everywhere, music and laughter filled the rooms, and it was fairly chaotic. Molly glanced up at Dom and noticed he wasn't particularly relaxed anymore either. He held her hand, and she held on to his strength as he guided her towards Cody and Suze, where they stood with Drake, Karl and a couple of people she didn't know. Molly wanted to hang back, but Dom pulled her along gently, his eyes meeting hers with a quick wink.

"Hey!" Suze looked up with a smile. "We wondered where you were."

Dom put his arm around Molly's shoulder and pulled her close, kissing the side of her face. "We just needed a few minutes of tranquility before we rejoined the masses."

"Tranquility? Is that what we're calling it these days?" Cody smirked.

"Hush!" Suze laughed at her husband.

"It's going to be great playing here," Drake Riser laughingly changed the subject, his surfer-style dirty blond hair moving in the wind as he spoke. He was a big guy like Dom, with an engaging smile and easygoing personality.

"You think?" Karl Martensson was another big guy, only with white blond hair and blue eyes. The six-foot-four Swedish backup goalie was a traditional Scandinavian, with pale skin, pale hair and light eyes, but seemed to have arms a mile long and a sexy smile. He was another good-looking guy, and Molly had to wonder if all hockey players were this good looking. Between Dom, Cody, Drake and Karl, they could be Chippendale dancers or movie stars. She'd always thought hockey players would be burly guys without any teeth; apparently, she was mistaken.

"Come on, it's an expansion team," Drake said with a grin, taking a pull from his beer. "There is so much potential here!"

"Potential for the rink melting in the desert sun and all of us being swallowed into oblivion," Karl muttered.

Molly snorted out loud and then clapped a hand over her mouth. "I'm sorry, but that was funny."

"Thinks he's a funny guy," Cody shook his head. "Listen, you're not going to be the backup forever. Rousch is thirty-seven, you're twenty-six. You're coming into your own. A couple of years and this team will be yours."

"Yeah, I know." Karl looked away, his big shoulders slightly slumped.

"It's better than sitting behind Price for the rest of your life," Drake said, referring to Montreal's stellar goalie, Carey Price. "You might never have gotten out in front of him."

Karl shrugged. "I could also play at home, in Sweden, and actually be a contender."

"The SHL isn't the NHL," Dom said firmly. "You know this is the best place for you. You're not going to be the backup forever."

"And you're sure as hell not going to be anyone's backup with the girls," Suze said with a grin.

"That's for sure," Molly nodded. "You'll have them swarming like bees!"

Karl gave them both a smile. "Thanks. That is definitely one of the perks of being in Las Vegas."

"What's a perk of Vegas?" Marco Rousch and his wife joined them unexpectedly. The red-headed starting goalie was from Switzerland and had a lilting accent.

"The restaurants," Suze said sweetly, smiling at him as she diverted the conversation.

Uncomfortable with Marco, Molly moved away from Dom and looked at Suze. "Let's go investigate the chocolate fountain." Tugging at her arm, Molly pulled her away from the men and headed into the other room.

The evening felt endless to Molly. Every time she found Dom, they got separated again. She met one person after another, and gave up trying to remember their names. Molly was glad to see Marco not circulating and making everyone as miserable as he seemed to make his wife. Cassidy spent most of the night with her eyes cast down at the floor while Marco drank until he was wobbling on his feet. Otherwise, everyone seemed friendly, if not outright curious about her, but most kept their opinions and comments to themselves.

Molly was just about to go looking for Dom when Sergei and Toli flanked her. Toli had had quite a few drinks and was grinning broadly.

"Molly!" He gave her a hug. "Do you like my brother?"

"I haven't had a chance to talk to him yet," She laughed as he swayed slightly on his feet. She'd never seen him drunk before, but he seemed to have an endless supply of vodka in his hand tonight. Maybe it was because Tatiana was here, but it was out of character for him in her opinion. She'd spent a lot of time with him this summer and had never seen him quite so out of control.

"Now is chance!" Toli winked at her and headed back to the bar.

"Is he okay?" She glanced at Sergei. "He seems pretty drunk. I've never seen him drink so much before."

"No?" Sergei smiled and shook his head. "We're Russian—we can drink a lot. This is probably the last time he will do that until after the season is over. He's very dedicated to the game—he doesn't drink much during the season."

"I guess I don't know that much about him as an athlete," she admitted.

"Yet he's very fond of you," Sergei said, his eyes meeting hers with an unspoken question.

"We're friends," she said for what felt like the hundredth time.

"So he says, but you are very important to him. Important enough to scare Tatiana into a trip to the U.S."

"I think I'm the closest he's ever come to getting over her," she said thoughtfully. "But we both realized that wasn't going to happen."

"Tanya's a great girl," Sergei said after a moment. "But I don't know if she'll ever be what he needs."

"Well, whatever happens won't be because of me," she said firmly. "Dom and I are together."

"I've heard." He nodded. "I hope it works out."

"What does that mean?" She glanced at him warily.

"Just what I said. I've watched him go through hell, and I don't want anything to put him back there."

"Is that a warning of some kind?"

"Maybe just a suggestion that you don't hurt him? He's like family to me—and your situation seems precarious. You've managed to catch one of the hottest bachelors in the NHL, as well as charm my older brother, who's never looked at another woman in 18 years."

Molly was speechless, forcing herself not to glare at him. "I'm not sure what *that's* supposed to mean," she said at last. "But I haven't 'caught' anyone, nor charmed anyone. I care about these people, and I'm going to assume you do too, since you're being a dick right now." She turned and huffed away from him, storming outside to the bar by the pool and getting another drink. The last person she'd expected to treat her like that was the infamous Sergei, but there it was.

"Hey!" Dom came up behind her, wrapping his arms around her waist. "Sorry, I keep getting caught up in conversations."

"It's okay." She took a sip of wine.

"What's wrong?" He turned her around so she was facing him.

"Nothing." She made a motion with her hand. "Just a little lecture from your buddy Sergei."

"Oh, hell, what did he say? Do I need to talk to him?"

"No. But apparently it's not just the women who think I'm too old for you!"

"He said that?"

"Of course not." She sighed. "Look, I'm going upstairs. I've had enough."

"I'll come with you."

"No, this is your job. Stay and do your thing."

"Not gonna happen." He grasped her hand firmly and pulled her back inside.

He scanned the room until he found Sergei and tugged at her until they were in front of him. "Okay, you two." He looked from one to the other. "Whatever it is, let's have it out in the open. One of my best friends and my girlfriend are not going to start out on the wrong foot."

Molly looked over at Sergei but said nothing. Sergei looked uncomfortable, staring back at Dom reluctantly.

"We don't know anything about her!" Sergei finally said. "First she moved in with you off the street, then she's living with my brother and he's getting arrested by her husband! I don't know what the hell is going on and, frankly, it seems like she's bewitched the lot of you!"

Dom stared at him for a moment and then burst out laughing. "Seriously, dude? You're worried that she's using me and Toli?"

"I don't know what she's doing, but you've never had a serious girlfriend in all the years I've known you, and Toli's never looked at anyone but Tatiana. Then suddenly she's pulling both of you around by the nose! What am I supposed to think?"

"That's she's awesome, and we both really like her. Except I like her a little bit more." He pulled her close to his side. "Look, Sergei, I appreciate your having my back, but Molly's one of us. Suze, Cody, Brad and Andra love her too—and you know that wouldn't happen if she wasn't on the up and up."

Sergei sighed. "I'm sorry, bro. It's just kind of hard to watch—I've never seen you in love before."

Dom chuckled. "Well, it was bound to happen, right?"

"If we're done, I'm going to bed." Molly started to pull away, but Dom gripped her hand.

"Come on, babe, don't be mad. He's just looking out for me—he hasn't had a chance to get to know you."

"Lucky me." Molly was mentally exhausted. She'd known it would be a different kind of evening, meeting so many people, but she hadn't expected the biggest attack to come from someone Dom considered family. It hurt, and she wasn't as forgiving as he was; she'd been hurt too many times in the past. Tim's friends had never been much nicer than Tim, and she hadn't worked so hard to crawl out of that dark place to now be in a similar situation with one of Dom's friends.

"I'm sorry," Sergei spoke quietly. "I didn't mean to upset you. Toli's been completely different since he met you—he barely saw his son this summer and he's never done that before! Our parents hit the roof when they heard he'd been arrested on a drug charge. I had to find out what was going on."

"I understand that, and I'm sorry for the trouble I've caused him." Her control was slipping, so she rose on her toes and kissed Dom's cheek. "I'll see you upstairs." She pulled her arm free and hurried out of the room.

"Sergei, what the hell did you do?" Dom glared at his friend. "I *just* got her to start trusting that I love her, and you went and scared her. Knock it off—just because you don't know her doesn't mean she's not good for me!"

"Dom, don't you realize how crazy this looks from the outside looking in?"

"No. I see you and Tatiana looking in from all the way in Russia, with your heads up your asses, not having any idea what's really going on, and making assumptions. Tatiana has the excuse of being jealous—what's yours?" With a grunt, he turned and followed Molly up the stairs.

2 1

MOLLY WAS SITTING ON THE BED, IN THE DARK, LOOKING OUT THE WINDOW. SHE'D locked the door, but Brad and Andra kept keys above the frames of several of the doors in case of emergency. Dom obviously knew where they were because he opened the door without any hesitation and slowly joined her on the bed. He didn't speak for a while, just gently rubbed her shoulders as she continued staring out the window. Finally, he pulled her up against him.

"I'm sorry," he said. "I didn't expect that from Sergei. He's normally a great guy. I don't know what's gotten into him. Toli said he's been kind of different, avoiding him on the phone and stuff, but he thought it was because of a woman. Something must be going on we don't know about."

Molly leaned against him wearily. "He's right, though. I've brought nothing but trouble since I've been here. You haven't really seen it because Toli has taken the brunt of it. And he's right—why would he do that for me?"

Dom tensed. "What are you trying to say? Is there something between you and Toli?"

"There isn't. Not for me anyway. I don't know for sure what he's feeling... he asked me out when we first met and we really hit it off. You know that, but I didn't feel that spark, the one I feel when I'm with you. He knew it right away, when I wouldn't let him kiss me—"

"He tried to *kiss* you?"

"Well, yeah, but that was before you and I were together!" She nudged him. "Come on—you had to assume he would try something when we spent the whole day in L.A. Anyway, he said it was obvious our hearts were taken, and that we were probably better as friends because lovers can leave, but friends are forever."

"What does that mean?" Dom frowned.

"It means I'm in love with you, but maybe he does have feelings for me. He wasn't happy to see Tatiana tonight. He got really tense when he saw her and Sergei, and now he's practically falling down drunk, which I've never seen before. We've been together all summer and he's never behaved this way. I don't how much of this is my fault."

"Okay, wait." Dom shook his head. "There is no way that's your fault. I've seen Toli drink—believe me, this isn't the first time. Maybe not this summer, but he's older now. He's also been out of the NHL for a while so he has a lot to prove. I'm sure he's just feeling off-kilter with Sergei and Tatiana showing up together like—" He froze. "Oh shit."

"Oh shit, what?" she asked, blinking at him.

"I'm thinking maybe there's something going on with Sergei and Tatiana and they're trying to throw the scent off what they're doing by going after you."

"That makes sense," she said thoughtfully.

"This isn't going to end well," he grumbled. "And we're going to be right smack in the middle of it all."

"You think they've been fooling around behind Toli's back?" Molly seemed stricken, heartbroken for her friend.

"Toli left Russia and told her he was done. They still talk, but he told me he knows she's not coming here and he's not going back there. Although he's hung on to some hope because they talk so often, it doesn't seem as though it's going to go anywhere."

"What do we do? There's no way in hell I'm going to sit back and let Toli get blindsided by this—especially with the season about to start!" She looked angry on Toli's behalf, and he put his hands on hers.

"Easy," he said. "If there's anything I've learned this summer, it's that you have to think before you act. Think about what the repercussions of what you're going to do might be. If you were to go down there and say something, there is a house full of NHL players and their partners—gossip would be all over the league within 24 hours. Toli's also drunk off his ass and that will only end with him and Sergei going at it like kids. This is definitely not the right time or place."

She nodded. "You're right, of course."

"We need to go back downstairs and keep an eye on both of them. I'll stick to Sergei and you stick to Toli, and we'll both keep an eye out for Tatiana. Hopefully we'll get through what's left of the evening without any issues. Tomorrow, we'll figure out if we're even right, and what to do next."

"Okay." She got up and reached for his hand. Together, they made their way back down to the party.

The phone rang far too early the next morning and Molly reached for it absently, trying to untangle herself first from Dom and then from the sheets. It had been after three in the morning before they'd finally gotten to sleep and it was just shy of 10:00 now. She was barely conscious, but she finally found her phone next to the bed and put it up to her ear blearily.

"Yes, hello?"

"Molly!" Toli sounded wide awake for someone who had only slept for a few hours after being so drunk.

"Toli, we're sleeping!" she murmured.

"Get up!" he said firmly. "We go to brunch. *All of us.*"

"All of who?" she moaned, falling onto her back beside Dom, who had opened one eye in annoyance.

"Everyone!" he said decidedly. "Please?"

"Toli!" she groaned, sighing heavily. "You don't want to be alone with them? Is that it?"

"Exactly."

"Here, give Dom the details." She handed the phone to him and then curled up against his side.

"What the fuck, Toli?" Dom grumbled. "We had a really long night!"

"Yes, yes, but this important. Noon, brunch at the Wynn." Toli disconnected.

"Fuck." Dom looked at Molly. "He's more *your* friend than mine, you know."

"I know, sorry." She took the phone and put it back on the nightstand. "How long do we have?"

"We need to be on the Strip in two hours for brunch."

"We need to crawl into the shower and then find coffee," she whispered.

"Fine," he chuckled, kissing her cheek. She nestled against him and for a few minutes they rested in silence, enjoying the quiet of the house and each other. It was nice going to sleep together and waking up together; they both sensed the ease with which they had fallen into that routine. Molly loved his quiet strength and the security he brought to her life.

"We've got to get up," she said, reluctantly pulling herself away from Dom. She glanced at his naked body with unabashed pleasure. "There is no way in hell I'd be getting out of this bed if I didn't think it was important."

He gave her an appreciative grin before getting up. "Do you think something happened after they got home last night?" Dom followed her into the bathroom.

"I don't know, but you know how Toli pretends he doesn't speak English and acts all goofy? Then when the cops show up at his house, suddenly he knows exactly what to say and puts them all in their place? I have a feeling Toli has been playing a similar game with Tatiana and Sergei."

"Is that bad?" He stepped under the spray of water and pulled her close to him.

"I guess we're going to find out." She wound her arms around his neck.

Arriving at the Wynn, the valet took their car and Dom and Molly walked hand in hand through the hotel towards the restaurant. She felt pretty in a slimming black pencil skirt, a black and white low-cut blouse and tall heels. She hadn't worn heels since high school, and she loved how Dom still towered over her even when she wore them. He seemed to like it too, the way he'd stared at her when she'd come out of the bathroom. They'd almost wound up back in bed, but she'd managed to get him out the door, looking equally handsome in a pair of well-cut slacks and a button-down shirt with several buttons open at the top.

Molly squeezed his hand as they walked. "I wish I knew more about Sergei. He sure isn't acting like the guy you guys all talk about."

"He's not," Dom muttered. "I mean, after what happened to Brian, graduation was kind of a downer, and then all of us took off in different directions. We kept in touch, of course, but he never really talked about his divorce or anything. That was about four years ago." He caught sight of Toli, Sergei, Tatiana, Cody and Suze, so he waved just as the hostess seated them.

Everyone seemed to be quiet and reserved, except for Toli, who talked non-stop as they got settled at their table and mimosas were ordered. Molly noticed Sergei and Tatiana looked uncomfortable, and she felt a moment of sympathy for Toli. It bothered her to see him behaving so strangely. She wanted to pull him aside and ask him what was going on, but she obviously couldn't right now.

As everyone began to scatter to fill plates from the scrumptious buffet, Molly remained seated, hoping Toli would stay as well. Dom finally got up, realizing she wanted a moment with Toli, and finally it was just the two of them. She gave him a look.

"Do you want to tell me what on God's green earth you're up to?" she demanded. "You know I will back you up on anything, but I need to know what's happening."

"Toli isn't sure yet," he said under his breath.

"You're not going to do something stupid, are you?" she asked, her eyes widening.

He shook his head. "No." He murmured something in Russian before looking at her. "No time to explain—please just support me?"

"Of course." She took a breath and focused on her drink. She was afraid to leave him alone because he was bound to say or do something he shouldn't, despite what he'd said.

Sergei came back first and eyed them with obvious suspicion. Molly really had to fight the urge to smack him but a knowing wink from Toli forced her to hold back.

"Do you two want to explain anything?" Sergei asked as he sat down, staring at them.

Molly couldn't stop herself from rolling her eyes.

"No," Toli said simply.

"You act like there's something between you," Sergei said. His English, unlike Toli's, was almost perfect. His accent was barely noticeable and it made him appear almost arrogant compared to his easygoing brother.

"I've been trying to tell you," Toli said, his eyes suddenly blazing with irritation. "Molly's ex-husband is a bad man—we have had many problems this summer but any day now divorce will be final! You just don't listen. Too involved with your *puck bunnies* to care." He made a face as he said the words 'puck bunny' and Sergei sighed.

"There are no puck bunnies," he murmured as Tatiana got back to the table and slid into the seat between him and Toli.

"What's going on?" she asked looking between them.

"Sergei doesn't understand how bad of a man Molly's ex is," Toli said.

"Why did you marry such a man?" Tatiana turned to Molly with a frown. "And more importantly, why did you stay?"

"By the time I figured out how horrible he was, I had no money, no friends and nowhere to go."

"And now you will live wondering when he will show up next?" Tatiana seemed genuinely concerned. "Is it not better for you to leave Las Vegas?"

"Dom is here," Molly said softly. "This is where his job is, so this is where I will be."

"For now." Dom had gotten back to the table and heard part of the conversation. "If I can prove myself, I can get traded somewhere far away and then we won't have to worry. In the meantime, we have a kickass lawyer who's going to make his life hell if he gives us anymore trouble."

"You would leave Vegas?" Suze had come back as well. "You can't leave us because of him!"

"We don't *want* to go anywhere," Molly said quickly. "Dom's just thinking ahead. Maybe Tim will realize we mean business and give up, but I don't know."

"It's ridiculous," Toli said firmly. "We will fix this. We must."

"And this is the crazy man who broke into your apartment and got you arrested?" Sergei looked incredulous. "You shouldn't be involved, Toli! A drug charge could get you kicked out of the U.S.!"

"Sometimes you must do what's right, not what is easy. Don't you agree, little brother?" Toli met his brother's gaze head on and another strange silence bridged the table. The brothers stared each other down until finally Tatiana stepped in.

"Enough," she said, her eyes suddenly very sad. "Please, this must stop, Sergei."

"Tanya!" Sergei looked horrified as he glared at her.

"What?" she asked simply. "Life is too short to continue this way. Besides, it's not just about us anymore."

"Tanya." Sergei's voice came out as a low growl.

"No." She shook her head. "This has gone on long enough. It's time to stop lying."

"Lying about what?" Toli asked, his eyes never leaving hers.

Sergei hissed something in Russian and Tatiana laughed. "The only person who has a stake in this is the only other person at the table who speaks Russian, Sergei!"

Sergei took a breath. "Tanya, this isn't the time or the place."

"Yes, I think it is," Toli said, finally looking at them. "I've suspected for a long time, so you might as well get it out in the open."

Sergei gaped at his brother. "What are you talking about?"

"You've been in love with Tanya for years!" Toli waved a hand in frustration.

"That's not true," Sergei huffed, his blue eyes dark and cloudy as he scowled at his brother.

"Yes, it is." Toli seemed extremely calm as he looked at his brother. "For years, you try to pretend you don't have feelings, but I know. You're my *brother*—I know you. I thought it was cute in the beginning, my younger brother having a crush on my girl. But the years passed and Tanya continued to put off a wedding, and then I realized why. She's engaged to the wrong brother."

No one spoke. The silence at the table was long and embarrassing, everyone waiting for someone else to talk. Tatiana stared down at her plate, completely quiet. Sergei looked like he was ready to flee the room, and Toli just looked from one to the other, waiting.

"How did you know?" Tatiana asked after what seemed like a long time.

"He's my brother—and I have known you more than half my life," Toli shook his head. "You think I take too many pucks to the head? Any idiot could see. Maria knew."

"Maria didn't know shit!" Sergei finally exploded, his eyes blazing.

"But she did," Toli shrugged. "She lives in Dallas now, not far from Anton's mother. I see her at the movies one night when I am visiting last year. We have coffee, and she asks me if Sergei is married to Tatiana yet. I laugh. She is embarrassed. Then everything makes sense."

"It's not what you're thinking!" Tatiana whispered.

"Tanya!' Sergei glared at her.

"What?" she demanded. "What do you want me to do? I love both of you, but I am only *in love* with one of you. Do I marry the wrong brother and make everyone unhappy? Or do I raise my child alone?"

"There's a *baby*?" Toli asked, looking surprised.

"Whose baby?" Sergei demanded, sitting up straight.

Tatiana made a face at him. *"Really?"*

Sergei's face changed slightly at he gazed at her. "When were you going to tell me?"

"When you decided to choose *me*, instead of hockey," Tatiana definitely did not struggle with the English language.

Sergei opened his mouth but apparently changed his mind. "You wouldn't marry Toli—why would I think you would marry me?"

"There's a reason I didn't marry Toli!" she said sadly. "And if you don't understand the difference, then I guess there's nothing to say."

"What does that mean?" Sergei demanded.

"It means she loves *you*, not me," Toli added helpfully, putting another bite of food in his mouth.

Sergei's head spun to stare at his brother, swallowing nervously. "I don't understand—you knew this yet you're sitting there so calmly? Aren't you angry? Aren't you hurt?"

"Toli was hurt a year ago when Tatiana cancelled wedding and Toli realized she is not in love anymore. Then Toli was angry because Sergei had to be reason she didn't love Toli, yet Sergei was sleeping with everything that moved. Now, Toli has a new home, new friends, and is happy. But Toli waits for brother to become a man."

"Shut up!" Sergei looked ready to spring out of his seat and Toli just eyed him.

"She's pregnant," Toli added.

"I'm sitting right here," Tatiana said, annoyed. "And frankly, I don't need him. I can raise a child on my own."

"That's not fair," Sergei turned back to her. "You didn't tell me! I haven't even had time to think about this and you're already deciding I'm not going to be involved?"

"I thought you loved me," she said. "But I guess I really did pick the wrong brother—twice."

Sergei frowned. "You announce there's a baby, at the same time you tell my brother I've been sleeping with his girl for the last year, and then you sit there acting hurt?"

"What do you expect?" she asked, shrugging. "I understood your reluctance to tell Toli about us before, but now it's done and you're still looking like a deer in the headlights. It's obvious that this, me and a baby, is not what you want."

"I have no idea what I want!" he protested. "Up until now we were seeing each other secretly—I need a few minutes to make sense of everything!"

Tatiana made a face. "Sergei, I don't need to pressure you into anything—I'm fine without you."

He grimaced, looking around the table in frustration. "I'm sorry all of you had to be here for this—I appreciate you just sitting there and letting us look like idiots." He took a breath. "But right now, I need some air." He got up and strode out of the restaurant.

"That went well," Toli said after a moment.

"You should go after him," Molly said finally. "He's your *brother*."

Toli sighed. "Brother needs a kick in the ass," he muttered, getting up. "But Toli will go." He ambled off in the direction Sergei had gone, leaving Tatiana at the table.

"I'm sorry," Tatiana said. "I wish that hadn't happened here."

Another uncomfortable silence followed as everyone got up to refill their plates. Molly stayed behind, still not finished with her first plate, and she picked at it as she sat at the table with Tatiana. Neither of them spoke, allowing the noise in the room to fill the silence. It was strange, Molly thought, to be so wholly immersed in these people after such a short time. It felt as though she'd known them for much longer than she really had, even Sergei and Tatiana. Toli spoke of them so often she felt a kinship with them despite the situation.

"You must think I'm a terrible person," Tatiana said, meeting her eyes.

"You can't control who you fall in love with," Molly said. "I just wish you hadn't given Toli hope."

"I didn't know how to tell him. We decided we would get married when we were sixteen and eighteen. He would play in the NHL and make lots of money while I went to school, and then after he retired, I would make all the money as a doctor. It was a plan, and for many years that's what we did. Then we began to grow apart. We grew into different adults than we were when we were teenagers, but he was always so loyal..."

"And you?"

"I was always studying and working," she admitted. "I didn't think about Toli too much—we had a plan and that's what I focused on. Two years ago I realized I couldn't marry him, because I didn't feel anything but friendship when we were together, and Sergei had always been around. We fell in to bed together the moment Toli and I decided to cancel the wedding, but he was still seeing other women. That was okay—I'm so busy all the time anyway—but we were careless. Now there's a baby whose father doesn't want to settle down. I thought about terminating, but it seems so senseless. I'm thirty-three and want children." She toyed with the food left on her plate. "Sergei said he loved me."

"Maybe he does," Molly said.

"I didn't know he was thinking about coming back to the US," she said, her eyes watering slightly. "I thought he was happy in Russia—with me. But it seems both the Petrov brothers are more drawn to the NHL than they are to me."

"Maybe you need to re-think living in Russia."

The two women locked eyes across the table. "Maybe." Tatiana looked up as Dom and Cody came back, and then she got up and headed off for the buffet.

22

DOM FELT GOOD AS HE SKATED OUT ONTO THE ICE A FEW DAYS LATER. HE WAS strong, probably in the best shape of his life, and ready to play. Though Saturday night's party and Sunday's brunch had left him, Cody and Toli slightly out of sorts, they'd spoken briefly while they'd been getting dressed and they were putting everything else aside as they prepared for the last few days of camp. The three of them had no worries about making the team, but they still had to make sure they played as hard as they could to set the pace for the season. Coach Barnett was counting on them to guide the others in the direction the team needed to go, and Dom was determined to be a leader this season.

He'd always been something of a black sheep on the teams he'd played for in the past, and this was his chance to change all of that. With Molly's help, he'd come a long way this summer in overcoming his guilt and anger about what had happened to Brian, and for the first time felt like he might be able to move on. The pain would always be there, but now it was just a dull thud instead of a pounding ache.

Taking a pass from Cody, he shot it towards the net where Marco stopped it with his glove and a smirk. Dom mentally rolled his eyes as he skated off and took a seat on the bench. Cody joined him a moment later and they exchanged a knowing look. Marco was a great goaltender, but he was simply an asshole. He spent as much time as he possibly could reminding Karl he was only the backup, and though Karl had a good head on his shoulders, Dom knew it had to be getting old. He was going to mention it to Coach Barnett because if Marco was riding Karl before the season even started, there was no doubt Karl would look to get traded next season, and they didn't want that. Karl represented their future and that had to be of equal importance as their present.

Chances they would make the playoffs this year, much less win a championship, were probably close to none, so they had to keep their younger players happy. The veterans were here to set a foundation for the younger guys, but it was guys like Karl who would shape this team going forward. And frankly, Marco was just a jerk. Dom hadn't known him before he'd arrived at camp, but he'd heard rumors. The Swiss net minder was arrogant, self-absorbed and not known for being a team player. Unfortunately, he was damn good at his job and until that changed, teams still wanted him.

A fter the practice game was over, they showered, dressed and waited for the coaches to arrive for their daily post-practice meeting. There were only a few days left and they would end training camp with a free scrimmage similar to what they'd done today, except it would be open to the public. They hoped to get the residents of Las Vegas excited about the sport and the team, so they had several community-friendly events planned between now and the end of October.

Thinking about their first road trip was the only downer for Dom. He could tell Molly was far more terrified about him leaving than she let on, and the truth was he was nervous too. She was hiding something, he could feel it in his gut, but he couldn't get her to open up. He had a feeling she was ready to run, and only her inability to ask someone like Toli or Suze for the money to do it kept her here.

He'd been desperately trying to make her believe he could protect her, but she was more worried about him than she was about herself and that was a problem. Whenever he tried to talk to her about it, she changed the subject or found a way to get them in bed, and he was guilty of allowing it.

"Why so serious?" Toli asked him as he and Cody walked out with Dom.

"Just worried about Molly. She's a nervous wreck about the start of the season and I don't know how to make her feel better."

"Try harder," Toli said, putting on his sunglasses. "If you don't, you will lose her."

Dom glared at him. "What do you know that I don't?"

"She believes Tim will strike as soon as we leave on the first trip, and she isn't going to sit around waiting for this to happen."

"You mean she's leaving?" Dom was alarmed.

"I don't know," Toli admitted. "But I do know she's very afraid for *us*, and that makes her an easy target."

"How do I make her safer?" Dom asked in frustration.

They all looked at each other, but no one had a good answer so they all went their separate ways for the afternoon.

Dom drove home thinking about how to get Molly to trust him to protect her. He hated living apart and each day only got harder. He understood her need to protect him and Toli, but they didn't need protection. It made him nervous she was alone with Andra a lot of the time, and even if Brad was home, he wouldn't be able to take on a bunch of police if they stormed the house with some bogus charge or a warrant.

He had to find a way to convince Molly she was safer with him, even when he was traveling. Maybe it was time to leave the apartment and think about buying a house where he could install top-of-the-line security and possibly even have guards on site. He could afford it, and Molly was worth it. She just didn't seem to think so, which had begun to make him crazy.

Pulling up at Brad and Andra's, he paused for a moment, trying to figure out what he was going to say. She was getting good at dodging the hard questions, so he was going to make sure not to let her deflect. It was time they had a heart to heart; he was already deeply invested in this relationship, and though he was sure she had feelings for him, he didn't know what she was thinking. He couldn't start the season worrying she was going to disappear the minute he turned his back, and it was time they talked about that.

Walking into the house, he found Andra and Molly in the kitchen cutting vegetables. Molly looked up with a smile, her eyes sparkling as she looked at him.

"Hey there!" Andra gave him a smile too. "How was camp?"

"Good. I think Coach has pretty much decided who's staying and who's going."

"He won't be home for hours," said Andra, "but you two should go spend some time together." She motioned with her head. "I've got this. Go do something fun."

"If you're sure." Molly put down the knife and quickly washed her hands. She dried them and then walked over to Dom, leaning up to meet his kiss.

"Let's go for a drive," he suggested.

"Okay, let me grab my purse." She picked it up off the chair in the corner and called out to Andra before heading out to his car. Getting in, she buckled her seat belt and glanced at him. "Where are we going?"

"My place?" He looked over at her questioningly.

"Sure." She smiled. "You have plans for us?"

He chuckled. "Yes—uninterrupted conversation."

"Okay."

They chatted amiably as he drove towards home, and he told her about the players and what they'd all been doing. They talked hockey and dinner plans until they were walking into the apartment. Molly looked around wistfully, realizing she missed living here. Brad and Andra had a beautiful home and had made her feel completely welcome, but it wasn't her house. More than that, it wasn't where Dom was, and she missed him. With their future up in the air because of the constant threat Tim would make a move, she didn't know what else she could do, but it was getting harder and harder to be away from Dom.

"Come sit with me," he said, pulling her towards the couch.

She followed, her hand in his, and they settled on the couch with her resting against him. She put her head on his chest, listening to his steady heartbeat and enjoying the firmness of his arms.

"I want to ask you a question," Dom said.

"Okay." She glanced up at his face.

"What do you want? If you take Tim and your divorce and all of that out of the equation, what is it that would make you the happiest woman in the world?"

"You," she said automatically.

He couldn't help but smile. "Yeah, but how? Friends? Marriage? A family? What do you want in your happily-ever-after with me?

"A family," she said with a faraway smile. "A big house we could host dinner parties in, with a big kitchen I can cook in, and a little boy or girl with big dark eyes like yours who would go running into your arms when you get back from a trip…" Her voice trailed off. "But that's not realistic."

"Why?" He lifted her face so he could look into her eyes. "You know I want to give you the world, right?"

"You can't give me a baby," she whispered.

"Yes, I can." He kissed her gently. "We could try to get pregnant right now, and see what happens. We could also harvest some of your eggs and have them put away for later, in case we need to use a surrogate or we find out you can't carry a baby to term no matter what. We could also adopt. We have a lot of options, babe."

Her eyes filled with tears. "You make me so happy," she whispered, burying her face in his chest.

"I know you're thinking about leaving and I need you to stop."

She closed her eyes and squeezed them tightly. "I won't be responsible for anyone else getting hurt," she said after a moment. "You know what that feels like, to be unable to help someone you love. You of all people know how it feels."

"He's not going to hurt anyone. I can take care of us, Toli can take care of himself, and Cody can take care of Suze and CJ."

"You don't know him!" she protested. "We're always going to be looking over our shoulders, and we're always going to have to think about where we are and what we're doing. After a while, that's going to wear on everyone."

"You need to leave that to me." He shifted his position so they were looking at each other. "I love you, Molly. Do you love me?"

"You know I do." Her eyes misted over as she looked into his handsome face.

"Then move home. I need you here, but if you're afraid when I'm on the road you can go stay with Andra. Or you could come with me sometimes. You can't travel on the plane with me, but you can come out to wherever I am and stay with me at the hotel. We spend a lot of time in the west, so it could be fun for you to explore some of the places we go. Suze could probably leave CJ with Andra sometimes and go too."

"I don't know," she whispered. "I want to come home—here, with you—but this isn't over. I know it as sure as I know the sun is shining outside. I still haven't gotten the final divorce papers, which means he's screwing with me, and he's going to do everything he can to draw this out. It wasn't supposed to take more than six to eight weeks and we're going on, what? Twelve?"

"Call the lawyer," Dom said firmly. "We'll find out what's going on and threaten to find another lawyer if he can't handle this."

"Dom, I'm so scared!" She met his eyes worriedly. "I want to be with you more than anything in the world, but—"

"There can't be buts anymore," he whispered. "You have to take a leap of faith, babe. I can't keep worrying about you leaving. I hate not waking up next to you or going to sleep with you in my arms. It's like our whole future is on hold, and it's not fair to either of us. Can you trust me to take care of you?"

"I do, but—"

"I'm not him," Dom said, starting to wonder if he was fighting a losing battle.

"I know!" She took a deep breath and put her hand on his cheek. "The problem is, how do I go on if Tim does something to you?"

"At some point, you have to let go of 'what if' and just think about now. I could die of a heart attack tomorrow, or you could get hit by a drunk driver. Are we going to stop living because one of us is inevitably going to die first? Come on, baby—you've got to give up this need to fix everything. Let me handle the hard stuff. I just want to make you happy—that's what *my* happily-ever-after looks like. Is that so hard to understand?"

She shook her head. "I guess not."

"So will you move home?"

"Okay." She wanted her happily-ever-after more than anything in the world. It scared her half to death, but Dom gave her strength she didn't know she had. Maybe, for once in her life, she could have her dreams actually come true. She had to believe it because the alternative meant never seeing this man again. She didn't think she could live with that.

23

"YOU NEED A CAR," DOM SAID THE NEXT MORNING AS THEY HAD COFFEE BEFORE he left for training camp.

"I do?"

"Unless you want to constantly drive me places."

"I wouldn't mind that."

"Yeah, but it would be better if you had your own car," he said. "I mean, at some point, I'm going to get home from a trip in the middle of the night, or have to leave at the crack of dawn and you'll be without a car while I'm gone. That's not fair."

"Dom, it feels like it's so much..." She swallowed. "I mean, I was kind of hoping I'd get money from the house so I could buy myself a few things."

"You can do that too, but you need a car now, before I leave on the first trip. I say we go car shopping tonight after camp."

"Okay." She didn't sound convinced, and he leaned over to brush his lips across hers.

"I can spend money on you if I want to. Must you fight me on everything?"

She nudged him. "No!"

"Good. Now go get dressed so you can drive me to practice and have the car in case you want to go somewhere today."

"You sure?"

"Yes!" He rolled his eyes. "Would you go get dressed already?"

"I'm going," she laughed, getting to her feet. He made everything so easy; she wondered if this was how all relationships were.

Going downstairs, Dom tossed her the keys and she took them with a grin. She'd never driven a Mercedes before, and she paused a moment before putting the key in the ignition. She slid the seat up a little since her legs weren't anywhere near as long as his, and flashed him a smile before backing out of his parking spot.

"Maybe you'd like to drive this?" he asked. "And then we could buy something a little more interesting as our other car?"

"Like what?" she asked, glancing at him.

"A convertible?" He grinned and she laughed.

"Weren't we just talking about trying to get pregnant?" she asked. "That's not exactly a family car."

"We'd put the car seat in *this* car," he said. "That doesn't mean we can't have a fun car too! Hell, we can have three cars if you want!"

"You really want to try and get pregnant?" She stared straight ahead, not daring to look at him.

"You want a baby, and although I don't think you're old, you're already technically in the high-risk age group, so we probably should do it sooner rather than later."

"We've only known each other a few months. Are you sure about this?"

"Of course." He reached over and laid his hand on her thigh. "I don't know what the future holds, but even if we decided we didn't want to be together anymore, I can't imagine any scenario where we couldn't share custody of a kid and still be great parents and friends. I'm not going to cheat or treat you badly, and I don't think you would either. What's the worst that could happen?"

"Well, that's a loaded question. But you're right—I can't ever imagine us not being friends."

"So, no more condoms?"

"I guess not."

"You should call the lawyer when you get home, and then maybe do some research on finding a doctor that can harvest your eggs. I think we should find a doctor in L.A. We want the best we can find, and we don't want anyone to see us coming or going from anyplace around here."

"Okay." She nodded.

"And I want you to relax, okay?" He squeezed her thigh. "Call Suze, or go shopping or something. I really, really want you to stop thinking so much and just be happy. Okay?"

"Okay." She reached down with one hand and put it on top of his. "Thank you. I love you—you know that, right?"

"I might be starting to believe it," he chuckled. He told her where to turn and she pulled up at the back gate of the arena.

"What time should I come back?"

"Not sure," he said. "I'll text you."

"Okay. Meet you right here?"

"Yup." He leaned over and brushed his lips across hers. "Have a good day."

"I will."

"Love you."

"Love you too." She watched him as he pulled his bag out of the back and then jogged into the building. Taking a deep breath, she wondered if she would ever get used to his being hers. He was so incredibly hot, he made her tingle all over.

Lost in thought, she made her way home and hurried up to the apartment, making sure to lock the door behind her. Despite the wonderful day she was having, safety and security were always in the back of her mind. She wondered briefly if that would ever change, if she would ever be able to drive to the grocery store without thinking about Tim, or hang out with friends without hoping Tim wasn't watching. Could she marry Dom and live happily ever after? It was almost laughable, because he made her believe it, but she still couldn't relax completely. At some point, she'd find a way to enjoy this new life, but she didn't believe that would happen right away.

W ith everything she had to do, the morning flew by. Before she knew it, it was after twelve and she decided to take a shower and put on some makeup before she had to go get Dom. He might be finishing soon, or it might not be until dinner time, but she wanted to be ready. Dom never knew ahead of time what time he would finish, and while it made it hard to make plans, she enjoyed watching him looking happy about going to work every day. He seemed to love being part of this new team, and she knew it had been a long time since he'd loved playing hockey. The Sidewinders were giving that back to him, and she was grateful she got to be part of it.

She'd just finished putting on some lip gloss when her phone rang and she picked it up with a smile. "Hello!"

"Hey, babe." Dom's deep voice always made her insides flutter a little.

"Are you ready?"

"We're packing up so I'll be ready by the time you get here."

"Okay."

"Did you eat lunch?"

"No, I was busy all morning."

"Okay, maybe we can go grab something and you can tell me about your morning."

"Okay! See you in a few."

She hung up smiling, and went to get her purse. Lunch with the sexiest man in the world sounded like the perfect way to spend the afternoon, other than maybe sex with the sexiest man in the world. But there would be plenty of time for that tonight. Grinning to herself, she headed back to the arena.

Dom was outside, standing with Toli and Cody when she pulled in and they waved as Dom headed towards her. She waved back, and unlocked the doors so he could get in. He looked hotter than hell in khaki shorts and a black Metallica t-shirt that pulled tight across his chest. His hair was still damp and she reached out to run her fingers through it as he kissed her.

"Hi," he said with a smile. "Did you miss me?"

"As a matter of fact, I did." She put the car in reverse and turned towards the exit.

"I missed you too," he said, taking her hand.

"We could skip lunch," she said slyly, glancing over at him. "You look kind of hot right now."

He chuckled. "We can definitely skip lunch," he said, running his fingers over hand. "Hell, we can skip dinner too, if we're going to spend the time in bed!"

"I kind of like the idea of baby-making," she said.

"Yeah?" He leaned over and brushed his lips across her cheek. "Me too."

She drove home as quickly as she dared. They practically raced up to the condo, tearing at each other's clothes the moment the door closed behind them. They were naked before they even got to the bedroom, so he scooped her up in his arms and carried her the rest of the way. He unceremoniously dumped her on the bed, laughing as she pulled him down with her. Their mouths fused together and they merged into a hot, sweaty kiss that left both of them panting.

"I should have mentioned babies weeks ago," he murmured between kisses.

"You should have," she agreed. "Apparently, it makes me hot."

"Baby, you've always been hot," he laughed. He flipped them over so she was on top of him. He ran his hands down her back, pausing to cup her curvy backside. Straddling him, she bent and kissed a trail down his stomach, hesitating slightly when she got to his erection.

Slowly, she traced her finger along his lengthy shaft, thinking she'd never done this for him before, and that she wanted to. He'd pleasured her in practically every way imaginable but she'd been too shy to do this. Tim had forced her to, and she'd thought it was disgusting, but as he kept reminding her, Dom was not Tim. Giving Dom pleasure brought her pleasure, and right now she wanted to make him feel the way he always made her feel.

"Honey, are you sure?" He was aware of all the things Tim had done to her in the bedroom, which was why he'd never pressed her to do anything like this.

"Yes…" Her voice trailed off as she ran her tongue along the tip of his penis and slowly took him into her mouth. She heard him moan, his hand digging into her hair. Encouraged, she found a rhythm he liked and ran her hands over it from the base of his shaft right up to the tip. It was incredibly satisfying to hear his groans of pleasure and she realized that with Dom she held all the power; it was the most delicious feeling in the world to mean that much to someone. Using her mouth, she licked and sucked until he was straining against her.

"I don't want to come like this," he ground out, gently tugging her hair. "I want to be inside you."

She let him pull her astride him again and he slid into her effortlessly. Her head fell back, her body melting against his in a familiar pattern. It had only been three months, but it felt like they'd been together much longer. She'd been foolish to think she could ever leave this man, no matter how much she would worry about him. He'd become her everything in such a short time, and when he made love to her she couldn't imagine these feelings with anyone else.

Feeling him moving inside of her left her breathless, her hands clutching at his shoulders. Sometimes they could move together for a long time and build to a climax gradually, but today she was unable to hold back after just a few minutes. Her body exploded around his just as he burst inside her, pumping hard before he groaned out her name. She fell against him, still reeling from such exquisite intimacy; she was completely in love with this man.

"I love you," she whispered against his cheek.

"I love you too." He wrapped his arms around her, loving the feel of her soft skin and silky hair draped all over him.

"Please don't ever stop loving me."

"I don't plan to." He kissed her then, slowly and lovingly, his tongue finding hers with gentle strokes that told her everything she needed to know.

"At some point," Dom said several hours later. "I have to eat."

She giggled, nestled under the sheets with him. She'd lost count of how many times they'd made love this afternoon. They were insatiable, and it went much deeper than just making a baby; she'd finally committed to him emotionally. She wasn't holding anything back anymore, and she wasn't going anywhere. Tim would have to kill them both first. It was that simple.

"Is that a yes-Dom-let's-go-eat giggle?" he asked after a moment.

"No, that was a this-is-so-much-fun-let's-do-it-again giggle!"

He laughed, kissing her chin. "I don't know if I have anything left—between Coach kicking my ass on the ice today and then you jumping me, I might not be able to perform again without food."

She reached under the sheets and found him already half-hard. She smirked. "I'm pretty sure I could get one more time out of you!"

"No way, you little nympho!" he teased as he slid out of bed.

"I could chase you and make you do me in the shower!" she called after him.

"That's actually a good idea." He stuck his head out the bathroom door. "We both stink of sweat and sex."

She got out of bed and padded into the bathroom, where he'd already turned on the water. She wrapped her arms around him from behind. His hands covered hers and she pressed a kiss into the middle of his back. Neither of them moved for a while, enjoying a moment of intimacy that was still somewhat new. It was almost palpable and he turned to face her, raising her chin with his hand.

"I never knew I could love anyone like this," he said.

"Me either," she whispered, her eyes meeting his in the fading light.

"We're okay now, right?" He searched her face. "You're not thinking about leaving me anymore?"

She shook her head. "I'm still scared, but I'm more afraid of being without you."

"Stop worrying." He buried his face in her hair.

2 4

THE END OF THE INITIAL PART OF TRAINING CAMP MEANT THE SIDEWINDERS WERE entering a whole new era, and Molly could feel the change in Dom almost immediately. With the big exhibition game tonight, he was completely immersed in all things hockey. Though he'd been working hard all summer, both physically and emotionally, the official start of the season meant he had to have his head completely in the game.

He was still as loving as ever, but she could feel the slight shift in his focus, the way he had hockey on his mind the last couple of days from the moment he woke up in the morning until he fell asleep at night. He'd explained it all to her, and she was glad to watch him do the thing he loved most in the world, but it was different.

After he'd left for practice Monday morning, she puttered around the apartment restlessly. She could have driven him so she could have the car, but he'd said practice wouldn't be a long one today and he'd be home before lunch since they would have to leave for the arena by five o'clock.

Her phone rang and she was happy to see Suze's name appear on the screen.

"Hey!" She settled on the couch.

"Hey." Suze seemed quiet.

"What's wrong?"

"Ugh." Suze sighed dramatically.

"What happened?"

"We had sex."

"We who?"

"Cody and I!"

"You mean, recently?"

"Last night."

"Why?"

"That's what I keep asking myself!" she grumbled. "Oh, God, it was so…"

"Good?" Molly supplied hopefully.

"Well, yeah, that." She sighed again.

"Would you just tell me what happened!"

"We had dinner, put CJ to bed, had a bottle of wine, watched a movie and then —bam! We were all over each other." Suze groaned. "And we didn't use protection! Oh, my God, what is *wrong* with us?"

"Nothing?" Molly tried not to laugh. "Come on—this has been a long time coming! I mean, how long had it been since you'd had sex?"

"Me?" Suze paused. "Probably four years."

"Four years?" Molly blinked. "Shit, Suze, how did you live with that man and not jump his bones for so long?"

"I was so mad at him for cheating on me, and I was heartbroken, and… we are such a mess."

"Did you talk afterwards?"

"No! We passed out. He got up before me and got CJ breakfast, and then he woke me up right before he left for practice to tell me he was taking CJ to school."

"Did he kiss you?"

"Yeah, but he always does that when he leaves the house, so that doesn't mean anything."

"Did he say anything *during*?"

"You mean, other than, *god baby you're so hot*?" She couldn't help but snicker, and they both giggled.

"Nothing romantic?"

"No! I told you he doesn't love me."

"You're so blind," Molly shook her head. "Everyone knows it but you."

"That's crazy." Suze sighed. "But I do want another baby, and he's a really good dad."

"Suze, you have to talk to him."

"I know. I just want him to romance me—is that too much to ask? After everything we've been through, couldn't he put just a *little* effort into it? I know we were a ready-made family after our one-night-stand, but he's still around, so why not act like he supposedly feels?"

"I think he does," Molly said softly. "I mean, the way he's so protective of you and CJ, the way he takes care of you and watches out for you? I think he shows you he loves you every single day. If I wasn't so crazy about Dom, I'd go out with Cody. I mean, if he wanted to." She giggled again and Suze joined her.

"He probably would, because he's a big fan of yours," Suze admitted. "In fact, everyone is! Toli is half in love with you, Brad and Andra treat you like family, Dom is head over heels for you, and I think Cody has a crush on you in a platonic way."

"Just like all your friends in college were in love with you, you mean?"

"I guess I never thought about it," Suze said after a moment. "I took one look at Brian and I never thought about anyone else ever again. Until the night I found the pictures on Cody's phone and realized he was sleeping around. That was when I realized I'd fallen in love with him."

"He cheated because he knew you were still pining for Brian. You have to be the one to make sure he understands you're over Brian. Otherwise, I don't think he's going to cross that line."

"You think?"

"I think."

"Ugh. He's going to be home soon and I have no idea what to say to him! You should come over!"

"No way!" Molly laughed. "Dom and I are going to be busy making a baby."

"*What?*"

"We decided to start trying to get pregnant. I'm forty—we don't have a lot of time so we stopped using condoms."

"Since when?"

"Recently?"

"And you didn't tell me?"

"I've been *busy!*" Molly said with emphasis.

"That's awesome!"

"Yeah, we'll see how awesome it is if I miscarry again." Molly bit her lip. "I hate saying that, but I've had twelve. It's a lot. If I have another one, I might be forced to have a hysterectomy and then..."

"Okay, let's not cross that bridge unless we actually come to it!" Suze interrupted firmly. "Think positive—think about all the fun you're having while you're trying."

"Well, there is *that!*" Now Molly sighed dramatically. "You have no idea—it's been crazy! We were like friggin' rabbits the first few days! Like six or seven times a day!"

"Wow, it's been a long time since I had any of *that* kind of sex!" Suze whistled enviously. "I mean, not since... well, not since I've been married."

"Again, you're going to have to give him a heads-up so he knows where you stand."

"I don't know how to do this," Suze said after a moment. "Brian was my first and only adult romance—we took one look at each other and knew! I don't know how this grown up stuff works. How do I do this?"

"I'm not sure either," Molly admitted. "But now that you've slept together again, it seems like it's time to talk about it."

"Can you imagine if I'm pregnant? We'll have a newborn and a seven-year-old!"

"Sounds wonderful!"

"You *would* think so!"

"Well, I'm going to shower and wait for Dom to get home," Molly chuckled. "Then if we have time, I think we're going car shopping before the game. He wants a convertible and I think I get the SUV."

"Nice." Suze said. "I guess I'm going to sit here and wait for Cody."

"Talk to him."

"I will."

Molly hung up and went to get ready.

Suze was still in the kitchen, checking email on her laptop, when she heard the garage door open. Feeling ridiculous about how nervous she was, she absently smoothed her hair down and took a sip of water. She hadn't been this nervous around him since the first week they'd been married. After that, they'd fallen into a routine and she'd been too heartbroken over Brian's death to think about much else.

At some point, she'd realized there was going to be a baby soon and she had to get ready to be a mom, whether she wanted to or not. Cody had been at her side from the day she'd told him she was pregnant, and he'd been the one to tell everyone. He'd been the one who'd listened to the snarky comments about him sleeping with his best friend's girl. He'd been the one who told Brad and Andra. He'd been the one who suggested they go to Toronto, far away from their old life in Boston and someplace they could start new.

His main priority from the day she told him she was pregnant was to take care of her and the baby, even though there was a chance the baby wasn't his. Cody had been a stand-up guy from the moment they got married.

The door opened and he came in, his bright blue eyes meeting hers.

"Hi." She swallowed nervously. "How was practice?"

"Good. Coach put us on two separate teams for tonight, and gave us a whole schedule of press crap we have to do before and after the exhibition."

"Are you excited?" she asked softly, walking over to meet him.

"A little." He looked down at her, unsure what to say after last night's drunken sex. He didn't know what had come over him, but it had been too damn long since he'd had sex, and she'd wanted it too. But this morning he'd snuck out like a coward, and he could see the pain in her eyes now.

"Can we talk?" Her voice was barely a whisper, but he heard her and nodded.

"Of course."

"I know you have a lot on your mind today—"

"I never have too much on my mind for you." He took her hand and led her to the family room. They sat on the couch, where they'd been sitting last night while they'd watched the movie.

"Cody, I—" She swallowed again. "I need to know what you want."

"I don't know what the means," he said slowly.

She frowned at him. "Dammit, do I have to spell it out?"

"Yes!" He ran his hand through his hair and then threw both hands up in frustration. "I've been walking on eggshells in my own house for seven years, Suze! I don't know what you want from me! You need to be the one to tell me—whatever it is!"

"I want you to act like you want me," she whispered, looking away.

"You want me to *act* like I want you, or you want me to really want you?" He asked gently, leaning over and forcing her to look at him.

"I want us to be—" She let out a curse as the doorbell sounded. "Dammit."

"Let me get rid of whoever it is," he said in irritation. "Wait for me." He threw open the door with a growl "What—" He stopped. "Sergei? What are you doing here?"

"I have to talk to you." Sergei looked exhausted, his eyes bloodshot and his hair sticking up more like Toli's usually did than his own normally well-groomed style. "Please, can I come in?"

"Cody, who is it?" Suze came around the corner and paused, her gaze landing on Sergei. "Sergei! You look terrible! What's going on?"

"Tatiana went back to Russia," he said. "She didn't even leave a note—she left while I was at camp yesterday."

"Oh, hell." Suze exchanged a look of frustration with her husband, but there was no help for that now. "Come in."

"You want a cup of coffee?" Cody asked.

"I don't know what I want. I didn't know what to do when I got back to the hotel and realized she was gone, so I just booked a flight out here." He sat down on the couch and looked at them. "What am I supposed to do?"

"Do you love her?" Suze asked.

"Of course I love her! I've always loved her! But she's my brother's girl—I wasn't supposed to love her, much less get her pregnant!" He stared at them. "What kind of person am I, sleeping with my brother's girlfriend?"

"They broke up," Cody said mildly.

"I was sleeping with her before that," Sergei said sadly. "I tried not to—I really did! But God, she's just..." His voice trailed off and he sighed. "She's everything I ever wanted. But I don't want to live in Russia—I want to play in the NHL. I came to the US to go to college because I wanted an American education, a serious college degree, and the opportunities it would afford me. I can't play hockey forever and this is where my future is—but she won't leave and now she's having my kid!" His eyes were wide and desperate, looking from one to the other.

"Did you talk when you went to Boston?" Suze asked.

"Some, but she was angry at me for the way I reacted when she announced she was pregnant. She pouted and I was too stubborn to grovel." He looked away. "I love her, but I want her to be *here*. I hate playing in the KHL." He looked so much like a surly toddler Suze almost laughed.

Instead, she took his hands in hers. "Sergei, you have to follow your dreams and your heart. If she loves you—and I think she does—she's going to give in. She can practice medicine here, but you can't play for the NHL there. Someone has to compromise."

"She wants it to be me," he said. "She wouldn't come to the US for Toli—why would she come for me?"

"She wasn't in love with Toli," Cody said.

"Boston offered me a contract," Sergei said miserably. "I told them I would need a few days to get my affairs in order in Russia, but I don't need to go back there for anything except her!"

"Have you talked to Toli?"

"No." Sergei looked down. "I don't know what to say! *Hey, by the way, sorry I fell in love with your girl?*"

"He knows that and he's already forgiven you," Suze said. "All you have to do now is tell Tatiana how you feel and ask her to be with you."

"You should have gone to Russia, not come here," Cody said. "You need to talk to her."

"I need to fix things with my brother," Sergei said. "Tatiana and I left for Boston without really talking things out with him, and I have to fix something."

"Toli and Drake are down at some radio station doing press this afternoon," Cody said. "You'll probably have to wait until after the game to talk to him, but you can come out to the arena with me, if you want."

"Yeah, maybe I'll do that. But I'll stay out of the way until after the game—I don't want to get in his head before the game."

"Why don't you go up to the guest room and take a nap?" Suze suggested. "You look tired. Cody can get your bag out of the car and I'll make sure you have something pressed and ready before the game tonight."

Sergei smiled at her gratefully. "Thanks, Suze."

"Go on upstairs. We'll wake you up in enough time to get a shower before we head out."

"Thanks." He nodded at both of them and then trudged up the stairs.

Cody took Suze's arm as soon as they heard the guest room door close. "We're not finished with our conversation."

"No." She shook her head. "But this isn't the time—Sergei's upstairs, you have your first public appearance as a Sidewinder tonight and CJ is going to be home soon---he's bursting at the seams with excitement."

"Suze." He took her by the shoulders and turned her to face him. "I need you to tell me what you want from me. Just tell me that much. I can't go into the game tonight if things aren't okay with us."

She smiled wanly, looking up at him. "I need to know if there's a chance of us ever being a real couple? I want to have more babies and I want—" She started when he bent his head and kissed her, his mouth devouring hers in a way he'd never done before. His hands dug into her hair and he pulled her so close she could barely breathe before he abruptly released her.

"Does that feel like someone who wants to be a real couple?" His eyes were blazing with intensity.

"Yes." She blinked up at him.

"Does it feel like a guy who would want to have more babies with you?"

"Yeah."

"Then there's your answer."

"Um, okay. You think you could do that some more?"

He laughed. "I've been waiting seven years to hear you say that." He scooped her up in his arms and carried her up the stairs.

SUZE PICKED UP MOLLY AT SIX. THEY WERE BOTH WEARING JEANS AND Sidewinders jerseys with Cody and Dom's names and numbers respectively. It would be Molly's first live hockey game, not to mention her first hockey game as part of the so-called wives and girlfriends club. She was nervous about hanging out with some of these women, but Dom and Suze had both promised her it would be okay. He didn't give a damn what anyone thought about their age difference, and Suze was a seasoned NHL wife who could give as well as she got; she would have Molly's back.

Pulling into the gate where guests of the players parked, Molly looked around the large arena with interest. Though she'd dropped Dom off and picked him up a few times this week, this was a new arena that had only recently been built for the team, so it wasn't a place she knew much about. The building was large and imposing, and she felt a moment of pride that Dom was a part of this historical team and whatever they were about to accomplish. She'd never felt anything like this before and she had to admit she was starting to get into the whole idea of being the significant other of a hockey player.

"What are you thinking?" Suze asked her as they parked and she pushed the button that lifted the hood of her convertible.

"That this is so cool!" Molly almost felt like a teenager again.

"It is," Suze nodded. "I've just been doing this so long—since my freshman year of college—I'm not as easily impressed. Although this new expansion team is a pretty big deal."

"I've watched a ton of YouTube this week while Dom was at camp, so I feel like I have a much better perspective of the game," Molly said, getting out of the car and following Suze to the gate. "But you're going to have to help me not say anything stupid and give me a clue when I'm supposed to cheer, because I still don't completely understand everything going on."

"No worries," Suze nodded. "I know this game inside and out—it'll be fun watching with someone who isn't jaded!"

"I really appreciate you passing CJ off on Andra so you could have my back tonight!"

"He'll be around," she laughed. "But he'll be up in the owner's box, so it's actually a little safer. Andra is so excited to have him in her life, she practically bounced up and down when I asked her if she wanted to take him to his first Sidewinders game."

Molly laughed too. "I can't wait to squish his little face when I see him," she said. "I'm sure he's excited."

"He makes you look tame. He talked from the minute I picked him up from school until I dropped him off at Andra's. He was sad he didn't get to see his Dad, but I think Andra's taking him into the locker room before they play so he can give Cody his usual pre-game hug. It's a thing they've done for as long as he's been going to games."

"That's awesome."

Suze smiled at the attendants as they walked through the underground area of the arena and into the VIP elevator. Molly looked around, taking everything in even as they talked.

"So this elevator takes us where?"

"Up to the level where our section is. We also have access to the owner's box, but not all the players' wives do—we do because Cody is going to be the Captain, plus my kid is up there with Andra."

"So when will they announce the alternate captains? Do you know?"

"Cody thinks at the first regular season game. In the interim, there are four of them wearing A's. Coach already told Cody he was going to name him Captain, but they won't make it official until opening night."

"Do you think Dom will get to wear an A?"

"I think so," Suze nodded, stepping out of the elevator and looking around. This was obviously her first time here too, but she'd been to so many of Cody's games, at so many different arenas, and they were all set up similarly.

"Okay, so who do think I have to watch out for?" Molly asked her. "You must know at least a few of these women."

"Actually, not really. We don't have anyone from Toronto here and I never really made friends with too many wives. I know a lot of them by sight or reputation, but I'm not really friends with them. Sergei will be sitting with us, though, so that should up the fun factor."

Molly frowned. "He's back? Does Toli know?"

"Toli knows because he got him the seat, but Sergei purposely didn't talk to him because he didn't want them to argue before his first game."

"Is Tatiana here?"

"No." Suze shook her head and told her what Sergei had told them.

"So she just left and went back to Russia?" Molly scowled. "I really dislike her!"

"I think she's just as confused as Sergei, and probably a little scared too since she's pregnant by a guy who hasn't exactly given her the warm fuzzies about the baby. She might be financially able to care for a kid, but that doesn't mean she wants to do it alone."

"The thought of getting pregnant again kind of scares me," Molly admitted as they walked. "The longest I've ever carried a baby was 15 weeks. That was my second pregnancy, which was a really long time ago, and since then it's never been more than 10 weeks. Now that Dom and I are trying, I'm as scared as I am excited."

"Well, this time no one is going to hurt you, and you're going to have the best care possible."

"We're going to L.A. to talk to a doctor about harvesting my eggs in a couple of days. Dom already told Brad he would need a day off and although he grumbled, Brad understands I can't wait until next summer at my age."

"If you can't carry a baby, I'll carry one for you," Suze said with a grin. "I just need to have one of Cody's first."

"You will?" Molly asked.

"Sure. Why not? I didn't mind being pregnant, and although I had about four weeks of morning sickness, my pregnancy was pretty easy."

"What about giving birth?"

Suze shrugged. "Ah, what's a few hours of pain for a beautiful baby at the end?"

"You're a good friend!" Molly felt tears threatening as she hugged her.

Suze hugged her back. "Come on, let's go meet these bitches and see what's what!"

Molly laughed. They stepped out into the aisle next to their seats and Molly's eyes widened at the fabulous view of the ice. It was huge, bigger than she expected for some reason, and there were already tons of people in the arena, talking and cheering. Lights flashed from the ceiling and the scoreboard, showing pictures of the team and support staff. Music was blaring from the speakers and there was an electricity in the air she'd never felt before. Thinking back, she'd never been to a professional sporting event. They didn't have any major league teams here in Las Vegas and of course she'd never travelled, so this was the most exciting thing she'd ever seen.

"Wow," she breathed, looking at Suze. "This is awesome."

"Yeah, it's pretty impressive." Suze looked around too. "Hey, there's Tiff!" She called out her name and Tiff waved them over.

"Hey, you guys!" Tiff got up and hugged them both. "I'm so glad you're here! It's going to be so much fun tonight!"

"This is my first-ever hockey game," Molly told her. "I have no idea what to expect."

"Well, it's just an exhibition between everyone who was invited to camp, but since this is an expansion team and it's supposed to be a full house, I think it'll be a lot of fun."

"I'm psyched." Molly looked around again, taking everything in.

"You guys, this is Jeannie," Tiff motioned to the woman sitting next to her. "She's engaged to Matt Forbes, who's going to be on the team with us."

"Hi!" Suze gave the woman a friendly smile, always willing to give someone a chance, although she usually remained aloof. You just never knew what you were going to get when you met the other wives, and you had to be careful who you got too close to. She'd learned the hard way her first year in Toronto. "I'm Suzanne— Suze to my friends!"

"Hi!" The woman looked to be in her late twenties, with curly brown hair that fell to her shoulders and light blue eyes. She was pretty, but didn't appear to be overly concerned with her looks, as she wore jeans and her fiancé's jersey, minimal makeup and no jewelry other than her engagement ring.

"I'm Molly," Molly took her cue from Suze and smiled too.

The women all sat down again and began chatting about the game. Tiff seemed to know everyone and everything going on around them, and she would either call out greetings or whisper something to their group. One of the women, Rachel Kennedy, was a fairly well-known actress now dating a player named Jamie Teller.

They'd been all over the tabloids after a video of them having sex made its way around the Internet. Supposedly, Brad had warned Jamie if there was so much as another hint of that kind of scandal, he wouldn't be in Las Vegas next season. However, while he was a center who didn't score a lot of points, he had amazing record winning face-offs, and that was something the team needed.

They watched Rachel move to her seat and sit down stiffly. She was obviously not comfortable in this atmosphere and seemed anxious to stay off everyone's radar. She was incredibly beautiful, Molly thought. Petite and probably a size zero, her auburn hair was swept back away from her face and parted on the side, showing off her big violet eyes. She had flawless skin, refined features and wore her makeup effectively. She was dressed down, though, in jeans like the rest of them, although she wasn't wearing Jamie's jersey. Instead, she wore a generic Sidewinders t-shirt.

"Should we invite her to sit with us?" Tiff whispered to Suze, who shrugged.

"Why?" she whispered back.

"Why not? Her fame doesn't scare me!" Tiff got up and approached the other woman. "Hi!" She sank into the seat next to her. "I'm Tiffany Marcus, Coach Marcus's wife." She held out her hand.

Rachel turned to her slowly, making no attempt to conceal the way she looked her up and down. Apparently she passed muster, because after a moment, she shook her hand and nodded. "I'm Rachel."

"Would you like to sit with us? We're all new to the team and Las Vegas, so I'm trying to make sure everyone gets to know each other."

Rachel glanced back at the others and then back at Tiffany. "I'm trying really hard not to call any attention to myself. Jamie is already in deep shit over that sex tape, and my job is to support him without making a nuisance of myself."

Tiff laughed. "Honey, we're hockey wives—we make nuisances of ourselves just by existing. But our group, this group at least, has no desire to make any headlines or cause any trouble. So if you'd like to hang out with the boring faction of the team, that would be us."

Rachel actually smiled. "Sure. I'm not going to be able to make all the games because we're shooting my show right now, but I wanted to be here tonight and for the home opener in October, so it will be nice to know some of you." She followed Tiff back to her original seat and Tiff introduced her.

"Are you going to stay in L.A. or will you move here?" Tiff asked.

"I'll be commuting back and forth for now. I'll keep my condo in L.A., but we're going to start looking at houses here. It depends on what happens this season, though. We don't want to buy a house if he's not going to stay."

"It's a great place to live," Molly said.

"Molly's a native," Suze laughed. "She actually thinks the desert is cool."

Molly stuck her tongue out at her. "Go ahead and move back to your winter wonderland in Toronto," she laughed. "I'll be here in shorts and a t-shirt while you're shoveling snow."

"Okay, you got me there." Suze grinned. "I'm not going anywhere that cold ever again!"

"Are you one of the coach's wives?" Rachel asked Molly.

Molly glanced at the woman and raised her eyebrows. "No, I'm Dom Gianni's girlfriend."

"The enforcer," Rachel said with a small smile. "And he's got the cougar thing going on—very cool."

Molly wasn't sure if she'd just been insulted or not, and she glanced at Suze with an unspoken plea for help.

"Actually, she's got our bad boy so settled down, I don't even know if he's capable of being an enforcer anymore," Suze said.

Rachel grinned. "There is nothing wrong with being a cougar," she said. "It wasn't meant to be a dig. I think it's awesome—in my business, by the time you're thirty-five they want you to play a grandmother, so I'm all about staying as young as possible, inside and out."

The women fell into easy conversation after that, and before long, the guys were taking the ice. Molly searched for Dom and finally spotted the number 16, clapping her hands together with delight when they introduced him.

"He looks huge out there!" she whispered to Suze.

"They're three inches taller in their skates!" Suze whispered back. She'd spotted Cody immediately, familiar with his body under the uniform and the way he moved on the ice. He wore the number 27 and she smiled to herself as she thought about their afternoon quickie before she had to iron Sergei's dress shirt and then leave to pick up CJ. Though it was too quick for her after so many years without sex, there was no helping that today. He'd needed to rest before the game and she'd needed to pick up CJ, but there was the promise of a lot more where that came from.

"Hello, ladies!" Sergei slid into a seat in the row behind the women and grinned at them. "Can I sit right in the middle of you?"

They all laughed and moved to make room for him between Tiff and Suze. He grinned like a cat that had swallowed a canary and he waved down at his brother, who had just been introduced and looked up in their general direction. He lifted his stick in acknowledgement and Sergei nodded his head.

"Sergei, this is Rachel, Jamie Teller's girlfriend," Suze introduced them.

"We watch *Vampire Legend* on Netflix in Russia," he said, nodding at her. "The guys are dying to find out what happened after last season's finale. They've got to wait a whole year!"

"Everyone dies," Rachel said with a wink and they laughed.

"That's a bummer," he said, flashing his most winning smile. Women tended to love him, and he knew it. He was a really good-looking guy, his eyes bright and blue, with thick, wavy blond hair. While Toli's teeth were crooked and gave him a look of perpetual mischief, Sergei's were almost perfectly straight, making him seem older and more mature. Toli was an inch taller, but Sergei was twenty pounds heavier, all of it muscle. They were built the same way, though, with long arms and legs, lean shoulders and muscular torsos. From the back, they were almost identical, and on the ice, you had to know them really well to be able to tell them apart.

They'd always been close, until Sergei started sleeping with Tatiana, and guilt weighed heavily on him now, especially tonight. He'd purposely avoided talking to Toli before the game because he was afraid it would affect his level of play if they argued, but at the same time, he needed to clear the air. Even if it meant giving up Tatiana, he couldn't imagine living the rest of his life being on the outs with his brother.

Realizing Molly was talking to him, he leaned over. "I'm sorry, I didn't hear you?"

"Did you talk to Toli?" she repeated softly.

"No." He got up and moved down several seats so he could sit on her other side. "I was afraid we would argue, so I wanted to wait until after the game. I texted him I was coming and asked if I could stay the night so we could talk."

"Oh, good," Molly smiled. "He's been really out of sorts since you and Tatiana left for Boston."

"I don't like fighting with him," Sergei admitted. "Believe it or not, we're very close. The last couple of years have been hard, but I'm going to try to make things right."

"So she went back to Russia?"

"Yup." He sighed. "I have to talk with Toli before I talk to her, though. Even though I'm crazy about her, I don't know that she truly returns my feelings, and I can't be with her if it means losing my brother."

"What about the baby?"

"The last thing she said to me before she left was that she probably wasn't going to have it." He looked troubled. "But I know she wouldn't have an abortion without talking to me. She was trying to piss me off, and succeeded, but she wouldn't do that."

"I'm glad you're here," Molly said softly. "I can hear the hurt in his voice when we talk, and I don't think it's because of her."

"I'll wait for him by his car in the lot," Sergei said. "And we'll straighten this out."

"I'm glad." She touched his arm. "He misses you."

"I miss him too." He smiled back at her, thinking she was a lot prettier than he'd initially thought. The more he talked to her, the more he understood why Dom and Toli were both so attracted to her. Though he and Toli hadn't spoken much when he'd been here last week, he got the impression his older brother would go out with this woman if given a chance. Unfortunately, she had eyes for no one but Dom and that left Toli firmly in the friend zone.

"Stand up for the national anthem!" Tiff called out.

Everyone got to their feet and Molly watched proudly as Dom stood in the middle of the ice with his teammates, many of them singing. She was happy to see him in his world, eager to start the most exciting season of his career. Personally, she'd never felt so loved or content, as if everything had simply fallen into place. She was positive he felt the same way; their coming together had been cathartic for both of them. He was moving past his grief, and she was walking away from a lifetime of abuse.

As the anthem ended, the girls started to cheer, yelling at the top of their lungs. The guys skated off to their separate benches. Dom was playing on Cody's team, with Jamie, Drake, and a bunch of guys no one knew, with Karl in goal. Toli was on the other team, with Matt, Zakk Cloutier, more guys they didn't yet know, and Marco in net. Dom's team represented the home team, wearing royal blue jerseys with black and gold accents. The other team wore their away jerseys, white with royal blue, black and gold accents. The colors were distinct and eye-catching, Molly thought, watching the activity on the ice.

Things happened quickly, and she struggled to keep up with the action once the first puck was dropped. She watched intently, but couldn't seem to keep her eye on the puck. How on earth did these guys move so fast? They were all in great shape, but watching them fly down the ice was mesmerizing. She'd never seen anything like it.

"You look flustered," Suze whispered to her.

"It's so fast," Molly breathed. "I can barely keep up."

"It's exciting. I've always loved watching the game. Even before Brian, I was a big hockey fan, which was strange for a girl from South Carolina. But something about it always turned me on."

"I think it turns me on too," Molly snickered. "Although those uniforms are kind of dorky."

"I just think about what's *under* those uniforms," Suze said with a grin and they laughed.

The game finished too soon, with the home team beating the away team. The guys seemed to be having a good time on the ice, and when it was over many of them handed out pucks or sticks to fans in the crowd. They were trying to establish a rapport with them, and this was one of many events they would be holding to do just that.

SERGEI STOOD OUT IN THE PARKING LOT NEXT TO TOLI'S SUV, AND GLANCED AT the time on his phone. It was getting late, but he hadn't wanted to get caught up in the media storm going on after the game, especially since he and Toli hadn't talked yet. He was happier to wait for him out here. It also gave him the opportunity to sneak a cigarette.

Tatiana had been trying to get him to quit for years, and he was down to only a couple a day, but he'd started smoking at twelve and the truth was it calmed him when he was nervous. He barely smoked at all during the season, but over the summer he picked it back up. So far, it didn't affect his ability to perform, but he figured his smoking days were numbered now that he was going to be a dad; his gut told him Tatiana was having the baby.

Checking his phone again, he pulled up his email as he took a long drag from the cigarette he'd lit. Nothing from Tatiana. He sighed heavily. He missed her, but he was tired of being caught between her and Toli. Although she didn't want to marry Toli, she didn't seem to want to completely break away either. Sergei had gone after her like a horny teenager when she'd confessed she didn't love Toli two years ago, and she'd been more than willing to fall into bed with him.

She'd promised him she was calling off the wedding, but it had taken her more than six months to do it, and then when Toli had told her he was moving back to the U.S. she'd actually told him she would consider marrying him if he came back. It drove him crazy to think she was playing games with them, and he couldn't figure out what she was doing. He didn't understand her and was tired of feeling like a fool.

Once he talked to Toli, he was going to give her an ultimatum. Either she wanted to be with him or she didn't, but he was done waiting and he wasn't going to stay in Russia. Although he would have preferred to be married to the mother of his child, he would find a way to take care of his kid no matter what happened with them.

He took another drag of his cigarette and guiltily put it out. He couldn't smoke once there was a kid in the picture, and even if he lived thousands of miles away, he still wanted to be a good role model. Assuming Tatiana hadn't already had an abortion. The thought made him a little sick, so he was startled when he heard footsteps behind him.

"Toli?" A deep voice called out in the darkness and Sergei turned. He and Toli were often confused, especially from the back, and he expected to see one of the players. Instead, he saw a uniformed security guard squinting at him.

"Can I help you?" Sergei frowned slightly. He didn't see the stun gun until he felt the excruciating jolt of electricity in his chest. He slid to the ground thinking he was going to kill someone for this. The pain was horrible, and he struggled to breathe through it. Somebody had shot him with a fucking stun gun and he thought his insides were going to explode. He tensed as he saw the man leaning over him, but he couldn't control his limbs. He saw the man's fist moving towards his face, but was helpless to defend himself. Then everything went black.

M olly woke up to the smell of fresh coffee and rolled over, stretching lazily. She and Dom had come home from the exhibition game last night and made slow, sexy love until she'd fallen asleep in his arms. Every morning when she opened her eyes, she looked forward to seeing his face and smiled now as he came into the bedroom with a steaming mug of coffee.

"You are the best boyfriend ever," she said hoarsely. She'd screamed so loud at the game she'd almost lost her voice.

"You sound pretty sexy when you're hoarse."

She rolled her eyes as she sat up and took the coffee. "Oh, that's good. Thank you."

"You're welcome." He sat on the edge of the bed, his long hair tousled and sexy. He'd showered when they got home last night so he'd slept with wet hair and now it was sticking up all over. She reached up to smooth down a few errant pieces and he made a face at her.

"Is it bad?"

"Nah, it's pretty hot." She winked.

He chuckled. "I think you're biased."

"Maybe I am." She raised her eyebrows. "You got a problem with me thinking you're hot?"

"Not at all." He leaned over to brush his lips over hers, his tongue briefly flicking her bottom lip before he pulled away. "But right now, I have to get dressed and get to a meeting. Some of the guys that are being sent down to the AHL were called in this morning and let go. So we're having a meeting with everyone that's left. There are still a few guys who won't make the cut, but they'll get to play the official pre-season games first."

"Aren't you already on the team?" She frowned. "I'm confused."

"Basically all of us that are already playing at the NHL level have contracts and we're on the team. However, there's always a chance that a younger guy from the AHL or even one of the rookies who were drafted this year, could earn a spot. So no matter what your contract says or how much experience you have, you still have to earn your place on the team. I'm pretty sure the core guys are all good—me, Cody, Drake, Marco, Karl, Jamie Teller, Zakk Cloutier, Matt Forbes—but there are a few guys who are going to have to fight for it. Why do you think Cody and I work out so hard over the summer? If you don't, you're going to get your ass handed to you during the regular season."

"Does it worry you?"

"Nah. It's what I've been doing since I was sixteen. Besides, now I have you, so hockey or no hockey, my life is pretty damn good." He kissed her one last time before getting up and going into the bathroom.

"What time will you be home?" she called after him.

"Not sure," he called back. "Probably lunch time. The first pre-season game is tomorrow night and Coach doesn't want to tire us out or risk injuries. I'll call if I'm going to be late."

"Okay." She got up and pulled on one of his t-shirts. It was almost a dress on her but she loved smelling his aftershave. Taking her coffee cup, she took it with her out to the kitchen and sat on one of the stools. She checked her phone for messages and was disappointed to see Toli hadn't called or texted. She'd been dying to hear what he and Sergei had talked about, and she knew he would tell her. When the guys teased him that he gossiped with Molly just like a woman, Toli always just laughed.

"I've got to go," Dom said, kissing her cheek as he brushed past her.

"Hey, tell Toli to call me after practice!" she laughed. "I'm dying to hear what Sergei said!"

Dom rolled his eyes. "I swear to God, you and Suze are going to cost him his man card!"

Molly laughed again. "I doubt it—he's just more in touch with his feminine side than you are."

He shook his head, grinning. "Love you!"

"Love you too!" She was still smiling as the door clicked shut behind him. She finished her coffee and an English muffin, and then got up to start getting ready. She usually met Suze on Tuesdays for yoga, so she pulled on yoga pants, a tank top and socks. She brushed her teeth, put her hair in a ponytail and stuck her backup cell phone in the small pocket on the inside of her yoga pants. She put her regular phone in her purse and grabbed her keys, which now included the keys to the SUV as well as Dom's new convertible.

She'd never heard of an Audi R8 until they'd looked at it, and she'd almost fainted when she saw the $119,000 price tag, but Dom hadn't seemed bothered at all. He'd simply given the man a credit card for the down payment and made arrangements for his accountant to handle the rest. She didn't know if she would ever get used to spending that kind of money, but Dom had laughed and told her she'd better. So now he drove the fancy convertible to practice and she drove his SUV. He'd offered to let her drive the R8 but she wasn't comfortable driving something that expensive or that fast. Not yet anyway.

Yoga lasted an hour and they packed up to go once it was finished. Normally they ran errands together or went for lunch, but Suze had a meeting at CJ's school, so Molly got back in the SUV and headed towards the grocery store. She usually shopped at Trader Joe's, but today she just wanted to grab a few things and get home to wait for Dom. She got what she needed and was in and out in less than five minutes.

Balancing the bag of groceries and her purse in one hand, she pulled out her keys with the other. She hit the button to unlock the doors as she heard a familiar voice hiss in her ear, "Keep walking or I'll kill you right here." She felt something hard and metal against her side and forced herself not to react.

"Tim, what are you doing?"

"You need to shut up and keep walking, or one phone call will put an end to your hockey player boyfriend."

"What are you talking about?" she cried, turning to face him. The next thing she knew something burned in her side. It was so painful she couldn't move, though her body tensed up so badly she thought she might be having a seizure. Once the initial pain stopped, she was so weak she couldn't stop herself from sliding into his arms. He picked her up and tossed her into the back seat of the SUV, taking her keys and purse from her as he got into the driver's seat. She tried to fight against the pain when the car began pulling onto the street. The pain was like nothing she'd ever felt before and she was afraid she was going to black out. *No, no, no,* she thought helplessly before her eyes started to close.

DOM WAS THE LAST GUY TO SKATE OFF THE ICE AFTER PRACTICE. HE HANDED HIS stick to one of the equipment managers and walked back to the dressing room feeling like it had been a good day. They'd worked on plays and tried out a few different lines before coach had called it a day. They would have an optional morning skate tomorrow, and then go up against the L.A. Kings in their first-ever pre-season game in the evening. He couldn't wait to get out there for real; it had been a long summer and he was anxious to get back into the game he loved.

He sank onto the bench and pulled off his skates, wondering what Molly was doing. Remembering what she'd asked him, he looked up and found Toli towel-drying his hair.

"Hey, Molly said you're supposed to call her," he called out. "She wants to know what happened with you and Sergei last night—*you fucking girl.*"

Toli instinctively shot him a bird but then glanced up with confusion. "Sergei did not come over last night—there is nothing to tell."

"What?" Dom paused. "Are you sure? Cause she and Sergei sat together during the game and they talked. She said he was anxious to clear the air with you —he wouldn't talk to Tatiana until after he made things right with you."

Toli frowned. "Really?"

"Just call her!" Dom shrugged. "That's what she told me."

Toli dug his phone out of his locker and froze. "Dom." His voice was quiet and stilted.

"What?" Dom looked up in annoyance; he hated being in the middle of this situation with Toli and Sergei; he was close to both of them.

"Check your phone."

"What?" Dom gave him a funny look.

"Dom, your phone!" Toli barked out the order loudly this time, making a couple of the guys around them jump.

"What the hell, Toli?" Dom reached for his phone and hit the button to turn it on. Then he froze too. "No, fucking no." His voice came out in a ragged whisper.

"You have the message?" Toli asked.

Dom felt the blood rushing to his head. "*Fuck!*"

"Do not panic." Toli was yanking on his jeans.

Dom turned and ripped off his jersey, tugging at the equipment he wore underneath.

"Hey, guys!" Brad, Dave and the new assistant coach, Yvon Gagner, came into the dressing room. "It was a good practice today. I think we're going to look good tomorrow against the Kings. Remember, win or lose, this is a learning experience for all of us…"

Dom wasn't even listening as he yanked at his clothes. *666.* The text had been sitting there for over an hour while he'd been trying to be a god damned team player, lingering on the ice. He'd programmed Molly's backup phone so she could send out a text to him, Toli and Suze by only having to punch a few keys. It was a group text with a pre-assigned speed dial number so she would only have to hit two buttons to bring it up, type in *666* and send. Three people would get the message, and hopefully at least one of them would see it immediately. They'd even done a test run to make sure it was easy and worked.

"Dom!" Cody came running in, his eyes wild. "Suze just called—what's going on?"

Dom realized Brad had stopped talking and was now staring at them.

"Coach, it's Molly!" Dom had pulled on shorts and a t-shirt and was throwing everything out of his bag as he struggled to find his keys. "He's got her. Jesus fucking Christ, he found her!" Dom pounded his fist into the wall in frustration.

"Easy, son." Brad moved to his side, and stopped his arm from swinging again with a firm but gentle grip. "Dom, look at me!"

"Coach, that lunatic *has her.*" Dom could barely choke out the words.

"How do you know?" Brad's eyes were alert but compassionate. They'd all come to love Molly this summer and though he didn't remember all the details, he knew Molly came from an abusive marriage.

"We had a prearranged text message set up if anything ever happened, and we just got it." He was practically hyperventilating as he imagined what Tim could be doing to her.

"We go *now!*" Toli was already moving towards the door.

"Wait a minute!" Yvon Gagner spoke sharply. "What are you talking about? You guys can't just leave!"

"I'm sorry, Coach." Dom gripped his keys. "We have to go."

"Wait for me!" Cody called out, pulling on a shirt.

"What are you boys thinking?" Brad asked, looking around.

"We're going to go get her!" Dom said gruffly.

"You can't go blindly into this—especially if he's dangerous!" Brad looked nervous but was trying not to show it; he'd lived through something like this once before with these boys and he didn't want to go through losing someone close to him ever again.

"We have to go…" Dom met his coach's gaze squarely. "We will *not* be too late this time!"

"Wait, what's going on? Did something happen to Molly?" Drake Riser had been across the room, but stood up now, his amber eyes narrowing with concern. "Do you need backup?"

"Yes!" Cody yelled, stepping into his sneakers.

"I'm coming too," Karl, who was already dressed, stood up and grabbed his wallet.

"I don't understand what's going on." Marco looked around the room, clearly annoyed. "You're going to go do, what, exactly? Your girlfriend is with her ex and you're going to ride in like the cavalry?"

"Fuck you, Rousch!" Dom didn't have time to deal with idiots like Marco right now.

"Seriously, Martensson?" Marco called out to Karl. "You think going out and kicking some poor schmuck's ass is going to help your career? You don't ever want to be the starter here, do you?"

Karl turned briefly, his blue eyes darkening dangerously, but he didn't say anything.

"Shut up, Marco," Brad fixed the redheaded goalie with a glare. "You don't know what you're talking about."

"Where the hell are these guys going?" Yvon demanded, his bald head glistening with sweat. "We have a game tomorrow. We don't have time for this personal nonsense and we're in the middle of a meeting. If you walk out that door—"

"Enough, Yvon." Brad held up a hand. "Go on, boys. Go get her and bring her home."

"Sergei isn't picking up his phone either," Toli said from the doorway. "Do you think…" His voice trailed off.

"He was supposed to wait for you by your car last night," Cody said, looking even more nervous.

"He was not there!" Toli looked angrier than Dom had ever seen him. He muttered something in Russian that made the only other Russian player in the room look up, startled.

"We have to go!" Dom was finally moving. "That specific code means she's at their old house."

"Do you know where it is?" Cody asked.

"Bet your ass I do." Dom nodded then swung his gaze back to Brad. "Coach, can you have Mr. Finch make some calls to the powers that be in Henderson? This might get ugly. Do you have all the information? I think they're at his house, but we won't know for sure until we get there."

"I'll take care of it." Brad moved towards his office with Dave on his heels and Yvon still glaring after them.

"We need to take your SUV and Toli's truck—mine is only a two-seater," Dom said to Cody. "I'll text you the address, Toli, in case we get separated, but try to stay close."

They were moving down the hall now.

"Wait up!" Zakk Cloutier, the twenty-two-year-old from the University of North Dakota, came down the hall after them. He wore jeans, a camouflage t-shirt and biker boots. His arms were covered in tattoos and his blond hair was partly shaved on one side and hung down to his shoulder on the other. He looked like he belonged in a motorcycle gang instead of a hockey rink.

"What's going on?" he asked, catching up to them. "Can I help? Where I'm from, we don't let our friends take care of trouble alone."

"You don't need to get involved, kid," Cody said. "This could be some serious stuff—"

"I'm pretty sure I can handle myself, whatever it is." Zakk looked at them, his green eyes moving from one to the other. "If one of your wives is in trouble, I'm in."

There was no time to argue, and frankly, Dom had no idea what to expect. For all he knew, there would be a slew of armed police in front of the house ready to shoot them. If this kid was willing to have their back, he wasn't going to say no. "Come on then!" he said as he turned and jogged out to the parking lot. He got in beside Cody, and Zakk climbed into the back seat. Drake and Karl went with Toli, and they pulled onto the street going well above the speed limit.

"Where does he live?" Cody asked, stopping at the corner.

"We need to get on the 515 south," Dom said in a tight voice. It was taking all of his self-control not to lose his mind. The idea Tim had found her scared him to death, but the idea she might be hurt right now made him want to kill someone. It had been ages since he'd felt this level of sheer fury, and the only thing keeping him from breaking everything in sight was the fact Molly needed him. If he lost control, she might die, and that wasn't going to happen. Not this time.

"Someone needs to call Suze," Cody said. "She needs to know what's going on."

Dom picked up Cody's phone and hit the speed dial, putting her on speakerphone.

"What's happening?" Suze shrieked into the phone. "She sent the 666 message. That means he took her to their old house! Dom, hurry!"

"We're heading there now." Dom said. "Cody's driving."

"You need to call Andra," Cody called out. "Tell her Brad is supposed to be trying to get Lonnie Finch to call his contacts in Henderson. We have no idea what we're going to find. None of us is armed, so we're potentially showing up at a gun fight with nothing but our fists—see if she knows anyone important she can call."

"Please be careful," Suze whispered into the phone.

"It's going to be okay, baby," Cody spoke with more confidence than he felt. "I love you, okay? Remember that."

"Cody..." She let his name linger before taking a deep breath. "I love you too. Both of you. Please take care of each other."

"We're going to be fine, we're going to get Molly, and we'll call you soon." Dom disconnected and took several slow, steady breaths.

"So, is this about your wife's ex?" Zakk spoke from the back seat, breaking the silence since he had no idea what was going on.

"Technically, my girlfriend's husband," Dom corrected mildly. "Her divorce has been in limbo for months—I'm going to fire that sonofabitch lawyer the minute we get done with this!"

"One thing at a time," Cody said. He picked up speed as they got onto the highway. He could see Toli right behind him and watched his speedometer creep past 70, 80 and then 90.

Cody's phone rang and Dom put it on speakerphone again. "Yeah?" Cody called out.

"It's Brad." His booming voice seemed to vibrate through the vehicle. "Just got off the phone with Lonnie's secretary, and he's on the phone with the mayor of Henderson right now. Hopefully you'll have backup from someone the mayor trusts, but if not..." He let his voice trail off.

"This is on me, Coach," Dom spoke with finality. "My girl, my situation—I'm not going to let any of the other guys get hurt. If we can't handle this like reasonable adults, then I'm going in alone."

"The hell you are!" Cody spat at him. "Molly's one of us now!"

"You have a family to think about!" Dom yelled back. "Somebody needs to be able to take care of Suze and CJ!"

"Coach will take care of them!" Cody was yelling too.

"Stop it!" Brad was yelling through the phone. "You do what you have to do to get Molly out of there, but if it's too late, you get the hell out of dodge. Do you understand me?"

"We got it, Coach." Dom said after a slight hesitation. "We're out." He disconnected and looked back at Zakk. "We're talking about a bunch of dirty cops, a wife beater and possibly a psychopath. You sure you're up for this?"

"Ready or not," Zakk said with a small shrug, "I'm not turning back now."

28

MOLLY CAME AWAKE SLOWLY, HER BODY ACHING IN WAYS SHE'D ALMOST forgotten. Her side still burned where the stun gun had shocked her. Her legs felt like lead and her head was pounding, but she didn't dare open her eyes yet. She listened intently for any signs Tim was with her, but she couldn't hear anything.

The last thing she remembered was pulling out her phone in the back seat of the SUV and sending out the *666* text. She'd heard Tim call someone and tell him he'd gotten her and was bringing her to the house. Though she'd been in a lot of pain, barely able to move, she'd managed to get the phone out of her yoga pants and quietly send the text before stuffing it back in. She'd slipped in and out of consciousness after that, but she remembered Tim carrying her out of the SUV and dumping her on the floor. He'd been screaming at her, kicking and shaking her. Luckily, she'd blacked out.

She had no idea how much time had passed, but she clung to the hope that even if Dom and Toli were still at practice, Suze at least had seen the text and was letting them know something had happened.

"Molly!" She heard her name in a hushed whisper. "Molly, you need to fight through the pain and wake up! I don't know how much time we have!"

Molly's eyes opened when she recognized Sergei's voice.

"Shh," he said, still whispering. He was sitting on one of their kitchen chairs, his hands tied behind him. There was an ugly bruise around one of his eyes, and dried blood under his nose and on his shirt. His shirt was torn and he had lost one shoe, but otherwise he looked better than she felt. "Tim went outside—he's been trying to wake you for half an hour."

"You're hurt," she whispered.

"I'm fine," he said quickly. "He thinks I'm Toli."

"Oh no!" She tried to sit up but a splitting pain in her arm almost made her cry out.

"How are you?" he asked. "He dropped you on the floor pretty hard and I think he broke your arm when he was trying to smack you awake."

"It hurts like it's broken," she said, swallowing.

"Do you know where we are?"

"This is my old house."

"Does anyone know this place?"

"Dom does—I gave him the address and he memorized how to get here, just in case."

"Do you think they know we're gone?"

"I sent out a text before I passed out."

"He took your phone and smashed it—I saw him." Sergei frowned.

"I have another one," she said under her breath.

"Is it on you?"

"Yes." She tested her left arm and winced; she could barely lift it. She slowly moved her right arm and slid her hand into her pants, her fingers finding the phone.

"Good girl," he said softly.

Though her hand was shaking, she managed to hit the speed dial code for Dom's number. She brought the phone up to her ear and leaned against the wall.

"*Molly?*" Dom sounded completely freaked out.

"Can you hear me?" She was whispering.

"I hear you, babe. Are you at the house?"

"Yes. Sergei is here too—Tim thinks he's Toli."

"Is he hurt?"

"Not too bad."

"Are you okay?"

"I think my arm is broken, but otherwise okay."

"Where is Tim now?"

"I don't know, but I'm going to leave the phone on and slide it under the couch. That way maybe someone can track us... or something."

"We're only a few minutes away!" he said. "Hang in there—I'm coming."

"Someone's coming!" Sergei whispered sharply.

Molly dropped phone and slid it under the couch a few inches just as Tim came stomping into the room. She turned slowly, looking up at him.

"Look who's awake!" he hissed. He moved towards her like a predator, and Molly tried not to let him see her cringe. She'd lived in fear for so long she didn't want that to be the last thing she felt before she died.

"Why are you doing this?" she asked.

"Why?" he shrieked, his face turning red. "*Why?* You left me, cheated on me, and then tried to humiliate me by showing my lawyer that damn video! Do you know how much trouble you've caused me?"

"Then why not just let me go?"

"Let you go?" He was blinking furiously, fists clenched at his sides. "And let

LAS VEGAS SIDEWINDERS: DOMINIC

you get away with what you've done?" He shoved her, and she fell over with a yelp of pain.

"Dammit, no!" Sergei felt the veins throbbing in his head as anger filled him. He'd been working on the knots of the rope that tied his hands, but he wasn't sure he'd made much progress.

"What are *you* gonna do, loverboy?" Tim laughed almost hysterically. He leaned over, close enough for Sergei to smell the whisky on his breath. "I'll tell you what you're going to do... you're going to watch while I fuck her—and then *she's* going to watch me kill you."

I n the car, Dom gripped the side of the seat so hard he could feel the leather ripping under his hands. Listening to the muffled conversation on the other end of the phone, he knew with every fiber of his being he was going to rip Tim apart, piece by piece. Gun or no gun, Tim would have to keep shooting because he would be dead before he let him touch Molly again.

"Breathe," Cody said as steadily as he could. Though he was as terrified as he'd ever been in his life, he had to help Dom stay in control for as long as possible.

"I don't know who this motherfucker is," Zakk sat forward in agitation. "But we need to get there."

"I'm going 85 on surface streets," Cody snapped. "We can't afford to get stopped!"

"It's around the corner," Dom said in a deadly voice. "Turn here and then stop. We don't want them to see us pull up."

Cody did as he was told. He could see Toli, Drake and Karl getting out of the car behind them. "Do we have a plan?"

"He might have his cop friends waiting to stop us," Toli said as they came together.

"You understand *nothing* is going to stop me?" Dom looked at his friends. "If they kill me, promise me you'll get her out."

"Dom—"

"Promise me!" Dom gripped Cody's arm. "Cody—I need to know if I don't make it, you'll take care of her."

"Yeah, of course." Cody swallowed and met his friend's eyes. "But understand *me*—we're *all* walking out of there."

"What's the plan?" Drake was standing next to the car, his arms folded across his massive chest. Drake was probably the only guy Dom knew that was bigger than he was, and he was grateful for these men who had followed him into this hell.

"We need to see what's waiting for us first," Dom said, joining them on the side of the road. "I can't believe he's there alone with Molly and Sergei."

"*Sergei?*" Toli's eyes darkened dangerously.

"Molly called—they think Sergei is you and grabbed him by mistake."

"They're okay?" Toli asked stiffly, taking a breath.

"For now, but she left the line open and from what we could hear, it's escalating."

"Okay, he can't have an army of cops in his front yard waiting to shoot us," Zakk spoke up. "My uncle is a cop, and you just can't do that shit. We need to call 911 and the press, to make sure there's too much publicity for him to get away with this."

"Hopefully Coach already did that," Cody murmured. "But yeah, why don't you call 911 and stay down here, a little way from the house? You can tell them what you know."

"Hell no!" Zakk glared at Cody. He reached down and pulled a knife from inside one of his boots. "I'm pretty sure I can take out at least two with just this baby." He palmed the knife and moved towards Dom. "Let's go get your girl."

Dom clapped a hand on his shoulder. "Let's do this." He turned to the others. "Here's the plan—if he has friends outside, you guys keep them distracted. Biker Boy and I will sneak around the back and see if we can get in without them noticing us. If the front of the house is clear, call 911 and knock on the door but keep your heads down—we know he's probably armed."

"I will lead," Toli said firmly.

"It's house number 422," Dom called after them. With a motion of his head, he and Zakk ducked between the two closest houses.

Molly fought the bile rising in her throat, trying to think of a way to distract Tim. If she could keep him talking, maybe Dom would get here before he hurt them anymore. She looked up at his red, sweaty face and for a moment she couldn't even remember what he'd looked like when they'd met. He'd been twenty pounds thinner and his hair had been thicker, but this man was a stranger. Right now his thin lips were in a flat line of displeasure as he glared down at her, and she looked up defiantly.

"Tim, can't we just go our separate ways?"

He laughed. "Really? You think you're going to get up and waltz out of here with your little commie boyfriend?"

"I'm not a communist!" Sergei grunted, following Molly's lead trying to distract him with conversation. "What the hell does that even mean?"

"You're a Russian, aren't you?"

"Well, I was born there, but I've lived most of my adult life here—and I'm a citizen." That was a lie, but Tim probably didn't know that.

"Bullshit!" Tim called his bluff. "I've had you checked out, *Anatoli Petrov*—and you're a Russian fucking national. You even had dinner with that commie President of yours a few years ago."

"Toli is his brother!" Molly interjected. She didn't know if telling Tim he'd gotten the wrong brother was a good thing or not, but it was all she had right now. "This is *Sergei* Petrov!"

"Oh, so you're doing *both* of them now?" Tim spun around.

Molly rolled her eyes; she couldn't help it. Unfortunately, she was rewarded with a backhand that left her tasting blood. She took a breath, not allowing herself to give in to the pain. "I'm not sleeping with anybody," she protested calmly.

"I saw you with this guy," Tim ground out through his teeth. "I saw you with him at a movie theater, and Hank saw you with him at the fucking Wynn having *brunch*! So don't fucking lie to me!"

The movies, she thought blandly. God, that had been back in July. Had he been watching her that long? And if so, how had he *not* seen her with Dom? He seemed convinced she and Toli were together, which was good for Dom, but very bad for her and Sergei.

"What, no more excuses?" Tim reached down and pulled her up by the hair, causing her to yelp. He pushed her against the wall, still holding her hair. She cradled her throbbing arm against her, but met his gaze without flinching.

"Now what?" she demanded. "You're going to rape me? In front of the brother of the man you think I'm sleeping with?" She laughed without humor. "Go ahead. You can't hurt me anymore."

"You think I can't hurt you anymore?" He slapped her so hard she saw stars, but she just lifted her head and looked back at him.

"You don't get it, do you?" She shook her head slowly. "It doesn't matter what you do to my body—I don't care about you anymore. I couldn't stop you from hitting me in June, and I can't stop you now. But if you hurt Sergei? His family—his *brother*—will hunt you down like an animal. You think I've caused you trouble? You have no idea what kind of trouble Sergei's friends, including the Russian *President*, will do once they figure out what you've done."

"Molly…" Sergei would have laughed at her comment about the Russian President if he wasn't so afraid of what Tim might do to her. Tim was on the verge of exploding, and she was goading him. Sergei struggled against the ropes around his wrists, looking around in desperation for something he could use as a weapon.

"Shut up!" Tim's fist smashed into Molly's face, sending her back against the wall, where she hit it hard and then slowly slid down, blood covering her face. Then she didn't move.

"You son of a bitch!" Sergei let out a yell as he lifted himself and the chair off the ground. He swung it around as hard as he could, catching Tim behind the knees and taking him down. He landed on top of him, kicking at the man's face as hard as he could. Twenty-five years of ice skating had given him thighs of steel, and he used every ounce of strength he had to keep the legs of the chair swinging back and forth across Tim's face.

"Sergei, look out!" Dom broke through the back door, rushing forward. Sergei briefly noticed someone behind him that was covered in tattoos, but he had no idea who it was.

Sergei threw himself out of the way as Dom landed on Tim in one flying motion, his fist connecting squarely with the older man's jaw. Tim swung back, grunting, but Sergei had tired him out, and Dom's furious blows soon had him motionless on the floor.

"Untie me!" Sergei hissed at the other man.

Zakk knelt beside him and made short work of the ropes. He helped him up and Sergei rubbed his raw wrists. He first thought was Molly and he swallowed hard as he moved towards her.

"Dom!" He called his name sharply, and then looked over at Zakk imploringly.

"I got this," Zakk said, reaching around Dom, who was still pounding into Tim. "You got enough trouble with the NHL—let me handle this." He picked up Tim by the shirt, punched him in the face several times to make sure his knuckles were bruised and smeared with Tim's blood.

"Molly!" Dom was breathing hard now, his heart practically beating out of his chest when he saw her. Her body was slumped against the wall, covered with blood, and he let out a howl of distress. He dropped to his knees beside her, pulling her into his arms. "Baby, wake up. Molly?" He pulled off his shirt and used it to wipe her face. He didn't realize he was crying until the room started to blur.

29

HE THOUGHT THERE WAS A LOT OF ACTIVITY AROUND HIM, BUT ALL HE COULD focus on was the woman he loved. He heard sirens and people talking to him, but his mind had already flashed back to the day Brian died. He could see Brian's face as plain as day, his brains splattered across the alley in Boston. As tears streamed down his face, heard his friend's voice in his mind. "She's going to be okay." He wasn't sure who spoke, but he was positive it was Brian's voice.

"Dom!" Cody was on his haunches next to him, grabbing at his arms to get his attention. "Dom, you've got to let the paramedics help her. Dom!" Cody finally smacked the back of his head.

Dom slowly turned, looking at Cody. "Is she dead?" he whispered.

"No." Cody gently pulled Dom's arms away as the paramedics began to work on her.

"You're sure?" Dom could barely speak.

"Dom?" Molly's voice was barely a whisper but both Dom and Cody whipped their heads around.

"I'm right here!" Dom reached out to run his hand over her forehead.

"Is Sergei okay?"

"I'm fine," Sergei spoke quietly from behind them. "Just let the doctors help you."

"Stay with me, Dom," she whispered, her eyes drifting closed.

"I'm right here." Dom stood up as the paramedics lifted her.

"Dom, you're going to have to talk to—" Cody started to say.

"I'm going in the ambulance with her," He said in a steely voice. "They can come to the hospital if they want to talk to me." He walked out beside her, not looking back, his bloody t-shirt still in his hand.

"We'll handle this," Toli said calmly to Cody. "Follow Dom."

"The kid—" Cody glanced over to where Zakk was standing in handcuffs, a smirk on his face.

"It's okay," Toli said firmly. "Dom needs you more. Toli will take care of the kid."

"Right." Cody gave him a grateful smile and then ran out to his car.

When Cody burst into the hospital emergency room, he found Dom heaving over one of the garbage cans. He looked around for help, spotting a nurse at the desk.

"Hey, could I get a towel or something?" he demanded. The nurse looked up, startled, but when she followed his gaze to the man covered in blood who was vomiting into the garbage, she quickly got up and produced a few towels and some ice.

"Thanks!" He shot her a smile and then rushed over to his friend. Taking the bloody t-shirt from his hand, he dropped it into the trash and put the towel with the ice on the back of his neck. "Come on—let's take this into the men's room."

Dom didn't move at first, but Cody managed to nudge him towards the bathroom. He pushed him through the door and leaned him against the wall. He wet the second towel and handed it to him. "Wipe your face, man."

Dom took the towel, but didn't move, eyes closed and chest still heaving as he leaned back. Cody let him have a minute but finally reached out to put a hand on his shoulder. "Dom, she's going to wake up and you're not going to be there. You need to wash up and get back to Molly, okay?"

Dom opened his eyes.

"You gonna be sick again?"

"No." Dom handed him back the ice pack as he leaned over the sink to rinse the blood off his face, arms and hands. He reached for a handful of paper towels and managed to dry himself off. He bent to rinse out his mouth, spitting out the vile taste of vomit.

"Cody!" From the hallway, Cody could hear his wife's frantic voice. He yanked open the door and stuck his head out. "Suze!"

She ran in his direction, throwing herself into his arms. "God, I was so scared! Where's Molly? Where's Dom?"

Cody gently kissed her before pulling her into the bathroom. "He's a little shaken up, but okay."

"Where's Molly?" Her eyes moved between them worriedly.

"I don't know," Cody said. "Dom needed to clean up a little—there was a lot of blood."

"Whose?" she whispered.

"Tim's and Molly's."

"How bad?"

"Tim? I have no idea," Cody shrugged. "But Molly was unconscious when we got there."

"You okay, big guy?" Suze went up to Dom and gently put her hands on his arms. His hands were shaking and she took them in hers, looking up into his handsome face as she tried to still them. "You're gonna need to snap out of this." she said finally.

"I know." He swallowed. "I just saw her laying there and all I could think about was..." He stopped.

"Brian." She wrapped her arms around his waist and pulled him into a tight hug. His arms went around her, his chin falling to his chest as he squeezed his eyes shut to try to stop the tears from coming down his face. "It's okay," she whispered. "It's not the same—she's alive, Dom."

"I keep seeing his face," he said. "I can't go to her until I shake this off."

"She needs you, buddy." Cody moved next to them, resting his hand on his friend's shoulder. "You can fall apart later—right now, she's going to be scared and she needs you to *man up*."

"You're right." Dom slowly moved away from Suze. He grabbed the towel off the sink and wiped his face again. "Can you find me a shirt? You have one in your car?"

"Yeah, I'll go get it." Cody jogged out and Suze wrapped her hand firmly around Dom's as she pulled him back into the hallway.

"Are you Mr. Gianni?" A small woman who looked to be of Indian descent approached him quickly, her white lab coat flapping as she walked.

"Yes." He looked down at her.

"I'm Dr. Patel," she said briskly. "Molly is quite agitated—she won't talk to anyone until she sees you. You're going to need to help us calm her. I don't want to sedate her until I can talk to her, but her injuries are quite extensive, so I'd like to make her more comfortable."

"Yeah, whatever she needs." He followed the doctor blindly.

The doctor brought him behind a curtain where Molly was crying on the bed. Seeing her bruised, bloody face nearly brought him to his knees, but he forced himself to walk forward, reaching for her.

"Baby, I'm here," he whispered as he knelt over her, brushing a kiss on her forehead.

"Is he dead?" she whispered back, reaching out to put her good arm around his neck.

"I don't know," he said, his eyes meeting hers. "Zakk hit him pretty hard..."

Her eyes narrowed slightly. Even in all this pain, she knew Dom had been the one hitting Tim.

"Don't worry about that," he continued. "Let the doctors talk to us so we can figure out what you need. Are you in pain?"

She nodded slowly.

"Tell me what hurts," Dr. Patel said in a quiet but efficient voice.

"My arm." Molly used her right arm to touch her left. "And my face is throbbing. I can't see out of this eye..." She pointed again.

"You're going to need x-rays and maybe a CAT scan." The doctor looked down at the frightened woman and spoke in a softer voice. "We need to see if the arm requires surgery or if we can just put it in a cast, and then we'll assess the pain in your face. I'm afraid your orbital bone may be broken."

"My..." Molly winced. "Is that the bone around my eye?"

"Yes." The doctor wrote something in her notes. "I'm going to give you something mild for the pain so you can relax but won't be completely out of it. Once we've done a few tests we'll talk about what we need to do next."

"Can Dom stay with me?"

"He can't go into X-ray, but he can wait right here. Don't worry—it won't take long."

Molly nodded and closed her eyes. One of the nurses put something into the IV and Dom could feel Molly start to relax in his hands. He kissed the top of her head and squeezed her fingers. "I'll be right here, baby."

He watched them wheel her away and sank into the nearest chair. The doctor approached him slowly. "Are you injured, Mr. Gianni?" she asked softly.

"Dom," he corrected absently. "And no. Any blood you see is hers."

"Your knuckles are bruised."

"I punched the wall a few times when I heard her ex-husband had kidnapped her."

The doctor raised her eyebrows but said nothing. Finally, she walked over to the cabinets and removed a few items. Pulling up a chair, she gently took his hands and began cleaning the dirt and dried blood from his raw knuckles.

"I can do that," Suze said, joining them.

"It's all right," the doctor smiled. "It's nice to take care of someone who takes care of others."

Dom looked up at her with a slight frown, but the doctor just continued her ministrations until she stood up, dumped everything in the trash, removed her gloves and slipped from the room. Dom watched her go and then looked at Suze. "Can you find out what's happening with... everything?"

"Hey, I got a shirt for you," Cody came in, handing him a t-shirt he'd found in his car.

Dom pulled it over his head. "Thanks. Where's Zakk? Did they arrest him?"

"They hauled everybody down to the station."

"What about Tim?"

"He's beat to hell, Dom," Cody said under his breath. "I don't know if you can let the kid take the rap for this."

"Just let me make sure Molly's okay, and I'll turn myself in," Dom replied automatically.

"Let's wait and see what happens first. It looked pretty bad, but apparently the mayor sent a special task force to handle the investigation."

"Should we call a lawyer?" Suze asked.

"Toli said he had everything under control," Cody said. "You know he's going to raise all kinds of hell about his brother being kidnapped."

For a while they were all silent, the only noises coming from out in the hallway. Cody sank into one of the other chairs and pulled Suze onto his lap, wrapping his arms around her. She rested her head against his chest and they sat, waiting for someone to come back.

When they wheeled Molly back in, Dom jumped to his feet. He leaned over her, taking her hand. "Hey, beautiful."

Her eyes opened slowly and he could see the drugs were making her sleepy. "Hi," she croaked. "Can I have some water?"

"I don't know," he said. "Let me ask."

"I'm right here." Dr. Patel came in, a Styrofoam cup in her hands. She handed it to Dom and he quickly put a straw in it before helping Molly lift her head to take a sip.

"What can you tell us, Doctor?" Suze stood next to Dom.

"Her arm has a very small fracture, but won't require surgery. We're going to put it in a soft cast and in six weeks or so it should be good as new."

"But?" Dom knew the look on her face wasn't good.

"Her injuries, as I suspected, are extensive. She has two broken ribs, a fracture in her jaw, and her orbital bone is indeed broken. Her nose is swollen so badly I can't even tell if it's broken yet. She's also bruised her left kidney and has a slight concussion. The cuts and bruises to her face are severe enough to possibly require plastic surgery."

"Whatever she needs," Dom said. "Please take care of her. I'll find a plastic surgeon to fix the damage to her face, but in the meantime, I don't want her in any pain."

"Dom." Molly's voice was soft.

"Yeah, babe?" He leaned over, taking her right hand between both of his.

"You need to make sure the guys are okay." She managed to open one eye, and looked at him intently.

"I'm not leaving you, Mol." He shook his head.

"I'll go..." Cody stood up.

"You sure, man?" he glanced at his friend.

"I should be there—I'm the team captain."

"I would go..." Dom's voice trailed off.

"You're staying right here." Cody shook his head. "We don't know if anymore of Tim's buddies might come sniffing around to finish the job, so I don't want the girls to be alone."

"Yeah, okay." Dom nodded.

Cody kissed his wife and then headed out.

30

AFTER THE CAST WAS PUT ON MOLLY'S ARM, SHE WENT THROUGH ANOTHER battery of tests. Everything seemed to take forever, and Dom paced for what felt like hours. They moved her to a private room so she would be more comfortable, and finally, late in the day, they gave her stronger pain medication to help her rest.

Dr. Patel told him she would probably sleep for the rest of the night. After getting something eat, Dom fell asleep in the chair next to her bed, his head resting on the mattress next to her. Suze fell asleep on the small sofa in the back of the room. Dom opened his eyes often, always on guard, but he managed to rest on and off. Sometime overnight, Cody slipped in and fell asleep beside his wife.

That's how they were in the morning when Brad, Toli and Sergei arrived. Brad gently woke Dom, who came awake quickly. Cody's eyes snapped open when Dom's chair scraped across the floor.

"Hey," Dom sat up, rubbing his eyes. "What happened?"

"Let's go outside so we don't—" Brad began.

"I'm awake, don't go," Molly whispered. "Could I have some water?"

Dom reached for the cup next to her bed and gently held her head again. She smiled gratefully.

Suze had gotten up too, and they looked up expectantly.

"What happened?" Molly whispered.

"We took care of everything," Brad said, nodding. "It was a long day yesterday, but I don't think Tim will be bothering you anymore."

"Is he in jail?" Suze asked.

"Well, he's in the hospital." Brad glanced at Dom. "But he's been arrested."

"Zakk?" Dom asked quickly.

"No charges." Brad shook his head. "We had all kinds of evidence against Tim and his friends. His partner, Hank, the one Toli hit over the head the night of the break-in, started singing like a fucking bird. Zakk told them what happened at the house: Tim was hitting Molly and Sergei tried to stop him, so while you went to protect Molly, Zakk put Tim out of commission."

"That's it?" Dom arched an eyebrow.

"Basically," Brad chuckled. He turned his eyes to Molly and they softened. "How are you feeling, sweetheart?"

"Like someone beat me with a hockey stick?" She tried to smile, but it hurt too much.

"Do you need anything?" Toli asked softly, reaching out to touch her hand.

"I need you guys to take Dom home and make him rest so he can play tonight."

"No way!" Dom shook his head. "I'm not leaving you! It's pre-season—they don't need me."

"He's right, honey," Brad said. "The game tonight doesn't matter."

"Yes, it does!" she protested. "It's the first *ever* Sidewinders game—it's historical and he's not going to miss it because of me!" Her eyes filled with tears as she looked at him. "I want you to play!"

He stood up straighter, brushing her hair out of her face as he traced a line along her chin. "You sure, sweetheart?"

"Can he play, Brad?" She looked to the older man.

"If that's what you want, he can play." He nodded.

She gave them a faint smile. "That's what I want. I want to see all you guys on the ice tonight. It'll be on TV, right?"

"Yes," Dom smiled faintly. He didn't know how the hell he was going to get out on the ice in nine or ten hours, but if that's what she wanted, he would find a way to make it happen.

"Suze, will you stay with me?"

"Of course." Suze nodded.

"I don't want you here alone," Dom said. "No matter what they say, I still don't trust that one of Tim's friends won't come looking for revenge."

"I'll stay," Sergei said automatically. "Those guys won't sneak up on me again."

"Don't you have to be in Boston?" Suze asked him.

"They thought I was in Russia," he shrugged. "When they hear about this I'll probably be in trouble anyway."

"I'll talk to your coach if you need me to," Brad said. "I can have our lawyers make a call to let him know you were a victim and not involved in anything you shouldn't be."

Sergei smirked. "I don't know about *that.*"

Toli snorted. "Probably you should say nothing."

They laughed together.

"Go get some rest," Molly said to Dom, squeezing his hand.

"I'll call you later," he whispered.

"Andra will be by after she takes CJ to school," Brad said to Suze. "So let her know if you need her to pick up anything for you?"

"Go home and get a shower," Molly told Suze. "Sergei will be here, so I'll be okay. You guys need to stuff fussing."

"If you think you'll be okay, I'll go home and shower, pack up a few things for both of us, and then I'll come back with my own car." Suze looked at her questioningly.

"Do that." Molly nodded. Her eyes started to close and Dom leaned over to gently kiss her bruised lips before slipping out.

S uze came back a few hours later pulling a small carry-on size suitcase with her. Molly looked over at her and would have laughed if it didn't hurt so much. "Are you moving in?" she asked.

"Smartass!" Suze smirked. "I have clothes for you, clothes for me in case I need to stay over, my laptop, slippers and pajamas for you, and a bunch of toiletries for all of us." She put her things in the corner and sat beside Molly. "Any news from the doctor?"

"They can't really do anything for the orbital bone," she said. "I just need to rest and give it time to heal. They've taped my ribs and they're watching to make sure there isn't any bleeding in my kidneys."

"That's good, right?"

Molly didn't say anything. Finally, her eyes met Suze's. "How bad is it?" she asked softly.

"What?"

"How bad do I look? Tell me the truth."

Suze hesitated. "I don't know, Mol. I mean, your face is literally swollen beyond recognition on one side and there are cuts and bruises all over."

Molly sighed heavily, a look of despair filling her eyes.

"They can fix it," Sergei said. "You'll find a good surgeon."

"I've caused so much trouble for you guys..." She bit her lip. "And now I might be disfigured..."

"Stop." Suze put a finger on her friend's lips. "Dom knew what he was getting into the day he and Cody found you. He was on a mission to save someone and he found you. Somewhere along the way, he fell in love with you. Since he met you, he's been the happiest I've ever seen him. His demons are fading, and you've become important to all of us. You can't worry about how you're going to look— I'm sure we can fix that."

"I've got that under control for you." Drake walked into the room followed by a slender blond in an expensive suit. He smiled as he extended his hand to Molly. "How are you, Molly?"

"Hanging in," she admitted.

"This is my sister, Dr. Mackenzie Riser. She's a plastic surgeon in Chicago, and she flew out this morning to take a look at you. After we found out you might need a plastic surgeon, I figured I'd bring in the best."

"Hi, Molly." Mackenzie leaned over and smiled, touching Molly's hand. "If you'll sign a consent form, I can take a look and see what's what."

"Um, sure, thank you." Molly blinked, glancing at Suze, who gave her a tiny nod. She signed the piece of paper they put in front of her and Mackenzie put it on the counter.

"Okay, let me look at you first." Mackenzie gently touched Molly's chin and lifted her head slightly. "So the orbital bone is broken and you have a fracture in your jaw?"

"That's what they tell me." Molly told her as much as she knew.

Mackenzie nodded. She picked up the clipboard at the end of the bed and read through everything, nodding to herself and making notes on the iPad she had with her. She checked the stitches on Molly's cheek and frowned. "I don't like these stitches—I think they'll leave a scar. But I can fix that."

"Okay." Molly was grateful for Suze's hand squeezing hers.

"Your nose may be broken as well, but there's so much swelling it's hard to tell."

"I can't make any decisions without Dom," Molly said softly. "And he has a big game tonight so I don't want to bother him right now."

"That's okay. I'm going to go over your x-rays and blood work, and then I'll be back to chat some more. You take it easy."

"Thank you. And thank you for coming all the way from Chicago."

"My little brother called, so I came." She winked and he smiled.

"Plus it means she gets to see us play tonight," Drake said, making her smile.

"Since I taught him how to play, I enjoy watching him."

Drake rolled his eyes. "Yeah, okay, sis."

"What?" She folded her arms. "Did I not put you on the ice for the first time when you were four years old?"

"Yeah—and then promptly went back to college!" He shook his head; Mack was 17 years older than he was, and insisted she had raised him even though she'd left for college when he was only a year old. They were, however, exceptionally close.

"Whatever." She turned away from him, and winked down at Molly. "So, now that I have your permission, I'm going to go find your doctor and see if we can coordinate some services."

"Thank you." Molly watched her easygoing efficiency and wished she could feel so calm about everything. She hadn't dared look at her face because she was afraid it would probably horrify her. Hearing she needed a plastic surgeon worried her—what would Dom think if she didn't heal right? She couldn't even think about it.

"You need to get that worried look off your face," Drake said gently. "My sister is a phenomenal surgeon. Google her and you'll see. She's one of the best in the country. In fact, she's so good she's moving away from traditional plastic surgery and working on a study to try out new procedures to help burn victims. It's cutting-edge stuff, so trust me when I say she will fix you."

"I appreciate your calling her," said Molly. "I appreciate your having Dom's back, too. I don't even know what you guys were doing there."

"When Dom and Toli got to the locker room and found your text messages, they went nuts," Drake said, settling into the nearest chair. "Once we figured out what had happened, Karl and I got on board, and then Zakk followed us out."

"So he didn't get in trouble? I know he wasn't the one who beat up Tim." Molly looked at him intently. "Even though I don't want Dom to get in trouble, I don't want someone else taking the blame either."

"They have statements that he was simply restraining your ex, and Tim fought back," Sergei said calmly. "Dom, Zakk and I all have the exact same story."

"What do I say?"

"You were mostly unconscious—you have no idea what happened once Dom and Zakk arrived."

"Okay." Molly nodded. "I'm surprised the police haven't been here yet."

Drake smiled. "Let's just say Toli has some *very* expensive lawyers involved, and they threatened to sue the entire city of Henderson if you were harassed after you'd been traumatized by a member of the police department. There were reporters there—it's all over the news."

"Oh, my God." Molly's eyes widened and Suze shot Drake a dirty look.

"Was I not supposed to say that?" He winced.

"Don't hide anything from me!" Molly looked at Suze in irritation. "This is my life—I should know what's going on."

"Don't worry," Sergei said. "The team has hired a crisis control publicist. She's flying out from New York to handle this for you and Dom."

"A *publicist?*" Molly looked upset again.

"Okay, that's enough," Suze said abruptly, noticing Molly's hands were shaking. "You don't need to worry about the details. Brad is handling everything and Dom isn't in any trouble. The truth is, the Sidewinders' PR department is eating this up. A bunch of guys on the team went out and took on a bunch of dirty cops, saved one of their girlfriends from being beat to death, and rescued a fellow NHL player who'd been kidnapped? This is a PR wet dream. The guys are already hometown heroes and they haven't even played their first game."

Molly was gaping at her. "Are you serious?"

"One hundred percent. So close your eyes and rest."

"You won't let me sleep through the game, will you?"

"Absolutely not." Suze squeezed her hand.

Deciding she couldn't do anything else until she saw Dom play, Molly closed her eyes and slept.

3 1

Waiting for the game to start, Dom paced around the dressing room impatiently. He was excited and nervous at the same time. Though he'd slept for several hours this afternoon, he'd been online and knew the press was all over Molly's situation and the team's involvement. Though no one knew he was her boyfriend, his was one of the names mentioned as being involved in the "incident." Toli and Sergei seemed to be getting most of the notoriety since Sergei had been kidnapped as well, and Sergei had stuck to the story he and Toli had apparently come up with: Toli and Molly were good friends, Sergei was in town visiting and Tim had mistaken Sergei for Toli, kidnapping the man he thought was sleeping with his soon-to-be-ex-wife.

There was speculation there was a romance between Toli and Molly, and for the time being Dom was okay with that. The people that mattered knew the truth, and after all the trouble Dom had been in with the NHL, it seemed easier to let Toli take the heat. Coach Barnett had been firm with the press, saying there would be no questions about the incident before the game and they would make statements afterwards.

In the meantime, Dom had spoken to Molly on the phone an hour ago, and though she'd said all the right things, he heard something in her voice he couldn't quite put his finger on. When he'd questioned Suze, she'd demurred as well, and he figured she couldn't tell him while she was with Molly. It bothered him, but not too much, because he would be going back to the hospital as soon as they finished here. Molly was most likely feeling insecure about the injuries to her face, and he was just going to have to remind her how much he loved her.

T he game was over before he knew it, and Dom barely remembered scoring the team's first goal or had a chance to enjoy the camaraderie in the locker room after they sent the Kings home with a 4-2 loss. Drake, Cody and Zakk had all scored as well, so they were a happy group until they sat through what felt like hours of interviews with the press.

Dom was surprised at how invested the media was in hearing Molly's story, and he quickly realized she wouldn't like the way it was starting to spin. She wasn't just a victim; she was also possibly to blame. After all, a woman who was dating a professional hockey player while still married to someone else had undoubtedly done something to antagonize a decorated police officer. Listening as reporters asked Toli question after question, Dom knew he had to get out of there before he lost his temper.

Gathering up his things, he went out the back door of the arena and got into his car. He drove straight to the hospital, still wearing the suit he was required to wear for press conferences. He left his jacket in the car and rolled up the sleeves of his dress shirt. He was coming down off the high of winning the game, and the press conference had left him with a headache. Part of him just wanted to take Molly and run away to protect her from all of this, but that wasn't in the cards. He had a career and they had a life here. This was home now, and he really didn't want to leave. He just hoped Molly still felt that way after she got wind of everything being said about her. Though Toli had handled everything beautifully, the fact she was still technically married had been brought up multiple times.

S he was sitting up in bed when he came in, and he leaned over to kiss her. He greeted Sergei and Suze, and asked them to leave the two of them alone for a little while. They were happy to comply and Dom took her hand as soon as they left.

"Hi." Molly gave him a weak smile. "You were good tonight. What a great game."

"It was pretty great," he agreed.

"What's wrong?" she asked him, noting the tired look in his eyes and the way he seemed to be avoiding her gaze. "Dom?"

"Have you had the TV on?" he asked.

"We turned it off after the game. Why?"

"There's just been a lot in the press about... everything that happened."

"You mean about me?" She blinked up at him.

"Yeah." He swallowed.

"Dom, just tell me." She met his eyes squarely.

"It's just, you know, everything about you and Tim is all over the press."

"Is the NHL mad at you?"

"No." He shook his head. "In fact, I'm hardly involved at all. This is all on Toli and he's been great, but..."

"But what?" She had a bad feeling about this conversation and she squeezed his hand. "Dom, tell me."

"The press has you under a lot of scrutiny—and you know how the media can be."

"I don't actually," she said slowly. "I mean, I know they sensationalize a lot of stuff with celebrities, but what part of my story is like that?"

"You're not divorced and you're dating a professional athlete. No wonder Tim lost his mind. Maybe you've done this before and the poor guy had just had enough. Then you got involved with your boyfriend's brother too." He looked at her guiltily.

Molly's mouth fell open. For a moment she couldn't even process what he was saying. Then her eyes narrowed. "Are you kidding me?" Her heart was hammering in her chest as she stared at him. "They're making me out as some whore who drove her husband to beat her?"

"Toli made it clear that wasn't the case, but there's still a lot of speculation and once they get hold of something, well..." He let out a breath and sat on the chair next to her. "The team's PR department is all over it and I've already got this publicist from New York working on my stuff, so—"

"So I'm getting thrown to the wolves?" She stared at him in disbelief.

"No!" He shook his head and leaned forward. "Babe, that's why I wanted to tell you what was going on. We're in this together."

"But I'm the one the press is calling a whore, and Toli is the guy sticking up for me." For the first time since she'd met Dom, she didn't understand him. Until now, he'd fought so hard for her, but she suddenly had the feeling he was more worried about his career than anything else.

"No!" He ran his hands through his hair in frustration. "Molly, if you want me to announce to the world we're together, I will. I just thought it would be better to let Toli handle it since—"

"Since he isn't in trouble with the NHL." She spoke icily as she realized he was backpedaling. "That's fine, Dom."

"Baby, I know you're upset but we can fix this. What do you want me to do?"

"Nothing." She waved her hand dismissively. "I'm a big girl. After what I've lived through, I can handle this."

"Molly, you make it sound like you're going to handle this alone, and that's not what I'm saying."

"But you're not really saying *anything*, are you?" She pulled her hand out of his.

"Molly, come on." He reached for her but she moved out of his reach.

"Just don't." She gave him a stare he'd never seen before.

"Please don't do this," he said wearily. "It's been a really bad couple of days and I just want to give you a chance to get better before we deal with anything else."

"Yeah, that's what I'm going to do." She turned away, staring at the open door. She couldn't believe this was Dom, calmly telling her to relax and forget about being called a whore all over sports media.

"You're mad at me, aren't you?" He took her hand again even though she tried to pull it away. "Molly, you need to look at me."

"No, I don't." She closed her eyes. "I'm really tired and I don't want to talk anymore."

He was surprised at her tone and gently let go of her hand. He'd known she would be upset, but as much as he wanted to make things right, he really didn't want to jump back into the fire. He loved her and had no problem going public with their relationship; he just didn't want to do it *now*. The season was just starting and he'd made a fresh start here in Las Vegas. If he made a public statement that he was the man she'd been seeing, it still wouldn't change the public's perception of *her*, and it would only put him back on the NHL's radar. There was no point in that, but he wasn't sure how to make her understand that without making himself look like a selfish jerk.

"You should go get some rest," she told him after they'd sat in silence for a while.

"Molly, do you want me to make a statement about us?" he asked. "If that's what you want, I'll do it."

"No, that's not what I want. There's no point in putting yourself in a negative light so soon after you were cleared by the league." She glanced at him. "I just need a little time, like you said."

He suspected that was a lie, but maybe if he let her think about it, and most likely talk to Suze, she would realize this wasn't his fault. They just had to lay low for a little while, and then the media would forget about this. He would talk to his publicist, Kate Lansing, and see what she could do as well. He'd find a way to fix this, and in the meantime, Molly could heal.

"I'm going to go home and sleep," he said softly. "But I'll be back tomorrow, okay? I'm going to talk to my publicist and maybe we can figure out a way to make this go away."

"Okay." Molly nodded.

"Babe?"

"Good night, Dom." She turned away from him when he tried to kiss her and he hesitated. "I'm fine," she said when he didn't leave.

"You don't seem fine."

"There's no point in talking about this—we can't fix it tonight. Go home; you look tired."

"We'll talk tomorrow, okay?"

"Yup."

Realizing she wasn't going to be rational about this tonight, he figured he'd give her some space. Kissing the top of her head, he headed out. Tomorrow would be a better day. They both needed a little time to think about everything that had happened and he desperately needed a good night's sleep. He ached all over, and they would be leaving the day after tomorrow to play in L.A. for their second pre-season game, so he couldn't afford to be tired this early in the season. After a good night's sleep, he'd talk to their lawyer and publicist, and then he'd be able to calm her down.

M olly sent Sergei and Suze both home not long after, telling them Dom would be back to sit with her. She hated lying to Suze, but she would probably get completely hysterical if she told Suze what had happened, so it was easier to be alone. Though it made her a little nervous, she didn't believe Tim would be able to send anyone after her after everything that had happened. Even if the press thought she was a tramp, it still didn't excuse a man from killing her, and one way or another, this would blow over.

What bothered her was the way Dom seemed to shut down on her. She'd never seem him like this and felt like a fool for trusting him. All his talk about making babies together and falling in love had been nothing more than a summertime fling while he worked out his issues. Now that everything had come to a head, he was going to turn tail and run.

She turned on the TV and found a sports station. As Dom had told her, she was all over the news in connection with the Sidewinders. They were using a picture of her from high school and she cringed. Though they were kinder than Dom made it sound, there was still a lot of speculation about who she was and how she'd become involved with Toli. Watching them talk about her on TV was the strangest feeling she'd ever had, and after half an hour she turned it off. She picked up the cell phone Dom had recovered for her, and stared at it for a moment. Her instinct was to call him, but she couldn't do that now. Not after the way he'd behaved. Instead, she texted Toli.

Can you talk?

It only took thirty seconds for her phone to ring. She answered softly. "Hi."

"Molly?" Toli sounded like he was half-asleep.

"I'm sorry, I woke you."

"No, is okay. Toli takes a long time to sleep after a game. How are you?"

His soft, concerned voice brought out all the emotion she'd been holding in and she completely broke down, sobbing so hard she couldn't talk.

"Molly?" Toli was awake now. "I'm coming—just wait, I'm coming." He hung up abruptly and pulled on a pair of jeans and a t-shirt. He grabbed his keys and headed out.

MOLLY WAS STILL SNIFFLING WHEN TOLI WALK INTO HER ROOM AND HE immediately reached for the box of tissues on the counter. He sat on the edge of the hospital bed and slowly wiped her face, careful not to hurt her. She looked at him miserably and he instinctively reached out to put his arms around her.

"What is it?" he whispered. "What's happened?"

The tears came all over again and he held her as she sobbed against his shirt. Somehow she managed to tell him about her conversation with Dom and he understood immediately. Dom was an idiot, he thought to himself as he stroked her hair. He was getting caught up in his career and not thinking clearly. Though he understood his need to get his career back on track, how could he sacrifice the woman he loved? It had definitely been a stressful couple of days, but Molly needed him now more than ever. Dom and Toli had tons of experience dealing with the bad sides of the media; Molly had none and he should know that.

"You must not hurt yourself, yes?" He gently pulled away, handing her another tissue. "Your eye is already swollen—you must not cry."

"I know." She tried to blow her nose but everything was still too swollen and the pain nearly made her cry out.

"Do you want Toli to talk to Dom?"

"No." She shook her head sadly. "If you have to tell him that he's hurt me, he can't possibly love me."

"Dom has never been in relationship before," Toli said. "Maybe Dom needs chance to explain."

"Maybe," she sighed.

There was a knock on the door and Dr. Riser stuck her head in. "Hey, Molly."

"Hi." Molly glanced over at her.

"Oh, my." Dr. Riser looked between them curiously, noticing how red Molly's eyes were and the wet spot on Toli's shirt. "Crying isn't good for you."

"Dr. Riser, do we have doctor-patient confidentiality?"

"Well, yes, I suppose we do since you've called me in to consult. But please call me Mack—everyone does."

"Does that include your brother, Mack?"

Mack hesitated. "Of course it does. What's going on?"

"I'm all over the news and I need to keep my life as private as I can."

"That goes without saying."

"I need to know how much you're going to charge me to take care of my face, and I need to make sure you don't send Dom any bills."

Mack blinked, unsure what was going on, but now that Drake had brought her into this situation, she couldn't just walk away. "I wasn't planning to charge you anything," she said finally. "There are some operating room fees and the cost of an anesthesiologist, but I took your case as a favor to my brother."

"If you'd rather not handle this—"

"Wait, Molly, I need to understand what's happening."

"Dom and I are no longer together, and I don't have any money until my lawyer gets me my share from my divorce. I need to know if you'll accept a letter from my lawyer saying you'll be paid after I get my divorce settlement."

"Molly—" Toli started to interrupt but Molly held up her hand to silence him.

"What happened?" Mack looked concerned.

"It doesn't matter," Molly said softly. "What matters is me getting on with my life." She looked at Toli. "I need a favor, Toli."

"You are being rash," he said just as softly.

"Will you lend me a few thousand dollars? I'll pay you back as soon as I get my money. In the meantime, I need something to live on."

"Toli will *give* you the money, but this is not—"

"I only want a loan. I've been a burden to people long enough, and it's time for me to start taking care of myself. But I have to get my face fixed."

Toli and Mack exchanged glances but didn't say anything.

"You told me we would always be friends," Molly whispered harshly. "Was that a lie like everything Dom told me?'

"No!" Toli looked like she'd slapped him. "This is not fair!"

"Then will you loan me the money so I can get away from this nightmare and try to get better without the media calling me a whore every day?"

Toli opened his mouth but then closed it again, swallowing. "Molly, you know Toli will do anything for you."

"Thank you." She looked back at Mack. "Can you arrange to get me released from here? Is there someplace cheap I can stay in Chicago while I heal enough for you to do the surgery?"

"Are you sure this is what you want?" Mack asked, frowning.

"I have to get out of here, as soon as possible," Molly said firmly. "I know people tend to blame the victims in abuse situations, but I didn't think it would wind up on the news like some kind of celebrity scandal! I never dreamed Dom would pick his career over me either. I thought I'd finally found the family I'd never had—instead, I'm nothing but a whore and there's a whole hockey team of heroes who saved Sergei. I think I've had about as much as I can handle."

Toli shook his head. "Molly, you are overreacting."

"Are you going to help me or not?" she demanded.

"Toli has already said yes."

"Mack?" She turned to the doctor. "It's up to you. Are you willing to help me knowing that you can't tell your brother anything?"

"Drake doesn't have any access to my patients," Mack said. "If this is what you feel you need, I'm here to help."

"Thank you." Molly looked around. "How long do you think before I can get out of here?"

"I think you need at least one more day before you can travel," Mack said. "And even then, you're going to be miserable on a plane."

"Toli will drive you," he said automatically.

"You have a game in L.A. tomorrow night," Molly said, shaking her head. She turned to Mack. "Can't you give me good enough drugs to get me through the flight?"

"I guess so," Mack nodded slowly.

"Then what do we need to do?"

"Molly, this has been a terrible ordeal for you, and I'm sure Dom said or did something really stupid, but are you sure this is what you want?"

Molly lowered her eyes, knowing she was being difficult, but her pride was pretty much all she had left. "I'm sorry," she said after a moment. "I know I'm being bitchy, but I pretty much lost everything today, and I'm hanging on by a thread right now."

"Oh, Molly." Toli looked at her sadly.

"Toli, I'm counting on you not to tell anyone."

"This is mistake, Molly."

"Toli." She met his gaze without flinching.

He muttered in Russian even as he nodded at her.

She squeezed his hand. "Thank you."

Molly wasn't sure how she got through the next day. Suze arrived bright and early, ready to spend the day with her, but Molly feigned nausea and pretended to sleep most of the day. Dom came after practice, but she'd refused to talk to him, much to everyone's confusion. She'd asked Suze to tell everyone she wasn't up for company, and Suze had done it reluctantly. However, after watching her warily all day Suze sensed something was wrong.

"Are you going to tell me what's going on with you and Dom?" she finally demanded.

"I'd rather not put you in the middle," Molly said softly.

"I thought we were friends?"

"Me, too," Molly turned away sadly.

"What's that supposed to mean?" Suze looked hurt.

"I'm sorry, I'm not mad at you. Dom and I had a fight and I'm just not up to talking about it. I cried all night, which is making my face hurt."

"Don't you trust me?" Suze asked.

"I do, and you're the best friend I've ever had," Molly said, meeting her gaze. "But I need a little space from everything to do with the Sidewinders. It's really hurtful to hear strangers on television insinuate you got what you deserved when your husband beat you, and then listen to them wax poetic about the brave hockey players who saved a teammate. Nothing about the woman bleeding on the floor—just the poor schmuck who was kidnapped by accident." She blinked away a fresh round of tears.

"Oh, Honey." Suze sat beside her and hugged her tightly. "You know that's not what we think, right?"

"I know it's not what *you* think," she whispered back.

Suze stared at her. "What did Dom say to you?"

"It doesn't matter." Molly shook her head. "Please, if you're really *my* friend, let me handle this the way I need to for my own sanity?"

"Dom did something dumb, didn't he?" Suze narrowed her eyes.

Molly nodded. "And I can't even explain how much it hurts."

"Why didn't you talk to him when he was here?"

"Don't you see? He's still fighting his own demons—I can't expect him to put my needs before his. And frankly, that's what I need. I need someone who can put me first. Dom can't right now and nothing anyone says to him is going to change that."

Suze hugged her as tightly as she dared. "What can I do?"

Molly just shook her head as she hugged her back.

If Dom thought Toli had been acting a little strange during practice, he knew it for sure on the flight to L.A. Toli sat on the opposite end of the plane, and when they landed he immediately exited and sat with Marco on the bus. During dinner, Toli sat with the other Russian player, Vladimir Kolnikov, and they seemed immersed in conversation, which was a first. Dom wondered if Molly had told him they'd argued, and he figured Toli was being protective of her. He'd known Toli would take her side if they ever fought, but he hadn't expected this much hostility from him.

Shaking it off, he focused on the game and was gratified that not only were they able to beat the Kings again, he scored another goal. Afterwards, he sat in the locker room listening as the media worked the room. Mostly, he just wanted to keep a low profile for a while, but he couldn't help but look up when he heard Molly's name.

"And what about Molly McCarran," the reporter was asking Toli. "Will you continue to see her?"

"She's my *friend*," Toli said sharply. "Of course I will continue to see her! This is ridiculous—perhaps the questions should be about her health, or how she's handling the emotional part of being kidnapped and beaten unconscious. Molly was a victim in case everyone has forgotten." It was never good when Toli started speaking perfect English.

"Don't you think you would have been angry if your wife of more than 20

years left you and started dating a professional hockey player?" The reporter
didn't seem to notice that the locker room had gone silent.

"If my wife of more than twenty years left me for another man, I would
wonder what I did to drive her away," Toli retorted. He held up a hand. "This
interview is over." He stalked out of the locker room and back towards the
showers.

D om watched Toli walk away in a huff and got a strange feeling in the pit of
his stomach. Toli and Molly were close, and he'd just put a journalist in his
place in front of a room full of reporters. Either something was very wrong, or
Toli was in a really bad mood. Thinking that Molly would know what was up,
he'd tried to call her, but it went straight to voicemail and he wondered how long
she was going to continue to give him the silent treatment. He'd been hoping a
few days apart would give them both time to come to terms with everything that
had happened, but she seemed to be avoiding him. She'd all but refused to talk to
him when he'd visited her at the hospital yesterday, and she didn't answer the
many times he'd tried to call today.

Frustrated, he sent her a text.

I know you're mad at me, but can't we please talk? I'm worried. Xoxo

He turned off his phone as the plane took off and closed his eyes. Tomorrow,
he would try to make things right. He'd had a long conversation with his publicist
this afternoon before the game, and she'd been sure she could turn this situation
into something positive for both him and Molly. She already had a reporter in
mind that would do an interview with Molly so she could tell her side of the story,
and she hadn't seemed worried when Dom had told her he wanted to come clean
about their relationship. Toli had taken the heat long enough and he needed Molly
to know he wasn't embarrassed to let the world know he loved her. He'd just
needed a few days to let the media storm die down. Now he was beginning to
wonder if giving her space was the best idea.

3 3

THE FLIGHT GOT IN TO LAS VEGAS AFTER MIDNIGHT, AND HE'D GONE STRAIGHT home to get some sleep. He got up at eight and after a quick shower, he headed to the hospital. He had to be at practice at eleven, but that gave him about an hour with her and he wanted to clear the air. He hadn't realized how much he would miss her in just two days, and it occurred to him that maybe she was starting to believe everything they'd been saying in the news. Celebrity gossip could be brutal, but he'd been sure she would ignore it. He wasn't paying attention to any of that, didn't she?

His walked a little faster as he got into the hospital, wondering if he'd handled the whole situation wrong. Molly wasn't like other women, and that was part of why he loved her. She was special, naïve about so much of the world, with a gentle heart that had been hurt too many times already. He wanted to make sure she was okay, and he stepped into her room anxious to see her. Instead, he looked at a neatly made bed that didn't show any signs anyone had ever been there. Confused, he stepped outside and headed for the nurse's station.

"Hi." He looked at the nurse on duty. "Can you tell me where Molly McCarran is? Room 227?"

The nurse raised her eyebrows. "She checked out early this morning, before I got on shift."

"Checked out?" he asked blankly. "Do you know where she went?"

"I'm sorry. She was gone when I got here at seven."

"Is Dr. Patel here?" he asked abruptly.

"I can page her." The nurse made a phone call and Dom paced impatiently.

Finally, he saw Dr. Patel coming down the hall. He hurried over to her. "Dr. Patel—did you release Molly?"

"I did." She looked up at him, her eyes inscrutable.

"Why?"

"She wanted to leave."

"But you said she needed at least a week so you could watch her—her kidneys and all that?"

"Sometimes a broken heart is more deadly than a broken body," she said.

Dom frowned at her. "I don't know what that means."

"Perhaps that is why Molly left without telling you."

Dom stared at her for a moment and then turned and ran out to his car.

O n the way to practice, he called Suze.
      "Where is she?" he asked as soon as she answered.

The silence on the other end told him this was much worse than he'd anticipated. Molly wasn't just upset in general; she was upset with *him*.

"Come on, Suze, I can't fix this if I can't find her."

"She wouldn't tell me because she knew you would get me to tell you." Her voice sounded tired.

"So she just disappeared, and you knew?"

"Yup."

"Dammit, Suze, why didn't you call and warn me?" he yelled, slamming his fist on the steering wheel.

"Do *not* yell at me," she said icily. "I'm not the one who fucked up here."

"What did I do?" he cried. "I was just trying to give her some time to rest and get through the worst of this. I told her I would make a public statement about us if she wanted me to."

"The fact you needed to know if she *wanted* you to is kind of the problem."

He let out a string of curses. "Suze, please—I love her. I fucked up, but I didn't mean to! Please, give me a clue to where she is."

"I swear, Dom, she wouldn't tell me." She paused. "But I'm sure there's someone who knows."

Dom paused, frowning slightly. "Toli," he said after a moment. "Toli knows." He disconnected and hit the gas. This damn car had better get him to the arena in short order.

H e was early and most of the guys weren't there yet when he stalked into the dressing room. Karl was the only one there, stretching, and he nodded in greeting.

"Have you seen Toli?" Dom asked him.

"Not yet." He glanced up. "Everything okay?"

"Molly's gone."

"Gone?" Karl stood up, frowning. "What do you mean?"

"I did something stupid, we had a fight and she left early this morning," he sighed. He threw his bag into his locker and glanced at his phone for what seemed like the thousandth time.

"Not answering your calls?" Karl asked knowingly.

"Nope."

"Well, whatever it is, you need to fix it," Drake said, coming around the corner. "Cause my sister left while we were in L.A. too."

Dom turned. "You think Molly is with her?"

"I don't know, but she hasn't answered my calls either, just sent me a text that she had a patient emergency and would be in surgery today."

"Toli knows," Dom bristled. "I'm positive of that."

"You think he's going to tell you if she asked him not to?" Drake started getting undressed.

"Fuck." Dom pulled off his t-shirt and started pulling on his gear. He'd never been good at relationships, but he hadn't expected this kind of drama from Molly. He thought she would tell him if she was upset. If she'd been angry with the way he was handling things, why hadn't she just said so? Of course, actions spoke louder than words, and her actions had spoken volumes; he'd just ignored them.

By the time Toli walked in, half the team was there and Dom was pacing like a caged animal. He was angry with himself, angry with Molly and really pissed off at Toli. He was positive Toli knew where Molly was, and equally sure he wasn't going to tell him, which got his blood boiling before he even spoke to him.

"Where is she?" he demanded as Toli walked through the door. Cody was right behind him and both of them stopped as Dom folded his arms across his chest, blocking the way.

"Get out of the way," Toli said in perfect English, his blue eyes glittering.

"The fuck I will." Dom glared back. "This isn't a game, Toli—she's got serious physical injuries and she's emotionally fragile to boot. I need to know where she is."

"She doesn't *want* you to know where she is," Toli didn't budge, despite Cody's prodding from behind.

"Guys, we don't need to do this here or now," Cody said, finally pushing his way past Toli into the room.

"Yeah, we do." Dom pointed a finger at Toli. "You were just waiting for the opportunity to pounce, weren't you? You couldn't wait for us to have a fight so you could swoop in and be the knight in shining armor. Well, guess what, buddy— like it or not, she's *my* girl."

"If she's *your* girl," Toli said evenly, "then why the hell was I the one on national TV defending her? Why was I the one she called when the man she loves broke her heart? Why was a team rookie the guy who got hauled away in hand-cuffs for something you did? Where the hell have *you* been through this?"

"I was right here!" Dom yelled, moving closer to Toli until they were face to face. "I asked her what she wanted me to do and she said she was fine! I didn't ask Zakk to take the blame for me either—he offered!"

"How convenient." Toli shook his head. "Everyone stepped up to protect you, so all you had to do was protect *her*, but you were so wrapped in yourself you forgot about the most important thing in the world—the woman who helped you get back to where you are."

"I didn't forget shit!" Dom spat at him, his fists clenched at his sides.

"You hurt her," Toli said, slowly dropping his bag. "And I warned you not to hurt her. I *told* you I would be unhappy if you did."

"What the fuck does that mean?" Dom ground out. "You think you're gonna take me on?"

"No one is taking anyone on," Cody tried to step between them but neither man moved. "Dammit, guys, this is not the place!"

"Tell me where she is!" Dom yelled, shoving Toli backwards. Toli came back fast, catching Dom around the middle and knocking him to the ground. Dom was six-five and two hundred and thirty-five pounds of pure muscle; Toli was six-two and two hundred pounds, but he was fast and strong. They rolled over on the dressing room floor, swinging wildly. Dom connected with Toli's jaw, but Toli came back with a blow to the chest that had Dom gasping for air.

"Dammit, stop it!" Cody grabbed for Toli and Drake stepped in to pull Dom back. Drake was probably the only guy on the team who could hold Dom back, and they did a short dance as Dom struggled to get away.

"*What the fuck?*" Coach Barnett stepped into the dressing room, his eyes blazing angrily. "Both of you—in my office now!" He turned on his heel after glowering at them.

Dom and Toli followed, Toli wiping blood from his lip and Dom holding his side. They didn't look at each other as they walked, and then stood on opposite ends of the room as Coach Barnett slammed the door to his office.

"Are you fucking kidding me?" he yelled, looking between them. "I thought the trouble on this team would be Karl kicking the snot out of Marco—not the two of you! You want to tell me what *the fuck* is going on?"

Neither of them spoke and Brad raised an eyebrow. "This is about Molly."

Again, no one spoke and Brad slammed his hand down on his desk angrily. "Somebody better start talking or I swear to God the two of you will be doing laps Herb Brooks style!" The reference to the 1980 US Olympic team didn't seem to faze either of them.

The two men glanced at each other and finally Toli spoke. "It's nothing. Dom and Molly had a fight and he thinks I'm trying to steal her, but I am not."

Dom stood stone-faced, still breathing hard.

"Dom, you gonna speak up or do laps until next week?"

"What do you want me to say?" he snapped. "Apparently Molly's mad at me, but no one will tell me what I did wrong!"

"And you brought this to work?" Brad rolled his eyes. "Dom, I thought you were good?"

"I'm good!" he practically snarled. "I just want to know where my girl is."

Brad glanced at Toli. "Toli, knock it off—this isn't high school. Don't get involved in their relationship."

"I'm not involved like he thinks," he said seriously. "They had a fight and she came to me because she didn't think she could go to him. She asked me not to tell him where she is and I'm trying to be there for her because she has no idea how to handle being in the middle of all this bullshit in the media. If Dom hadn't been so busy thinking about his career and how he looks to the NHL, maybe he would have been there for her instead of me." He shook his head. "She doesn't love me,

Dom—she loves you—but you hurt her and I'll be damned if I abandon her in the middle of all this. I would never go out with your girl behind your back—you should know that."

For a while no one said anything and Dom finally sank into a chair. "I don't know what I did," he said. "I swear to God, I thought she needed time to rest and let the worst of this blow over. She told me—all of us—to go out and play, so that's what I did."

"That was *before* they called her a whore on TV," Toli interjected.

Dom blanched, realizing how ridiculous he sounded right now. God, he'd fucked this up royally. He rubbed his hands down his face and sighed.

"So are you two okay?" Coach Barnett shook his head. "Dom, you can't be doing this shit. I'm cutting you some slack because the last few days have been hell, but this is it. You understand me?"

"Yeah, Coach."

"Will you tell Dom where she is, Toli?" Coach Barnett asked.

"I cannot." Toli shook his head. "If I betray her trust, she will run from me too, and then what will we do? She has to have someone who has her back right now —" Dom started to interrupt, but Toli stopped him. "Right now, I'm all she has— if I betray her, she will be alone."

For a moment they were quiet. "Toli—thirty laps. Go." Brad motioned with his head and Toli headed out.

Dom started to get up but Brad held up his hand. "Listen to me. As your coach, I have to give you thirty laps just like I gave him. But as your friend, you need to get your head out of your ass and fix things with Molly."

"I don't know where she is or how to get her to listen! I've called and texted a hundred times."

"You're a smart guy with money—use your resources, son."

Dom nodded wearily. "What happens if she doesn't want me back?"

"She will," he said. "You just need to prove to her you're going to step up to the plate—NHL or not. This wasn't on you, Dom. You did a good thing; you're not in trouble with the league."

"Fuck." He was frustrated.

"You're still holding your stomach. You all right? Can you skate?"

Dom gave him a wary smile. "A head butt from a Russian isn't enough to keep me down, Coach."

Brad just shook his head. "Go."

3 4

L YING ON THE COOL, COMFORTABLE BED, M OLLY WAS GRATEFUL TO BE ABLE TO rest. She and Mack had flown in this morning and even with the drugs she'd been in pain. They arrived in Chicago and Mack immediately checked her into the private clinic where she did surgery and her patients subsequently recuperated. Molly was tired and sore, her face throbbing and her ribs killing her. She started to doze off almost instantly, even as Mack checked her temperature.

"You have a fever," she murmured. "I'm going to start an IV and get you on a low dose of antibiotics. If the fever continues, I may have to call in someone else. We were concerned about internal bleeding, but I don't have the equipment for that kind of thing here."

Molly sighed, too miserable to do anything but nod.

"Molly, if I have to take you to a regular hospital, there will be bills."

"I know. I talked to my lawyer yesterday and he said I'll probably be getting a lot more than what we originally thought since Tim is being prosecuted, so he'll do a letter for me saying the money will be coming, it just may take a while."

"Okay." Mack hesitated. "Are you sure you want to leave things like this?"

"With Dom, you mean?"

"With everyone. You left your whole life behind, without a backward glance. That can't feel good, and although Dom let you down, I don't believe he doesn't love you."

"I don't know what I believe," Molly whispered. "I trusted him and thought he was going to be my everything—then he just ducked for cover when the shit hit the fan."

"I think he's a little gun-shy."

"I know he is, but at the end of the day, his career and his reputation were more important than me, and I can't live like that."

"I don't blame you, but I also don't think you should write Dom off just yet."

"I feel so crappy right now I can't even think about him." Molly closed her eyes and Mack felt her forehead.

"You're really warm. I'm going to start the IV and let's see how you feel in a few hours."

"Okay."

Mack worked quickly and efficiently, all the while thinking about her options. Molly needed to have someone here with her. This wasn't a simple plastic surgery case, and while Mack was happy to help someone in need, she was beginning to think Molly's injuries might be more serious than they'd first thought. Although she'd seemed okay in Las Vegas, now it was looking like something else was happening. Her kidneys had been severely bruised and Mack wracked her brain trying to think of a nephrologist she knew here in Chicago. There were a few, but no one she was close to and Molly's lack of insurance could be a problem. She understood her need to be independent after everything that had happened, but this wasn't a time to be proud.

Reluctantly, she went down to her office and picked up the phone. She might regret this, but she wasn't sure she had a choice.

The locker room was quiet after their morning skate on Friday. San Jose would be in town tonight for the next pre-season game, and the team was trying to stay focused on keeping up their winning streak. Karl would be in goal tonight, and Marco was stomping around the room in a snit. Toli and Dom were keeping their distance, making the vibe in the room different than their first two games. Cody watched them with concern, wondering how they were going to play together with the tangible friction between them. The others were picking up on it too, and that wasn't good.

Drake was the first one dressed and he looked at Cody. "Hey, you got a minute?"

"Sure." Cody followed him out into the hallway where Drake paced restlessly.

"Look," he said. "There's a situation."

"What's going on?" Cody looked worried.

"It's Molly."

"You heard from her?"

He sighed. "She's with my sister and she's had a complication. I don't know who to tell. Mack is between a rock and a hard place—she thinks Molly might need surgery and without insurance..." His voice trailed off.

"Shit." Cody groaned.

"Molly doesn't know she told me—technically, she's breached patient confidentiality but it's either that or Molly might die."

"Is it that bad?" Cody's eyes widened.

Drake nodded miserably. "She spiked a fever yesterday and today they had to admit her to the hospital. They think maybe her kidney has disconnected from a blood vessel or something. Mack's been trying to find a surgeon who'll take her pro bono."

"Dom needs to know," Cody said without hesitation. "This ends now." He turned and went back into the locker room. "Dom. Toli. Now." He turned and walked back out again, heading to Coach Barnett's office.

"What's going on?" Dom demanded.

Cody didn't say anything until they were in the office. Coach looked up in irritation, but Cody shook his head slightly. He shut the door and looked at them. "Okay, here's the deal. Molly's taken a turn for the worse, and she can't get a surgeon to see her because she doesn't have insurance. You two are going to have to figure this shit out, because Molly's in trouble."

"She hasn't called me!" Toli said before Dom could react. "Toli would have sent money—you know that!"

"How the hell do you know this?" Dom demanded of Cody.

"Drake heard from Mack."

There was a moment of silence before Dom spoke. "Tell Drake to give his sister whatever money she needs and I'll pay him back." Dom said. "Is she in Chicago?"

Cody nodded.

"Do you know where, exactly?"

"No, but we can find out."

Dom turned to Coach Barnett. "I have to go, Coach. She needs me and I'm going to be there."

Brad nodded. "Go."

Dom looked at Toli. "I'll tell her you kept her secret."

Toli made a slight motion with his head. "Take care of her," was all he said.

Dom turned and left the room.

A rriving at the airport in Chicago late that evening, Dom rented a car and drove to the address Mack had given him earlier. He had no idea what he was going to say to Molly, but he had to figure it out. Being without her even these few days had been miserable. He'd been so angry and frustrated, both with her and with himself, he didn't even know what to do anymore. The idea she believed he would pick his career over her was crazy; he didn't understand how she got that idea.

Yes, he'd wanted to lay low but not because he didn't want to stick up for her. In fact, it was quite the opposite; his going public about their relationship would only confirm to closed-minded people that she had technically been cheating on Tim. Everything Tim did to her would be forgotten amid the reality she'd been cheating. However, he'd taken steps to rectify the situation before he'd left Las Vegas, thanks to Kate.

He pulled up to the hospital and hesitated slightly before sending a text. Then he walked into the building. Mack was waiting for him as she'd promised and he was surprised to see how tired she looked.

"Hi, Dom." She smiled as he hugged her and kissed her cheek.

"Thanks for taking care of her—how is she?"

"We had a bit of a scare," she admitted. "She was bleeding pretty badly and the surgery to correct the detached blood vessel took longer than normal, but Dr. Halpern says she's doing better now."

"Can I see her?"

"She's tired and doped up—you're going to have to tread carefully."

"I promise," he said somberly.

"Let's go." She led him to the elevator and they rode up to the top floor. Walking together, Mack motioned she would walk in first. He paused outside the door as she went in.

"Molly?" Mack's voice was soft in the dimly lit room. "How are you feeling?"

"Like I got beat up again," Molly whispered. "What time is it?"

"Almost ten. You've been asleep most of the day."

"You should go home," Molly felt herself getting drowsy again.

"I need to tell you something first," Mack said gently.

"Am I okay?"

"You're fine, but I need you to understand I did something you're not going to like."

"What?"

"I had to get someone to pay the surgeon or you might not have gotten the care you needed—you could have died, Molly."

"Did you call Toli?"

"No." Mack hesitated. "Dom, come on in."

"Oh." Molly sighed even in her drug-induced haze.

"I'm sorry," Mack said gently. "But I had to make sure you had access to the best doctors." She turned and quietly left the room, touching Dom's arm as she went.

"You didn't have to come," Molly said, feeling tears well up in her eyes as she looked at him. He looked so damn handsome, but there was sadness in his eyes she'd never seen before. Instinctively, she reached out her hand to him. He took it and gently leaned over to brush his lips across her forehead.

"I'm so sorry, baby," he whispered. "I didn't mean to hurt you. I don't know what I was thinking, but I'm going to do whatever I have to do to fix this."

"Maybe it wasn't meant to be," she whispered. "Maybe you need to work on you—without me."

"No." He shook his head vehemently. "I love you. I didn't mean to screw things up. I made a mistake, but I'm new to relationships too—you've got to give me another chance."

"Dom?" Molly's voice was barely audible.

"Yeah, babe?"

"I need Mack…" Her voice trailed off as her eyes rolled back in her head.

"Mack!" Dom bolted for the door, his stomach seizing in panic.

Mack came running in and suddenly there were people everywhere. Dom stepped out of the way, unsure what to do as several nurses and another doctor came in.

"She's bleeding again," someone said.

"Page Dr. Halpern," Mack said quickly.

"We need to prep her for surgery."

"We need to move her stat." They began wheeling her out and Dom stared, paralyzed by fear.

"Mack, what..." His voice was barely a whisper.

"The kidney is bleeding again," she said. "But Halpern is one of the best. He'll take care of her."

"Oh God." He sank into the nearest chair feeling nauseous. "I don't understand —what's happening?"

"During the beating, some of the blood vessels in her kidney were fractured and disconnected. She was bleeding and they operated to stop it, but the surgeon said he was afraid there might be more he couldn't see because of swelling. Apparently, he was right because she's bleeding again."

"But how will he see them now if he couldn't see them before?" He stared at her in despair.

"We have to trust him." She took his hand in hers.

It felt like hours before the doctor came out and Dom thought he was going to lose his mind. He paced until his legs hurt and then he stared out the windows wondering what he would do if she died. He called Suze and booked her on a 6:00 a.m. flight out of Las Vegas. Then he sat and waited, fighting the urge to scream at the top of his lungs.

This was the kind of panic he'd felt the night Brian died, as they'd all been waiting for the doctor to come out and verify he was gone. After this past summer and meeting Molly, he'd thought these memories were long gone, yet here they were again, making his pulse race and sweat drip down his back. By the time the doctor came out, Dom almost couldn't breathe.

"She's doing well," Dr. Halpern said, shaking Dom's hand. "Better than expected considering everything. I think we've got it all now, and she should be able to rest comfortably. However, there was something in tonight's blood work that didn't show up on the records she brought from Las Vegas."

"What is it?" Dom felt his stomach clench again.

"It appears that Molly is pregnant."

"Oh my God." Dom felt dizzy and Mack quickly pushed him into a chair.

"Dom? Is that possible?" Mack touched his arm.

"We've been trying..." His voice trailed off. "She has a history of miscarriages —she's not going to handle it well if she loses another baby. How did they not notice before?"

"The levels aren't very high, so she's just barely pregnant—maybe a few weeks? Most women wouldn't be getting a blood test this early on."

"Yeah, that's all it could be," he whispered. "We decided to start trying because she's..." He swallowed. "Because she's 40."

"With the amount of blood she's lost, I think you need to prepare yourself for the worst with regard to the pregnancy," the doctor said gently. "But everything else is good."

Dom closed his eyes and nodded. He could feel Mack's hand on his shoulder, rubbing gently as he struggled with another bout of nausea. It was like reliving a nightmare, and this time he was to blame. He got there in time to save her, but maybe not the child they both wanted so much. He had no idea how he would tell her.

D om woke to laughter in the hallway and a crick in his neck. He stretched slowly, cognizant of Molly sleeping close to him. She'd woken in the middle of the night and asked him to lie next to her, so that's what he'd done, despite the tiny bed and his huge body. Carefully, he lifted himself out of the bed and stretched.

"About time you woke up," Mack came in holding out a cup of coffee.

"Thank you, God," he breathed, taking it from her gratefully.

"You can call me Mack," she chuckled, smiling. She looked fresh and alert this morning, wearing a tight black skirt and red blouse. She wore her lab coat over her clothes, and probably looked a lot better than he felt, but she couldn't have gotten much more sleep than he had.

"Has the doctor been by at all?"

"As a matter of fact, he was here about an hour ago and we just let you sleep. Molly's fever is gone and everything looks good. He thinks she's going to be fine."

"What about the baby?"

Mack gave a slight shrug. "So far, there's no change."

He nodded. "I'm going to try to freshen up. Will you stay with her?"

"Sure." Mack sat down in the chair next to where Molly slept. A moment later the door opened and Cody and Suze came in. Mack put a finger to her lips and they all stepped back out into the hall.

"What's happening?" Suze asked. "Dom sounded frantic last night."

Mack explained everything that had happened just as Dom came out to join them. He hugged Suze and Cody put a hand on his shoulder.

"How are you holding up?" he asked.

"I'm not really sure," Dom admitted. "She scared the crap out of me last night when they rushed her off to surgery..."

"I have patients to see today," Mack said. "But I'll be back this afternoon. Call my cell if you need anything, okay?"

"Thanks." Dom hugged her tightly. "For everything."

"You're welcome." Mack nodded at Cody and Suze and swept down the hall.

"You look exhausted," Suze said softly. "What can we do for you?"

Dom sank into a chair. "She's pregnant."

"What?" Suze's eyes opened wide. "How?"

Dom gave her a look. "The doctor said we should expect the worst, after everything she's been through. He doesn't think the baby will make it, between the physical trauma, the blood loss and two surgeries."

"Oh hell." Cody sat by his side and put his arm around his friend's shoulders. "Does she know yet?"

"No." Dom shook his head. "The levels in her blood are low, so they think it's probably just a few weeks."

"Has she seen the press conference?" Suze asked, sitting beside him.

"No. We barely had time to talk before she started bleeding again. She woke up long enough to ask me to lay next to her about five this morning and that was it. What time is it now?" He looked around, confused.

"It's after ten," Cody said. "We got here as quick as we could."

"How'd we do last night?" Dom asked, remembering the game against San Jose and desperate to hear about something normal in his world.

"Sharks went home with their tails between their legs," Cody said with a grin. "Karl got the shutout."

"Good for him." Dom nodded. Despite being happy about the win, he was so tired. Hockey was the last thing on his mind, but he needed to think beyond these sterile walls and the pain they represented both now and in the past. All he'd been able to think about was how close he'd come to losing her. He needed her to be okay, and it scared him to think she might not come through this.

"I'm going to fly out to meet the team in Colorado tomorrow morning," Cody said after a moment. "Coach said to tell you to take whatever time you need. We still have 10 days before the regular season starts, but if you need more time he'll work it out."

Dom nodded absently. He couldn't imagine leaving Molly right now, much less getting on a plane to Colorado. He wouldn't leave her until she was okay.

"Have you thought about marrying her?" Suze asked him, leaning over and resting her chin in her hand.

Dom blinked. "Well, yeah. But she's kind of mad at me right now, not to mention barely conscious."

"I think you should pop the question as soon as she wakes up."

"I don't have a ring."

"Then I could go ring shopping for you!" Suze wiggled her eyebrows and Dom managed to laugh.

"She's not divorced yet." He frowned. "We've got to talk to that damn lawyer."

"Actually," Cody pulled an envelope out of his jacket. "Coach made some calls and we got this. Technically, she's been divorced since September first, but the court clerk was in Tim's pocket. Lonnie Finch got an attorney involved when Coach mentioned the delay in the divorce papers, and apparently the judge signed off on everything on the 1st but his clerk conveniently forgot to send out the papers. They got this for you yesterday."

"Thank you." Dom took the papers with shaky hands and put them on his lap. All he wanted was to hear Molly's voice and know she was okay. Divorce papers in hand, he slipped back into her room.

Molly was awake and he leaned over to kiss her lips. "Good morning," he said.

"I woke up and you were gone," she whispered.

"Sorry, I needed to go to the bathroom and get coffee." He held up the cup he still held. "And then you got visitors." He let out a low whistle and Suze practically bounded into the room.

"Suze!" Molly's face lit up and she reached out her arms. Suze hugged her gently.

"I was so worried about you."

"I'm so happy you're here." She glanced at Dom. "All of you."

"Everything's going to be okay," Suze said.

"I don't even know what happened," Molly rubbed her eyes, wincing at the pain that was ever-present in her face. The drugs kept everything at a dull roar, but she couldn't touch her face without some reaction.

"You had more bleeding in the kidney," Dom gave her an abbreviated version of what had happened.

"Why do you all look like you're hiding something from me?" She focused on Suze, because she would cave faster than the guys.

"I have lots of things I haven't told you," Dom said quickly. "But I'd like to tell you in private…"

"We're going to go get some food," Suze said, standing up. She kissed Molly's forehead and grinned. "Let the big lug grovel for a while—it'll be fun and I wish I could watch, but Cody says I can't." She winked at her husband, who chuckled.

"You're coming back, right?" Molly asked worriedly.

"Of course!" Suze waved and Cody squeezed Molly's hand before they left.

For a moment, neither Dom nor Molly spoke, simply gazing at each other with a little bit of trepidation. He had no idea where to start, and Molly couldn't figure out what he was thinking.

"So," he cleared his throat. "Are you still mad at me?"

She smiled faintly. "I'm too tired to be mad at anyone—that would take energy I don't have."

He slowly stroked her hair. "I'm sorry about all of this, baby. I guess I was thinking more about how we would have handled things if you weren't in the hospital. I was thinking it would be easier for us to lay low until the lawyers sorted stuff out. My biggest fear about announcing to the world we were together was that it would make all the assholes out there right—technically, you were still married when we started sleeping together. I don't give a shit about what people think about me, but I didn't want that for you." His eyes bore into hers with so much emotion, she nearly sucked in her breath.

"I'm sorry," she said after a moment. "I needed you and you were suddenly so distant…"

"I was scared," he admitted. "Everything happened so fast, and I kept thinking about Brian when I was holding you and you were bleeding everywhere. I needed a little distance from the smell of death." He hung his head. "I'm sorry. It wasn't you—it was my demons coming back to kick my ass."

"I should have come out and told you what I needed," she admitted. "I expected you to read my mind because basically that's what you've done since day one. I was in trouble and you knew I wanted to be saved, that I didn't really want to die. I kept saying it couldn't work between us because of the age difference, but you knew I wanted you. Since the beginning you've been able to tell what I needed, and I thought that since you didn't this time, it meant something different."

He shook his head. "I love you, baby; I was just overwhelmed. But I've got my head on straight now, and I've got your back." He went over to his bag and pulled out his iPad. He took a minute to connect to the internet and then pulled up a web site.

"What are you doing?" she asked.

"Can you sit up a little?"

She nodded and he used the remote control to lift the bed. "Before I left, we had a press conference. Me, Cody, Toli, Drake, Karl and Zakk, since we were the ones involved. There are a few lies in my speech, but that's because we can't go back now and change what we told the police since Zakk could be charged with perjury, and we don't want to go there, but the rest—especially with respect to you —is true. I guess I lied about when our relationship started, but that was about protecting *you*, not me. I'm a guy—taking into account the fact I was single when we met, no one is going to look twice at me getting laid, even if you were married. So the only details I changed were to protect you." He put the iPad on the tray table and rested it against the box of tissues so that she would be able to see it.

Molly watched as a clip came up on ESPN, showing a long table where Dom, Cody, Toli, Drake, Karl and Zakk all sat. They wore suits and looked so somber and professional she felt a moment of discomfort.

"Thanks for coming." Dom spoke in a steady, firm voice and then introduced everyone. "First, I want to make sure you understand there will be no questions at the end of this. We're here to set the record straight about the incident with Molly McCarran and Sergei Petrov, and that's all. Cody and I first met Molly when I arrived in Las Vegas in June. We came upon a situation where Molly was being beaten by her husband, Tim. Cody was quick enough to start taping that incident." He motioned to someone off to the side and a videotape came up on a screen off to the side of where they sat. It was the tape of the day they'd met and Molly had to swallow her distaste as she watched. Dom squeezed her hand as the press conference continued.

"We kept this video out of the media because we wanted to respect Molly's privacy, but now there has been so much speculation about who she is and what happened, it's time to clear this up. When I saw what was happening that day, I knew I needed to help her. I couldn't let her go back to that life. What happened after that isn't a huge surprise. She moved in with me for a few days, and then she stayed with Cody and his wife for a while. We became friends. We helped her put divorce proceedings in place and started helping her get her life back together. When Toli arrived from Russia, he had just broken up with his long-time girlfriend, and they became friends as well.

"Molly was afraid her husband would find her, since he had a long history of abuse, so she used Toli's address in her divorce papers, even though she was really living with Cody and Suze. It was a matter of safety, and all of us took that threat seriously. As the summer went on, Molly and I formed a bond and got to be close friends. I started to have romantic feelings for her, but we both wanted to wait until the time was right. Her lawyer kept saying the divorce was final, but the papers never arrived. At some point, as we got close to the beginning of training camp, Molly and I realized we were in love. The lawyer assured us her divorce was just a glitch in the system so we went ahead with our relationship. Neither of us is ashamed of it—she filed for divorce back in June and moved on with her life.

"On the day of the incident in question, Molly was at the grocery store when her ex-husband used a stun gun to kidnap her. The night before, he had accidentally kidnapped Toli's brother, Sergei, who was in town visiting. From a distance they look a lot alike, and Tim thought he was Molly's new boyfriend since she'd been using Toli's address. There was nothing going on and they had nothing to hide, but in his mind, she was cheating. Molly had been at yoga that morning, and had her cell phone stuck in a pocket inside her yoga pants, so she managed to get out a text letting us know she was in trouble. When I got the text in the locker room, these men beside me were the ones who stepped up to help me go get her. As you all know, I have a bit of a temper." There was light laughter in the press room before Dom continued.

"We showed up at Tim's house and there was a group of officers outside. Zakk and I snuck around back to see if there was a way into the house. Cody and the others called 911 and the media, while they stood outside keeping Tim's friends too busy to notice us sneaking in. When we got inside, Molly was already unconscious and bleeding on the floor. Sergei heard us and even though he was tied up, he threw himself at Tim to give us a chance to get to them. I ran to Molly while Zakk restrained Tim. There was a brief fight, but Zakk did what he had to do to help Sergei get away and to keep Tim from doing anything else.

"That's the whole story, in a nutshell. Molly never cheated on Tim, and my understanding from our attorney is that she was free to start dating after she filed for divorce, which she did on June twentieth. She and I didn't start actually dating until sometime in August—I didn't write the date down in my calendar. We went from friendship to something more over the course of the summer and then her ex-husband did something really heinous. This is the real story, and I'm hoping you're going to let us move on, both personally and professionally. The Sidewinders are three-and-oh in the pre-season and we're really excited to bring NHL level hockey to Las Vegas, so that's where we'd like the focus to be."

"Are you and Molly still dating?" One of the reporters called out as Dom started to get up. He paused and looked back.

"I said there would be no questions, but I will answer that one: Yes, we are still dating and plan to be together for the long haul. I would appreciate it if you would respect our privacy right now while she's healing from her injuries. She's had three surgeries since the incident due to internal bleeding and—"

"What are her injuries, Dom?" someone else called out.

Dom sighed. "Our PR department will release a statement about all that. Thank you." He and the others rose and filed out. The clip ended.

Molly looked at Dom with tears in her eyes. "I love you," she whispered. "I'm sorry I doubted you."

"I'm sorry I gave you reason to doubt me." He reached for her hand and brought it to his lips.

"Then why do you look so sad?" she asked softly, watching his eyes.

"Because I have something else to tell you," he said in a ragged breath.

"What is it?"

"Well, we hit pay dirt in our quest for a baby."

"What?" She cocked her head. "What do you mean? We didn't stop using condoms until a few weeks ago..."

"They had to do a lot of blood work and even though it didn't show up when you first got to the hospital, it's showing up now; elevated levels of HCG."

"Why is that sad news?" she asked slowly.

"Because of everything that's happened, and your history of miscarriage, the doctor said..." He couldn't believe he was getting choked up. "The doctor said we should expect the worst."

Her eyes widened slightly and then she closed them. "Has there been bleeding?"

"Not that kind—you had all kinds of internal bleeding, but not vaginally. The doctor just said that between the beating, the bleeding and multiple surgeries, the chances of this pregnancy staying viable are low."

"Damn." She bit her lip and blinked away a few stray tears.

"Don't cry," he whispered, laying his head on her shoulder. "We can try again or find a surrogate. I don't care—I only care about you."

"I'm sorry I'm broken," she said raggedly.

"You're not," He shook his head. "I promise you, no one will ever lay a hand on you again. You're never going to feel broken again."

"Can we just pretend it's going to be okay?" she whispered suddenly, swiping at her eyes.

"The baby?"

"Yeah. Can we go forward acting like it's going to be okay? We won't tell anyone—that would be too hard—but I want to enjoy it. If I have another miscarriage, they might have to do a hysterectomy, so this might be the only time I can be pregnant with your baby."

He nodded as he swallowed a huge lump in his throat. "Sure. Except Suze and Cody already know.'"

"That's okay—I would have told Suze anyway." She stroked his hair, thankful he was with her again. "So what do you want? A boy or a girl? And do *not* say you just want a healthy baby—you have to have a preference!"

He smiled. "A boy, of course! Someone I can teach to play hockey!"

She smiled too. "That's what I was thinking too. Can we name him Dominic, Jr.?"

He wrinkled his nose. "Do we have to?"

"You don't like your name?"

"It was my dad's name, and I hate to carry on his legacy with our baby because he was an asshole."

"We can name him whatever you want."

"I want to name him Brian," he said softly. "Since *his* biological son is actually named Cody, I'd like my son to be Brian."

"Brian's a good name," she nodded.

"What if it's a girl?" he asked.

She laughed. "I want something really funky—like Savannah or Taryn or something like that!"

He shook his head. "Why something so trendy?"

"I don't know—I want her to grow up strong and independent, and a name like that will help her kick ass and take names."

"So Mohammed Ali?" he joked.

She giggled. It was such a beautiful sound he leaned up and kissed her.

S itting in the arena with Suze, Andra, Tiff and Rachel, Molly was excited to be out in public again. It had been a long seven weeks since the incident with Tim, but she was finally eating solid food and able to walk without pain. Her arm wasn't in a sling anymore, her kidneys were healing nicely and she was ten weeks pregnant. So far, to the amazement of all her doctors, the pregnancy remained healthy. An ultrasound had revealed a strong heartbeat and she and Dom were trying desperately not to get their hopes up, but with each passing day, the baby's chance of survival grew.

Looking down at the glistening engagement ring on her finger, she was happier than she'd ever been. She and Dom had secretly eloped as soon as she left the hospital in Chicago, with only Cody and Suze in attendance. Being married would give her access to his health insurance, which had to be a priority right now. Though he had plenty of money, medical costs added up quickly, and with such a high-risk pregnancy, they decided it would be better to be covered. In the summer, after the baby was born, they would have a real wedding and go on a honeymoon. In the meantime, only a handful of people knew they were married and she was having the time of her life planning a wedding with Suze.

"Let's go Sidewinders!" Suze yelled beside her.

Molly had strict orders to take it easy but she was enjoying herself. She'd been on partial bed rest since she'd come home from the hospital, both because of her healing body and the pregnancy. She did almost nothing all day, but she'd finally been cleared for light yoga, so she and Suze had gone this morning. Though she was stiff and sore, it felt good to finally get back to some semblance of normalcy.

The other fun news was that Suze was pregnant too, nine weeks along and thriving. Their due dates were only a week apart so Molly pushed down thoughts of losing yet another baby, thinking about how much fun it would be to have their kids close together.

As the Sidewinders took the ice, Molly watched Dom intently, skating out behind Cody and Toli. Cody had been officially named Captain, wearing the C proudly on his jersey. Dom and Toli were the two Alternate Captains, and Molly had known wearing a jersey with an A sewn on the shoulder had been a high point in Dom's career. Though she'd been forced to watch all the other games on TV, she'd finally gotten permission to come tonight and it took all of her self-control not to jump up and down. She was healing well, but her priority was keeping the baby safe.

She saw Dom look up in her direction and lift his stick. She waved, a big smile on her face.

"God, you two are ridiculous," Suze teased her.

"And proud of it," Molly grinned.

"I thought sure you two would run off and get married the moment you got out of the hospital," Andra said.

"I didn't get a real wedding the first time," Molly said with a secret smile. "And I'll be damned if I don't get one this time."

"When is it?" Andra asked.

"August," Molly said.

"I'm already excited!"

Molly and Toli were as close as ever, and she was grateful for his presence in her life. He and Dom had buried the hatchet so she felt okay about spending time with him. Now that Sergei and Tatiana were officially together, he'd been more okay than she'd thought he would be. They were meant to be, he'd told her, and though she knew he believed that, it still left him unsettled. He'd been in a relationship for all of his adult life, with a few exceptions during times he and Tatiana had broken up; hence when Anton was conceived. But now he was completely single and about as interested in dating as he was in having a root canal.

"Women are difficult," he'd told her wryly.

Watching Zakk score the first goal of the night left the girls cheering loudly and he turned to point his stick at them, making them laugh in delight.

"How many girls do you think he's sleeping with?" Suze stage whispered to their group.

"A lot!" Tiff laughed. "He's soooo hot. Good thing I'm happily married, cause I'd get me a piece of that if I wasn't!"

They laughed again. Molly looked down and saw Dom turn back from where he sat on the bench. He found her eyes and winked; she blew him a kiss before he turned back to the game.

I got my happily-ever-after, she thought to herself, and Dom got his life back. They'd climbed out of the darkness, together, and found their way back to the light. Today was the first day of forever and she couldn't wait to find out what happened next.

EPILOGUE

Dom took slow, steady breaths as he buttoned his shirt. Focusing on the task of getting dressed was the only thing keeping him from running to the bathroom and losing his breakfast. This was going to be the hardest things he'd ever done and it suddenly felt like everything he'd done in the last year had led up to this moment. Ten long months that had brought the most remarkable changes to his life, even though he wasn't sure if he deserved them.

Shaking off the melancholy thoughts, he looked over to where Molly was fixing her hair in the bathroom. Her face was almost healed since the beating and the subsequent plastic surgery she'd had no choice but to have. Her nose had been broken so badly she couldn't breathe, and the fractured jaw made it impossible to eat. They'd met with every possible specialist to ensure the baby she carried would be okay, but in the end they worried if her jaw healed wrong she would be both disfigured and in pain. Somehow, everything had come out okay, including the baby.

She looked as beautiful as ever and he stole up behind her, wrapping his arms around her expanding waist. He rubbed her small stomach gently, resting against her. She smiled up at him, her eyes narrowing slightly when she felt him tremble.

"You're shaking," she whispered, turning to him. She grasped his hands in hers and met his eyes directly. "He can't hurt you now," she said softly. "I'm here, Cody and Suze are just downstairs, and Toli and the others are nearby. We've got your back, and you've got this."

"I know." He took a deep breath. "I just want it to be okay."

"It's going to be." She touched his face. "If it wasn't, he wouldn't have agreed to meet with you."

"What if he wants to sue me or something?" he whispered.

She shrugged. "Then we pay him. He doesn't have any power over us, babe. It's just money."

He nodded, though he felt sick.

"Come on." She pulled him by the hand and grabbed her purse. "Let's go."

They took the elevator downstairs and she held his hand tightly until they got to the small hotel conference room where the meeting would take place. Cody and Suze were there waiting for them, and he looked at his friend gratefully.

"You don't know how much this means to me," he said softly.

Cody smiled. "Yeah, I do." He motioned with his head. "He's already in there —let's do this."

Dom swallowed hard, but nodded. He turned to Molly and pressed his lips to hers.

"I'll be right here," she said softly. "I love you."

"I love you too." He squeezed Suze's shoulder as he passed her. He and Cody paused at the door and looked at each other.

"Whatever happens, it's going to be okay," was all Cody said.

Dom opened the door and stepped inside.

Bobby Thomas was sitting in a chair, his curly blond hair slicked back and the jacket of his suit unbuttoned. His eyes met Dom's and after a slight hesitation, he got to his feet, extending a hand. Dom walked forward slowly and shook it. Neither of them spoke and finally Bobby's companion, another player for the Canadiens, cleared his throat.

"Thank you for meeting me," Dom managed to find his voice. "Uh, this is Cody Armstrong."

They made introductions before they all sat down, the four men staring at each other with an awkward silence.

"I'm not sure why we're here," Bobby said at last, his eyes moving from Dom to Cody and back again.

"Because I owe you an apology," Dom said. "A real one—not the bullshit mandated by the League. What I did was fucked up, and I needed you to know that, man to man."

Bobby nodded, seeming just as nervous as Dom. "Okay."

"I don't expect forgiveness, or that we're going to just bury the hatchet and pretend like it never happened," Dom continued, trying to still his shaking hands. "But I wanted to sit across from you and give you my word that nothing like what I did to you will ever happen again."

"Good to know."

"And if you ever need anything, whatever it is, I owe you."

Bobby took a long drink from the glass of water in front of him and the room fell into silence once again. He glanced at his teammate, who hadn't said a word since Dom started talking, and got to his feet. He began pacing, looking every-where but at Dom

"When I woke up in the hospital they told me my neck was broken," he said after a minute. "They said the spinal cord hadn't been severed but that I would probably never play hockey again." He turned and fixed Dom with a stare. "I hated you. I was so fucking mad, the only thing that got me through those first days was hoping I could get well enough to kill you." He paused. "And then I started drinking and partying, making an ass out of myself. I figured some guy broke my neck—I had the right." He was still pacing, gazing out the big conference room windows.

"Bobby, I—" Dom got up but Bobby held out a hand.

"Let me finish." He turned. "One night I picked up this girl. She was great—really hot, smart, funny—and she could suck the chrome off a tailpipe." He shook his head, a faint smile playing on his lips. "We'd gone a couple rounds when I went looking for my bottle of Jack Daniels, but it was empty. I told her to go get me some." He shook his head. "I didn't ask her—I told her. We were both too wasted to drive, and when she fought me on it, I lost my temper, started calling her names, threw stuff at her..." He took a breath. "I didn't hit her but I almost did. I was a complete asshole, and just before I closed the door in her face, she said, 'wow, I guess now we know why Dom Gianni broke your neck.'"

The room was quiet for a minute before he continued. "The next day I called a friend and he got me the tape of the game. I watched that play where I slashed you in the back of the knee over and over, until I was having dreams about it. What the hell was I thinking? I didn't have an answer then and I don't have one now, but the one thing I knew was you weren't the only one who fucked up that night. I was so busy trying to pretend I wasn't the rookie, I wasn't the new kid, and that I *was* as good as the rest of the team, I lost sight of the game. I lost sight of everything except getting over on you. For whatever reason you were in my sights and I wanted to go at it, one way or another."

"No matter what you did," Dom said, trying to wrap his mind around what Bobby was saying. "I still left my feet and charged you—something we're never supposed to do."

"And even though they tell us not to put our heads down from the time we're five years old, I did it anyway." Bobby shrugged. "Whatever went on that night was on both of us."

"That night changed my life," Dom admitted. "It sucked for a while, but it's the best thing that could have happened to me. Now that I'm through my probation and all the therapy, I love hockey again, which is something I lost along the way."

"Last week they told me I could play again," Bobby said. "I don't know if I'll get back to NHL level play, but I'm going to try my hardest, and I hope I can find love for the game again too."

"I'm really happy to hear that," Dom said.

There was another awkward silence when Bobby finally walked over to Dom and stood in front of him. They looked at each other for what seemed like a long time but was probably less than a minute, and Bobby slowly extended his hand again. Dom looked down at it and then reached out to shake it.

"I was really surprised when I got your message," Bobby said. "But I'm glad you reached out. It means a lot."

"I'm glad you agreed to meet me."

"I guess I'll see you around," Bobby stepped back and glanced at his friend, who got up.

"And I meant what I said," Dom said. "If you ever need anything at all..."

"I may need a job when this is over," Bobby chuckled.

"Give me a call." Dom nodded before following Cody out of the room.

As soon as he stepped into the lobby Molly was on her feet, moving towards him.

"I felt the baby move!" she whispered excitedly, pulling his hand to her stomach.

"Really?" He gazed down in awe, noting that his hands were no longer shaking. She was almost five months pregnant now and they had yet to feel the baby. *Until now.*

Molly glanced up as Bobby Thomas paused in front of them, his eyes moving to her stomach as well. She smiled brightly, deciding she didn't need to ask what had happened.

"I'm Molly," she said to the younger man. "Dom's fiancé. It's good to see you up and around."

Bobby inclined his head. "I didn't know you were expecting, Dom. Congratulations."

"It could be the best thing that ever happened to *you*, too," Dom spoke so softly Bobby almost missed it.

Then he smiled. "Yeah, I hear ya. Take care. Nice to meet you, Molly." Bobby turned and got into the elevator.

"What did you say to him?" Molly asked, looking at Dom curiously.

"I'll tell you later." He kissed her. "Come on, let's go celebrate!"

"Tell us everything!" Suze said, falling into step with them.

"Nothing to tell." Dom glanced at Cody and just grinned.

EXCERPT FROM "DRAKE"

October 31, 2012
  Chicago

Coming off the ice, Drake Riser felt a brief moment of triumph as his team, the Las Vegas Sidewinders, notched another win. This was the last game of their first road trip, and they were undefeated. For an NHL expansion team, they had beaten all the odds, getting through six pre-season games and 12 regular season games so far. They were bound to lose eventually in an 82-game season, but not tonight. They were going home with another win and a whole lot of energy.

It had been a wild couple of months since he'd taken the leap of faith and gone to Las Vegas. He'd been happy in Detroit, but he was in a rut and needed a change. When the opportunity came around, he'd been interested in something new. It was an added bonus that one of his best friends, a goalie named Karl Martensson, was going too. Add to that several other friends that he'd played with over the years, and he was on board.

Jumping into his new life with both feet, Drake had been having a blast—both on and off the ice—but he was restless. If he was honest with himself, he was lonely, and it was hard for a guy like him to meet decent women. Sex was easy, but women who weren't after his money or the status of becoming the wife of a professional athlete were hard to find; he'd already been through one marriage like that, and at 31, he had no desire to do that again.

"Coach said you're not flying home with us," Cody Armstrong, the team captain and one of Drake's good friends, came up beside him as he got dressed.

"My sister has this charity thing tonight and she expects me to show up since we're in Chicago anyway," Drake shrugged.

"Oh, yeah, that masquerade ball," Cody grinned. "Better you than me!"

Drake grinned. "Alcohol, attractive women and a happy older sister—I'm thinking it's not that bad."

Cody laughed. "When you put it that way..." He clapped him on the shoulder. "See you day after tomorrow."

Drake nodded and slipped out to the waiting taxi. He would get back to his hotel room, change into the tuxedo his sister had rented for him and then walk across the street to the venue. It was already after 10:00, so he was running late, but her big events always ran until the wee hours of the morning. If she hadn't become a top-notch plastic surgeon, she could have been a fundraising guru. His older sister seemed to be good at a lot of things, especially trying to find him a new wife. She'd been attempting to set him up on dates for a few years now, and he was glad he was too far away for that anymore. It had been a nightmare when he was still in Detroit and she'd been able to set him up on dates, sometimes several in a week.

Tonight his mind was only on one thing: sex. He wasn't kidding anybody with his monk routine. He'd gotten tired of one-night stands, so he'd stopped having them, but it had been months since he'd gotten laid and that was getting old too. Here in Chicago, his hometown, there had to be a sexy socialite interested in one night with a good-looking hockey player. At least he hoped so; he wouldn't be going to this dance otherwise.

Erin stared at the beautifully dressed people, stunning decorations and luscious tables of food without any interest. The Halloween-themed masquerade ball had been a last-minute invitation by the new plastic surgeon she'd come to Chicago to meet with, but now she was having second thoughts. The only reason her friends had been able to coax her out to such a social event was that her Victorian ball gown covered the burn scars down the right side of her body, and the elaborate mask she wore covered the scars on the right side of her face.

She never went out socially anymore. She had returned to desk duty at Quantico just six months ago, and only left the townhouse she shared with one of her best friends, Kate Lansing, to go to work or to the dozens of doctors she saw on a regular basis. They said she had PTSD, or Post-Traumatic Stress Disorder. The death of her best friend combined with nearly debilitating injuries and an ugly divorce had been hard on her and she hadn't been the same since it happened.

Then there was the physical therapy to get her strength back and work through the pain of the burns. She'd had multiple surgeries to remove the flesh that was no longer living with the hope that new skin would grow in its place. That hadn't happened to the extent they'd been expecting, though. Nothing had healed as well as they'd hoped, even after five surgeries and dozens of doctors.

"Are you going to sit here all night?" Kate demanded, giving her a look, her brown eyes sparkling with excitement. "Come on, you're in disguise. No one can see anything. Dance with someone. Have a drink. Do something. *Anything!*"

"I'm going to have fun!" Her other friend, Tessa Barber, gave her a pointed look.

Erin rolled her eyes. "I'm here, aren't I? You don't have to babysit me! Go dance. Have fun. I'm fine, you guys."

"If you don't have any fun, I'm calling Liv!" At that, Kate flounced away, her dark hair swinging behind her, Tessa close on her heels. Kate had given up so much to take care of Erin over the last 18 months; that's why Erin had felt guilty enough to come to this stupid dance. That, and the compelling invitation from her new plastic surgeon.

Erin really hadn't wanted to come, but Dr. Riser had been so sweet and generous. This was a huge fundraiser for a local children's hospital and the tickets were normally $500 per person. Lots of celebrities and professional athletes were supposed to be here, and she recognized many despite the disguises. When Dr. Riser had offered tickets to Erin, Kate and their friend Tessa, who lived here in Chicago, they'd convinced her that this was the perfect setting to get out socially. After all, she was almost completely covered—no one would be able to see the scars under the big Victorian-style dress and the elaborate gilded mask that covered most of her face.

Erin had come to Chicago to meet with Dr. Riser after her ex-mother-in-law, Jan Gentry, had told her about this doctor's specialty in burn victims. She had a new procedure she was testing and needed subjects who were willing to let her try it on them. In Erin's case, it was not like it could hurt. Almost the entire right side of her body was severely scarred from the explosion in Afghanistan. Her right eye drooped slightly and the skin on her right arm and leg was brown, mottled and ugly. The scarring started at her temple, went all the way down her arm, and started again mid-thigh, stopping several inches above her ankle. Her torso had been mostly spared because of her bulletproof vest and Liv's quick thinking, rolling her on the ground, but the rest of her was ruined. She could barely stand to look in the mirror anymore.

Divorced and basically broke after so many medical bills, all semblance of what had once been her life was gone; she went to work, therapy, the gym, and the rest of the time she hid at home. After Liv had been moved to a unit in Hawaii, her friend from college, Kate, had left her thriving New York City public relations firm to come live with Erin in Virginia. Though she traveled back and forth quite a bit, Kate, along with Liv and Tessa, had decided that Erin shouldn't be alone. The trauma of the explosion, coupled with her disfigurement and losing Shay, had been more than she could handle by herself. Liv had been unable to stay in Quantico any longer, and was forced to transfer to Hawaii. Tessa had been pregnant at the time, so it was Kate who had offered to uproot her life and moved to Virginia.

Erin had tried to fight them, but in the end, they were right. Without Kate, she would undoubtedly be curled up in a corner somewhere feeling sorry for herself.

After being released from the hospital in Germany, she'd come home to the U.S. to have her husband serve her with divorce papers. In lieu of taking her share of the million-dollar home she and Clay had bought, along with their assets, she took a mere $50,000 payout that she used as the down payment for her condo, and instead of alimony, Clay paid the $5000-a-month nursing home bill where Erin's father had been when she'd been deployed. With advanced stage Alzheimer's, it didn't seem that he would live much longer, and although Clay had balked, somehow Jan had talked him into it.

Thank God for Jan, she thought as she sipped the fruity drink Kate had stuck in her hand. Clay would have left her with nothing, but Jan had somehow gotten her the down payment for the condo and worked out the deal to take care of Erin's father. Though she'd made good money while deployed, and she still made a good salary now, Clay had spent every dime of their shared monthly income decorating the house and entertaining. She hadn't even realized that he'd spent her paychecks as well as his own while she'd been gone. Unfortunately, she'd signed a prenuptial agreement before they married restricting her from getting any of his healthy trust fund.

Ironically, Shay had a life insurance policy for $500,000 that had Erin as the beneficiary. Clay was currently in court fighting to take it from her, but she hadn't even shown up to the hearing. She didn't care about the money—she'd gladly trade it to have Shay back. Two years later, it was still unbelievable to her that he was gone.

Drifting back to the present, she looked around the room and caught a glance of herself in a mirror. In all fairness, she looked lovely. The sapphire ball gown covered her right shoulder and had a long embroidered sleeve that went to her wrist. The other shoulder was bare, as was her arm, and the dress came with a corset that accented her already slender figure. The skirt was full and enhanced with a hoop skirt Kate had forced her to wear, completely covering the scars on her right side. Her dark hair was swept up in an elaborate updo, covered with bejeweled pins, and curling tendrils framed her face. On her face was a gorgeous gold and crystal-laden half-mask that almost completely covered the right side of her face, while leaving her undamaged side glowing prettily, with the exception of the wired portion that rode just above her right eyebrow. Honestly, it was the first time in two years she'd been able to look at herself without wincing.

"Hi." A sandy-haired man with amazingly long-lashed hazel eyes, who was wearing an incredible tuxedo with tails, approached her with a smile. He was at least six feet five inches with shoulders that seemed to take up the whole room. She was momentarily stunned by his large form and rugged good looks.

"I'm Drake Riser," he continued. "My sister said she would tell our mom on me if I didn't ask you to dance, and she's my older sister, so I do what she says." He leaned close and stage whispered, "She kind of scares me."

"I do not!" Dr. Mackenzie Riser nudged her much younger brother with a laugh. She leaned over to give Erin a hug. "This is my younger brother Drake. I figured I'd introduce you since he doesn't know many people here and, other than your friends, neither do you. So, Erin meet Drake, Drake meet Erin." With a grin, she moved away towards another group.

"Sorry," Drake laughed. "She hosts this shindig every year and always wants everyone to have a good time."

"She's very sweet," Erin smiled.

"How do you know my sister?" He leaned back against the wall next to her comfortably, his large frame dwarfing hers.

"I, er, well, I came to Chicago to talk about her new study." Erin took a breath and waited to see his response.

"Oh." His eyes met hers with genuine concern. "Her burn study?"

"Yes." She looked away. "My unit hit an IED in Afghanistan."

"I'm sorry." He looked genuinely contrite. "I didn't realize—I know she has patient confidentiality; I didn't even think..." His voice trailed off. "I'm really sorry. I shouldn't have asked."

"It's okay." She shrugged. "It's been two years—I'm not ashamed of seeing a plastic surgeon to help me."

"Well, I don't know what's under the dress," he shrugged. "But you look pretty good to me."

"I do?" Erin blinked. Then she laughed. "God, I'm sorry. That was an idiotic thing to say! Thank you. But yes, there's a lot of damage under the dress."

"Would you like to dance?" Drake abruptly changed the subject. "I promise, no more stupid questions and I won't look under your dress."

In spite of herself, Erin laughed again. "I'd love to dance."

She let him take her hand and lead her to the dance floor. He moved easily on his feet and she let herself get lost in his strong arms and handsome face. It was the first time in years that she'd thought of anyone but Shay as handsome. God knows, though Shay and Clay looked alike, there was always something ugly underneath Clay's smile. She'd spent the last two years wondering why she hadn't noticed that until it was too late.

"You looked awfully serious just now," he said lightly.

"Thinking about my ex-husband and other things I shouldn't be," she admitted.

"Anything you'd care to share?"

She shook her head and focused on enjoying the sensation of a man touching her, even if she was covered from head to toe. It had been nearly three years since she'd had sex, and for whatever reason, this man made her miss it. Between her multiple surgeries, physical therapy, visits to the psychologist, work, and of course dealing with both Clay and her father, she never thought about sex. Mourning Shay had pretty much sucked the life out of her; if not for Liv, Kate and Tessa, she wasn't sure where she would be.

"So how long have you been divorced?" Drake asked, cocking his head. "We might as well get all the hard questions over with."

"Legally? About a year, but I got a letter from him while I was in Afghanistan, asking for a divorce a little over two years ago. The day of the explosion."

"Shit." Drake shook his head. "You mean you came home from Afghanistan with burns all over your body and he still filed for divorce?"

"Well, he'd *already* filed apparently, but his mother made him wait a year. She and I are still close. If not for her and my three best girlfriends, I never would have made it. It's been the worst two years of my life, and to add insult to injury, Clay tried to say that it was my fault."

"An IED in Afghanistan was your fault?" Drake narrowed his eyes. "What kind of asshole were you married to?!"

She smiled wanly. "A big one, apparently." She shook her head. "Let's not talk about me anymore, okay? Let's talk about you. You know I'm a Marine—what do you do for a living?"

"I play in the NHL." He paused. "Hockey."

This time she scowled at him. "I'm a woman, not a dunce—you think I don't know what the NHL is?"

"A lot of girls give me a blank look when I say that," he said. "Unless they're puck bunnies, and I'm too old for that shit."

"Puck bunnies?" She frowned.

"Girls who hang around the rink trying to sleep with hockey players."

"Oh." She made a face. "*Groupies*."

"Exactly."

The music was fading and he took her hand. "Come on. Let's go for a walk. It's hot in here and I would prefer to escape before my sister tries to set me up with someone I don't like—I've had to suffer through three terrible dances already."

"Was she playing matchmaker with us?" Erin looked up in surprise.

"Why not?" He smiled down at her. "You're beautiful, intelligent, and successful—what's not to like?"

"She's seen me naked!" Erin muttered. "Why on earth would she want to subject her baby brother to someone who looks like I do?!"

"Does that mean I get to see you naked?!" he asked, his eyes glistening with amusement.

"Hell no!" She laughed though, finding it easy to do with this giant of a man who seemed so kind and gentle.

He guided her out onto a beautiful balcony that overlooked the grounds of the country club where the ball was being held. Lit by hundreds of tiny candles, it was romantic and peaceful.

They leaned over the railing and for a while, neither spoke. "So, who do you play for?" she asked. "Chicago?"

"No. This is my hometown, but I was drafted by Montreal and then played with Atlanta and Detroit. This past summer I was traded to the new expansion team in Las Vegas."

"How's that been?" she asked. "I don't follow them, but I remember thinking it was an odd place for a hockey team."

"It's actually been pretty cool. The city has really stepped up to welcome the team, we get a ton of tourists at the games, believe it or not, and the guys I play with are stellar. Really special group of guys—we're like a family, and in the 11 years I've been in the NHL, it's never felt like this before."

"That's wonderful," she nodded. "That's what my last unit was like. My ex-husband's twin, Shay, and I were best friends all through college. When we graduated, I married Clay and got assigned to Quantico, and Shay deployed. A few years later, they put him in charge of a top secret mission and he had to put together a special team. He asked for me to be his security chief—that's my specialty—and so he handpicked our unit. It was a really great team." She paused. "Obviously it didn't end well, but anyway, why are we talking about me again?"

"I like your voice," Drake said softly. "I like you. You're pretty, you're funny, and it seems like you've been through hell, so I don't mind listening. Plus, I have a confession to make."

"Uh-oh," she looked at him suspiciously.

"It's not a big thing!" he chuckled. "I noticed you and asked Mack who you were. She said I should come over and ask you myself. Of course, I got suspicious and asked her why she wouldn't tell me who you were, and then I kind of guessed you were a patient, but when I started moving your way, she stopped me and told me about the PTSD. She said she was only telling me because—" He grimaced.

"Because?" she prompted.

"She knows me well," he squirmed. "And I like women. Since my divorce—"

"Divorce! You didn't tell me *you* were divorced!" Erin frowned at him.

"I'll tell you about it," he said solemnly. "Just let me explain. She told me about the PTSD so that I wouldn't try hooking up for the night. Don't be mad— she knows there have been a lot of women since I've been single and she didn't want you to be a number."

"It's been so long since I've had sex, I think being a number might be necessary," she murmured, before realizing what she'd said and turning red. "Crap, did I say that out loud?"

"Yup." He grinned. "But honest, I noticed you first. *Then* she told me. It wasn't intentional."

"It's fine." She shrugged and looked up expectantly. "Your turn."

"Typical story." He shrugged. "She was a puck bunny." It felt odd talking about his ex to someone; he'd never talked about the divorce to anyone, but Erin seemed like exactly the kind of girl he could talk about it to.

"We met when we were both 22, and I had been picked up by Atlanta. I met her at some charity thing. She was a model, catalogs and such, and we hit it off. I was offered a pretty good contract that year. Within the year, I bought her a massive engagement ring and a Mercedes, and bought us a gorgeous condo in Buckhead." He shook his head. "*Then* we got married. And you know, spending all that money would have been fine if she hadn't done what she did." He stared out at the beautiful grounds in front of them.

"If it's awful, you don't have to tell me," she said gently, touching his forearm.

He glanced down at her. "Seriously? After what you've been through? My story is a piece of cake. Just a case of being young and stupid." He shrugged. "We were married within a year. I got picked up for two more years for two million dollars. We got married, furnished our place and the nine months we dated plus the six months we were married, were actually pretty good. We had fun. She was a model, but she wasn't stupid, and she liked to work out so we did that together. She traveled for her work, and I traveled of course, so she wasn't clingy or whiny when I was gone. My parents didn't love her, and her mom is a crazy drunk that we saw maybe twice the whole time we were together, but we were a little family." He looked down at her and sighed. "And then I went on a 12-day road trip. I pulled a groin muscle on the second day and flew home. I'd tried to call her but she didn't pick up so I just hung up and got on the plane—I was tired and in pain.

"I got home and the condo was dark and quiet. Her car was in the garage, so while it was possible someone had picked her up, it was odd that the alarm wasn't on. I got into the kitchen and turned on the lights. There were a bunch of papers on the counter, along with some pain medications and one of those bracelets they give you when you're at the hospital. Her name was on it, and I stared at it, wondering how she'd been at the hospital yesterday but hadn't called me. So I looked at the papers and I kept reading the words, but didn't understand them. And then it hit me. She'd had a D&C; fancy name for an abortion."

"Oh, Drake." She winced. "You didn't know she was pregnant?"

"Nope. And while I was just 24 and we'd only been married six months, I was furious that she didn't even give me a choice, didn't trust me enough to talk about it! I probably would have agreed—neither of us was ready—but she didn't even tell me. She killed my kid without a second thought, and planned it perfectly so I'd be away for 12 days and I'd never know."

"Was the fight terrible?"

"No." He shook his head. "I slept on the couch and when she got up in the morning she found me there. She realized I knew what she'd done and tried to make excuses, saying she couldn't have a baby and all the stuff I knew she'd say. But I couldn't trust her anymore. I couldn't even look at her. I told her to pack up her stuff and go. I didn't care about the ridiculous money I'd spent on her and told her she could keep the ring and any of the wedding gifts she wanted, but the house and furniture were mine. I told her if she fought me I'd tell the whole world what she did. She left. I got divorce papers from her lawyer about a week later with exactly what I'd said. No alimony since we were only married six months. That was seven years ago and I haven't had a steady girlfriend since."

"And now you're a bad boy," she said with a soft smile. "Who has lots of one-night stands."

"Sometimes." He grinned sheepishly. "It's not like a new girl every night, but it's usually a few times and then I move on. Women are hard, you know? I guess I'm telling the wrong woman about that, though."

"Men are hard too," she agreed sadly.

"But now we're both divorced, and we're here." He reached for her hand and intertwined their fingers between them. "Do you want to take a walk on the grounds or is it too cold?"

Erin didn't know if she was excited or incredibly nervous, but his touch was both sexy and comforting. "No, I'm fine." She let him lead her across the balcony, their hands linked between them. She had no idea why she was holding hands with a man she'd only known for half an hour, but something about him made her feel good for the first time in a long time. It wasn't just his good looks either; he seemed so solid and reliable. It was kind of ridiculous to feel that way since she had no idea what he was really like, but right now she didn't want to think about it and didn't care anyway.

They made their way across a path that wove around the country club. There were intermittent streetlights that made it romantic instead of creepy, and while it was unseasonably warm for this time of year in Chicago, it was still chilly. She had never really liked the cold, but tonight it didn't bother her. Maybe it was the man beside her or the fact that it was the first time she'd gone out in over two years, but for tonight she was happy to go with the flow, wherever it led her.

"So, what's it like being a hockey player?" she asked as they walked.

"I love it," he said. "It's all I've ever wanted to do. Are you a fan?"

"I am," she nodded. "Not a huge fan, but I follow the Capitals since I live outside of D.C., and we used to go to a lot of games in college. It's fast-paced, so I think it's exciting."

"Do you play any sports?"

"A little volleyball and basketball," she shrugged. "Before the accident anyway. Now I do mostly strength-training and weight lifting, and I've been starting to run again. I kind of stopped everything after I got back from Afghanistan."

"What do you do for fun?" he asked lightly.

"Not much," she admitted. "I haven't been the same since the accident."

"No boyfriends?" he stopped walking, turning to look at her.

She shook her head slowly. He made her nervous when he looked at her with his beautiful eyes that were actually more amber than hazel now that she saw them up close. He was tall and she could see his broad chest and muscular arms through his jacket. She had the strangest urge to run her hands over his biceps so she forced herself to focus on his face.

"What were you thinking just now?" he asked, his voice a little huskier than before.

"I, uh," she swallowed hard. "I was just thinking that you have great shoulders. I like broad shoulders."

"I like tall brunettes with blue eyes," he murmured, moving his hands around her waist and pulling her a little closer, his eyes never leaving hers.

"I'm broken," she whispered. "My body is hideous—truly. Tonight you see a lot of makeup, a fancy dress and a mask, but it's really bad. I also have PTSD and nightmares. I can't be alone for long periods of time. And there is absolutely no way I could take my clothes off in front of you. I don't have anything to offer a guy like you."

He paused, confused as to why he still wanted her after everything she'd told him; he just did. "I still like you."

"So you want to be friends?" She glanced down to where his thumbs were making little circles around her waist.

"I want to kiss you," he said softly. "But I don't want to scare you away."

"I'd like you to kiss me," she breathed softly. He lowered his head and his lips found hers; gently, so much so that she reached up to pull his head closer. His tongue slipped between her lips and found hers. For the first time in years she felt her stomach flip over and her heart pound in her chest, in a good way. This was not a panic attack—this was pure bliss. His touch was tender but sexy, encouraging her in a way that made her want things she hadn't even thought about in a long time.

"Oh boy," she breathed heavily, leaning against him as she broke away. "This is not going to end well for either of us."

He chuckled, a rich sexy sound. "Because you won't take your clothes off?"

"Exactly."

"So if I found a way to get inside your panties but you could still keep all your clothes on, would that work?" He had no idea what made him ask her that, but once he did, he became acutely aware he wanted her more than he wanted to admit. Something about her vulnerability, and the shadows beneath the mask, went way beyond just getting laid for him. His gut told him she needed him to love her tonight, even more than he needed to break his dry spell.

She gave him a look. "Seriously?" She tried to look stern but a giggle escaped and she'd never giggled before. *What on earth was wrong with her?*

"I'll make you a deal. You get to keep your clothes on, we can keep the room dark, whatever you don't want me to see I don't see—but we both get lucky. Come on, three years is too long for anyone, especially with a hot body like yours."

"I...I don't know..." she stammered. "I mean, how..."

"Do you want to have sex with me?" he whispered against her ear. "Forget about your problems—just right here and now—do you want to make hot love and have a bunch of orgasms?" It was suddenly very important for him to convince her he could make this work. He wished he understood why he wanted her so badly, but it was a subconscious need that went beyond anything he could put into words.

She gulped nervously, but focused on everyone telling her that she had to start living again. And this guy was so incredibly hot. "Yes. Very much."

"Then come on."

"Drake, I want to, but I don't know if I'm ready for this kind of thing." Her eyes searched his.

"My sister will beat me upside the head if I'm unkind, and anyway, that's not my style. Me, you, one night of sex, and then we decide if Cinderella wants to see me again after the ball." He met her gaze intently.

"Just like that?"

He touched her cheek with his fingers. "It's not complicated. We both want it and I'm willing to play by your rules. I won't hurt you, Erin."

"Where would we go?" This might be a mistake, but he was right that they both wanted it.

"My hotel is across the street." He tugged at her hand.

She sent a quick text to Kate, so she wouldn't worry, and then closed her hand firmly around his.

Visit my website for buy links to read the rest of Drake and Erin's story...

www.KatMizera.com

66347738R00124

Made in the USA
Middletown, DE
06 September 2019